With one swift move, he grasped her arms, pulled her across his lap, and turned her on her back.

The mischievous twinkle in her eye defined who she was: swift, cunning, sexy, loyal, and spirited beyond the norm. She was the most beautiful thing he'd ever seen and to have her in his arms was far more than he deserved. Lucian tucked one arm behind her back to cradle her head, while his other hand held her chin.

"Can you read my mind now?" he asked. Serina began to lift her head to kiss him when he stopped her in her tracks. He grinned. "Not so fast, m'lady." He dipped his head to greet her, his mouth finding solace on hers. He pulled away licking his lips. "God, woman, you're so sweet, I feel as if I may lose myself in you, and I've only just kissed you. Is this part of your magic?"

"Lucian if I held that force, I'd have men knocking down my door all the time, yet you, sir—" She nodded towards the remains of her front door. "—seem to be the only man intent on doing just that!"

Eden's Black Rose

by

Jaclyn Tracey

This is a work of fiction. Names, characters, places, and incidents are either the product of the author's imagination or are used fictitiously, and any resemblance to actual persons living or dead, business establishments, events, or locales, is entirely coincidental.

Eden's Black Rose

COPYRIGHT © 2009 by Jacqueline Kearney

All rights reserved. No part of this book may be used or reproduced in any manner whatsoever without written permission of the author or The Wild Rose Press except in the case of brief quotations embodied in critical articles or reviews.
Contact Information: info@thewildrosepress.com

Cover Art by *Nicola Martinez*

The Wild Rose Press
PO Box 706
Adams Basin, NY 14410-0706
Visit us at www.thewildrosepress.com

Publishing History
First Black Rose Edition, 2010
Print ISBN 1-60154-757-9

Published in the United States of America

Dedication

To the man who led me through Eden's gate, Steven: the twinkle in your eye and your smile each morning makes getting up worth every second of the day. I owe you everything, for without you, my dream would never have seen the light of day.

To the two loves of my life, Caitlyn and Christopher, and my support group, Kayla, Crispy, Adam, Ashley, Jenn and all of you who moved into my office with me, thank you for your unconditional love, inspiration, company and reminding me the flowers got fed more than you did... I promise some day to venture back into the kitchen, but in all honesty, you did learn the fine art of take-out!

To Callie Lynn Wolfe, my editor and dear friend, thank you for your encouragement and believing in me. You are the only person who has ever asked me to do something and I did it—no questions asked.

To Wayne and Patricia Bowers, I tried my best to immortalize your generous hearts and spirits. I'll love you forever. Cheers!

To all my family and friends, if you see a name in here you recognize, I borrowed it.
If you don't see it in this book, I'm just getting warmed up! Big grin ☺

Chapter One

London, 1896

Running a brittle, anorexic finger along the dew-drenched metal of the park bench held a refreshing quality in the midst of the heat wave. Oh, he thought, what he wouldn't give to go home and find his casket filled to the rim with ice. Adding to that delightful idea, he threw in a cold stiff one for a late night snack. She'd be roughly five and a half feet in height, with meat on her bones. Something to sink his teeth into. Excited, he gripped the back of the seat. The cold penetrated his lichenified shell. Inhaling something foul, he cast an estranged eye around yet found no one in the vicinity. Besieged by a flurry of delirious flies acting as if they'd found a giant pile of manure, he decided the warmer weather indeed created unwanted havoc. He shielded his face with his hand and watched the insects swarm to him like iron to a magnet. With the speed of a lizard, his tongue shot out and snagged a dozen or more of the winged nuisances. After a few crunchy chomps he swallowed, satisfied.

Waiting for her to exit the restaurant, he tapped out a lonely tune in the dirt with his foot, one solitary note at a time, lifting tiny plumes of dust into the air in rhythm to the quartet playing inside. Afflicted by dust since childhood, he sneezed and the force shot his red-marble eye out of his head like a tiny cannon ball. He scurried across the ground to retrieve it, and after a quick spit-shine he popped it back in its socket a bit gritty.

For the past four years, he'd had nothing more than broken dreams of her to comfort him. So many evenings he slept on the floor...so damned close, lending her his bed, for what? Nothing, he conceded. The only thing his generosity produced was a sore wrist from too much time spent beneath his covers fantasizing.

He'd taken his time, plotted, made diabolical deals, and given the ultimate sacrifice for her, his life, to bring him to this juncture. Tonight she would be his. No mistakes. No turning back.

Four years ago, he'd underestimated her.

Never again.

He watched through the picture window as his lady danced with strangers. Repulsive, spineless, heathens hidden behind the stature of wealth and social class, attempting to fondle her as they held her soft, curvaceous, body close. He slammed his fist into the bench, the wood splintering beneath his fury. It should be him in her arms, his body pressed against hers. He shook his head and refocused, the flies dispersing in one chaotic cluster and then settling again in his hair.

The yellow silk ball gown flowed graciously around her ankles. With every step she took, the dress clung to the soft ripeness of her hips and small firm breasts. Having already seen what secrets lay beneath her gown, he knew there stood a pair of legs that were long, slender, guarding the entrance to what he claimed as...his.

He imagined her once again bare, with her long, ebony tresses flowing over him as she straddled him and rode him hard. Only in this fantasy, things would work out swimmingly to his advantage.

He envisioned her breasts firm and her nipples peaked with desire. He'd take her ripe buds into his mouth and taste, suckle, and then sink his teeth deeply into them. Her muscles would tighten and clamp down to grip the full length of him as he drove into her silky entrance. He'd start slowly at first, then harder and harder until wave after wave of sheer pleasure would wash over her. She'd be hot and slick and growl his name over and over until they were both sated. He knew he could and would satisfy her. Tonight, he'd make her his. After he finished with her, she would never desire another man.

Ever.

His tongue slithered across his lips in anticipation. He watched her laugh, whisper in strangers' ears, her hot breath on their skin, while his stolen blood roiled beneath the surface of his flesh. Beneath his trousers his prurience was about to burst. He fidgeted, playing a mean game of pocket billiards, squeezing out what little life his dick had left. He fondled his only testicle, remembering how he lost the other one.

Jesus, she had one hell of a grip on me that night.

He ran his free hand over his face, resting on the hole where his eye once called home. He went back in thought to his first and last date with Raven St. James, thinking their night together wasn't as magical as he'd promised her. What would he promise her tonight? Eternity? Immortality? A living hell? And then some!

The door to the restaurant opened, jarring his thoughts. As people sauntered into the streets, he shoved his body from the bench, stretched his long, lanky legs, and took to pacing at a good clip down the street. Coming upon a darkened alleyway, he turned brusquely to relieve his now throbbing erection. Shaking off the slime, he watched his nob wither before his eye. Back into the street, he slipped into her carriage to surprise her, only once inside he was the one surprised.

"Jasper?" His gray ugly eye cast the other man an unappreciative gaze. His red marble glared eerily ahead.

"Master." Jasper bowed his head in respect. "I thought this task would be easier on you if it were done by someone other than yourself. This way, when Raven sees you after such a long respite, you'll be her knight in shining armor."

He pondered the idea, a malicious grin forming. For once in his moronic existence, Jasper made sense.

"Fine, but let me speak to her first. I must have her..." He attempted to finish his thought but repeated, "I must have her."

"What of Lucian, my master?" Jasper asked, anxious.

He cringed at the very name. His jaw tightened, the muscles of his neck taut, his smile gone. Oh, how he loathed the man.

Lucian...The relentless thorn in his side.

Lucian...Mister Tall-Dark-And-Handsome. No doubt having an incestuous relationship with his goddess of a twin. The lucky bastard. In all likelihood, the reason Raven never came to him.

Lucian...Soon to be out of his life forever.

Hatred for this man stockpiled for the past eight years, and tonight he'd finally rid Lucian of his last breath.

Tonight, it was all about him. A small whistle escaped his nose. He hissed, "Obliterate him."

Jasper's laugh penetrated his soulless shell the same way he would penetrate Raven this evening. A frenzied feast culminated by her sweet surrender.

****

Not ten seconds after being jarred from her dreams by a choir of unharmonious magpies outside her bedroom window, Dr. Serina Spencer realized she was about to have one of those days. It was laid out in front of her, literally. She slid out of her bed and when she planted her foot on the floor, her toes sank into something warm, mushy, unexpected. Unwanted! The neighbor's cat snuck in the window again and left her another present. Serina's voice echoed throughout her home. "You little furball! If someone sees you in my home, it's me that burns at the stake, not you. I don't want anyone thinking I have a familiar. If I catch you, you'll be down to eight lives." A few days prior, the carcass of a headless mouse awaited her on the kitchen table and before that a garden snake on her pillow, its guts displayed in a vivid disarray. Reminded her of her first autopsy, a sloppy mess. Why was she always getting dead things dropped off at her door? Was it not enough she dealt with such matters at work? "What's one more?" she'd asked, sarcasm-laced.

After steeping the perfect cup of black tea and adding two heaping spoons of sugar, Serina reached inside her new cooler, pulled out a glass bottle, removed the cap and poured the... "What the h—?" The congealed liquid plopped into her cup with a solid *kerplunk*, the fluid now all over the countertop. She gagged. "So much for the new cooler." The soured concoction was heaved down her drain, where it clogged the opening. Serina headed off to work, tealess.

Definitely not the banner morn she'd anticipated.

****

After thirteen grueling hours spent in Hell's garden, Serina's affectionate name for the morgue, she'd had it! She'd seen enough blood and guts to last her a lifetime or at least the rest of today. She couldn't wait to escape the confines of these walls.

Glancing around the room through weary eyes she bid, "Sweet dreams," to the decomposing cadavers, praying none responded, although it wouldn't surprise her. She pulled the door tight, locking it behind her.

Serina's mind took a small detour with the sound of the latch.

Do locked doors keep bogymen out?

No but they keep out handsome suitors, not that you'll see any in this century!

Do closed windows laced with garlic keep vampires at bay?

You could ask the guy from this morning, but oh—wait a minute, you muted him permanently.

How 'bout holy water and crosses?

That's a Father Butler question.

Have I really lost my marbles? Was that demon real? And do I really want the answers?

Yes. I hope not and no, respectively.

Thinking back, her afternoon had been born in the bowels of Hell. No other explanation befit the day. Her assistant fled shortly after they took down a newly turned vampire. The dead man blasted out from the cooler, like a boxer taking to the ring, snarling, scratching at everything and everyone. He had no clue as to whom or what he was only that he thirsted for someone's blood. Eyeing Serina, he licked his lips in anticipation. She still couldn't believe it.

Earlier, she'd placed the man on ice, his ribs cracked open and a nice slice separating his skull from his brain. Before her disbelieving eyes, the man refashioned himself. His rib cage closed in like a giant Venus Flytrap, securing the rotted organs inside, while his teeth popped out one at a time, clanking on the floor like loose change. He sprouted four heart-stopping dents in their place and gave Serina a little flash of fang.

After securing her dignity so that she did not wet herself, Serina wasted no time and screamed bloody murder. Realizing that wouldn't correct the situation, she swiftly beheaded the man, ripped out his heart and stuffed him in the incinerator. Serina concluded he'd died from a newly discovered blood disorder, hemophilia.

Apparently not.

Days like this one, she could do without. Hated being wrong.

With the heat beleaguering her, she decided to go straight home. Normally, she'd have already been to the orphanage, helping out, but the mere thought of little people climbing atop her, all hot and sticky, well, she quelled the idea fast.

****

Once home and settled, feet propped up on an adjacent chair, Serina read by candlelight her cherished book by John Waller, *The Discovery of the Germ: Twenty Years That Transformed the Way We Think About Diseases*. Most nights candlelight relaxed her. Tonight, the little bonfires roasted her bum. Misting, Serina tried to decide if she should keep her favorite, lacy robe on or trot about in her birthday suit. Misting, her endearing word for sweating. Sweating conjured up pictures of filthy rogues, or her after a day like she had at the morgue. Misting seemed delicate like the morning dew on her beloved rose bushes. It was feminine and soft, like her. She chortled at the very idea of her being feminine. There wasn't an ounce of grace to be discovered within her.

Her dressing gown, gathered in the back, resembled the train of a wedding dress. Black silk rosebuds adorned it. The front of her robe needed no decorations. Her generous endowment had that covered and then some.

An hour earlier, she'd struggled ridiculously to get the two buttons closed, exhaling all her air, hoping to deflate her chest just enough to hook them.

"Finally," she'd said triumphant. "Although to breathe no longer seems an option. At least I'll look ravishing when someone finds me out cold on me floor, a lovely shade of blue." After she sucked in a huge gulp of air, one of the buttons broke free and flew across the room. Frustrated, she got down on her hands and knees to search the floor. What she found left her red-eyed and runny-nosed. Maybe tomorrow she'd dust and sew the button back on.

And then again?

****

In an attempt to hop right back into her book, Serina found her own skin an uncomfortable fit. With her hair glued to her like tentacles of an octopus she remembered why she always wore it up. Blythe and her brilliant idea! "Wear your hair down, Dr. Serina! You're too finicky, too matronly. You'll wind up a spinster surrounded by hundreds of cats."

"Why do I listen to her? I most certainly will not have cats for company. Spinster?" She grunted as she made her way to her kitchen for a wet cloth. Bringing the cool, moist rag to her, she wrung it out across her neck. The brief respite from the heat as the water trickled down between her breasts was enjoyable until the robe became soaked and transparent. Serina glanced at her chest. Her nipples, now perky and wide-awake, appeared ready to burst through the robe. She tweaked them gently. "You old girls hot enough? You're bloody well big enough!"

Laughing at her foolishness one moment, doubled over the next. Her sixth sense was never a gentle breeze coming to call. It was a hurricane with an urgent message. A storm approached.

Serina's skin burnt with a prickly, insatiable energy she couldn't vanquish, much like poison ivy. The combination made her all the more certain she would indeed be knee deep in *shite* soon. The cool water that only moments ago caressed her now felt as if it could boil her flesh. At that moment she was certain nothing could satisfy her. She immediately reneged, knowing a large bowl of crème ice would do nicely.

Crème ice...her answer to a tumultuous day or a lonely night. It worked better than most of her spells and, if she were truthful, all her spells! Her margin for error grew wider by the day. Being ambidextrous, dyslexic, and colorblind didn't help either.

With a swift change in direction, Serina set her sights on her icebox, anticipating the vanilla flavor, almost tasting it as she opened the door and found everything inside melted into one smelly unrecognizable pile of, "Sh..." She slammed the door shut. She added to her procrastinate-today-pay-tomorrow list. Tomorrow. Not that she was one of those, but...if the shoe fit? She would get someone in to look at the icebox and possibly clean it...sew on a button...and take the time to dust. Frustrated, she rolled her eyes.

In the far-off distance the clacking of horse's hooves against the cobblestone announced someone's arrival. Subtle voices in her head drew her to the window. Peeking out into the street, she saw dimly lit homes that cast a yellow haze around a barren carriage held up in the middle of the road.

One of the voices inside the carriage was inaudible. Serina sensed the voice to be a male, gurgling—drowning, neither one good. Trying to read his mind proved futile. The man had the attention span of a gnat in a windstorm. Then she heard another male. Fear saturated his every word. A definite mixture of yelling and gurgling between the two men filled the air, a combination she didn't fancy.

Hold pressure. I'll find us a doctor, please just hold on. Don't you dare go die on me. Damn it, or I'll kill you me self!

****

The driver of the carriage, Duncan Thomas, groped his unraveled wit's end. He couldn't help it. Once he'd had seen the state of the two people he considered his brother and sister, all reason abandoned him. He'd have rushed these two to their family physician had he not seen the elderly doctor being carried out, from the same party they'd attended, completely inebriated and not aware of his own name. Couldn't begrudge the man, the celebration had been in his honor for years of service to Her Majesty. Desperate, Duncan would have propositioned the flu-faker if he'd happened by. And since Duncan didn't get on well with the sight of blood, he'd given praise he hadn't fainted dead away.

This atrocity delivered him to the side of his wife, the night she bled to death giving birth to their breech daughter. He'd never seen so much blood...until tonight.

Witnessing his baby suffocate with the umbilical cord knotted around her delicate neck stymied a chunk of Duncan's heart forever. And here, his best mate was busy doing both, bleeding and choking to death. He screamed at the top of his lungs for help.

A haunted chill scraped Serina's spine upon hearing the man's despaired pleas. She suddenly regretted using her powers. Bathed in blood and frantic, the injured man fought for every molecule of air he could suck into his lungs, yet the gentleman's lady companion lay still, seemingly untouched. Hopefully, she'd only fainted. Somehow, Serina knew it wasn't going to be that easy. It never was.

That thought didn't bode well. With her palms to the skies she begged, "Please, no more dead. Is it not enough I have to go to work and face this, now they're getting delivered to my door? I was kidding this morning! Oh Goddess, just once can't I have a man land on me stoop? Alive! Betrothed to no one? In one bloody piece. Happy to see me? I finally get it. 'Tis not what I wish for, 'tis how I wish for it!" With her nose pressed to the glass, Serina noticed curiosity seekers doing the same thing she did, peering out doorways and windows. She watched a tall man in a black cloak and top hat run sporadically from door to door, rattling them, pounding on them, begging for assistance. He stopped in the centre of the road, hysterical and screamed, "Is there a doctor anywhere, please, anyone, we need help," before he dropped to knees and wept.

Doors slammed in his face and no one came, all because of a well-known madman and serial killer, Jack the Ripper. People steered clear of coaches and strange men.

Serina took two steps, stopped and turned around. She felt underdressed. Overflowing, to be more precise. A corset would have worked, but she despised the bony bodice, vowing to never wear one, regardless of her buxom appendages. She grabbed her afghan from a chair and wound it around her shoulders and chest. Heat or heatstroke, there'd be no peep shows. Hands on her little black bag she headed out the doorway.

"I'm a doctor. What's taken place?" she called out as she ran into the street. Sizing the man up, Serina felt no intimidation in the least by him. Yes, she was eye level to his navel. Yes, he was acting like a stark, raving loon, but his eyes, they held a genuine concern that touched her.

Duncan stood, mouth slightly ajar, saying naught, staring at her.

"What?" Serina barked. "Sir." She snapped her fingers at him. "Please, tell me what has taken place."

Impatient by nature, she strutted to the

carriage, and tripped over the afghan. She struggled to keep her balance. *Aren't you just the most graceful being? Not quite prim and definitely not proper.* No, she was certain beyond a reasonable doubt no one could ever accuse her of being proper. Prim? She had no clue of the meaning of the word.

"I was driving my lord and lady home from the gala this evening when something...no, someone...no, something, well, I am not sure what in bleedin' hell it was, but it blew right past me with such speed and force it knocked me on me arse, then commanded me to lay quiet with its ghastly voice. I couldn't move, couldn't protect me family. A bastard of a thing," he explained no longer staring at her, but glancing up at her as he plopped down on the road and rubbed his bloodied forehead. "I'm not even sure, Miss, how long I lay on the ground. Time was stolen away. The creature's eyes were the deadest pools of hatred I've ever seen. The bastard laughed as it floated off. I still can't believe me eyes, Miss. It floated. I swear I've had neither grog nor mead this eve. An ale, yes, but nothing more. Two, I'll confess to, but that was it, I think."

She took in the shaken man, his arms locked around his body, rocking himself. He would be of no use. Serina approached him. Bending eye level with him, she peeked under his hat to find his injury. A gash above his brow that didn't need sutures. He could wait for mending. The two in the carriage couldn't.

"Your name, sir?"

"Duncan Thomas."

From the corner of her eye, Serina watched her neighbor approach, half apprehensive, half eager, it seemed. The woman would run a few steps and stop. Then she'd run a few more, each time pivoting back toward her home. From Serina's standpoint, the woman obviously didn't know if she was coming or going.

Serina had never spoken with the woman before but saw her out occasionally with a fat little cat that looked like a cow and acted like a dog, following closer than her shadow. Probably the pesky pussy that left her the housewarming gifts. In a heartbeat, Serina knew she was going to place the carriage driver in her charge and have the woman run supplies if needed. This way Serina could attend to the two in the carriage with no watchful eyes surrounding her, no one questioning her methods of medicine or magic.

Serina extended her hand. "Hello, Miss. I am Doctor Serina Spencer."

"Molly Baynes," the woman replied, shaking Serina's hand with a solid grip, crushing her fingers. "Pleasure's all mine. Heard oodles of you."

"*Ouchhowdoyoudo.*" Serina shook her fingers behind her back to rid the pain without offending the woman. Taking a deep breath she asked, "Molly, would you be so kind as to take Mister Thomas here back to your home? Tend to him, and bring me some clean cloths and all the water you might spare?" Gently, Serina nudged the woman toward Duncan.

Molly didn't hesitate and escorted him toward her home.

Reluctant to leave, he continued to turn back to Serina, but Molly nudged him forward, saying, "Let the little slip of a thing help them. They'll be fine. 'Tis been said she's a true miracle worker."

Serina steadied her nerves hearing Molly. Seems her secrets weren't as safe as she thought they were. She flung open the carriage door and peered inside. The smell coming from the carriage impaled her. It was the morgue all over again, only sickeningly sweet in a repulsive, dry-heave-her-breakfast-lunch-and-supper sense.

Serina ran for cover. The contents of her

stomach surged forth. She made her way back to the carriage, not sure whether she felt better or worse. She leaned toward worse.

Peering inside the carriage, Serina stepped back, her eyes wide. Blood covered the man, the seats, and pooled around his feet, but not a single drop lay on the woman. Was she unconscious or drained dry? And did she want the answer to that? The man's vocal cords glistened in the moonlight. How he was breathing between gurgles seemed nothing short of Divine Intervention. Feral eyes glared at her. As he attempted to speak, thin bubbles formed and popped, one after another from the hole in his throat.

"Mister, you're a bloody mess. I don't usually chat with people once they're as bad as you. They're either halfway to heaven or hell by now, and from the looks of you I'm guessing you weren't allowed passage to either. Tonight your lucky star shone in my window."

His petrified look clearly stated otherwise. All of two seconds passed before he attempted to scream, flailing his arms in the air.

Before he clobbered her, she ducked. For all his efforts, the only thing he produced was more frothy bubbles.

"Oh, how I loathe bubbles. Hold that thought, Mister." Serina shoved her index finger inside his neck, instantly stilling his motions. She watched the shocked expression cover his face. Within seconds, her spirit and energies were busy sealing off the holes in his esophagus and lungs forcing every extra bit of energy she could squeeze out into his pleural cavity. "How in the name of Goddess did he miss your trachea? He got everything else," she muttered, poking her finger around in there.

With all good intentions, Molly came carrying cloths and two large buckets of water, but when she looked into the carriage, she immediately turned tail and fled.

Serina mumbled, "Oh, I'll bet that didn't look good."

Serina tried to reassure him with a gentle mind push that she wanted to help him. A bundle of loose nerves, he moved all over the carriage with her finger still probing within his neck. He grabbed her hand and, with a sucking pop, tugged it from his throat. Head tilted sideways, he looked curiously between her finger and her face.

Joined with her, a warm unexpected jolt of power passed between them. He dropped her hand in fright and backpeddled to put distance between them.

"Yeah, Mister, that scared me too," she admitted. "Listen, I am going to give you something to help you relax. I don't usually need to, but you're worse than me in a dentist's chair." She fished around in her bag and found a jar of ether. After saturating a cloth, she aimed for the man's nose. "It will make you want to close your eyes. I promise not to hurt you."

He blocked her wrist with one hand, his other hand still clutching his neck. Locking eyes with her, he desperately needed her to understand something.

Serina read his mind and glanced to the unconscious woman. She reassured him, "She's still alive," and prayed she hadn't lied.

He actually attempted a small smile, throwing Serina off guard. His strength alone amazed her, and once cleaned up, he'd be rather bonny.

Serina called to Molly. With great trepidation, her neighbor trudged back, Duncan trailing behind.

"Molly, I need two things from you, dear. Just don't look too closely at these people and breathe very shallow. One, lay your index, ah, pointer finger and your middle finger on the woman's neck." Serina instructed, "I'll show you." Serina placed Molly's hand on the woman's neck. "You're trying to feel a slight bump beneath the skin. Leave your fingers there and count to sixty."

Molly kept her fingers glued to the woman's neck, her eyes closed tight and counted as Serina mentally prepared herself. His healing would be done from the inside out, even though others would want or actually need to see stitches and bandages.

Look and act like a normal doctor, Serina, or tomorrow you'll be the belle of the ball, hung out to dry and once again with no escort.

"Molly, are you well?" Serina asked absentmindedly.

"No, Miss," Molly answered, her hand firm against her nose in a useless attempt to block death's stench. Blood has a scent all of its own and, once inhaled, it's never forgotten.

"Splendid," Serina said focused on the gentleman. "Is there any movement under that woman's skin? Do we know these poor souls' names yet?"

Ready to enter the man's body a second time, she was seduced by an overwhelming urge to know more about him, everything, his wants and darkest desires, things he held closest to his heart. And, for the strangest reason, she wanted to be in his heart and be every one of his dreams and desires. That thought made her pause and scratch her head.

A little flustered, she asked, "Could I have their names, please?"

Duncan answered, "Lord and Lady St. James, Miss."

Married. A pout covered her lips.

Duncan added, "They're twins. I'm the caretaker, and these two are me family."

Twins. Did he say twins? Serina's lips changed direction.

"Miss, she's as cold as ice," Molly answered through chattering teeth.

One look at Duncan, hunched over with his head between his legs, hyperventilating, and Molly ready to collapse, Serina had to get them out of there before she had two more to care for.

"Molly, finish tending to Duncan. Keep him occupied. Ask some of the neighbors if they've any spare trousers and shirt for this gent. And all the more water you can spare? Ta."

Molly grabbed Duncan's hand, helped him stand, and retreated for the safety of her home.

Serina looked to the man for whom she now had a name to go by. "Lord St. James, sweet dreams!" And with that said she placed the ether-soaked cotton over his nose and held him as he drifted off to sleep.

Laying her hands lightly upon his shoulders, Serina focused on his interior body, allowing her healing powers to sift through him to mend the ruthlessly damaged ligaments, muscle, organs, arteries and veins. Moving on to his bowels, Serina's eyes watered and her stomach bucked. She would not vomit again.

Wrong!

Serina stuck her head out the door and heaved. Pulling the windows open and pushing the doors out, she prayed for frigid air and moments later, an arctic blast ripped through the carriage, chilling her to the bone.

So much to learn, so little time.

Serina wasted no time and directed her powers to the man's abdomen, watching as his intestines folded neatly, securely back into his body cavity and that foul, vile stench dissipated. She sent a warm, static heat through his blood to kill any bacteria that harbored there.

After scanning Lord St. James' body, Serina

strategically placed some bandages, just in case anyone had questions. As she neared completion, she noticed two things that piqued her interest.

His left hip held a birthmark shaped like a crescent moon with a star-shaped spot wedged between the two points of the moon. It was perfect, as if someone had painted it on him, but then, she noted, everything about him was perfect.

Her second more noticeable point of interest lay between St. James' thighs. She took a deep breath as she eyed his endowment and fought back nervous giggles. The sight of him lying there spread out before her made her think things she'd only heard whispers of from others, never having experienced them herself. He wore one long, thick erection, almost too long, almost too thick. Serina licked her lips.

Even dying he's erect. Typical male.

In the distance, Molly and Duncan's voices brought her back to an all-too surreal reality. Serina patted her chest. Exhausted and completely misted a second time today, she washed him with cool water to rid any residual stench that clung to him. Ripe? Indeed he was.

Serina's last task was to replenish his blood loss. She decided to use her blood even though it differed from mortals. Serina dug through her little black bag and retrieved the necessary bottles and tubes and needles. She tied off her arm with a leather strap that, one, hurt like the dickens, and two, made the veins in her arm and hand throb and bulge.

Watching the needle pierce through her skin, she whined, "I really despise sharp objects aimed at me." Serina had no clue how much blood to give the man, but taking in the bloody carriage, she transfused one full bottle. Giving him that much left her shaky, cold, and nauseous. He, on the other hand, appeared rosy and warm. She reached for a ladle of water and gulped it down to replenish some fluids.

Glancing at his tattered trousers and what lay so close, enticing her, Serina grabbed a dark silk shawl she'd spotted earlier crumpled into a ball in the corner of the seat. She draped it across his lap and tucked in the edges under his belt, giving her eyes respite and thus returning his dignity.

While waiting for Lord St. James to come around, she tended to Lady St. James. Serina found the woman stunning regardless of her putrid color. Black, silky tresses draped down to the floor of the carriage. Ebony eyelashes blanketed her alabaster cheeks in a complimentary contrast.

With her examination, Serina found Lady St. James' uterus had been damaged, so badly the woman would never be able to bear children. Serina swallowed the lump of bile in her throat and let her energy flow throughout the woman. She reshaped the muscle, removed the adhesions, returning to her the opportunity to bring life to this world.

To get her healthy glow back—"Not again?" Serina gnawed on her bottom lip. The woman needed a transfusion too.

Watching her blood replenish Lady St. James, Serina had a moment to feel good about what she'd accomplished tonight. She'd given two strangers a second chance at life. It was the polar opposite of working in the morgue. Her moment cut short when her head filled like a hot air balloon and started lifting off towards the stars. "Just let me get through this," she prayed as she undid all the tubes and bottles and packed them into her bag.

Her stomach in a tumultuous knot, Serina yanked out handfuls of cloths before she chucked the bag into the street. Picking up the last bucket of water, she chugged the fluid and then dowsed Lord St. James and the carriage, cleaning both as best she could. She didn't want them to see a bloodbath that would scare the daylights out of them when they came to. At most, she thought they'd be disoriented. She certainly was. With that last viable thought, she passed out facedown into Lord St. James's lap.

Lucian St. James pried open his heavy eyelids, feeling as if the weight of the world rested upon them. Confused by his surroundings and unable to get a grasp of the evening events, he instead grasped a woman. He tried to recall what happened, but he drew blanks. His night became a jigsaw puzzle with missing bits and pieces. He was at a loss as to why there lay a scantily dressed female in the carriage with him with her face pressed precariously close to his groin.

Doing what? he wondered. Had she fallen asleep? A curl touched his lips. "Could I have fallen asleep?" He scoffed at the very idea.

Lucian found this situation most amusing. And so it seemed, the more amused he got, the more aroused he got. On the opposite seat his sister lay quiet. Completely out of her character. Chatting with no one conscious he said, "Please let Raven be asleep. Don't wake up now. Good God, how much champagne did I consume? And who is this little slip of a thing?"

Lucian ran his fingers through Serina's wavy auburn locks to rouse her. With a gentle touch, he traced the outline of her body, over her back, her ribs and lower to her hips. He slid his hand over her bottom, and enjoyed the soft, supple firmness. For a split second, he envisioned her naked, lying across him while he gently spanked her. He laughed aloud.

He thought about undressing her in her febrile state. All right, he agreed "feverish" was a lame reason, but if she came around that's what he was sticking with. Then better judgment kicked in and he decided to keep her clothed...for now. What if she woke up naked and began screaming? Glancing at his soggy predicament of tattered trousers, a black shawl draped oddly across him, his shirt shredded, frustration set in. He squinted, while his fingers puttered with his five o'clock shadow and his free hand slapped her lush little behind.

Lucian went back to his puzzle. Who was this woman with soft sensuous curves he would love to skim with his fingers and memorize with his heart? Why was she face down, buried within his loins...asleep, no less?

Why was his sister snoring to the high heavens in the carriage? He'd seen her at the party with a shandy in hand, and he knew all too well it only took one to get her glassy-eyed and giggly. Therein lay his answer.

Where the dickens did Duncan disappear to? He rubbed his jaw in thought. Oh wait, the last time he saw Duncan he'd been playing craps with a few friends with a nice mountain of winnings in front of him. Probably enough to buy London Bridge, not that England would *ever* sell her.

And more importantly, was this little woman going to finish what he hoped she'd started? She'd obviously attempted to rip off his clothing in a heated passion. *Wish I remembered it.*

"Excuse me, Miss." Lucian gave her a gentle shake. "Would you be so kind as to remove yourself so as I may try to regain my composure? Mind you, you were a tad bit rough with my attire. These did have buttons on them at one point."

Serina stirred.

Dizzy and disoriented, Serina couldn't quite figure out where she was. Blinking, she tried to see past some large, silky, dark object blocking her view.

After she rubbed her eyes, Serina reached out to examine what obstacle threatened to poke her eye out. With a solid grip on the steel shaft Serina froze.

Slowly, she rolled her eyes upward at the tumescent erection still blanketed in silk. She couldn't move a muscle to save herself, but then, obviously, she couldn't stay there with her face buried in the man's loins, either. Her fingers opened with reluctance.

What do I do to get out of this sticky situation with my dignity intact?

Nothing came to mind...Well, that wasn't exactly true. One thing came to mind. Her eyebrow lifted in a non-prim, non-proper fashion.

Serina licked her lips. Truth be known, she'd read his mind and had seen what he'd wanted from her. He wanted Serina to take him, all of him, into her mouth, lick the length of him, taste him, nibble her way down his shaft and capture his more delicate parts, and ultimately drive him over the edge. She was pretty confident she could grant his wish.

Instead, heart racing, she turned her head away.

"Sir, I know this looks completely enormous..." *Dear God!* Serina bit her tongue and covered her mouth, disbelieving she'd uttered such gibberish.

Lucian laughed wholeheartedly which compounded her embarrassment.

"I mean outrageous. I know this appears scandalous, but please give me a minute of your time before you say anything or judge my reasons for being here like this. I swear 'tis not as it seems."

"I believe, Miss, you've already had a minute or two from what I can see. I'll leave the final judgment until you're finished." He smiled smugly.

Someone thought his vain sense of humor funny. Serina rolled her eyes.

"Oh no, Sir. Is that what you think? I was not! A lady would never." She attempted to sound appalled. *Oh, Serina. You lie. You most certainly were thinking that and you would...* "Let me try this again. Lord

St. James, I am Dr. Serina Spencer. Your sister and you sort of fell into my lap and were in need of emergent care." She gazed up at him, a wall of muscle, and she felt like the little slip of a thing she'd heard Molly call her. The man was sheer, rugged beauty she wanted blanketed across her body, stoking her already heated desires.

"Well, Dr. Spencer," Lucian gestured to her position in the carriage. "Your story is backwards, dear, for who is in whose lap?"

Lord St. James wore a grin the devil himself would envy. She realized he was toying with her and enjoying every second of it. Oddly, so did she. Serina decided to get up and out of the carriage before anything more embarrassing happened. With one arm to each side of his body, she pushed away from him and lost her footing in a puddle of water. About to say, "Oops," she slipped fast and forward directly onto the man's welcoming silken-covered erection. She became all arms and legs trying to get off him.

Lucian grabbed her forearms and steadied her.

"Oh, by the Goddess, I'm so sorry," she prattled. "Oh, I'm so..." Serina tossed the shawl aside and grabbed his penis a second time, lifting his warm shaft to inspect it...Still solid! "I didn't hurt you, did I? I'm utterly mortified." Feeling a slight pulsation coming from beneath her fingers, she glanced back towards her hand. He was bubbling over with joy, literally.

The small gestures of her hand along with the warmth of her breath was all it took, and Serina knew Lord St. James was in no way injured, and that all body parts worked just fine. His head fell backwards, and he sucked in a huge gulp of air with a languorous glaze to his eyes.

Good thing you fixed his airway, Serina.

"Oh, Sir!" Serina gasped along with him, no longer overwhelmed with guilt for hurting him, or thinking she had, but now for touching him.

"Umm!" He cleared his throat and gave the chin nod towards his groin.

She released her grip on him, again!

Lucian placed a gentle finger to her lips. "Shush, m'lady. I'm fine. You've more than seen to that. You've a most peculiar bedside manner." He couldn't help but smile as he straightened the shawl, covering himself once more. "I must confess to you, it is very stimulating, finding a beautiful woman in my lap...And a first."

He placed his fingers beneath her chin and tilted her head upward to get a closer look. He found her ravishing, with a small, slightly turned-up nose, soft facial features, unforgettable glistening, green eyes and lush full lips made for him alone to kiss. That thought caught him off guard, but then it seemed everything about her did. When she laid her head back down on his shoulder to regain her composure, he knew she was thoroughly mortified. With that small movement, Lucian wasted no time and placed his hand back in the silken strands of her hair, savoring the moment.

"I would think that you and I might need a more informal introduction after this evening, m'lady. My name is Lucian and you could start by looking at me. My promise to you, I'll try not to make any more wise comments or embarrass you more than you already appear to be, but on the rarest of occasions, as my dear sister claims, I speak before I think. You've been forewarned."

Serina glanced up from beneath her lashes just as he winked at her.

Lucian's gentle whisper sought her out and touched her where no man ever had. He caressed her soul and took possession of her heart.

Oh, bloody hell, what's wrong with me? Well, genius, how 'bout blood loss and the heat. The heat, yes, indeed, he is an inferno.

"I do have some serious questions for you, though." Lucian brushed her hair from her face, adding intimacy to the desire that swiftly overcame her.

"My name? Oh, ah...call me Serina." She shyly met his striking silvery blue eyes. They shone, as if the sun beat directly on them. Melting mercury, she thought. The man definitely had the capability of making a few things melt, her being one of them; her drawers a dead giveaway. Serina stifled a gasp. She could actually differentiate his eye color. Color blind from birth, she hid it as best she could, memorizing everything in life her mother had taught her, like apples are red, grass is green, dead people are bluish-grey...the important things, to be sure.

His lips, she decided, looked like an invitation to heaven. Serina wanted to kiss that bottom lip and nibble on it just a bit—all right, maybe more than just a bit—have them explore every inch of her body...for starters.

Even through what was left of his trousers the solid muscle of his thighs looked inviting. Serina slid her hands over them once more, just because she could. What was a little more guilt at this point?

Isn't she a cheeky one? He bit his tongue thinking that only moments before, he'd done the same to her delicate behind. He sat in awe of the woman, wondering how fate had intervened and given him this little gift so nicely wrapped in a scantily-laced robe. His heart had a strange tug to it as he watched her every move. For the first time in his life, he felt alive, possessive. Urges demanded he take her and run. Run far away from everyone in his life and get to know her, to make love to her on the beach as the setting sun cast a golden glow to her soft, flawless skin. Wake with her in his arms and warm her where the sun didn't shine!

What in the name of the Queen happened to me tonight? Not as much as I'd have liked to! Lucian, you've only just met the woman. Act like a gentleman.

Having never before experienced anything remotely like this, Lucian found himself in a quandary. He'd never given another woman the time of day, let alone a second glance. He'd had a vision years earlier of a woman, his passionate mate. And here she sat flashing him with the most remarkable smile, an interesting attitude, and those bountiful breasts. *Jesus, they're so inviting. So soft. So sensuous. So in need of my undivided attentions.* Lucian threaded his fingers together for fear he would actually reach out to fondle her without an actual invitation to do so.

Just the thought of Lucian... His name spelled divine. Oddly her breasts began to ache, her nipples firm and pressing free from the robe. When a cooler breeze hit her she glanced down. Her jaw dropped.

Out of the robe! For the love of God.

"Don't get embarrassed, Serina. Casually look down and just tuck the only thing that's bigger than your mouth back in its place. I realize 'tis the challenge of a lifetime you'll spend eternity fighting."

Lucian grinned. "Personally I think they're beautiful and wouldn't mind seeing them more often."

Serina snapped her head up. "Excuse me?" Her eyes went wide, taking the man in. "Did you just see my—never mind that. Did you read my mind?"

"As much as I wish I could read minds, Serina, especially yours, I cannot. You just said all that nonsense out loud, luv. Once you're all tucked back in, would you answer some questions for me? Need any help? Willing and able, at your service."

I bet you're able! The weight of his gaze as he sat back and stretched reminded her of a prowling cat, hungry to devour its prey. *That, I imagine, would be a fancy feast!*

"Lucian, let me start by telling you what happened here tonight and then see if you've any unanswered questions."

Lucian interrupted, "I wish Raven would come out of her stupor. She's had a little more drink than she's used to tonight. She sleeps like the dead. This is rare for her. And where, in the name of God, is Duncan? Last time I saw him, he had enough coins in front of him to...He's probably met some woman, or at least I hope he did. The man's been to hell and back, but that's a story for a different day."

Lucian's demeanor changed before her eyes. The smile—gone. His silver-blue eyes—the calm before the storm. "Is that what you think happened to you tonight?" She asked confused. Could the man honestly have no clue what happened to them? "Both you and your sister will be fine. Mr. Thomas is safe with my neighbor. Lucian, listen carefully to what I'm about to tell you. A vampire attacked you both. You were both in pretty rough shape. But tonight, Sir, was your lucky night, in more ways than one."

Lucian glanced to his sister, then to Serina, studying her.

"Did you say 'vampire'? How much spirits have you indulged in, Madam?"

Serina raised her voice, "Pardon me? Do not doubt me, Lord St. James. These creatures are very real and very deadly."

Lucian gently brushed Raven's bangs from her face. He tilted her head to the side and gasped upon seeing a large bloody bruise with two puncture wounds in her neck.

"She's fine. Trust me."

"Doesn't look fine." Lucian stared in disbelief. "You wouldn't lie to me? Then why hasn't she come round? A vampire you say?"

Serina continued, "She's gaining her strength. I

swear to you, I took care of her." She leaned over and placed her hand atop his, hoping to calm him. She found the spark still there, ready to be rekindled as a warm pulse flowed between them. The look he gave her when the jolt shook his body almost made her laugh. "That's a story for a different day, luv." She smirked. "I gave you both a blood transfusion. She'll likely require another one tomorrow. Theory has it that it takes three bites in a relatively short period of time to become an indentured servant to a vampire. All it takes is one nasty blood-drenching bite to become undead." Serina poked his chest with her finger. "You came close. I put you back together again, hopefully better than Humpty Dumpty."

"Humpty Dumpty? What a pathetic name."

Serina cocked her to one side. "You're pulling me leg, right?"

"About what?"

"About Humpty?"

Lucian shook his head no.

Serina inhaled his fragrant breath. With that thought, she realized she was in trouble. She grabbed his rugged chin covered with a faint shadow of whiskers and raised her eyebrows as she looked into his eyes. "Fairy tale published in 1810?" she said with a question in her voice. "Please tell me you know fairy tales. Come on, Lord St. James. Every child has been told it. Humpty Dumpty sat on a wall…" Serina waited to see if he would finish the tale or if he truly hadn't heard it. A few more seconds passed. "Later, I'll read you the tale. There's two theories. First is about an egg and the second about King Richard, murdering wastrel that he was."

"Ooh, a bedtime story?" Lucian winked. "You don't care much for the royals, do you?"

"They're all daft. Incestuous group, I've been told. Just look at the Queen's husband. Too many uncles and brothers in that pot. Anyway," Serina continued, "I believe that creature wanted you dead." *I certainly wouldn't. Worn out atop me definitely, but never dead.* Again, she smiled coyly. "And your sister, well...count your blessings. Your driver's rattled, but he's fine."

Raven St. James stirred. She blinked a few times and then rubbed her eyes. Her fingers lightly rubbed the wound upon her neck and she winced.

"Lucian?" Raven's voice sounded raspy, and raw. She looked around the coach, her eyes wide as she noted a few bandages on her brother. Setting her sights on Serina, she asked, "What's happened to us? Are you all right? Why've you a naked woman in here? Did she hurt you? What did you do to his clothing?" she accused Serina.

"I'm not naked," Serina snapped in self-defense, knowing she really didn't have a leg to stand on with that remarkably oh-so-intelligent rebuttal. "And—" she paused, pointing her finger at Raven while she attempted to think of something—anything that made some sense. Instead she gave Raven an ill-fated grin.

Seeing Raven's facial expression, lips scrunched, both her eyebrows arched towards her hairline and her finger pointed at her see-through robe, Serina tried again to secure the garment. Failing miserably, she went in search of the afghan. Out in the street. Serina groaned. At this point she no longer cared about her attire, or lack thereof.

Raven pulled herself into the corner of the seat and hugged her knees to her chest. "Lucian, answer me."

Lucian reached over to Raven and pulled her to him.

"Lucian, where's Duncan? Is...?" Raven's voice quieted.

"Ray, this beautiful woman saved our lives, and

we owe her. I only have a limited version of the evening's events, but she believes a vampire attacked us."

"A what?" Raven squeaked. "Don't even tell me you believe her."

"Vampire. Let me finish, Beauty. She was kind enough to give you and me her blood."

"You've gone stark, raving, mad, Lucian St. James," Raven declared.

Serina extended her hand. "Raven, my name is Serina Spencer. I'm a doctor. I work at the hospital's morgue. They are real, the vampires, trust me. I dealt with one just this morning."

With a hint of sarcasm, Raven asked, "This one's a gem, Luce. Where did you find her?"

Lucian and Raven exchanged a glance in which he clearly stated Raven should back off. He added, "I do believe her, Ray."

"Truly?" Her tone defeated. When Lucian nodded, Raven made the sign of the cross over her heart.

"Why don't the two of you come into my home and freshen up? Raven, would you care for tea? I really need to get out of this coach and replace some of the fluids I gave you two, before I pass out again." She glanced at Lucian, a small curve formed upon her lips. "Please, come in."

Lucian let go of his sister and jumped out of the carriage. He found it hard to believe that moments before he had almost met his death. He felt better than he had before the attack. He held out his hand to Serina to help her down. The moment she slid her small hand into his, power rippled through his body. He embraced the energy. Letting go of her hand, Lucian wrapped his hands around her tiny waist and brought Serina to him, allowing her to slide down the front of him—slowly, as she brushed against the thickness of his unwavering erection until her feet hit the ground. He held onto her for a moment, not at all embarrassed in showing her he had feelings for her...until he realized the silk shawl she'd draped across him now lay on the road by his feet.

Serina picked up the afghan she'd started out with. "You need this more than I do." She wrapped the heavy cover around Lucian's waist, all his personal parts concealed yet again. "At least until you find some trousers. You'll be getting more than you bartered for, wearing these." She reached up and ruffled his silky curls.

Serina watched as he bent toward her and prepared herself for the kiss she knew he was about to deliver. She wet her lips and closed her eyes...

He whispered behind her ear, "I am truly grateful for all you've done tonight. This should seem like the worst night of my life, yet it is the complete opposite. And I believe you to be the very reason." He moved his hands to her cheeks, his thumbs brushing her soft skin. "Regardless, I want to spank you." Lucian choked, and Serina burst out laughing. "I mean, thank you." His cheeks burned a lovely shade of red.

"We're quite the pair, you and I," Serina conceded.

"Indeed." And with that said, he placed a delicate kiss on her cheek. This was the first time he'd ever kissed a woman. Really enjoyed it. And didn't think he could stop himself from taking her right then and there. A shudder of need ricocheted the length of his spine from his brain to his loins. Oh, how he just wanted to take her away and make her his. Lucian glanced around for a private spot. Regain your brain, the head atop his shoulders nagged. *Take your time with her.*

His other head, the one below the afghan was not about to go down without a fight. *You'll be sorry if you don't throw her over your shoulder and run! I'm not going anywhere all evening. That you can believe.* A small groan escaped him.

Her first kiss ever. Trapped, like a fly in honey, she couldn't have moved if she'd wanted to, and she didn't want to. His aim, however, was shoddy. Serina wanted a real kiss, but she didn't want to give the impression of being a tart, either, although bumping into and grasping his silky erection negated she should still worry. That minor catastrophe didn't really count, since it was an accident.

"Strangely, I know how you feel. I'm glad I was able to help you, but Lucian, you owe me nothing. The pleasure of your company, even under the most dire circumstances tonight, has been quite memorable." Without even realizing it she snuggled into his frame, arching backwards to gaze up at him. Maybe he'd attempt another kiss and perfect his aim. She batted her eyelashes at him.

About to close the distance to Serina's tantalizing lips, he turned at the last second and whispered, "You need to scoot while you still can." Reluctant, he bowed, allowing Serina to escape him.

Her disappointment hidden behind a forced smile, she turned and walked away from him with exaggerated sway to her hips, until she stumbled on the uneven slate and fought once again to keep her balance.

Lucian enjoyed the view. She definitely had a nice bottom! Images bombarded his mind of more intimate acts he wanted to do with that fine little arse...and the rest of her. Lucian wanted Serina. He needed her. He would have her. Didn't he deserve love for himself? He'd spent the past eight years raising Raven. He'd seen to her safety, cared for her and placed his life on hold day after day after their parents were murdered. The sensation of eyes burning a hole in the back of his head prompted him to turn around and find his little beauty standing in the carriage eyeing him curiously.

"Oh, do tell! What exactly did I miss tonight, Luce? I don't ever recall seeing that look on your face. Ever." Raven kicked at her brother. "Are you going to get me out of this oven?" Lucian swung Raven around to the ground and hugged her.

"Can we go inside, Raven?" Lucian pleaded.

"You're an imbecile, Luce. But I feel it, too." Raven had her hand over her heart as she spoke, "She's different, all right." Giving her brother a quick glance, she wrinkled her nose. "Nice trousers, Luce. Do I want to know why you've got this wrapped like a kilt?"

Lucian shook his head no.

Raven grabbed the afghan. Lucian held tight. Regardless, it became a tug of war between sister and brother with Lucian winning as Raven fell into a fit of hysterical laughter. "I don't even want to know what happened to you tonight, but if that woman saved you, then I owe her. I don't ever want to think about losing you, Lucian. I'm willing to share you, but never to lose you." Raven tossed her arm around her brother's waist and began walking towards Serina's home. "God, Lucian, you smell absolutely rancid." Raven chortled.

"She saved you as well, Ray. Vampires? I'd heard a few tales, but I thought they were just that—tales." They proceeded up the pathway arm in arm, surrounded by beautifully thick black rose bushes.

Chapter Two

Once inside Serina's home, Raven went to work, the professional snoop she was. She needed to find out everything about the woman because, from her shoes it looked like her brother had met his match. Everywhere Raven looked vases filled with both fresh and dried blooms hogged the tables, the floors, the windowsills, even a player piano. Family photos were lost behind the bouquets. Intricate bottles filled with fragrant oils cluttered another table and gave the home a heavenly scent.

Serina entertained a unique style when it came to her home décor. She possessed a bold passion for the unusual bordering almost on atrocious. Not one thing matched. Wallpaper boasted yellow roses with light green leaves and vines that crept across the walls. A sapphire colored velvet couch and love settee held plump, orange taffeta toss pillows. The pink paisley curtains? What was this woman thinking?

Raven thought her words carefully. "You have a flare for the unusual, Serina. The flowers are breathtaking." Raven raised her voice, uncertain where the doctor had gone. "Who is your gardener?"

"Me," Serina answered from a small room off her kitchen. Coming out in a clean yellow linen blouse with a purple and black striped skirt, that accented her figure without flaunting it, she carried a tray of tea into the room and placed it on the table.

"My background may be in medicine but my true passion is chemistry, the way things are put together and why. I'm still working on how the black roses came to be. My mother sneezed on one of them and it turned black. They used to be white. Her sneeze began a reaction that went from one rose to the next and so on, just like dominos as they tumble."

Raven's eyes went wide with disbelief. "You are, of course, joking."

Serina shook her shook. "I swear it. Strangest thing I've ever witnessed. Anyway, from the black roses I've developed a fragrance. Would you care to try it? 'Tis sold in the markets. I've named it Eden's Black Rose after my mother. She told me I'd recreated Eden's garden." Serina handed Raven a small ornate rose-colored bottle. Raven started to shake her head in protest of the gift, but Serina pushed the gift into her hand. "This way you'll always remember me."

Raven gave Serina a warm hug. "Thank you for everything you've done for us tonight." Raven set off to finish her journey through Serina's home. "Lucian?" Raven's voice echoed through each room. "Ah—Lucian, what a stunning garden." Raven shoved past him and slammed him into the doorframe to get out to the back garden and in passing tugged at the pink and purple garment still secured around his waist. English yellow roses climbed to the heavens with black roses interspersed. The petals of both bushes covered the ground with a silky veil.

'Tis a bumble bee's paradise. You'll never see the little buggers until it's too late." Raven laughed alone. Lucian shook his head at her.

"My fair, Raven, your mirth endears me. Your humor enchants me. Your logic evades both of us."

"Did you know Serina's also a chemist? Maybe she could make a pill to help your hubris, Luce." Raven nudged her brother with her elbow.

"If I could do that, Raven I'd be living better

than the Queen herself. Not that I believe you need a pill, Lucian." Serina gave him a coy smirk before turning to Raven with a conspiratorial wink.

"Right, so this is how it's to be. For once Raven has someone to side with. Go ahead ladies, have your moment." He gave both women a wide toothy grin, before he pretended to choke his sister. "Is Duncan still with the woman across the road? We should probably retrieve him, Ray, and let this woman get some rest. We don't want to wear out our welcome."

Never happen!

Inside, he pulled up short in front of the yellow roses and plucked one from a vase, then handed it to Serina. "These roses you surround yourself with are beautiful, m'lady, yet pale in your presence." Lucian took her hand in his and brought it to his mouth.

Oh how he wanted her. Then. There. That second. He honestly didn't believe he'd be able to leave her house, to leave her unless he was kicking and screaming. Then he thought he might be a tad bit melodramatic. Yes, she was beautiful. Yes, she was smart. Yes she was oh so incredibly sultry, alluring and those twinkling eyes. Jesus, the woman had enchanted him, snuck up on him and stolen his heart. And he didn't care. God help him, it was love at first sight, of that he was certain. He'd never been in love before, and if this was love, he was in trouble. Serina didn't stand a chance!

"Hello, hello, Lucian, Raven?" Duncan's voice carried over well before he approached the front door. "I've got you some clean trousers, Lucian, and a shirt. A gentleman living next door to Miss Baynes said you could have them. Said he's put on some extra weight since his wife became with child, and he can no longer squeeze into them. I believe they've got their roles reversed." Duncan crushed Lucian to him. "I thought I'd lost you. Luce, you can't die on me. Promise me. I'd be lost without me best mate."

"Your only mate!" Lucian returned Duncan's hug. "Not to worry, old man. You can't get rid of me so easily. 'Twas naught more than a flesh wound," he joked.

Duncan shook his head and released a large pent-up sigh. He tossed the clothing to Lucian. "That flesh wound you speak of resembled something more akin a gutted rhino. Please hurry and change, Luce. I see you've been dressing with Raven's clothing again? Pink kilts?" Duncan turned to Serina. "Dr. Spencer, thank you for saving me girls."

Lucian wasted no time swatting the back of Duncan's head. "

Through laughter Duncan added, "I don't know what you did to help them, but I am grateful. You are a miracle worker." He gave Serina a small bow at his hips. "The roses are beautiful, might I?" Duncan picked a yellow rose from the vase and ran out the door, mumbling something about Molly.

"May I use your washroom, Serina?" Lucian held out the clean clothes in front of him with a slight shrug his shoulders.

"Come with me, Sir. It's up the stairs." Serina held out her hand to Lucian. He wasted no time accepting her offer.

"You've a washroom on your second floor?" Lucian asked curious. Most of the homes in this area were plain, simple with watersheds in their garden.

"Yes. We have a large water tank in the attic that fills with rainwater—or me if there's no rain. Me Mum wanted a modern home and trust me, she always gets what she wants."

Lucian looked back to his sister. "You all right if I leave you?"

Raven shooed her brother off. "I'm fine, never been better, truly."

Lucian couldn't help but admire Serina's

backside as they climbed the stairs, the way the material on her skirt hugged each curve, caressed her thighs, cinched her waist and accented her tight little tush up close and personal. What he wouldn't give to be her clothes, with her flesh slinking across him. Her choice in her wardrobe though, the eccentric color combination, left him wondering if she'd dressed in the dark. "Do you live alone, Serina? Where is your family? How is it a beautiful, young woman is a doctor and has no one to care for her? You don't do you?" Lucian was almost afraid of the answer, but he had to know everything.

"I live alone. I'm twenty-one. My parents are off on an adventure to America. I am on staff at the hospital and when I'm not there, I'm either in my garden or at the orphanage." Serina made it perfectly clear no one pined for her affections other than some starved-for-attention children.

The intensity of Serina's emotions left her uncertain how to act. And a doubting Thomas didn't suit her life. How did she become a brilliant young doctor, a psychic and know nothing of love or relationships? Reluctant, she released his hand. *I'm no good at soul searching. Give me a dead body any day of the week, but don't try to figure out me.* "The washroom is here. I'm going to keep your sister company. I trust you'll be fine." As Serina turned to leave, her foot caught in the hem of her skirt. She was launched head first into the wall. "I'm fine," she announced, other than the embarrassed ego splattered all over the wall.

Lucian covered the distance and embraced her from behind. She melted against his chest. His arms felt strong and warm, and for the first time, Serina felt safe and comforted. Wasn't it only an hour or so ago she was dead set against having another human touch her? Extra body heat? It was one thing to have the orphans climbing all over her. Lucian was an entirely new bedtime story.

His whiskers caught in her hair as he settled his chin atop of Serina's head. "You've a funny way of going down stairs, m'lady. There are easier ways. Trust me. Don't move a muscle, and I'll see to your safety." Lucian spun her fast in his arms to face him and tapped his index finger gently to her nose. "Stay put, little one."

"Right, then." Serina watched his beautiful sculpted body walk away. She fought every wild urge not to give chase. Her head became clouded with thoughts of him behind that door, in only his birthday suit—and oh what a present. She ruffled her hair into total disarray, just as her mind was. She dropped to her knees to pray for guidance, or even a lucid thought would even have done the trick, with neither happening. "Dear Goddess…"

Not privy to Serina's confession, Lucian said, "That's an odd compliment, Dr. Spencer, but trust me, Goddess, I am not if you've not noticed." He pointed to his groin with that sinful grin she'd simply fallen in love with. "Aren't doctors supposed to know the difference between Gods and Goddesses?"

Lucian's eyes danced with mischief and his smile held deep intimate thoughts of what the two of them would share soon. Serina bit her bottom lip, her mind busy playing out the possibilities.

"There is a dinner in town Raven and I must attend in a few nights. You would honor me as my guest?" He bent down and picked her up. "Up we go," he said as they headed down the stairs.

Serina tossed her arms around his neck and for just a moment nuzzled her face to the side of his neck. She enjoyed being this close to him, and now that he'd cleaned up, his scent tickled her fancy. "What will I do without you tonight to help me get back up these stairs to bed?" Once she realized how that sounded she gasped.

Tart with a capital "T." That's me! Ah, what the hell. Serina leaned back, and batted her eyelashes at him. Lucian stopped about halfway down the stairs, turned around and headed back up them, his pace faster.

"This night, then?"

"For as much as I would love that, I'm going to ask you to turn around once more and head back down the stairs, although I really don't know why. Lucian, I've never..." Serina hesitated looking down at the floor. "I've never lain with a man before." She wasn't sure if it was a confession or an apology. She wanted to prepare him she was a virgin and knew nothing in the ways of lovemaking so he wouldn't be disappointed if they ever....

Lucian sat down on the steps and snuggled her in his lap.

"Serina, neither have I." He gave her a puckish grin. "Seriously, I've never been with a woman. So we'll take this slow. Get to know each other better, and then I'll tuck you in tomorrow night."

"You're very funny. You—never been with a woman? Were you locked away your entire life? Or are you a eunuch?"

"I believe we've crossed that bridge. You stole me best kept secret from under me black silky shawl. No eunuchs under there." Lucian winked. "But seriously, I've never met the right woman." *Until tonight.* Lucian twirled strands of her hair around his fingers as he lost himself in her gaze. "I do believe you've bewitched me, doctor." He bent forward, and with a little tug of her hair, she landed inches from his face. With only a whisper in her ear, and his hot breath against her skin, he said, "I'd like to kiss you." His hand splayed across her cheek and jaw in a soft caress as his lips brushed against Serina's lush mouth. He nudged his tongue through the parting in her lips to taste her. To swallow her. To savor her all in one kiss.

Oh! The man is making me insane. Serina wanted to throw caution to the wind. Something she'd never done a day in her life. To date, her existence had been so bloody predictable, so sheltered, so lonely. Just once, she wanted to live, to feel what it was like to be with a man and not have her life or reputation hang in the balance. Not have her mother hanging like a noose around her neck, waiting to snuff out her last breath.

Serina lay in Lucian's arms, his desire for her pressed firmly against her bottom. She wiggled into that mass and bit her cheeks when he swallowed a gasp. *Do it once more, Serina. See what happens. This could be fun.* She pressed her bottom in closer. Lucian threw his head back and wore a look Serina wasn't entirely sure was pleasure or pain. She scanned his thoughts and smiled. Pleasure.

He bent to her once more, lips parted, his eyes hidden beneath long black lashes. His scent reminded her of the air, fresh and clean, after a rainstorm. When his lips pressed against hers, he moaned as he deepened the kiss. Concerned she did something wrong, she broke away from him. "Did I hurt you?"

He rolled his eyes up every scrumptious inch of her. "I don't believe you could ever hurt me, unless we never get to finish this some time soon." Lucian's face was all male. The want, the desire, the need etched into his very being. "M'lady, I know we can't, well...No, actually we could do this, but not tonight. Not like this. I want everything between us perfect when that time comes, so for now, I'm going to carry you the rest of the way down the stairs."

Serina kissed his cheek. "Thank you for not sullying my reputation tonight. I'd love to have dinner with Raven and you. What should I wear?"

"Nothing comes to mind, m'lady, literally nothing."

Serina slapped at his chest. "Lord St. James, please try to be serious for just a second. If you're to begin wooing me, then I want to look ravishing for you." She raised her eyebrows a few times in jest.

"What's that, my wild rose? Begin wooing you? And here I thought I all ready had. I'll have to work on my charm." He kissed her again, long and deep, because he wanted— no needed to. He broke away and asked, "Do you have a gown?" almost afraid to after seeing her attire tonight. He realized the other women at the dinner would eat her alive if she showed up looking anything less than royalty. They were sharks, and she'd be fresh chum dangling off a hook in front of them. He'd seen the aftermath of such a frenzy when some poor woman was led into their little clique of self-righteous, pompous, duplicity and tossed out, looking worse than a two-bit strumpet without a quid in her pocket after an evening in the tunnels with a group of drunken sailors. "'Tis a formal affair. I'd rather pass on the evening, but my stature within the House of Lords states I must grace them with my presence." He snickered alone. Serina didn't bat an eyelash. "Raven shall have the pleasure of your company during dinner. Then afterward, you'll be my dessert. Fair enough?"

"Fair enough." A small smile curved her lips as she met his gaze. "I've never had need of a dress for such an occasion. I'll have to see what I can put together."

Lucian's heart thumped with nervous agitation. In haste, he offered, "I'll bring you a dress for the evening. And your favorite color is?"

"You don't have to buy me a dress, Lucian. I'm very capable of dressing myself. Your offer overwhelms me."

"Serina, let me do this for you, please? I'd really love the opportunity to dress you." His innocent smirk changed to that a devil would envy. "Undress you, actually," he whispered. "This is truly the least I can do for you." Hands clasped, he pleaded to her to allow him this small favor.

Serina nibbled on her bottom lip. "Green. I think my favorite color is green. Or possibly purple. Red might be nice. I love the color of your eyes. They're blue right?"

She's color blind?

Humbly she added, "And you don't need to spank me." She snorted so loud Lucian jumped. "I mean thank me. I'd have done the same for anyone."

"All of it?" Lucian asked, as he thought back only a short time ago to their time together in the carriage.

"My bedside manner, Lord St. James, is my best attribute," she teased, as she brushed his silky curls from his face.

"No arguments there, luv."

Serina started to crawl off Lucian's lap when he grabbed her waist and pulled her back to him.

"I still owe you an escort down the stairs, m'lady." With an awkward stance and her draped in his arms, he carried her to the bottom of the stairs. The uncomfortable bulge in his trousers would prove to be a constant reminder tonight would be long and lonely.

Lucian pressed his lips to hers once again in a hungry kiss. When he pulled away, he said, "Hopefully that one will hold me over for a bit, but I doubt it." He set Serina down and whispered, "Look," as he pointed to her couch. Duncan held Raven fast asleep in his arms.

"How long have you two been here?" Lucian asked overcome with guilt and embarrassment.

Duncan grinned. "Not long, Luce. She came over

to Molly's home to give you two a little privacy."

More embarrassment, less guilt.

Lucian turned to Serina. "I will begin my wooing rituals in the near future. Sweet dreams, m'lady. Come on, my old man, let's get our sleeping beauty home." Lucian scooped Raven into his arms and carried her out the door.

Duncan held the carriage door open for Lucian and his sister. Once they were inside, he turned to Serina. "Good night, Dr. Spencer." He bowed before climbing atop the carriage.

Forehead to the glass, Lucian watched Serina grow smaller with each step the horses took from her.

Serina stood at the edge of her lawn with one foot in heaven and her other foot dancing lightheartedly on earth as she watched her future roll off in the carriage. The sky dazzled her with stars. Each more brilliant than the next as they shimmered like tiny diamonds strewn across black velvet. The full moon's glow replenished her energies better than the sun on a bright warm day. A simple grin graced her cheeks. What was this feeling that invaded her? Lust or love? Or was it just the heat and one handsome, gentle man with the most dreamy eyes she'd ever lost herself in?

Her merry thoughts faded as she worried over Lucian's attacker. Even with the heat, shivers bit into her spine like the blustery March winds on a rainy day. Serina retreated inside and locked all windows and doors. She wasn't sure at that point if it was easier to die from heat stroke or a vampire attack. Serina went with heat stroke. It seemed the lesser of the two evils.

Curled up in her bed, she lay quiet under her quilt, feverish and sweating, yes sweating, her knuckles woven into the quilt for a sense of security more than anything. She began to rethink the night's events and was astonished with the outcome. She'd saved a very handsome, eligible man, his sister, and even gotten a dinner proposal. Not to mention her first kiss. She could still taste him on her lips and what a rare delicacy. Serina drifted off to sleep hoping to dream of the new man in her life, but her dreams were not so kind.

Chapter Three

The first dream of many began with strangers pointing accusatory fingers at her. "Witch...she's a bloody murdering, whore of a witch. Kill her," they cursed in unison.

Nothing like a good tongue lashing to get your blood to boil. "I am not a whore," she cried out in her sleep, arguing with no one in particular. "Why wouldn't you defend yourself against being a witch?"

The fact that she didn't have a brilliant hypothesis irked her.

The rocks these heathens launched, as she hung on the wooden stake about to be crucified, filleted layers of her skin. It didn't take long before her flesh resembled one of her autopsies, except she happened to be quite alive and very unappreciative of the pain. Her tormentor's lifeless faces, with their eyes pecked out from their sockets, and necks ripped open, accused her of the one thing she prayed she was not. But in complete honesty, Serina had questions. How could she do the things she did, to heal the deathly ill or read people's minds or adjust the weather? All right, she still had to work the kinks out of the weather. It never turned out as sunny as she wanted.

Serina didn't have the answers, but those ruining her good night's sleep did.

Witch.

At least they're no longer calling me a whore.

"Whore of a witch!"

Dammit!

Serina's dreams dragged her through the wee

morning hours and ended when she awoke screaming. Her heart thumping loudly, Serina lay as still as the proverbial church-mouse, drenched. A none-to-subtle headache prodded her mind, and left her feeling as if she were up to her eyeballs in quicksand.

What the heck?

After a frantic few minutes, she'd figured out the culprit was dehydration. The previous evening depleted her. Roughly five feet away she spotted her destination; a nightstand with a water pitcher. The quilt went first. Serina dangled her feet over the bed and attempted to cross the room. Stepping onto the floor, she found the quicksand beneath her. With every step she took the deadly granules sucked at her, surrounded each toe and weighed her feet down. She pulled each leg up and placed it in front of her, in an attempt to walk, but her thighs burned and her toes turned into knotted cramps. The water pitcher may as well have been a mirage.

Her reflection in the looking glass, parched lips, cracked and bleeding stuck out better than a mad cow alone in a field tripping over its four feet. She ran a gentle finger across the rough flesh. Lucian wouldn't want to kiss her today. She pouted and her lips split wider. Desperate, she lunged forward and grabbed the nightstand. She tried to lift the pitcher, but her arms felt like anvils dangled from each one. Pain riveted down her arms to her hands. She set the pitcher down to work out the cramps. *What the hell is wrong with me?* How humiliating would it be to die of thirst in her own home with a full pitcher of water smack dab in front of her? Then she realized if she died, humiliation would be moot. Trying a second time with both hands, she was able to pour the water, except a dark viscous liquid sloshed into the cup. The container and its contents tumbled over. Soured clots splattered like broken eggs on the floor. A burnt, coppery odor violated her little nose. Accustomed to the scent, she was certain blood painted her legs and feet. Serina's last thought before blackness swallowed her was to aim for the bed.

****

The warmth of the morning sunrise which Raven usually enjoyed, today did a bit more than gently coax her awake, it lambasted her. Raven lay very still in her bed, wide awake and very much in misery. Her eyes clamped shut, streams of water seeped out the corners and ran off her cheeks soaking her pillow. Someone had to have snuck in and placed her head in a vice grip. She was beyond confident that at any moment her brains would burst through her nose, ears, and mouth. The mere idea of lifting her head to get a drink was out of the question. Raven tried to call for Lucian, but found both her voice and strength waning. She tried to give him a little mental mind push they often used for communication between them, but even that proved futile. Against better judgment, she attempted to climb out of bed. On borrowed energy, she flopped one leg at a time over the edge of the bed. She sat upright holding on to the mattress's edge with all her might. She tried to stand but instead met the floor with an alarming thud.

****

Awakened by a loud crash, Lucian jumped from his bed in desperation. He fought back the panic that waited, like a snake coiled in the grass, ready to strike. As he headed to Raven's room, he found the length of the hallway grew longer rather than shorter with his every step. The carpet runners purposefully reached up in attempts to trip him, and inevitably doing so, Lucian careened into a Louis XIV table in the hall. The priceless treasure tipped sideways along with the candelabra that it once held. Bits of shattered glass added to his mayhem.

"Bloody hell," Lucian uttered as he looked at the bottom of his feet. After some painful moments, picking out glass from his feet and fingers, Lucian attempted to touch Raven's mind but she was like a closed book. Any other day of the week, their ability to psychically communicate came as a blessing. Today it vexed him.

He found Raven on the floor, unconscious with the appearance of death already upon her. Her flawless, alabaster skin had a taut, frigid appearance. He wondered how she could be so cold when the room sweltered? Lucian fixated on the window...wide open. How? He'd personally locked it. He stripped Raven's quilt from her bed and wrapped her. Carrying her limp body, he headed for the stables and managed to find the remainder of the broken glass in the hallway. Bloody footprints trailed behind him like a broken shadow. Tears blinded him as he dropped to his knees in front of the carriage. "Duncan." His voice cracked with anguish.

Coming up behind Lucian, Duncan took Raven. No words were exchanged as Duncan carefully placed the woman in Lucian's lap and slammed the door shut. Then, Duncan drove the carriage towards Dr. Jones's home pushing the horses so hard he knew he'd be walking home.

Pulling up in front of their family doctor's manor, Duncan jumped from the carriage before it stopped rolling, and ran as hard as he'd driven the horses towards the door. Pounding on the heavy wooden structure did nothing to bring anyone to the door, nor did it do anything to improve his temperament. From the side of the home a frail, petite, grey-haired woman hobbled with the aid of a wooden cane towards Duncan.

"G'day, Mr. Thomas. If 'tis the doctor you'll be

needin' he's off to the O'Donnell's. They're having their baby today."

Duncan left her standing alone pointing her cane in the air. "We have to go to Serina's, Lucian. I'll explain later," he yelled back through the carriage window.

Numb to the core, Lucian brushed Raven's hair from her face, while his thoughts drifted to a time four years back when they were both still at university, and how he nearly lost Raven. He hadn't allowed himself to think about the sick events that almost killed his twin because even behind closed eyes he could see the nightmare all too vividly.

****

Four Years Earlier 1892

With only days until graduation, Lucian sat beside Raven on a bench outside the men's dormitory at the university, both quiet watching as families and friends prepared for the commencement ceremonies.

"I do believe, Luce, you and I are the only ones here with no family," Raven mumbled as she watched an ant drag an object much bigger than itself deep into a hole. Raven back-filled the bug's little doorway to the world without a second thought.

"You've got me, Ray, always. Mum and Dad would be so proud of you."

Raven sat up and cut Lucian off, placing her fingers to his lips. "Of us, Lucian. You're fantastic. Mum had dreams for you, but you surpassed them all. You are smart, suave, and dashingly handsome."

Lucian cut Raven off. "Raven, don't ever call me handsome. Smart and suave are fine. Definitely dashing, but sisters aren't supposed to notice things like that, but thank you." Lucian gave her a half court bow with the tip of his finger from his forehead.

Raven pushed at his chest playfully. "I'm not lusting after you, dear brother, that's simply vulgar. Comparatively speaking, look at that roommate you've had all these years, Xavier Sinclair. He is truly the most undesired, depressed man I've ever met. Let's just state the obvious and go from there. His eyes look like water after you've had your bath."

Lucian placed his hand over his heart. "Me?"

Raven stifled a smirk. "His lips are so thin and red. They look like they were painted by an artist who'd run out of paint. His teeth remind me of a shark, too many and too sharp. His body is identical to the skeleton hanging in the science lab. Neither meat nor muscle on him. I hope someday soon modern science can help him and his hubris. Unreal! He believes himself to best any man. You ever see him around women? No sane woman would willingly hand over her dowry for him."

Lucian threw his arm around his sister's shoulder and tugged her to him. "No worries, Ray. Your dowry's a tad bit skimpy as it is." Lucian teased, pointing towards her chest. "No man is good enough for you. I'll take care of you forever."

"Lucian!" Raven blushed. "I love you, but there's a limit, and you are pushing it."

"Well, speak of the devil and sadly the ugly scalawag does appear." Lucian twisted her head in the direction of the man. "Xavier, we were just talking about you." Lucian extended his hand toward the emaciated man.

Raven sat quiet, her cheeks trapped between her teeth.

"All good things I'm sure, Lucian," Xavier stated as he returned the shake. Xavier's glance covered Raven head to toe. He bid, "Raven, good afternoon. Sad to think there are only days left 'til we part our ways. I assume you'll not be following me to my home to toss me out of my bed any longer. I truly regret you never once let me lie by your side." Xavier grinned, showing off all those teeth Raven had no use for. "I found it cold on that floor all those nights I lent you my bed."

Raven's stomach rolled at the very idea of ever lying with him. "Trust me, Xavier, it would have been colder in the bed." Raven tried to make light of the statement, but she was dead serious, and her smile frozen. As Raven would've guessed, Xavier never seemed to notice.

Good comeback, Raven. Lucian tossed to her mentally, while his eyes never left Xavier's face.

Raven's lips thawed enough to give him a slight grin.

"Hello, hello, my lord and lady." A loving voice welcomed Lucian and Raven. They turned and eagerly closed the distance.

"Duncan, so great to see you. We hoped you'd make it." Lucian hugged him. Standing a good four inches taller than Duncan, it appeared as if he could climb on top of the man and smother him.

"Air, Luce, I need air. Your grip's grown stronger boy...finally. And your legs, longer, if that's possible." As he spoke to Lucian, Duncan grabbed Raven and brought her snugly to him. "'Ello, me beauty. I've missed you, not your cooking mind you, just you. Heard there was a fire at the main kitchen. That wasn't you, right?" Duncan looked up too late to see Lucian motioning behind Raven's back for him to hush. "Oh dear."

Tears welled in Raven's eyes. "'Tisn't as awful as the tabloids made it out to be. No one died and a new building replaced the old smoke house." Raven sniffled.

"Change of topic then? Did you two actually think I'd miss the biggest day of your lives? Ah Ray, don't cry." Duncan wiped away Raven's tears. "Come, my little cry babe. Show me around this university and then let's get a bite to eat. 'Tis a long dusty ride here, and I'm a hungry boy." Duncan, with an arm around the two of them whisked them away, ignoring the last man standing, Xavier.

"Long ride here my a—" Raven tried to tease, but Duncan covered her mouth before she could finish her sentence.

"André's a long ride. We're a hop, skip, and a jump, old man," Lucian finished.

"The Queen sends her best," Duncan subtly slipped in.

"Who?" Lucian asked.

Duncan gave Lucian a disappointed glance. "Still not speaking with her, are we?"

"Not in this lifetime, old man."

****

After dinner and a stroll throughout Piccadilly, investigating all the new and upcoming boutiques and bakeries, Lucian and Duncan escorted Raven with all her packages back to her dorm. Lucian planned to catch up on old times with Duncan. He needed to know his friend would be all right after his tragic loss. A new little person in the manor would have been so welcome and loved, but instead things went terribly wrong and a funeral for both his wife and baby was arranged. One large casket and one tiny white casket lay side by side in their private cemetery. Lucian hated reliving that day, yet he could never forget it or the broken look on Duncan's face when his family was laid to rest.

But tonight, Duncan looked superb. The two men walked to a local pub for an ale or two, to relax and enjoy life. They'd lost track of the time talking, when Raven invaded Lucian's thoughts, scared and screaming. Lucian grabbed Duncan's arm and dragged him from the pub, the mug still clutched in Duncan's hand, his ale spilling out, Duncan muttering gibberish.

****

The unexpected knock on the door startled Raven. What could her two boys want or have forgotten, she wondered. Raven opened the door and took a step back. In the hallway, with a starved barracuda-toothed grin upon his face, Xavier lurked.

Her voice cracked, "Xavier? 'Ello. What can I do for you?" An uneasy feeling punched Raven in the very pit of her stomach. His cold, lifeless eyes gave her a morose feeling. Xavier didn't look right, not that he ever did, but this night he had more of a disheveled appearance. She thought about slamming the door in his face and locking it, but poor judgment gave way. For a moment, she felt foolish. This man had never been anything but a gentleman to her. He'd been her brother's roommate for all the years they lived at university. She never liked his appearance, but had never imagined him dangerous.

"Raven, may I speak to you for a moment? I've a graduation gift for you. Might I come in?"

Raven watched his bony fingers twist, and the tips blanch white. She pressed her hand to her abdomen and bit back a grimace. "Xavier, thank you for the thoughtfulness, but you shouldn't have. I've nothing for you."

"Oh, you do, Lady St. James. Trust me."

When Xavier's tongue wet his lower lip her flesh turned to raw chicken skin, clammy and bumpy. She backed further into the room. He followed.

"For years now, I've watched you grow into a beautiful woman, and I've waited for you to come to me. So many lost opportunities, Raven." Xavier nudged past her as he spoke. "You never came, Raven. So now, I'm coming to you. I've been most patient, but there are only days left till we part our ways, and I want to—no I need to show you how I feel. I know you feel the same way. You just could never tell me because your precious brother was always around. Now he's not. It's just you and I, finally alone."

Raven wiped his spittle from her cheeks. His rigid body language oozed violence, better than a festering sore. Seeing his skeletal fingers coming towards her, she backed away, her mind a flurry of thoughts.

What in hell is wrong with him?
He couldn't possibly want—no—sex?
He's a bleedin' pilchard if he thinks...Lucian!
Why the hell did I allow him in? Lucian!

She didn't know whether to scream bloody murder or reason with him. She told herself to remain calm and just talk to him, then everything would be all right. "Xavier, I'm sorry if I've ever misled you about my feelings for you. I've always considered you a friend." *Dammit, men get so insecure with the word "Friend."* "What of your family? I've heard mention of the Maestro and your brother Xanti. Are they coming to the ceremonies? I just love how you call your father the Maestro." Petrified, Raven prattled, hoping to stall Xavier until her brother could get to her. Sweat beads slid down her neck and into her cleavage. She followed Xavier's eyes as he watched. Then the one thing she didn't want to happen—happened. Tears replaced sweat drops.

"Stop it, Raven. Stop acting like a child!" Xavier yelled. He shook his head back and forth, fists clenched. When he refocused, he smiled, but it was a smile Raven didn't want directed at her.

Ever.

"No Raven, no family this time. My father and brothers really aren't morning people. I'll see them after the ceremonies."

"Xavier, really, you need to leave now. It's late, and I'm tired. I've been very busy today and tomorrow will be the same with Duncan here and all the pre-ceremony activities taking place. The ladies and I are preparing an early tea." Raven's hands trembled as she pointed to the door.

Lucian, come to me now. I'm in trouble, real trouble. Raven sent the thought to her brother again and again. A silent mantra. She headed for the exit. "I'll get the door for you."

Xavier blocked her. "I don't think so, Ray. You and I aren't going anywhere for a while. I told you I want to show you how I feel for you. Now," he spit out as he grabbed her arms and thrust her onto the bed. With one forceful blow, he backhanded her across the face.

Welts blossomed across her cheek.

"I like the tears on you, Ray. I'm going to lick them off you, one by one. And for our finale I'll make love to you until you scream my name. You'll never want another man nor have another man, Ray, if it's not me."

The last thing Raven saw was his fist coming directly at her.

****

One of the housemothers heard the pleas and got to Raven's room just as some beast fled Raven's room covered in blood. She yelled at the top of her lungs, "It's Jack, it's Jack the Ripper, bloody God help us," as she took chase after him and chucked her tea cup at his back. Xavier vanished, leaving the woman staring into the empty hallway. The woman swung around dizzily and began screaming, "It's Dracula" and passed out.

****

At the entrance to Raven's dorm, Lucian noticed two women in the hall, whispering. He heard only a few words, beaten, bound, and raped, and he blew the door open in a blind rage. Raven sat on the bed with two women tending to her. Her eyes swollen, and bruised. Blood trickled from her nose. Her clothes stained red and torn to shreds. The strand of pearls their mother had given her for her sixteenth birthday, gone. Raven had never taken the necklace off from the day she received the gift.

Bite marks covered Raven's chest and abdomen. Her right arm dangled in such an unnatural state, Lucian knew the surgeon would have to be called to mend it, not to mention everything else on her battered body.

Sitting beside her, Lucian went to hold his sister's hand, but she pulled away from him, her head hung. Her black hair matted down by blood concealed her anguish. A constant stream of tears rushed off her. The very sight of her ripped open Lucian's heart.

Her hand to her jaw, Raven managed to whisper, "Lucian, I know you have questions, but not now. I am too disgraced to face you. He has stripped my very soul from within me."

Overwrought with emotion, Lucian didn't know what to do or how to help his sister. He didn't have the right words to say to her and he'd never experience that before. They'd shared every aspect of their life together never holding anything back from one another. Now Raven sat before him despondent. Then his tears came. He turned away. She couldn't see his pain. She'd worry about him. That was her nature; everyone else came first. So badly, he wanted to hold her, take away the hurt in her beautiful blue eyes.

"Ray, I know you feel many things now, I can see into your mind. This is in no way your fault. Never blame yourself for this, my beauty." Lucian had all he could do to keep his voice neutral, but an edge to it gave him away. "Please just give me a name, and I'll make sure he never hurts you or any other woman ever again."

"Why, Lucian? What bloody good would it do

now?" Raven's voice carried such rage it took Lucian aback. Hatred and bitterness shielded her now.

"The damage is done. The bastard's probably ruined any hope I have at having children. Lucian, look what that monster did to me. Look, Lucian." Raven yelled hysterical. So much, in fact, she spread her legs apart and pulled her torn pink skirt up past her thighs.

"No, my beauty, don't do this," Lucian choked at the sight of the damage to her. He covered her, closed his eyes and prayed he could forget the heinous vision now imprinted forever behind his eyelids.

One of the women in the room threw an arm around him fearing he might faint. He shrugged her away.

"Ray?" Lucian went to place his arms around her, but she pulled away again. Lucian was certain death was upon him. He let the monster get her, when he'd promised for so many years to protect her. He let her believe he was her knight in shining armor. He'd failed her. He was no better than the monster that did this to her.

Don't think that, Lucian. You still are my knight. Just rusty. I love you.

That one thought tipped the scales. Tears fell as if the levy gave way. He loved Raven. There she sat, broken, saturated in her own blood, and she was trying to make him feel better. He pulled her against him, protectively.

Duncan eased his way into the room. He couldn't believe his eyes. Choked up, his knees buckled, and he landed on the floor beside Raven. He reached for her hand. "My little beauty, I will get the man who did this to you, I swear this on me life. I love you, Ray."

Duncan got off the floor, hugged Lucian and staggered into the hall. The pain on Raven's face...He couldn't bare it. He did not want her to witness the rage he felt. And with everything Duncan had been through, he couldn't trust his emotions to stay resilient and strong for her.

After the surgeon arrived, Duncan broke the news that it was Xavier who had attacked Raven. He told Lucian, "Raven put up the fight of her life. The women in the hall saw the tail end of the attack and tried to help. They told me Raven gouged one of his grey eyes from his head and tore off one of his testicles too. Xavier ran from the room holding his nob, screaming like a baby. His broken ball is splattered on the floor in there." Duncan pointed back over his shoulder to the room. "His eye hung from a tethered nerve." Knowing she'd gotten a piece of the bastard, made Duncan feel better. Now it was his turn to get a chunk of the bastard, his head. Preferably both.

****

Within a day's travel, André St. James arrived in London. He'd heard Raven's screams, felt her distress just as Lucian had the second the attack happened because he shared the same mental pathways his cousins did. He dropped everything, fled France and came to offer his support for Raven and a swift sword for the monster that hurt her.

The three men searched for months but found no leads to Xavier. It was as if the rogue disappeared from the face of the earth.

****

Present, 1896

Molly headed across the street mid-morning, her little black and white cat winding its way between her feet with each step. She knocked on Serina's door, calling to her new friend, but the door remained closed. Molly didn't seem too concerned thinking maybe the doctor went to work and had gotten an early start. She turned to leave when the pounding of hooves in the distance caught her attention. She looked down the road and saw Duncan at the helm of the carriage fast approaching. Dirt and rocks spit out from under the wheels. A wake of unsettled dust hung in the air. Molly started back towards the house.

"Have you seen Serina today, Molly?" Duncan yelled as he jumped from the carriage.

"No, Duncan. I don't think the doctor's home."

Lucian jumped out from inside the carriage, with Raven crushed against his chest. Before he could ask, Duncan took Raven. Lucian stormed up to the door and began pounding on it. "Serina!" He yelled, as he slammed his shoulder into the door a few times. The door cracked beneath his weight, and Lucian shoved his way through. Charging, he made his way up the stairs to her bedroom, where he found Serina face down on the floor. Beside her, a broken pitcher lay in a puddle of water.

He lifted her from the floor and headed back downstairs to the kitchen. "Duncan, bring Raven into the parlor."

After Lucian lay Serina on her kitchen table, he placed cool, wet cloths on her face and chest trying to bring her around.

Finding herself in the arms of a very handsome man once more would have been a nice start to Serina's day had she not been soaked and chilled to the bone or had the sudden urge to vomit all over everything. Lucian included.

"Please forgive me, Lucian," she offered mortified. "You're going to need a new wardrobe if you keep coming here. What's happened to get you back to me so soon? Better question, why am I on my table soaking wet?" Serina wiped her mouth off with a rag supplied by Lucian.

"Raven was attacked again. She needs help,

although after seeing you, I'm not so sure you can help her. I found you on your floor." Lucian wiped Serina's stomach contents from his shirt.

"Help me up, and I'll get things ready for another transfusion. Is Raven awake?"

"Barely. To touch her, well it's as if she were..." His voice trailed off. "Please help her, Serina. Use my blood."

"Lucian, go ask Molly and Duncan to go to All Hallows Church on Byward Street. I need them to bring Father Butler back. After they've left we need to talk."

"Only if you use my blood."

"Bribery?" Serina wrinkled her nose at him. He returned her wrinkle with a shifty eyebrow and then tapped a finger to his arm, reiterating his desires silently.

She argued and ran nothing short of a filibuster that Lucian wasn't strong enough to donate after losing so much blood last night, but he insisted and made a liar out of her by the time they were finished. He was a spry one.

****

"Hello, my child." Father Butler greeted Serina with a quick peck on her cheek. Coming in from the blustery morning what few hairs the man held were windblown and stood on end, his cheeks a ruddy purple. The portly little man carried a smile big enough for all of them until he saw Raven's grave appearance. Shortly thereafter, the priest administered her last rites.

In the corner of Serina's kitchen, Lucian stared into space. Lost.

Last rites.

Father held little hope for her. Lucian's heart ached like never before. Yesterday they danced at a ball, laughed, enjoyed their friends, spoke of future dreams, and today...the Grim Reaper loomed outside. He wiped the foul tears from his cheeks as he watched Father Butler pour the blessed water over his sister. With each bubble that boiled from the holes in her neck, the acid within his stomach rose. He swallowed hard.

Not long after, Father Butler told him Raven may not respond to his exorcism or the transfusion, but if she survived, she may show signs of turning into a vampire.

Lucian listened to Father tell him things he'd never thought possible. It was as if someone wrote a horror novel and he was the main character, Raven the poor waif, destined to a gloomy ever-after. When Father Butler told Lucian he had to pour the blessed water on him too, Lucian decided his gloomy ever-after was looking a little too surreal for his liking. He never uttered a sound as the water burned through his flesh to rid the evil incubus from his body.

Serina couldn't watch. She worried that Father Butler was right to give Raven her passage to heaven. She'd seen cadavers in the morgue come in looking better, even the bloke she beheaded. Was that only yesterday?

Father Butler tapped Serina's shoulder jarring her thoughts. "I've done all I can for your new friends. You be safe, little girl. You are my heart."

"I won't allow anything bad to happen to them, Father."

"Little girl, the bad things have taken place. There are some things you truly have no control over."

"Ye of little faith, Father. You don't give me enough credit." Serina stepped closer and kissed Father's cheek. "Thank you for your help."

"I've seen your work, dear. You're years away from enlightenment. 'Tis a shame your mum left in such a tizzy. So much to learn, so little time." Father attempted a small smirk and quickly lost it. "For you, Serina, I'd lie down and die if you needed me to."

"There's a gloomy note to end the day on. Love you, Father. Give my babies at the home one of these for me." Serina hugged the man to her.

He broke away. "If you have need, call." Father Butler handed each of them a silver cross, said a silent prayer and then left, his step much slower than his racing mind.

Hours passed and morning turned to early afternoon. Raven spent the majority of the morning teetering between lucidity and lunacy. Lucian had carried her upstairs to Serina's spare room. Worn out, he too stretched out on the floor beneath his twin. The last thing he saw before he drifted off to sleep was Serina curled up in the seat by the bay window reading.

Upon awaking, Lucian asked Duncan to run to the manor for fresh clothes. The remnants of Serina's stomach contents lingered on his shirt, and the scent did not resemble the fine cologne he usually dowsed himself in.

Serina met him at the base of the stairs.

"I'm going to check on Raven. Coming back up?" She held her hand to him.

Lucian grasped her fingers and trailed after her. A shrill squeak escaped the door's hinges when Serina shoved it open. Both she and Lucian jumped. Raven never flinched. "She sleeps like the dead." Lucian pushed past Serina and went to his sister's side, then sat upon the bed. "I probably should rephrase that!" He sighed.

Serina walked to the opposite side of the bed and pressed her palm to Raven's forehead. Raven was clammy and her clothing smelled of strong urine. "Excuse me a moment?" Serina turned and left the room. When she returned she held a stack of white linens, some clean undergarments and a night-dress. She set the pile down beside Raven. "Lucian, would you excuse us for a few minutes?" Serina didn't want to tell Lucian that Raven had soiled herself.

Lucian stood in haste. "Why?"

"Your sister needs dry clothing, that's all."

"I'll do it. I'll change her."

Puzzled, Serina asked, "Wouldn't she rather a woman change her?"

Lucian shook his head adamantly no. "I said I'll do it."

Serina backed away, both angered and hurt by his shortness. After all, she was only trying to help.

"I hadn't meant to sound so bitter, but my concern for Raven has gnawed away my last nerve. She'd die a thousand deaths if she knew anyone ever saw her."

"But, Lucian, I am a doctor and a woman."

Lucian fingered the stubble on his chin before he spoke. "You don't understand. How could you?" He tossed his hands in the air, at a loss. "Raven wears scars across her body that she wants no one to witness. Ever. She was raped four years ago and came close to death. The bastard chewed chunks from her, Serina. She allowed only myself to care for her as she healed. She clings to her dignity. If she knew you saw her, she'd worry you would think less of her or worse—pity her. So if you'll give us some privacy, I'll attend to my sister." Lucian gave Serina the full weight of his gaze.

Serina's heart immediately went out to Lucian. To carry such a burden and such love for his sister, showed true unconditional love. Serina closed the distance and embraced him. "I'm sorry," she offered as she glanced directly into his chest. She couldn't help the small curl to her lips. Their height differences made standing together somewhat awkward. "I should have asked, not just presumed I would provide her care."

Lucian grabbed Serina and held her. He even went as far as to plant a small peck on the top of her head. "It is I who should apologize, m'lady. I am just so used to doing everything for her. It is hard to let go. Harder to let others in."

"Possibly you could start now, by letting me help you. Maybe in time Raven could grow to trust me as well." Serina backed out from Lucian's grasp and left to get water.

Lucian felt a small piece of his soul relax. This little woman he'd found was a rare, special creature. Her caring and generosity took him by storm, but then again, everything about her had.

When she came back into the room he asked, "Are you certain you want to see this? It is truly inhumane."

Serina braced herself for whatever Lucian revealed as he lifted the covers. Serina stared in disbelief at Raven's scars for some time. And then tears flooded in her eyes.

"You all right?" he asked.

Serina shook her head no.

Lucian tilted her chin to bring her face into view. "Maybe now you understand why Raven doesn't want anyone to see this."

"Lucian?" Raven called out.

Lucian dropped the coverlet in haste. "'Ello, Beauty. How you faring?"

Raven licked her lips. "Parched comes to mind. A cup of tea would hit the spot." Her smile was weak, but there. "Mind filling me in why I'm in a strange bed?"

"I've got the tea. You two catch up." Serina offered a little too fast. On her feet and headed out, Lucian grabbed her wrist as she passed him.

He whispered, "Nice. You're leaving me with the

real dirty work of explaining?"

"Beauty and brains, m'lord. A rarity to be sure." And with that she scooted out the bedroom door.

Lucian eyed his sister with great apprehension. "You certain you want tea? Not blood?" he asked absent of any humor.

Raven backed up on the pillow. She eyed Lucian oddly. "What the 'ell is wrong with you? 'Ave you lost your mind?"

"What do you remember of last night, Beauty?"

"You tucking me and then I awoke here, only minutes past, so begin your explanation, dear brother. You've piqued me curiosity. And don't even attempt to tell me any more vampire tales."

"Oh my fair, Raven." Lucian lay beside her, and plucked one of the pillows from behind her head for himself. "Lie back and allow me to attempt to explain the unexplainable."

Serina returned with a tray filled with steaming Earl Grey tea, crumpets and garden-fresh, raspberry jam. She fast realized she'd be dining alone. Raven lay curled within Lucian's strong arms, both of them sound asleep. She briefly wondered what it would be like to nestle within his arms, and wake every morning beside him. Heaven came to mind.

Early evening, Lucian ventured to the kitchen to find Serina with her nose buried in a book. Noticing a tray of food on the counter, he bee-lined for it.

"'Ello," he said as he jammed a mouthful of a crumpet into his mouth.

Serina wiped a few crumbs from his cheek. "Hungry? Duncan and Molly are across the road cooking supper for us. They'll be here shortly. How's your sister?"

"Burning up."

Serina slammed the book closed, crossed her kitchen and pulled out a canning jar filled with yellow powder.

"Curry?"

Serina shook her head no.

"Mustard powder?"

Another nod side to side. Deep in thought, she placed a finger to her lips and shushed him.

"I placed more cool cloths on her forehead and changed her again. She comes and goes." Lucian told her as he followed on her heels.

Serina tapped her finger to the jar. "I've got something to reduce the febrile state." Minutes later she had a cup of tea and the powdery substance beside it in a small apothecary bowl.

Lucian dipped his finger into the powder, tasted it and scrunched his face. "'Tis bitter. What is it already?"

Serina smirked at his facial expression. "Salicylic acid. It comes from a willow tree's bark. Not to worry. It's not black magic or anything so medieval. I've sweetened her tea so when I add this, she'll never taste it."

They took the tea to Raven. Lucian scooted behind Raven and held her steady while Serina helped her take small sips until the cup was empty. Within minutes, Raven's eyelids fell closed.

At the sound of her back door opening, Serina picked up the empty dishes. "I think our supper is here. Will you join us or shall I bring yours to you?"

Lucian stretched out his legs and yawned. Without censor, he glanced at Serina and said, "You are truly lovely. Would up here be all right? I don't want to leave her."

Serina nodded. "You don't have to make up compliments to get me to do things for you."

"I made up no such thing, m'lady."

Tray in hand, Serina curtsied, wobbled on one leg, which caused the china to topple over into a heap on the floor. Serina plunked down beside the broken dishes, too embarrassed to move. "Would you like to replace lovely with lubberly? I am a true klutz."

Lucian crossed to her, and slid his arms underneath hers. With a little lift, he had her on her feet again. "No I would not. Maybe you should get some rest."

Before she had time to protest, he cleaned up the broken china and carried it down stairs.

Serina traipsed behind this time.

"Supper's in here, Luce," Duncan offered from the dining room.

"Old man, what have you cooked up? It smells..."

Duncan covered Lucian's mouth as he looked him dead in the eye. "Molly made us some steak and kidney pie, Luce. Been a long time since we've had that, hey?" The grin, if it was really one, warned Lucian to tread lightly.

"That it has," Lucian answered. *Just not long enough!* "I'm going to take mine upstairs if you don't mind. Ray's in a state, and I need to be there when she wakes fully."

The twinkle in Duncan's eye faded. "Your clothes are in the washroom. I'll be up shortly to relieve you."

"We're good, Duncan, but thank you." Lucian turned and hugged Molly for her thoughtfulness and carried his bowl of steaming organs up the stairs, holding it an arm's length from his nose.

Serina looked between the flaky pie and her half-eaten crumpet. "Molly, please save mine for later? I'm going to take Lucian up on his offer and rest. You two, make yourselves comfy. There's some of Father Butler's homemade wine in the pantry. It packs a wallop, so be careful."

"Serina!" Lucian yelled from the top of the stairs. "Come quick!"

Serina hiked up her skirt and took the stairs

two at a time with Duncan one-step behind her. They entered the room and found Raven hunched over the bed in distress. Serina rushed to her aide. Lucian knelt down in front of his sister, and swept her hair from her face.

"What is it, Raven?" Serina asked.

"The tea, it's poisoned. It's ripping me stomach in half." Raven vomited, covering her brother in curdled tea. "I'm sorry, Luce." She began to cry.

"It's all right, Beauty. I'm getting used to it. I'm going to draw a bath for you."

Raven nodded. "Serina, I'm sorry I'm making a muck of your home."

"Raven, everything is washable, your brother included. I should've known better. Sometimes the medicine gives people an upset tummy without food." Serina hugged Raven to her. "Come on. I hear Lucian and Duncan trying to draw your bath. Since when does it take two men to turn on a faucet?"

"They are joined at the hip. It takes one to think of something and the other one to act upon it." Raven attempted a grin but it never left her lips. Instead, she finished emptying her stomach.

After Serina helped her into the bathroom, Duncan offered, "I'll take her from here, Serina."

Serina pointed. "I'll be right in that room." Her bedroom was adjacent to the bath.

Raven grabbed Lucian's and Duncan's hands. "I'll be fine on me own. Really. I'm feeling a bit more human since I tossed that stuff up on you, Luce. You need this bath more than I do."

Lucian swept his arm from Raven to the tub, gesturing, "Ladies first. Holler if you need me. I'll be right outside."

"Hey, Ray?" Duncan tapped her on the shoulder, "Want some pastries? I'll run out and grab them. No problem."

"You're a love, Duncan." Raven pushed everyone

out of the room and locked the door behind her.

One hour later, Lucian sat with his back against that very door, his leg bouncing off nervous energy as he waited to hear any signs of life. Worried, he knocked on the door. "Raven?"

No answer.

"Raven?" He pounded louder.

Feeling the walls vibrate from Lucian's fists *a-rat-a-tat-tatting* on them, Serina ventured out to the hall.

Annoyance defined Lucian's face. "She's locked the door and isn't responding."

"I'll go grab the key. Don't bust anymore doors down." Serina tried to lighten his mood, but Lucian didn't respond. She returned holding the key out. "Here you g—"

He snatched the little skeleton fob from her hand, twisted the key and pushed on the door. It didn't budge. "Raven?" he screamed.

"There's a door from my parents room. Give me the key back." Serina took the key and ran down the hall. "Lucian? Get in here fast."

Raven's unresponsive silhouette was a bold contrast against the cold white tile. A steady stream of blood flowed from an open laceration on her calf with a straight-edged razor beside her foot. Serina grabbed a few towels and placed a pressure dressing across the wound, then sent her energies inside to cauterize the wound without anyone the wiser.

Lucian's jaw dropped. "She tried to kill herself?" Confused he mumbled, "Ray? What the hell are you doing?" He picked her up from the floor and headed back to the bedroom.

Serina eyed Lucian. It was a toss-up as to who looked worse. Serina grabbed a clean cloth and dabbed sweat from Lucian's brow, then lifted his thick mane of curls from his neck and wiped the cloth across him. "Feel better?"

Lucian gave her a sluggish nod. "Why? Why would she do this?" Once he had Raven tucked in, he walked to the hearth, knelt down, and gathered some kindling. It didn't take long for the room to fill with a sweet aroma of black cherry wood once the fire took hold. Tired, Lucian rested his head on the side of the bed.

Understanding the type of day he'd had, Serina suggested, "Lucian, why don't you go freshen up. I'll make us some hot tea."

Lucian lifted his head to meet Serina's gaze. "Better idea. You go freshen up and I'll make the drinks. I've seen your balancing act. I'd like to drink it, not wear it." He winked. "You've done more than humanly possible for us today, Serina. I can ask no more of you." Lucian stood and walked to her. He snuggled her in his arms and regardless of circumstances, a shudder of need engulfed him. With his head atop of hers, he let his lips linger. This, he could get used to. Forcing himself away, he told her, "I'll draw your bath. Stay put."

"Don't you need Duncan?" Serina asked.

Lucian smiled. "Funny!"

With a few minutes to kill and a sore back, Serina stretched out next to Raven. The heat from the fire found her a welcome target.

After filling the tub with some of Serina's scented oils and placing rose petals in the water, Lucian sought out Serina only to find her sound asleep beside Raven. He looked over both his ladies. He loved one dearly, since the day they were born. The other, he knew he would love until the day he died.

He grabbed Raven's toes and wiggled them. "Ray, wake up. We need to chat."

Serina stirred. "Lucian?" She climbed from the bed and motioned him to follow her. "Come to me." She opened her arms to him and waited.

Lucian wiped his eyes, but he didn't move. Because right now—if he moved to embrace her, he was certain he couldn't stop himself. He needed Serina right now more than he needed air. He wanted to lose himself in the woman and forget the day's past events, and that wouldn't be fair to her. When he did make love to Serina it would be from passion and a mutual trust, not sympathy. Lucian stood, took her hand and placed a gentle kiss on her palm. "I'll send Duncan up now." He walked out without turning back.

Serina's arms fell to her sides. Her tears followed, stinging her cheeks. She moped down the hall like a scolded dog with his tail between his legs. Serina wanted to comfort, to hold him close and let him know she was there for him, that whatever he needed she would provide. Instead, she'd been cast aside like a pair of old shoes that were too small or not the right color or just plain ugly.

"Hi, Doc," Duncan said as they passed. "Guess I'm on watch for the night. Lucian left. Said he needed air, a lot. Want to fill me in?"

"Not really."

"Anything specific I have to do?" Duncan asked.

"Just be there when she wakes. I'm turning in for the evening." Serina entered her room, closed the door, threw herself atop her bed and attempted to drown herself in tears.

Chapter Four

Magpies squabbled outside her bedroom window louder than a marching band. Serina pulled the covers over her face. It didn't lessen the boisterous birds' cackles, but it did knock out the sunshine telling her it was well past her time to rise and shine. Eyes clamped shut, she attempted to go back to sleep. She found no reason to hurry out of bed and subject herself to one, Lord St. James. She couldn't face him, certain he'd laugh in her face after his blatant rejection last evening. He was probably still rolling on the ground laughing.

"I must have appeared so fatuous to him. Why would any man want me? I'm color blind, clumsy and a-b-s-o-l-u-t-e-l-y ignorant to men and their needs," she said to no one.

Her toes wiggled without her doing. "Oh, God no!" She rustled all her courage and inched her way from under the safety of her covers.

"G'afternoon, m'lady. Definitely color blind and clumsy, but ignorant doesn't become you."

Serina's eyebrow shot upward. Lucian had a definitive drawl that one acquires after consuming more than their fair share of spirits.

Lucian stared at Serina from the foot of bed, glassy-eyed, his hair windblown and his breath...Well it wasn't as fragrant as Serina remembered two nights past. She was willing to bet he'd found Father Butler's stash of wine and chased that down with water from the horses' trough.

Serina stared back.

"I'll say it again, possibly louder this time so as

you might respond? I'll even enunciate. Good afternoon, m'lady."

"Did you say afternoon?"

"Yes, I believe I did." Lucian dug into his pocket after his timepiece. When he pulled the watch out loose coins hit the floor and rolled under the bed. "Look. Look there. See it?" He attempted to tap on the face of the watch twice, missing each time.

"You've left no doubt where the phrase *drunk-as-a-lord* comes from. You're groggy!" Serina sat up and grabbed the watch from him. She held it so she could read it. "'Tis only quarter past nine you daft sod, not three forty-five." Serina tossed the watch back to him. It bounced from his fingers to the floor.

"Why did you throw that at me?"

Serina bit her cheeks, but she laughed regardless. The look on his face was precious. His eyelids drooped obscuring his vision and his pouty lips sulked. Oh, how she wanted to kiss that look off his face, ah but...she almost forgot, she was thoroughly upset with him. Done with the likes of him!

Serina tossed the covers from her bed and began to trudge past the drunken giant.

"Where do you thinks you're headed?" he asked as he hoisted her in the air and tossed her back onto her bed.

"Away from you." Serina raced to reach the other side of the bed on her hands and knees, but Lucian caught her foot and dragged her back to him, covers and all.

"What do think you're doing?" she shouted.

"I want you..." Lucian fumbled as he attempted to secure her hands.

"'Tis good to want, Lord St. James. It gives purpose to a person. Now let me go," she yelled. "I'm going to check on Raven." Serina kicked her way free, stomped out of the room and down the hallway.

"She's not in there, and I'm not deaf," he mumbled. "Just a wee inebriated."

The spare room was found vacant. She tramped back to her bedroom. Hands on her hips, she demanded, "Where is she then?" to a second empty room. "Lucian?" Serina spun around. Before she had time to think, Lucian had her over his shoulder, securing her with his hand pressed hard into her bottom as he headed back for the bed.

"You're insane if you're thinking what I think you're thinking," she screamed.

"What?" Lucian scratched his nose with his free hand. "I was last night when I walked out and left you. I won't make that mistake again."

"No you won't because I'm walking out on you—just as soon as you put me down." She punched at his backside.

"Bloody bugs are out." Lucian tightened his grip on her bottom while she tried to wrangle herself free. "Physics, my wild rose. Pure and simple. I am bigger and stronger than you." He slapped her little bum.

"Did you ever hear of David and Goliath, you big oaf? Did you just attempt to spank me?" Serina squirmed unsuccessfully.

"I will if you want me to." Lucian secured her legs and whipped her around to his chest so she lay in his arms.

He gave her a brilliant grin, one she wanted to knock off his face if she could just get free. He proceeded to toss her flat on her back and cover her with his two hundred-forty pounds of dead weight.

"I don't want to hurt you, Lucian," she warned. Lucian's mirth only enraged her more. "I mean it. Let me go." Serina began to cry. "Please, I don't want you..." She never got the chance to finish her sentence, like this, drunk.

Lucian covered her mouth with his hand.

"Shush! You don't mean that." About to cover her lips with his, Lucian stopped and studied her two heads and four wild, ferocious eyes. "I would never hurt you. I just want to kiss you. Trust me...that's all that could happen right now. I only want to tell you I am sorry I left you last night. I wanted you to want me for me. Pity was plastered all over your pretty little face."

Serina pushed at his chest, grunting. "Get off me! I need to find Raven."

"She's with Duncan at Molly's. Whatever you did to her helped. She's back to her old chipper self and spry as the kitten in your kitchen playing with the mouse. Nor did she try to kill herself. Seems she reached for the soap and the blade fell from the window sill and since she doesn't get on well with blood she passed out."

"Please get off me? I can't breathe." She lied through clenched teeth.

"Not so fast." He dipped his head towards her, testing the waters. If she truly didn't want him, he'd know soon enough, when she clobbered him. "Serina?" From behind sealed eyes, tiny water droplets ran off her cheeks. Drops he'd caused. "I'm going to kiss you, just once, and then I'm pretty certain I'm going to pass out."

"As you wish, m'lord." Serina was finished fighting both him and her head. Her heart would win this round. Being stubborn was one thing. Being stupid was not an option. When his lips covered hers all her anger, self-doubt and lack of self-esteem disappeared. He moved her to unchartered territories. She'd never lay beneath a man before, and she found this divine until his tongue dragged across her cheek and left behind a slippery cold trail. Then his head bumped into hers, and she heard him snoring—that fast.

"Oh bloody hell. He's got me pinned beneath

him. This is not happening." Serina took in slow, deliberate breaths of air. With only her fingertips free to move, she twirled them in an upward motion and envisioned a gentle wind to lift and carry Lucian to the other side of her bed. Short of breath and anxious when nothing happened, she spit out, "Any day now!"

Lucian's snoring intensified, sounding like tiger purring in her ear.

Swearing and thoroughly upset she tried a second time. "Winds of change, pick up your pace. Place Lucian St. James into outer space."

Everything happened so fast Serina didn't have time to react. She blinked and Lucian spun horizontally above her, in a cyclic fashion. First, his head whipped past her, then his feet, then his head again, and he kept going like her Victrola at nauseating speed.

Fully awake, he screamed for his life, "M'lady, I beg of you, stop this," as he grasped at air.

"There's a slight problem, Lucian," Serina yelled, "I've never done this incantation before. They rarely work as they should. Case in point, of course, being you." She tried to duck seeing him coming directly towards her.

Lucian latched onto Serina as he circled. Now they were both caught in the windstorm within her bedroom. Lucian's feet slammed into Serina's coatrack. Splintered. Serina's nightdress caught her oil lamp and tore it from the dresser. There would be no more flicker from the shattered rubble.

"You have to stop this," he screamed petrified.

Without giving it another thought Serina spit out, "The eye of the storm, a twist of fate, land us inside my garden gate."

Inside one second, outside the next, and falling fast towards thousands of thorns and roses. "Hammock," Serina bellowed a split second before they ruined her precious flowers. Never mind looking like a pincushion, the flowers came first. Serina had her priorities.

Serina shoved back her hair from her eyes and caught her breath. "Wow! I've never done anything quite like this before. What do you think, Lucian?" Serina asked exhilarated. "Lucian?" She tapped his cheek.

Lucian attempted to focus.

"I can explain," she said. "You're not hurt, right?"

Lucian stared in disbelief. He did however, find he fancied the position in which they landed. Serina was buried under him for a second time this morning with her legs spread to both sides of him, and her nightdress scrunched beneath her hips.

"Do you want me to tell you what happened?"

"Serina, after the past two days there's nothing—absolutely nothing you could say that would surprise me. The cat's out of the bag. I tried with the ignorance card pretending not to notice a few things, like the way Raven miraculously stopped bleeding last night or this feeling I can't shake that you were—are still inside of me. And the funny thing—I'm quite sober now, thank you. I can't even blame this on the wine or the whiskey or the scotch I got into last night thinking my sister attempted suicide after we were both attacked by vampires. This little excursion through the air was fun. We'll have to get a magic carpet the next time though. Duncan told me I should, by all rights, be popping up daisies, yet here I lie! Not that I mind this position." Serina opened her mouth to speak, but he placed his fingers to her lips. "Just tell me I haven't lost my mind. We'll go slow. I'll swallow one dose of your reality at a time, Dr. Spencer. Fair enough?"

Serina nodded. "Fair enough. Can we go inside and sit down?"

Lucian bumped noses with her. "Just don't point at me or say anything that rhymes." He winked, but he was dead serious.

Pushing his leg off to one side of the hammock to get up, Lucian trapped his foot in between the crocheted knots and lost his balance. They went into second spin. One second he was on top of Serina and the next she lay atop him on the ground hysterical with laughter.

"You are truly something else," he said as he reached up to brush her hair from her face.

Serina straddled him. Her new perch, she found empowered her. She also found out very fast that this was the direct route to relieve the itchy, tingling between her thighs. She rocked her pelvis over his groin, trying to be inconspicuous. Seems she wasn't the only one that liked their new position.

He returned her *not-so-inconspicuous* thrust with one of his one. "What's up?" he asked, his voice low and seductive.

"I am." Serina jumped, her face flushed. "I'm going inside. I can't do this here."

"Do what?" he teased.

"This—outside."

"Oh, but you could do it inside?"

"What was that name your sister calls you every chance she gets?"

"Imbecile. *Touché*," Lucian answered with a nod of his head.

"Yes, that's it. You coming in or sitting here alone?"

"I'm up too," he announced as he brought up the rear.

Seeing a significant rise in his trousers she thought, that you are. "I'll be right back. I need to change."

****

"Where to begin?" Serina made herself comfy on

her couch next to Lucian. "As you've witnessed, I was able to heal you and Raven because of special powers. I can also read people's minds. I read all four of you."

Lucian couldn't help it, he fell more in love with her as the day went on. Every move she made stole his breath, like the way her lips curled higher on one side or the ever-present twinkle her eyes held. His favorite was the way she nibbled on her lower lip when she looked at him as she did now. "You're a nosey little witch aren't you?"

"There's more…"

He sighed. "Isn't there always!"

With her lips slightly parted and her eyebrow arched, she finished, "Anyway, with the three of us doing blood exchanges we are all now connected to one another. I can hear you if you call to me and vice versa."

Lucian couldn't focus on anything other than how the sleeveless, black, lace blouse Serina wore accentuated her breasts. With each breath she took he watched, mesmerized by the rise and fall of her creamy flesh. Oh, what his tongue could do for her if strategically placed on or around her nipples.

"Remember, m'lord, I can read your mind."

A coy smile swept across his face. Nabbed! "You're not the only one, Serina, albeit it's different for me. Raven and I and our cousin, André have always had a special way to communicate with one another. Ever since we were children we've been able to read one another's thoughts. André's mum was our mum's twin. Runs in the family I guess." Lucian took her hand in his and stroked her fingers.

"Lucian, see if you can read my mind right now."

Her voice was a siren's sonnet that settled right in his groin, but then, wasn't that the whole point of the seductress?

Serina stifled a grin as he strained not to blink.

"Don't look at me as if you're going to burn a hole through me, just try to feel with your mind and heart at the same time." She scooted closer and began a slow lazy stretch of her arms over her head, with every intention of nudging her endowment forward. An invitation she hoped he'd accept.

He blurted, "Your desire shall be your death if you don't kiss me soon." Lucian puckered up and leaned into the lady. His advances were halted when Serina placed a firm hand to his chest..

"Not so fast, sir." She winked.

"All right, my desire shall be my death if I do not feel the promise of dreams your lips offer." Lucian returned the wink. With one swift move, he grasped her arms, pulled her across his lap, and turned her on her back.

The mischievous twinkle in her eye defined who she was: swift, cunning, sexy, loyal, and spirited beyond the norm. She was the most beautiful thing he'd ever seen and to have her in his arms was far more than he deserved. Lucian tucked one arm behind her back to cradle her head, while his other hand held her chin.

"Can you read my mind now?" he asked. Serina began to lift her head to kiss him when he stopped her in her tracks. He grinned. "Not so fast, m'lady." He dipped his head to greet her, his mouth finding solace on hers. He pulled away licking his lips. "God, woman, you're so sweet, I feel as if I may lose myself in you, and I've only just kissed you. Is this part of your magic?"

"Lucian if I held that force, I'd have men knocking down my door all the time, yet you, sir—" She nodded towards the remains of her front door. "—seem to be the only man intent on doing just that!" Serina wrapped her arms around him. "Kiss me again?"

"Where are my manners?" He moved a breath

away from her. "You'll never have to ask again." He snuggled beside her, crossed one leg over her legs, propped himself up on an elbow and gazed into her eyes. He began fidgeting with the buttons on her shirt, loosening them one at a time, waiting in between each one to see if a protest of sorts came. When none came, he advanced higher to the next button. Lucian left the last few buttons closed, more for her modesty. He found no corset beneath the shirt and silently thanked the Gods. He'd seen the torturous devices hanging in the wash room and knew if he were to ever have to remove one, well, the woman would be years older by the time he figured its secrets out. He slid his fingers across her ribs and abdomen and beneath him she shivered and tiny goose bumps formed.

"Chilly, my wild rose?" He blew a warm breath over her tummy.

Her thought went to him. *Quite the opposite, m'lord.*

"I got that, m'lady. Life is going to be interesting between us. I am most flattered and shall continue to fulfill your desires."

"You're a cocky SOB."

"You'll find out soon enough just how cocky." Lucian bent his head toward Serina's stomach and with the swirl his tongue inched his way across her sweet flesh. When he got to the last button he nibbled at it. Surprising them both, the button flew across the room leaving Serina baring all and laughing. "Oops. I'll stitch that back for you later." Lucian never took his eyes from Serina's face as he took her breast into his mouth, teasing her with his tongue, first with a quick flick then a light graze of teeth.

Opening her mouth to speak, Serina found her vocabulary reduced to moans, unable to form coherent thoughts from the pleasures he bestowed upon her. She caressed his cheek with her finger as his tongue caressed her breast. She loved the way his mouth feathered over her skin, and caused a deep, warm need between her thighs. She tried to relax, to just breathe, to enjoy these new sensations but she needed an outlet.

Serina went to work exploring Lucian. She ran her hands through the silken texture of his hair, then marched her fingers up and down his back, to her final destination, his scrumptious derriere.

That one gesture caused Lucian to change positions. He slid across her stomach and covered her with the weight of his hips.

She wiggled impatient. She needed his heated desire once more pressed hard against her mons either to relieve the incessant itch or rub her raw before she lost what was left of her sanity. This lust or hunger now awake within her, screamed for his undivided attention. Luscious little sensations reached well into her private lips and struck a chord. She ached to have his fingers, his mouth or the silky-smooth shaft she'd held in the carriage, buried within her to dance and resonate deep inside her.

Being this close to her, Lucian had to regain some control or this, his first time, would well be over before it began. Serina made him feel like a man for the first time in his life, made him feel things he'd only overheard others brag about in their conquests. This was no conquest. He was giving his heart to the woman.

"Can you read my thoughts now, m'lady?" He pressed his hips into her and gave a wiggle back and forth spreading her legs further apart until he nestled comfortably between them, and hit that one spot she itched to have scratched. He kissed her neck, lightly at first and then harder as he lost himself. Her delicate skin and the fragrance of blooming roses, intoxicated him. He thrilled listening to the small sounds of pleasure she made. This, without a doubt, he could get used to.

Everything Serina felt at that moment intensified tenfold as his lips ravaged her. She found out fast, her neck had a direct path to the deepest part of her body, where all her wants, desires, and dreams lay secretly locked away and his lush lips were the key. Serina returned a slow swivel of her hips. With all the movement between them the black skirt she wore ended up well up past her hips. She didn't remember how it got there only that she wanted it gone. Her satin drawers and his trousers were all that separated her from her dreams.

"Lucian," Serina asked. "Would you make love to me, now? Here? P—"

Lucian closed his lips over Serina's, silencing her pleas. His kiss was deep and long as passion drove his instincts. He broke away to see a smile on her lips. "I already told you, you'd never have to ask me again. I meant that. Are you sure here and now? I mean don't get me wrong, m'lady, I'm willing and able, but I want you to be positive."

"I've waited my entire life for you. My heart and head tell me I'm right. And trust me they rarely agree on anything. I've had dreams and desires that I've never thought I'd experience until I met you. I know you feel the same way. And not just because of this." Serina met the firmness of his erection when she pulled him closer.

With her fingertip, she traced the outline of his lips. "I fancy your lips kissing me here." Serina pointed to her mouth. She kissed him lightly. "And here." She pointed to her neck. She gave him another light playful kiss. "And here." Again, she covered his mouth with hers and delivered one deep, luring kiss, then she broke away, and she made a trail with her fingertip down between her breasts. "And definitely here." She slipped her fingers across her nipples watching him with a curious anticipation as he followed her finger. With a slight shift of hand, Serina grabbed Lucian's chin. With her eyes closed she met his mouth, hers slightly open, and slid her tongue to his and began the mating dance.

By this time, Lucian had Serina's drawers down, well past her hips, and on their way to their final destination, the floor. His disappeared just as quickly.

"I want to see you. I want to touch you, to make love with you, Lucian. And I want you to do the same to me." Serina was in no way embarrassed by her words. Confidence ruled her.

He stood before her, firm, lean muscles everywhere. "You are incredibly beautiful," she said staring in awe at his penis. She swiftly lifted her gaze before he caught her being so bold.

"You failed to mention one minor detail, m'lady." Lucian slid his hand over the length of his erection to give Serina a show of what he had to offer her.

Serina licked her lips. The length and breadth alone would not disappear inside her without a fight. Half of a grin worked onto her lips. The fight would be well worth the effort.

"That's not minor, luv," she teased as she wrapped her fingers around him and squeezed.

Lucian's body quivered.

Serina climbed from the couch and slid the blouse from her shoulders. It fell to the floor. The skirt vanished as well.

Lucian's intention? To ravish every inch of the woman from her thick, auburn hair, to her sparkling eyes, and those full, firm creamy breasts! And her mind. He loved her mind. She was brilliant, caring, compassionate, witty, desirable...

He closed the distance. His hands on her face, he tilted her chin to gaze into her eyes. He ran his fingers through her silken locks, and tugged her head back, exposing the luscious line of her neck. With only the warmth from his lips on her neck, her body stiffened with anticipation. The pulse beneath her skin raced as he kissed her. Had he not been so intrigued with every aspect of making love to this woman, the idea of her pulse should have bothered him. He'd touch on that subject later.

Until it, her scent, and the little *thump-thump—thump-thump—thump-thump*, ate at him and consumed what was going to be his first erotic moment of his life.

"You know, m'lady being a vampire may not be such an awful fate for you if I actually end up becoming one. I love the reaction I get when I kiss you here." Lucian kissed her neck. "And here." He kissed her cheek. "And definitely here." Lucian covered her breast and lapped at her nipple. He nibbled harder, flicked his tongue around her areola and suckled drawing her ripeness out. "Just think what would happen if I held special powers as you do and nibbled here?" He slid his hand between her thighs and pressed into her mons.

Serina moaned beneath his lips.

"Trust me, Lucian, you are special." The only thing that took a second or two to register was the fact he'd said something about a vampire. She couldn't quite recall if he said he was one or if he wanted to be one. At that point, she didn't care. She really didn't. If he did turn, she'd find a way to follow him—to the gates of the graves if that's where they ended up. Serina lapped at his nipples, now firm from her ascension and the tastiest little treat she'd had in her mouth, thus far.

Positive her knees were about to give out from under her, she slid her hands down and held onto his tush. She teased him as she slid her fingers between his cheeks, pinched him, patted him lightly and moved lower. When she grasped his sac, its squishy texture hardened.

"Everything turns to stone when I touch you."

"Everything but my heart." Lucian kissed the tip of her nose then crept back to her collarbone.

With his erection pressed against her stomach, firm, thick and hot little tremors sprinted through her as Lucian's lips worked their magic. "You're going to leave one of those little marks on my throat that tells everyone I've been up to no good, Lucian." She leaned backwards with a little moue.

"No good? And here I thought I was being so very good." He mimicked her pout. "I like the mark I've given you. I think it'll be one of many. The rest, however, will not be open to public viewing, luv." He slid his hand between her thighs again, and weaved his fingers through her dark curls. A warm moist invitation awaited him. When he ran his index finger and middle finger over her *cresson* and pinched her little nubbin, her teeth clamped down harder than vise grips onto his nipple. "Ooh!" An intense thrill settled in his groin.

He caressed her womanhood, stretched her, searching for that spot deep within her that would assuage the blissful pressure in her. From her body's reactions and the gentle groans she whimpered, he knew he'd discovered something.

Her muscles tightened and gripped his fingers. Tenderly, he eased two fingers inside her. He didn't want to hurt her when he entered her, knowing this would be her first time...his, too.

Serina didn't look hurt. Her smile reeked of shameless satisfaction. He continued to slip his fingers in, out, around, and over that one soft little fleshy nub that left her body trembling in his arms. Lucian thrust his tongue into her while his fingers caressed her private lips. Exact opposites on each end of her body.

About to lift her, movement through Serina's

window caught his eye. His dream of their first joining and his erection shattered. "Do not hesitate, and run for cover."

"Huh? What?" she asked one step away from a trance.

"We've company in about ten seconds. Move your dainty little arse unless you want Duncan viewing it."

One moment Lucian had Serina beside him and the next, he stood alone, naked, in her parlor. "Where are you?" he hollered.

"Upstairs, hurry." She giggled. "Oh that was close."

Lucian skulked into her bedroom and plopped down atop her bed. His long face made Serina bite the inside of her cheeks.

"What's the matter, m'lord?"

"You have to ask?" He motioned to his naked body. "All my things are in a heap on your floor. Not to mention, we didn't..."

"We will when the time is right and not before. Let me cover meself and I'll go get your knickers." Serina kissed Lucian softly before she headed out. "I rather fancied that downstairs, m'lord. Thank you."

"Lucian St. James, at your service! Before I forget, Serina, tonight is the dinner I asked you to attend."

As he sat with his hands strategically cupped across his loins, Serina had all she could do to not go to him, remove his cover and finish what they began downstairs.

"You will turn many a head with your beauty and elegance, Serina."

She choked on laughter. "You too shall turn many a head if I don't go retrieve your clothing."

Teasingly, he flashed her a quick peek of the remainder of his withered shaft. "You think?"

"Oh, Lucian!" Serina bent to kiss him one last

time because he looked too handsome in only his birthday suit. "After supper tonight, don't forget you owe me dessert. You are my dessert." She bit him lightly and walked out of the room.

Chapter Five

After Lucian returned from the manor with fresh clothing and gifts, Raven flat out told him she wasn't about to waltz into the restaurant looking like the zombie she felt like and having to answer every busy-body's question in the establishment about her horrendous past few days. Even though she felt better, her appearance left nothing to the imagination that she'd been to hell and back. Her neck held four distinct puncture wounds she couldn't explain without getting hauled off to the asylum. Her plan? She would stay with Duncan and Molly and be a third wheel, like it or not.

"Serina, I've something for you. You'll be needing it soon unless you were planning on taking me up on my idea and wearing nothing at all to dinner." Lucian stood in the hallway to her bedchamber with three lavish boxes, wrapped in silver and gold paper.

"Is it only you up here or do we have company?"

"Yes, and why would that make a difference?" Lucian's voice held an edge of amusement to it. Again excitement built within his body by her voice alone, and a single hope of what may come. Both of them sweaty, breathless and sated like never before worked for him!

The door to the bedroom opened to Serina wearing only a mischievous grin. She warned, "Enter at your own risk," as she reached for him and dragged him wide-eyed into the room.

Lucian closed the door behind them and placed the gifts on the dresser, then stood before her speechless.

Serina extended her hand to him and whispered, "Where is everyone?"

He had to clear his throat a few times before he managed, "Umm...in your garden, awaiting your beautiful presence."

"Then they'll have to wait a bit longer." Serina drew Lucian to her, and with her index finger, she motioned him closer to her mouth. "I'm not asking this time, m'lord," she whispered as she undid the buttons on his shirt. Once she could touch his chest, she began to lick him, soft caresses to his nipples, barely grazing them with her teeth. She enjoyed the way they swelled and protruded as she suckled. She had the same effect on hers. As her mouth explored his chest, her hands found the buckle of his trousers. Easily they slid to the floor. A small smile graced her lips. His nipples weren't the only thing that swelled. Serina slid his shirt from his shoulders, and admired the man before her. "I don't want you to move a muscle, Lucian. I want your legs to go weak, the way mine did earlier."

"I believe that's already been accomplished, m'lady."

"Before we were formerly introduced, m'lord—" Serina sank to her knees in front of him, and tossed her hair off to one side. "—and I was snoozing in your lap, or so you thought." She stroked the smooth muscle before her. "I read your mind and you thought I had an entirely different purpose for being in your carriage." Serina gave a long steady stroke over the length of his shaft.

"Umm." He grabbed her hair to steady himself.

Serina flicked her tongue over the tip of his penis, and then covered him with her mouth. He was soft yet hard. A fabulous conflict. As she tightened her lips and slid him farther into her throat, she tapped into his mind to find out what he experienced. She needed to know if what she was doing was what he wanted. All he could focus on was her mouth and how rapturous this was. She eased her way back up his shaft and swirled her tongue fast over his swollen head. His grip tightened in her hair.

So far so good!

Again she descended, harder, deeper until he was well past her tonsils. As she ascended she licked his shaft like he was a crème ice, and she enjoyed him just as much if not more. With pursed lips she went down again. How she did it she'd never know, but she consumed the entire length of his shaft and she even managed to tickle his sac that hung below.

Throughout her wily endeavor, he squirmed, laughed and pleaded, "Please don't stop!"

She wasn't about to. Knowing she could bring this man to his knees in ecstasy empowered her.

"More, Serina. Bite me. Lick me. Take me into you."

Serina took him at his word and nibbled, licked and sucked with unrestrained fury as he thrust his nob repeatedly down her throat. The quickened rise and fall of his chest and groans that echoed through her room suggested the end was near.

"God, woman!" He groaned. "Either I've died and gone to heaven or you're the ultimate devil in disguise." Watching the little enchantress in front of him working her magic, sucking his essence from him the way she did, he realized what he thought would take place in the carriage and what she did here and now, well, there was no comparison. The pressure built and his climax erupted.

That fast. Short but sweet.

Serina closed her surprised eyes as a hot, thick liquid exploded down her throat. She stumbled briefly, but regained her rhythm and for the first and only time in her life, gracefully, finished what she started.

Lucian pulled her to her feet, lifted her in his arms and tossed her atop her bed. He followed and blanketed her with his body and her lips with his.

"I thoroughly enjoyed that. Thank you."

"I had a sneaky suspicion you did." Serina leant forward and kissed his chin.

"M'lady, I've never felt this way before. I know my heart belongs to you. Don't answer me until after dinner tonight; think this through." Lucian got up from her warm body and walked over to the boxes handing her the smallest of the three. He knelt down on one knee.

Serina glanced between Lucian and the box, and she fought the tremors going through her body. *Is this how love works? I find this beautiful man almost dead, save him and his sister and then begin to make the kind of love one only dreams of in their heart with him? And now, here he is on his knee before me proposing while I'm still naked and sweaty—oh for the love of God! I'm sweaty? Doesn't this just happen to everyone, every day? Well doesn't it?* Her mouth hung open. Not her best look, but if he was serious about the proposal he might as well get used to it.

Serina opened the shiny box and just stared. The ring, it belonged on a queen's royal delicate finger, not her calloused one. She looked at the princess cut diamond, surrounded by two trillion-shaped dark stones in awe. "How did you know I've dreamt of this very ring?" Her eyes filled with tears.

Lucian placed his fingers to Serina's lips. "I love you. Some things in this life are disputable, questionable, even doubtful. My feelings for you are none of those. You make my heart beat, you make me laugh and you most assuredly drive me crazy. I have felt nothing for so long I feared I never would until I met you. You opened my world to me three days ago." He shrugged his shoulders. "Would you give me your heart to share, your soul to mate with, your love to cherish for an eternity, your desires mine and only mine to fill? Spend each day and night allowing me to love you, to make love to you? Hourly works!" Lucian winked as he brought her hand to his mouth and kissed every knuckle.

"I don't have to wait." Serina scooted to the edge of the bed. "I want to be able to look into your eyes for eternity, Lucian. They are a direct path to your soul, and mine recognizes yours as if you've lived inside me. You have my heart as I have yours. And my temple is yours any time you want it. As for the hourly arrangement? You've forty-eight minutes until our next joining." Serina kissed Lucian with every ounce of love she could pour into him. "The ring, Lucian, what color are the two stones on the sides?"

"Emeralds, the exact color of your eyes, a deep, earthly, green. Do you really adore it?"

"It is perfect. What are the other two boxes?"

"Don't know. Let's have us a look, shall we?" Lucian sat on the edge of the bed watching her reactions, hoping he'd made her happy.

Serina opened the two remaining gifts only to stand there wide-eyed. Her dress was a graceful mix of silk and satin with delicate lace. The front had a scoop neck allowing minimal cleavage to peek out, which suited her just fine. Crystal beads embellished the bodice of the dress and the back of the gown was gathered, held with a clip of white gold with inlaid gems. Serina had never seen anything so elegant, let alone wear it. The shoes were satin with pointed toes and a slight heel making it easy to walk or dance the night away in. *If only!*

"Lucian, this is the most precious thing I've ever seen." She held the gown in front of her, admiring it. "What exactly would you call this color?" she asked, feeling her face flush. "In case someone asks."

"The dress and shoes are chartreuse, a slight cross between yellow and green. It's all right, Serina, I'll coordinate your clothing for you every day so you needn't worry. We can make labels for your clothing to match colors or keep certain outfits hung together and washed separately."

Serina closed her eyes, mortified. She admitted, "Me mum used to do that for me, set me clothes out for me that is. It's been dreadful without the help. I've no clue what I'm wearing. I can tell black and white but that's all, other than your eyes. Father Butler gave me a light sapphire ring a while back and told me it was sky blue. Oddly, he told me I'd meet a man with the same color eyes and your eyes look the same shade. Am I right?"

Lucian brought her hand to his lips and kissed her. "Yes, you are. Father said that, hey? Smart man. I'll always be there to help you. One box to go!" He inclined his head towards her dresser.

In her last box lay a necklace of emeralds and diamonds that left Serina beyond flabbergasted. "Lucian, did you pinch these gems from London Tower? I'm serious. The Queen will certainly be looking for these." Serina placed the jewels to her neck and glanced in her looking glass. "We'll be needing some of the Bobbies to escort us about town this eve. I'm almost speechless. 'Tis truly a rare occasion."

"I have no doubt," he teased. "Go dress, m'lady. I'll go freshen up and await you in your garden. I do realize that you will look stunning in the dress and the jewels, but they do not make you beautiful, for you already are. You are the icing on the cake, and that is my favorite part!" Lucian gently kissed Serina's cheek and reluctant to leave her, headed to the bathroom.

****

When Serina entered into the garden, Lucian

couldn't take his eyes from her. He stood, and crossed to her.

"My dear family—" Lucian held his arm around Serina's shoulder. "I would like to introduce my fiancé, Dr. Serina Spencer, to you. She has accepted my proposal of marriage this afternoon." He couldn't contain the grin on his face.

Raven flew across the garden to Serina and hugged her. "I won't mess up your hair or dress, Serina. I promise, but I have to hug you. These past days of our lives have been hellish, yet I believe everything happens for a reason. Serina, I've always wanted a woman for my brother who is a lot like myself. I'm teasing, Luce." Raven peeked out around Serina and gave her brother a devilish wink. "No really, someone intelligent, funny, sincere, and beautiful inside out—me again." Raven fanned herself, laughing.

Lucian tapped the back of Raven's head.

"And my brother found you. I am honored to call you my sister." Raven chastely kissed Serina.

"Raven, I've always wanted a sister."

"Well now you've got one," Duncan piped in. Duncan approached Serina and lifted her off her feet. Holding her eye-level, he said, "May the gods help you, Serina, you've got a sister all right." Duncan lifted a mischievous brow to Raven. "I've cared for and loved these two my entire life, Doctor. You are now placed within my heart and my care for all time." Duncan planted a big kiss on her forehead and set her down. He made his way to Lucian and tossed his arms around him, and proceeded to pull Lucian away from everyone's ears. "We should head to town soon, Luce. You two will miss your dinner altogether if we delay much more. Oh, I heard through the grapevine there's a storm brewing. Watch out for your black cloud." Duncan thrust his hands palms up, gesturing, who knew!

"Nothing, my old man, shall spoil my evening, not even her."

"Just watch yourself. Or more so, watch your lady. That other wench is a viper."

Lucian noted his concern, sparking his own. "I know this is an odd time to bring things up but, Duncan, stay close by the women tonight, please? What if that thing comes back after Ray?" Seeing the worry in Duncan's eyes, Lucian realized he'd scared him. He felt guilty for doing so, but he wanted them safe.

Hearing the tail end of their conversation, Raven butted in, "We'll be fine tonight, Luce. Now you two ride off into the sunset, have a nice supper and bring us impoverished folks home some scraps and peppermint patty-cakes, got it? Skedaddle now." Raven pushed them toward the carriage.

Chapter Six

Serina rode beside Lucian on top of the carriage taking in the sights, enjoying the evening air. Looking upwards towards the sun, she closed her eyes a moment, and allowed the waning warmth to settle into her soul.

"This is my favorite time of the day. I love the warmth of the sun, even on a chilly day, it finds you. I could sit and stare at it all day without so much as batting an eyelash. Well—you know, not exactly stare at it. I'd go blind if I did that now, wouldn't I?" Serina rested her head on Lucian's shoulder, to snuggle up to him, but she found the ride uncomfortable. With every bump in the road and jar of the wheels, her head bounced from his shoulder.

He laughed, tossed his arm around her and reined her in tighter.

"What?" Serina asked.

"You, my wild rose. You cannot possibly be comfortable, yet you continue to rattle your brains about just to be close to me. I assure you, m'lady, you will get your chance to be close to me again soon enough."

Serina mumbled, "Our hourly joining is well past due."

Lucian's perfect smile showed off those lush, full lips that she needed on her again. Serina couldn't get over how incredibly handsome he was with his hair tied loosely back. His silk shirt matched her dress color and his black linen pants got lost under the tails of his double-breasted silk jacket. Serina loved the way he looked yet the jacket covered up one of her favorite anatomical parts, his bottom. Damn formal events and all clothes for that matter, Serina thought, miffed that she couldn't get the full view she wanted.

"I got that one. You really like my arse, hey?"

"Lucian St. James!" Serina gasped. "Aye, but indeed I do love watching you walk. Coming or going you are a sight for sore eyes." She pat her cheeks as they flushed.

"After everything we've shared today you blush? You amaze me. Are you ready to be introduced to my world, m'lady? We're here." Lucian jumped from the carriage and held his hands to her. "May I introduce you as my fiancé? Or would you care to wait and have a more formal coming out party?"

Serina looked forward seeing what was nothing short of a miniature castle. Stained glass windows of deep vibrant reds and purples decorated every wall in intricate detail. Glancing to the tower, she saw a guard watching over the entire city. The gent looked as every bit as pretty as some of the women she'd seen entering the building. He wore a frilly, white-lace shirt, white knickers, white leather boots with black buttons and a white velvet jacket. His hat, Serina decided, was a cross between a pirate's cap and one of the Three Musketeers. Plumes of feathers decorated the hat so it appeared as if a flock of birds nested atop his head.

"Let's play it by ear. I want to see how many beautiful women you attract this night, before I go breaking too many hearts." She gave him a half-cocked smile.

Lucian pulled her off the carriage directly into his arms, her feet dangling above the ground. "You are the only beautiful woman here. Remember that. Oh, if the Queen shows up just cover up your throat and hide your left hand for a bit, right?" Lucian kissed her cheek. With the look she gave he realized she honestly didn't know if the ring and necklace were hers or the Queen's. "I'm teasing you. I did not beg, borrow nor steal to get your jewels. Raven and I are very wealthy."

"How wealthy?" Serina asked nonchalantly as she paused her steps checking herself over, smoothing out her dress and trying to fuss with her hair, which she decided she didn't like wearing up.

"Very. Stop your fidgeting. You are ravishing. There will be an entire room of envious women tonight, Serina. Not because of the ring on your finger, but your beauty will be theirs to want and mine to have. Shall we go inside?"

"I've actually got butterflies smashing into each other in my stomach, Lucian. I've never felt this before. It's sort of nice in a maddening way."

Lucian looped his arm through Serina's and led her to the doorman who wore the same blinding white attire as the tower guard. Once inside, they were introduced formally to a curious crowd as Lord St. James and Dr. Serina Spencer. A hush covered the room like a wet wool blanket with all eyes upon them. Whispers from women in all corners of the room found Serina.

For one thing, Lord St. James had an escort, other than his sister, a beautiful stunning creature, and secondly, a doctor. Most of the people amused Serina. The women thought Lucian would never find a woman because of Raven. They weren't sure exactly how far their relationship as brother and sister went. The single women spent their conversations trying to pick her apart from her dress to her hair to her make-up, which she worried over as well. Most of the married women found her a perfect compliment for Lucian. Serina smiled in spite of her tummy's trembles. Her alter ego soaked up each and every flattering remark.

Stepping into the stateroom Serina let out an,

"Oh my," as she ran a gentle finger across the table. The lavish room reeked of regal wealth. Rich, silk drapes with threads of glittering beads adorned the windows from the ceiling to the floor.

Tapestries and paintings from all the famous painters, van Gogh, Monet, Renoir and Degas, graced the walls. Renoir had always been her favorite. Even though she couldn't make out the colors, she could visualize what he attempted to express, by the emotion of the portrait. Serina found his paintings laden with romance and a sensual serenity. Looking up, she noticed little cherubs hovering over everyone's heads, like guardian angels. This certainly beat the little black and white magpies that waited on her window's ledge of her home, bombing her occasionally.

About to pick up a glass of water and chug it to relieve the bone-dry mouth, Serina noticed the intricate roses carved into the crystal goblet. Suddenly she felt like a pauper in a jewelry shop, completely out of her league. The moment brought her right back to charm school and all her blunders as a young girl. The cruel laughter from the other girls in the class at her shortcomings because she wasn't as dainty or schooled in etiquette or because she voiced her opinion instead of biting her tongue stuck with her. On any given day of the week, she couldn't walk across a room without tripping over one of her two left feet. And she was certain beyond a reasonable doubt the women here wouldn't want to know the daily goings on of a morgue or carry on a conversation about the orphans she cared for. Even if she did have a hundred stories she'd love to share about how loving and wonderful they were. Mist formed above her lip. She wiped it away plagued.

The atmosphere left her frazzled; she'd never been to anything so formal or beautiful. All the dinners she'd ever attended at the hospital were hosted by a bunch of stuffy men who sat around with pipes and cigars, blowing smoke up their own orifices, slurping down glass after glass of brandy, talking amongst themselves in an attempt to pretend she didn't really exist in their world. For a moment, she wasn't certain she fit into this one either. "This place is fit for the Queen, Lucian. She could actually dine here."

"Serina, this place is the Queen's." He bent over her and kissed the top of her head lightly.

"If you're trying to make me feel at ease, that wasn't the correct thing to say." She gave him a grim grin.

Lucian adored watching her walk about, taking in everything to the smallest detail in child-like wonder. Her refreshing outlook on life was the polar opposite of every woman in the room. One in particular, Contessa Van Holstein. What a nag, Lucian thought. How could two women be so very different? Contessa, an overtly zealous woman, cared for nothing other than the narcissistic reflection in her looking glass. His Serina was beautiful inside and out, caring, giving...his list could go on.

Serina, on the other hand, found each woman breathtaking. Gowns made from the finest materials of silks, satins, taffetas, and fine laces graced each woman, with cost obviously not a factor. She noticed most of the women were much larger framed than her, leaving her feeling malnourished and down-right trodden. The only thing that saved her from running out the door was the man that slid his arm around her waist and pulled her into his warm, inviting shelter. Serina's heart began to slow down. She shyly asked, "Why me?"

"Your heart and soul belong with me, Serina. I knew it the minute I found you in my lap. These women are fallacious. They only care how far up the food chain they make it. Love is not in their vocabulary. Lust may indeed be there, but lust does not love make, m'lady. And I want love. I need only you. These women think of material possessions as being most important. You know the old adage, 'he who dies with the most money wins.' Wins what? You can't take it with you when you're gone, unless of course you're a vampire." Lucian quieted and shrugged his shoulders as he pondered the possibilities. "I wonder if people are writing a clause into their wills these days to hold settling their estates until three days after their funerals, you know, just in case they do come back and want to reclaim monetary and material possessions."

"You honestly believe you're going to end up one of them don't you? Let me refresh your memory, Lord St. James. You are not dead. You did not die. Damned close but I saved your arse. Yes, arse." Serina poked her fingers into his rock hard abdomen, bending them backwards. Annoyance masked her features. "Remember any of that? Please do not speak of death tonight. Today we celebrate life and our love. I want to enjoy you without worry for at least one night. Pl—"

Lucian quickly grabbed Serina and covered her mouth with his before she had a chance to finish. His kiss was tender, loving. "I apologize, m'lady. There will be no more talking about you know what for this night. Fair enough?" Lucian gave a quick glance about the room and put his cheek to Serina's and whispered, "Look around." It seemed their one kiss had stolen the attention of the entire room. "I see a few raised eyebrows. Would now be an appropriate time to announce our intentions or would you like to make them all wonder just a bit more?"

Mischief made his glance.

"You did that on purpose!" She turned herself into the shelter of his body, gazed up at him, and giggled. "Now, Sir, these people do not know me and are probably not having the purest of thoughts. Let's clean up my act."

"'Tis no act, m'lady, I assure you." Lucian cleared his throat and grabbed Serina's left hand and brought it to his lips. "My lords and ladies, I would like to share with all of you the woman who has entrusted her heart to me. Dr. Serina Spencer has accepted my proposal of marriage." The room went still, all for one very upset woman who cried in hysterics as she strutted from the room, slamming a door behind her. An older gent standing close said, "Such theatrics, Contessa," as she blew by him. He then lifted his glass and chanted, "Cheers, Lucian and Serina!" Others followed suit. People approached to congratulate them, hug them, and peck cheek after cheek with kiss after sloppy kiss.

Serina began to feel like a wet rag. She'd had enough of strangers slobbering all over her, even though their gestures were earnest. Enough was enough!

"Let the musicians play a waltz for these two," a woman hiding under a bee-hived, white-powdered wig shouted.

Panic.

It slammed Serina full force. Maybe the slobbering kisses weren't so bad, even from the one gent with blisters covering his lips. She was certain she had a spell to make them disappear. Or was it create them?

Either way, Serina had no clue how to dance. Had never danced. Had two left feet. Had always been too busy playing doctor, reading her books, dissecting anything dead left on the ground, messing up every spell she attempted to cast. Too busy studying when other girls were learning things that now seemed a necessary evil like how to curtsy with a saucer upon one's head or to sip from a soup spoon and not slurp, or how to *dance*. Serina cursed under her breath as Lucian took her hand and attempted to escort her to the floor. He ended up dragging her, heels scraping against the marble.

"Lucian..." She attempted to backpedal away from the center of the floor.

"Just hold onto me, Serina. I know you are nervous."

"Nervous? This isn't nervous. This is petrified. I can't do this." She growled, "I've never done this!" So many people watched!

"Trust me?"

"Yes. But—but..."

"No buts. Think of dancing as just getting to hold someone you love closely, in front of a hundred or more people watching and just waiting for you to slip up."

"Lucian! You're not funny. I always slip up!" She smiled despite her nerves.

"Honestly, just hold onto me and follow me. I'll go slowly and you'll look amazing."

"How did you learn?"

"Raven taught myself and André, but not before we crushed her toes more than a few times."

"This isn't so awful," she mumbled once she settled comfortably into his chest. Serina wrapped her arm around Lucian with nothing short of a death grip and laid her head against his chest. He held her steady and with his other hand swept her around the floor.

Serina held her breath, praying for her equilibrium—just this once—to work.

Lucian talked, occupying her thoughts as they glided across the dance floor. There were only two, possibly three times, she tripped, but Lucian caught her and whisked her around the floor, with no one the wiser. Couples sashayed toward them, and gave their best wishes. A few comments were made to

Lucian that he was indeed the luckiest man in London, if not the entire world.

Yes, her hat size was definitely getting bigger as the night continued.

The woman who had previously run out of the room crying, returned and waddled over to Serina with her eyes blazing, and blatantly asked how she won Lucian's affections the second Lucian left Serina's side.

Taken aback, Serina asked, "Good evening Miss...?"

"My name, you tidbit of a harlot, is Contessa Van Holstein. My friends call me Tess. You will not." The crass woman all but spit the words in Serina's face.

Serina stepped back, examined her carefully. The woman's dress left nothing to the imagination, which Serina deemed was not in the woman's best interest. The white satin, skin-tight dress left barely any breathing room. Rolls of flesh rippled and puckered the material. The woman's complexion had a multitude of skin-colored papules bursting from beneath her skin. They reminded Serina of barnacles growing on the docks at the seaside. Lumps, some the size of grapes protruded from under her hair. Serina could feel her face twisting into an ugly scowl. She coughed lightly, patting her chest.

"You do not belong here with us. And how is that you are here with our Lord St. James? Where is the Lady St. James? I wouldn't go picking out your china patterns so quickly if I were you!" She snorted, her nose high in the air with indignation.

Serina's eyes went wide. *By the Goddess! She could have at least blown the thing before she came out. Nose dandruff, ewh! The lovely views one gets from being so petite.*

Miss Contessa was not taking Lucian's engagement well. Serina found the woman full of guile. Dear old Tess wanted Lucian all to herself, and Serina just threw a giant anvil into her dowry. Pity!

Serina crooked a finger to the other woman and when Tess was close, she discretely whispered, "I'm not one to kiss and tell. Oh!" Serina covered her mouth with one hand and feigned laughter. "Allow me to rephrase this. I did kiss him. More than once mind you! Whew! By the Gods, you have no idea what you're missing. His tongue—" Serina paused. "—it's easily six or seven inches long. Other body parts, if you get my drift, are twice the size, wink, wink." Serina nudged her with her shoulder.

And just when Serina thought the woman's disposition couldn't get any uglier, she hated it, but she had to admit she was wrong. Flaming red face, eyes narrowed, and spittle leaking from her lips, Serina tapped the woman's jaw shut and left her to return to her fiancé. Serina's new favorite word.

"Besides being ignorant, the woman is cursed with elephantiasis."

"Oh, she's cursed all right. What's that?"

"You must have heard of Joseph Merrick, the gent they called the Elephant man? Passed away six years ago. An associate of mine at London Hospital took care of him. Dr. Fred Treves. I never met Joseph. Bit too young. But he left an impression in my head and heart forever. Your Miss Van Holstein's got it all right. And then some. What a shame to go through life with such a debilitating malady. 'Tis no wonder she has such a dreadful disposition."

"Serina, she's not mine. She's a miserable wench that followed me around all spring like a bad case of chats. Enough of her. Dance with me. It gives me the free excuse to hold you closely." Lucian held his hand out to Serina and sent her into a spin that landed her body pinned against him when he finished.

Serina smiled. The man knew how to dance. Thankfully, at least one of them did!

Serina ranked this the most enchanting evening in her life. He'd courted her, he'd asked her to marry him and they came *s-o-o-o* close to consummating their relationship, but there was more. Lucian attentively catered to her every need. He treated her as if she were the only person in the room with him even though there were over one hundred people there. One hundred people all watching them closely, like ants behind the glass walls, waiting to flatten them at any second with the heel of a shoe. All right, truth be known, the only person that really looked like she'd enjoy flattening her was Tess.

After dinner, Serina had her first glass of champagne. She enjoyed the way the bubbles popped in her mouth. After her second glass, she ended up with a slipped smile on her face. "Lucian, would you show me to the powder room? I believe the bubbles are attacking me from the inside out. They tickle."

His grin hogged his face. "I want to be the only one who tickles you from the inside out."

"Now?" Looking beyond Lucian, she scrunched her eyebrows together as she focused on someone on the opposite side of the room. "Who is that man in the corner by the little statue of David? Lucian, and I do mean little. Poor man. How would you like to be immortalized by the world etched in stone that tiny?" Serina spread her fingers about an inch apart as she eyed the statue then she glanced towards Lucian's groin and smirked. "Not that you would, mind you. A bigger stone would be needed. Much bigger." She attempted to adjust her fingers to an appropriate length.

"Serina!" Lucian whispered. "Up here, luv."

Serina blushed and peeked out from a guilty set of smoldering eyes.

Lucian said nothing, but shook his head, enjoying her antics.

Almost as quickly as that thought came, it vanished. "I love saying your name Lucian...*Looshaan*. If we were to have a child, a little girl, we could name her Lucy." Serina let the name roll off her tongue slowly in the same fashion she'd just done to his name.

Lucian bent his head down to meet hers. With his nose pressed against hers he said, "No..."

Serina pouted. "No children?"

"Children, yes, all girls as beautiful as you, but no Lucys. M'lady, I must agree with you that bubbles have attacked you. Come with me, my wild rose. Do you want me to escort you inside or wait out here for you to return to my arms?"

"I'll be fine, but Lucian—really, who is that man? He's been watching you all evening, and with not the friendliest of faces. He's not right. He and Tess would get on together fine."

"I do not know him. I'll ask around while you fix up something, although I can see nothing out of place on you. You're stunning."

"That's what I wanted to hear!" Serina tapped her finger on the tip of his nose and disappeared.

Having the powder room to herself, she stared into the looking glass with a silly grin plastered on her face lost within her thoughts until she heard two men talking. Lucian's name mentioned more than once piqued her curiosity. She glanced upwards noting a small vent between the two rooms. Without realizing what she'd done, she climbed up on the counter to get closer to the opening, which she found tricky in an evening gown and heeled shoes. If anyone walked in now she realized she would have some explaining to do.

With one ear pressed tight to the vent, her gut twisted hearing the men's voices. An urgent sense to protect Lucian, to run fast and hide him away forever from everyone swarmed her senses. She'd heard one say, "I can't believe it, Master. He should be covered in dirt today, yet here he is looking healthier than you and with a fiancé who no one's ever had the pleasure of having. I wonder where Raven is. He's never left her. Never! Maybe she didn't survive. But don't you worry, I'll finish this. You can count on me."

Then Serina heard another voice, more like a low guttural growl that shot up the hairs on the back of her neck and pricked sharper than the thorns from her roses.

"Raven had better survived, or I'll lie back and personally watch my wolves shred you limb by limb. Am I perfectly clear?"

"Yes sir, very clear."

A loud cracking noise followed whimpers. Having heard enough, she hopped down from the countertop and ran from the powder room directly into Lucian's arms. Unable to control her trembling, she whispered, "We must leave immediately."

"What is it, what's happened?" Lucian drew her to him hoping to quell her obvious fear.

Serina squeezed her arms around his waist, as she walked him backwards toward the exit. She explained, "I overheard two men in the powder room talking about you and Raven. They said that you should be dead, but since you're not, they'll finish you. Lucian, we need to get out of here, get Raven and go somewhere safe. Egypt should be safe, plenty of sun! Those things don't appreciate sun, right? Why do they want you dead? Why?" She felt anger build within her...not a good thing from where she stood. Her control and her powers didn't quite mesh when she felt threatened.

Serina's first malignant thought passed through her head. From the day she took an oath to care for people proclaiming no malfeasance, she wondered now if she'd be able to live up to it. She could walk into that room and make the hearts that belonged to the voices cease to beat. She could will it so. The men would be dead. Lucian and Raven would be safe. Serina turned to walk back to the powder room when Lucian caught her wrist and pulled her back to him.

"You cannot do this, Serina. You are not like the animal that tried to kill Raven or myself. You could not live with yourself."

"I won't live without you, Lucian." Serina turned in his arms, never taking her tear-filled eyes off him.

"You won't live without me. Ever if I died, I would make my way back to your arms. Death cannot separate us, m'lady. Only time and circumstance."

"You're not God, Lucian. You don't get the luxury to pick how and when."

"God has naught to do with this, Serina. God does not have vampires for his disciples, rest assured. So yes, for now I shall pick my time and how and it won't be at the hands of some bloody beast." He rested his chin atop her head, catching his wits. He needed time to absorb their situation, but it seemed a luxury he was no longer afforded.

"Did you see two men go into the restroom?"

"Only one."

"Well, one is better than none. Did anyone know him?"

"He is assumed a streetwalker in search of scraps. Speaking of scraps, let's stop by the kitchen on the way out, and we can kill two birds with one stone. We can ask the chef if he knew who he gave food to, and we can pick up dessert for our misfits at home."

Hands on her hips, Serina asked, "Even in the midst of a life and death crisis you think of food.

Men! Are all men as obdurate as you, or am I the only woman lucky enough to have a man think such things?"

"A man's gotta eat, luv, and then there's dessert." Lucian marched his fingers down her back to her bottom, patting her. "And then there's dessert." Lucian's smile spoke of hours of nothing but the two of them together; romantic images and thoughts conjured within his head fast and furious, regardless of his situation.

"Lucian!" Serina shoved at his chest, though for all her effort he stood unmoved. "Please, be serious for one moment." She threw her hands into the air. "Would you stop? Get that image of me out of your thick head for the time being."

He offered an innocent smile.

"I just overheard two men devising a plan to kill you and all you can think of is food and me. I believe the champagne did you in. For the love of God, what if they actually succeed? You came into my life like a tornado and blew my world wide open. I don't want you sucked away leaving only death's destruction behind. I won't lose you, do you understand?" Serina crossed her arms under her chest, which by default, she realized accentuated her breasts even more but there wasn't much she could do about it. They were what they were, buxom. She looked as stern as she possibly could, until she noticed his focus remained on the rise and fall of her chest. "I'm up here you daft sod." She kicked at his ankle. She wasn't budging until he started to take her seriously, and he had no idea of just how stubborn she could get. Serina leaned against one of the kitchen tables, fuming.

Lucian approached, batting his big baby blues willing her to smile.

Nothing.

"I know you're frightened, but I can't go to the

constable telling him of the past few days' events. It would place you and Raven in danger, not to mention myself. I can't tell him we were all but killed, and you saved us. Serina, they'd have the Sorcerers Squad knocking down your door before we returned home. Do you want that? Want those murderous scoundrels hanging you out to dry? I most assuredly don't."

"I can take care of myself. You're already in danger, Lucian. So is Raven. She's two sets of marks on her neck to prove how much danger she's in. Three sets and we're all up to our necks in trouble. No pun intended. You need protection. I can save you as long as you've got a pulse, luv, but I cannot do the reanimation thing. I'm not Dr. Frankenstein."

She roughed up her hair frustrated. Then her pacing kicked in, getting her in the way of the head chef. She grabbed his coat in passing and read the embroidered name on his lapel aloud. "Nice name—ah, Payton." She slapped his chest, and gave him a slight shove out of her way continuing with her rant.

Payton gave Lucian a weary glance, one blond eyebrow arched. He watched patient, backing into corners when Serina neared. He had every right to kick them out of his kitchen, but then he may have been just a bit intimidated by this insane little woman who'd taken over his kitchen. He realized she meant business. Glancing at the King's nephew, he looked amused and there in lay the problem.

"Lord St. James, begging me pardon for eavesdropping, although I don't much have a choice, but, Sir, your lady...she makes sense. The man's ne'er been here before this night. I'd liked to have been able to help you, but you clearly need to visit the constable, Sir." Payton looked down at the floor, scared to face the man. He'd all but insulted royalty. Tomorrow, he knew he'd be looking for a new position as a pot scrubber somewhere if he still had a head atop his shoulders when he woke up...If he woke up!

Serina decided then and there, she'd recruited an ally. She liked Payton and adored the way he'd called her Lucian's lady. And more importantly, she was thankful that he sided with her.

"Payton, your wisdom is worthy of someone taking heed. Hopefully Lord St. James will listen to not one, but the two of us." She cast Lucian a reprimanding glance.

"Serina, I will speak with the constable tomorrow. I promise."

Serina gave him the look.

"Cross my heart and hope to die!"

"Ah! Don't say that. Hope to die? Do you have a death wish?"

"Can we please go now?" He crossed his eyes as he walked past the chef. "Payton, I'll take your words to heart. I appreciate your honesty. Most people treat me with kid gloves, always afraid to approach me. Thank you for treating me as a man, not some daft nephew of the Queen. 'Tis refreshing."

Serina's jaw hit the ground for a second time. Payton held the same pose.

"If you ever tire of the work here you are welcome at my manor as chef. I've enjoyed many of your meals. Lord knows my sister and Duncan can't cook." Lucian added, "We're at a loss. Come by tomorrow if you would like to look about. But you better hurry up before 'they' kill me and you lose your offer." Lucian tried to make light of the situation, but his smile faded fast. "Come, Serina." He held his hand to her.

"Excuse me—did you just say the King's nephew? Oh, bloody hell," Serina muttered. "These are the Queen's gems aren't they?"

"Actually, I said the daft nephew of the Queen. There is no blood that binds me to the King

Consort."

"I'm marrying an almost prince?" Serina said dreamy-eyed. "How did I miss that?"

"Lord St. James," Payton called, snapping Serina out of her mini trance. "Would you be so kind as to give these to your sister? I know how she fancies them. I hope she is well." Payton handed Lucian a bag of the mint Pattie cakes.

Lucian nodded. A knowing glance passed between the two men. He fast realized Payton would indeed be stopping by tomorrow to acquire the position in his manor, just as long as his new position wasn't atop his sister, he'd be fine.

Having said their farewells and blowing Tess a quick kiss, Serina headed home, her fiancé safely tucked by her side. From the carriage, she watched people strolling the sidewalks, holding hands, some in intimate chatter cuddling, others laughing and enjoying the cool night air. It left her ripe with jealousy.

"This isn't fair, Lucian. We've just met. I can't believe someone would kill you just because you've royal blood running through you. It makes no sense." Angry little tears blurred her vision. She scooted closer on the seat, needing to feel him beside her.

"It makes absolute sense, Serina. For centuries people have killed and been killed to wear the illustrious crown of jewels, to be placed upon a pedestal and told you are worthy of treatment that does not befit the rest of your countrymen? No man is above another. We are all equal in the eyes of the Lord. I realize this goes against every social class and moral I've been raised by but 'tis what I believe. Most days it, the crown, reminds me of Jesus' thorned headpiece. Power, freedom, glory, servants at your beck and call, never having to apologize or have a worry, well, other than the obvious—losing your last breath to some scoundrel. This life is believed to be Utopia by many. It has been this way since the dawn of time. Cleopatra, Julius Caesar, Queen Mary...We take the good with the bad with a stiff upper lip. Ha! I have ne'er wanted the responsibility. I will not place my family in harm's way, ever."

Finished with his rant, Lucian slowed the carriage as they passed a small lake. With the full moon glowing and a light breeze, shimmering waves sailed across the water, Lucian pulled the reins on the horses and the carriage rolled to a stop. He hopped off.

"Come with me? This is one of my favorite hideaways. No one ever bothers me here." Lucian helped Serina down.

After spreading a blanket under a tree, Serina snuggled between Lucian's legs and leaned back. They relaxed by the water for quite some time without speaking, both content. "Are you warm enough?" he asked as he rubbed her arms.

"It's beautiful here. I'm fine." Serina bent her head back to see Lucian's face. That small movement sent her hair falling down over her shoulder and into her face. Lucian swept it back, tucking it behind her ear.

"Would you look at the manor on the opposite side of this lake? By the goddess, it's fit for the Queen. Wonder who lives there?"

To tell her or not to tell her the home was his? Surprise won out. "I am so sorry I've dragged you into my personal wars with would-be assassins. I should have told you I live with this threat every day of my life. There are seven of us that still have this hanging over our heads like a guillotine; the Queen, her three daughters—best to avoid them if you can, and our cousin, André. He resides in Paris. Once in a blue moon if we're lucky we hear from him. My mother and her twin, Chyna, are the Queen's younger sisters. My parents were murdered, and my aunt Chyna went missing just before their death and ne'er resurfaced. The Queen has naught to do with Raven or myself. Hasn't for eons. I believe she's responsible for my parents' execution. She knows this so she won't come near myself, as she fears for her own life. I've cared for Raven for the past eight years now."

"Lucian, I'm sorry your life has borne witness to such tragedies." She reached up and touched her lips to the tip of his nose. "To new beginnings."

"Cheers, m'lady." Lucian bent forward and found her lips soft, warm and inviting. His heart heavy with the knowledge she feared for him, it upset him that the magic of their first evening together had been ruined, that he couldn't promise her the fairy tale would last forever. He couldn't have promised her that even if he wasn't royal.

"You are the spark to my flame, Serina. You ignite my very soul. You are a cool and gentle breeze, calming and tranquil, and you most assuredly are the eye of a storm. Everything about you radiates an untamed spirit. I want to lie here with you for the rest of this night and watch the sun grace every sensuous curve of your body in the morrow. Would you do this for me?" Lucian pulled her onto his lap and moved his hands to her face. He whispered, "I love you, Serina Spencer, and I've ne'er loved another." He kissed her again, finding her tongue, deepening his kiss, and memorizing her sweet essence as if it were their last kiss.

"Just promise me one thing, St. James."

Lucian held his breath waiting...expecting any second that she would bring up the constable, and he didn't want get into that discussion again. Choking out each word he said, "Whatever m'lady wants, it is so."

"You're a lousy liar, Lord," she teased. "Don't let

any spiders crawl on me. I really loathe them. They'll send me running in ten different directions. And about the constable...We're still on for that trip in the morning." Serina kissed him before he could protest. "You forget my powers, silly man."

Torn between going home and staying right where he was, Lucian made a quick mental check on his sister.

Raven, is all well?

We are fine; all for our sweet tooth still has cravings. You at the lake?

How did you know?

Lucian, I'm in your head more than you most days, sweetie. Speaking of which?

I've your mint cakes, little one, although if you continue to eat them I'll no longer be calling you little one. As long as you're fine, we'll see you in the morn. Good night. Sweet dreams, Ray.

Good night, my imbecile.

Lucian enjoyed the evening, talking, laughing and eating all the treats they were supposed to bring home to Raven. With Serina asleep, entwined within his arms, he nodded off not long after her.

Lucian awoke dodging acorns as squirrels dropped the tiny bombs while ravaging the tree for nuts. He glanced over his lady. She lay comfortably on her side with him spooned perfectly to her back.

He pushed Serina's hair away from her neck and kissed her, then nibbled. His lips traveled over her shoulder, over her collarbone and made their way back to her neck.

His arm had other plans. By its own design, it began a slow descent around the front of her dress finding the firm swell of her bosom. Her breasts felt soft and smooth under the satin and silk fabrics. Yet with the slightest caress, he found they awoke hungry for his attention. Her reactions instigated his body's reaction. He hardened in mere seconds.

"Good morning, my wild rose. Can you think of anything, anything at all that you might possibly want or need this beautiful morning that I, Lucian St. James, may personally take care of for you?"

Serina attempted to whip her head around to face him but only made it half way. The damned grin upon his lips was irresistible, his disheveled morning hair as untamed as he. Her heart flip-flopped. "Only one thing comes to mind, my lover."

"What's that?"

"You're on my hair. I'm tied down." Serina pointed to the locks under his arm.

"One of my other fantasies!"

Lucian's eyebrows shifted. Serina recognized the non-prim, non-proper suggestion, and she bit at the smirk forming on her lips. Wasn't a bad fantasy at all as long as it involved silky restraints and a promise of passion. "Of course one other thing does come to mind."

He shifted to free her hair. "Please don't say the constable."

"We'll discuss him, but not until you've taken me in your arms and had your way with me. Fair enough?"

Lucian wasted no time and crawled to her feet. "Fair enough." He sorted through the layers of fabric her dress held until he found flesh. "My, what delicate feet you have. All the better to..." He popped her toe in his mouth and sucked on it through her giggles. After kissing each little digit he ran a nail down the center of her sole. Serina laughed, bucked and squirmed trying to break his grip but he tightened his hold.

"Ticklish, try again."

"You lie back and watch the clouds and listen to the birds sing while I wash away every lucid thought you own."

"Aye, you're a wee bit cocky don't you think?"

Lucian glanced to the solid bulge and taut material his trousers held. With a charlatan's pout he asked, "A wee bit? Oh, m'lady, you'll find out soon enough." He proceeded with a slow sensual massage, his fingers kneading their way up the length of her calves, inching his way up her thighs and still farther north. Lucian took cover beneath her dress and disappeared.

Serina laughed. "You remind me of a kitten stuck under the covers of a bed."

Lucian purred. "I believe I've found some catnip under here." Wrapping his hands around her ankles he lifted her legs over his shoulders, leaving her open to him and baring all. He bent down, pressed his mouth hard against her private lips and lapped away at her as a kitten does cream. His tongue probed and prodded her entrance. This left her lifting her hips to meet his overtures.

"What? That's not catnip, Lucian...Whew!"

Lucian crawled out from under the gown licking his lips. "No, 'tis not, but then being a fine physician, you know what body part my lips have found."

"Most aware," she grunted. "Stop talking!"

"As you wish." Lucian returned to his destination and proceeded to kiss the delicate flesh on the inside of her thighs. With a gentle graze of teeth, he nipped at her as he moved closer to her warm, sweet temple. He slid his tongue over her private lips, barely a whisper of a touch until he picked up his pace and the pressure of his kisses. Each deliberate sweep of his tongue was erotic, and hot, to excite and pleasure her.

Serina moaned, rotating her hips. "Umm. Whatever you do, don't stop." She slid her fingers into her hair, lifted her hips and pressed his mouth even closer.

He did as he was told. He slid his tongue deep inside her enjoying the sweet taste of her. When a slight contraction squeezed his tongue, desire filled his loins. Each time he plunged farther into her, her hips surged up to meet his rhythm. He continued his ministrations allowing her no time to catch her breath. Her reaction to his affections made not only his chest tight, but other areas as well. Critically tight.

"Lucian, just exactly—how long is your—tongue?" Serina found her speech strained. "I feel—" pant, "as if—you're tickling my tummy from the inside out. It's—wonderful." She sucked in a large gulp of air and held her breath through the mounting pressure between her thighs and stomach.

I told you last night I wanted to be the one who tickled you. Do you really want me to stop what I'm doing and show you or can it wait?

Merged completely with him, she felt his joy, that he was able to bring her such pleasure. Serina enjoyed the closeness, the intimacy of being able to talk as if no one else on the earth existed. Serina shook as waves of her orgasm teetered on the brink of the precipice, so close to abandonment. His lips sucking on her was delightful to say the least, but, release would not come. She needed him buried deep within her. Today, it had to happen! She searched to find something to anchor onto, but Lucian safely buried himself under the layers of her dress. Serina began to laugh and couldn't stop.

Lucian popped his head out, a curious look upon his face. "What, my little lover, is so funny?"

"Could you switch positions? Now?"

"Hold that thought!" Lucian ducked under the dress giving her one last kiss as he slid his tongue deeply inside her again making sure she was ready for him. He dragged his tongue slowly and stiffly over her mons, flicked it hard then bit down and shook his head back and forth until she screamed.

"Lucian, now!"

When I'm ready and not a second sooner.

He drew her little button taut between his teeth and tugged.

"Lucian!" She screamed again and pounded her fists into the dirt.

"So impatient, little one." With two fingers he flicked her from the inside while his tongue mirrored the same actions over her swollen nub. Her body convulsed and quivered as she writhed beneath him. Releasing her, he crawled out and stood in front of her. He liked what he saw, Serina flat on her back, panting better than a dog basking in the hot sun.

May not have been polite to stare, but his size both scared and intrigued her as he undid his trousers to reveal a firm, silky erection. Was she seeing things? His shaft grew thicker and wider before her disbelieving eyes. She gnawed her bottom lip with both anticipation and desire to have him fully inside her. Another minute and she'd lose her mind. She mustered her best "come hither look" and in a low voice asked, "Do you have any idea what you do to me? I need you now! This very instant or it may be too late."

Thoroughly enthralled, this moment had to last. His undid the remaining buttons of his shirt and flashed one side of his chest. He rubbed his nipple and fought the urge not to laugh as he played. Switching sides, he continued toying with her. With a little spin, the shirt fell and he showed off a firm, flat abdomen, and dark curls that got lost beneath the confines of his trousers. Then he dropped the trousers and flashed her a quick peek of that arse she'd admitted to fancying.

"You put the strip-tease artists to shame, m'lord."

"That I do," he laughed. He licked his lips and tasted her essence upon him. "Serina, you are the sweetest nectar I've ever tasted. I have found my dessert buried deep within you."

"That's nice—really luv," she grunted from clenched teeth. "I'm done with my appetizer, now might I enjoy my dessert? Ple—"

Lucian bent down and pressed his fingers over her lips stilling her. "Ah, ah, now, m'lady, what was that I said 'bout you asking? Ask again and I'll have to place your luscious little bum over my knee and paddle you."

"Whatever it takes, m'lord! Just stop your taunting."

Lucian laughed long and heavy, as he blanketed her body with his. "You're absolutely positive?"

Serina giggled. "Ask me again and I'll say no."

"Right then, relax." Lucian crushed her and slid his penis between the folds of Serina's private lips and pressed into her mons, then ever-so-gently inched his way inside her. He took his time and eased his way out, getting her used to having him inside her. "Wrap your legs around me. Oh, my wild rose!" Lucian closed his eyes, a strained look on his face. "I ne'er imagined this could feel so...unbelievable," came out heavy, breathy. "I'm not hurting you?"

"Quite the opposite, m'lord."

With each thrust he gave, she returned the favor with a upward bump and grind. The mixture of prurient and graceful moves of her body almost became his undoing. He slid his hands beneath her bottom and pulled her hips closer to him, pressing harder and deeper into her. Her orgasm exploded around him with that tiny change of position. Muscles deep within Serina contracted, tightened and squeezed him repeatedly until his release followed, spilling his seed deeply within her.

Lucian propped himself up on his elbows and eagerly kissed the woman he'd flattened beneath him. "I think we should do this again and again.

Later today?"

"Lucian, don't move quite yet. Something's going on." She pointed between her thighs. "Oh, 'tis delightful." She closed her eyes with anticipation. "I'm becoming ripe all over again.

Just from Lucian's laughter, and the slightest of movement of his body brought Serina a second time. "I can see later happening quite nicely."

Exhausted and sated, Lucian lay quiet encased in his lover's arms, waiting to regain his strength so he could at least crawl back to the carriage if need be.

Yes, the lake would be his all-time favorite hideaway.

Serina wiggled her way from under Lucian and laughed.

"What? Why do you insist on laughing at me?"

"You kept your word to me last night, but there is a giant spider on your bum."

Not a split second passed and Lucian found an abundance of energy. He danced out of synch to the world, brushing his arse and legs off. He admitted unashamed, "I absolutely loathe anything that can hide on you, take a chunk out of you and then crawl away laughing. Speaking of which, do you want to jump into the lake before we head home?" He flashed her a quick grin.

Shaking her head a frantic no, she blurted out, "No...no lakes. Ever! I hate the feeling of my toes sinking into the muck and slime on the bottom, knowing full well it's mostly fish excrement and dead bugs in a watery grave. But you go in...Really. I'll watch safely from this spot. Enjoy your dip." She gave him a smug smile as she waved her hand toward the water, shooing him off.

"M'lady, I fear I cannot allow you to sit here all alone." Lucian bent over and scooped Serina up into his arms. She kicked and screamed as they headed for the water. "Why do you fight me, little one? I'll hold you so your feet don't sink, just mine and then we'll both be effectively trapped in the water until the fish start to nibble at you..."

"Why me? Why can't they bite your bum? Lucian really...I can't do "S" words. No swimming, sailing, skiing, skating, cycling—I know that doesn't start with an "S" but..." Serina prattled on through her wiggling, in an effort to get away from Lucian as he waded her deeper into the water, "Lucian, this beautiful dress. It'll be ruined. Please take me back." Serina's last ditch pleas fell upon deaf ears.

"Little liar. I know one "S" word you do rather well. I'll have another dress made for you. Hold on and relax. I promise I'll be the only one that nibbles on you."

The water rose up and over her waist as Serina lay across Lucian's arms, hanging on for dear life. Lucian bent over and whispered, "Hold your breath."

"Wha—" She never finished her question. Under they went.

Lucian came up laughing. Serina emerged gasping for air and spitting out water.

"See, you didn't drown." He covered her lips with his before she could launch further protest, and he held her until she stopped shaking.

Breaking away, she watched the waves come up and blanket their bodies. She relaxed slightly, and attempted to enjoy the tranquil atmosphere. Later, when she was safely out of the water, she'd find a daddy long legs and place it on him.

Setting her down on dry ground and watching her regain her land legs, Lucian said, "You are truly the most beautiful drowned rat I've ever laid eyes on."

"I can't believe you just did that." Serina bent at her waist, and shook out her hair like a dog would his coat. She straightened her posture and then tried to peel the dress from her legs so she could effectively take some steps.

Lucian glanced at her every curve. "I like what happens to you when you get wet."

"Which end of me?" Serina asked, feeling sexy.

"Both. Definitely both."

Lucian mimicked Serina, sending black, silky curls wildly about to rid the excess water. His soaked clothes showed the hard, masculine outline of him as well. "Well, my little mop, shall we make our way home?"

Serina mouthed the words, "little mop," back to him and pushed him back into the lake. He sunk up to his neck in the water, his eyes wide. She turned and sprinted toward the carriage laughing, until her foot caught a root sticking up and she tumbled face first to the ground. Then it was Lucian's laughter she heard moments before he rescued her from her entanglement.

****

Sound asleep in Molly's parlor, Lucian found Raven on a chaise lounge, and Duncan and Molly sandwiched on the couch.

"Good morning sleepy heads, the day's half gone," Lucian whispered to the three of them. He walked to Raven and bent down to kiss her cheek. "Wake up."

Raven glanced between Serina and Lucian. "Good morning, my knight. Is it raining? You're both soaked to the bone."

Lucian shrugged his shoulders. "Everyone up. We need to get back to the manor and take care of some things. No rain, Ray, we were at the lake."

"Luce, you still need a bath today. Swimming in muck doesn't count."

Lucian sniffed his armpit and winked. "I'm good for a few more days," he jested, as he followed Serina out the door.

"Serina will you come and spend the day at the manor with me? I want to show you everything our home has to offer." Lucian wasn't going to take no for an answer. The very idea of her being apart from him, for even a moment, left his heart racing. He knew he was in trouble then. How could he go back to work or do anything if she wasn't tied to his side?

"Give me a few minutes to get out of this soggy dress and look a little less like a mop." Serina gave him a slight shove as she waltzed passed him.

"Need any help? Willing and able, here at your service," Lucian offered, but Serina trudged forward, ignoring him. "Serina, you didn't answer me, want some help?" Lucian asked trying to undo the buttons on the back of the dress as they crossed the road to her home.

"Lucian," Serina turned, serious. She swatted at his philandering fingers. "Could we get inside first? How long do you plan on waiting before you go to the constable?" She purposefully batted her eyelashes at him, in hopes of persuading him. "Also, I should pop in at the hospital to check in. We could kill two birds with one stone. Do you think you and Duncan could fix my door today?" she asked heading up her stairs. Lucian brushed passed her and went to her closet, pulling out a matching skirt and blouse.

Serina dressed in front of Lucian before he realized he'd missed his opportunity to have her again. Lucian threw himself atop her bed, and patted the area beside him. "How did you do that?" He was beginning to think himself quite the lothario.

"So, your intentions to help me out of the dress were solely for your own reward?"

"I would definitely reward you too." He puckered up and hoped she met him half way.

Unable to resist those lips, Serina walked over and kissed him, and then turned to walk out of the room.

That didn't go quite as he thought it might have. "Hey!" Lucian patted the bed again with his eyebrows raised.

"Lucian, my body needs a few hours of recovery time. Not much, mind you, but a bit more. I don't think I could walk if we were to make love again."

"I'll carry you all night. Your dainty little toes shall never touch the floor." He sprung from the bed and followed on her heels.

"You, sir, are incorrigible. Is this how we are to spend our days and nights?"

"M'lady, I do hope so. I can think of no other place on earth I'd rather be, than wrapped up in your arms with your legs securing you to my body." Lucian dropped on his hands and knees and lifted the hem of her skirt.

"Hello—hello...Lucian? Serina? Your chariot awaits." Duncan's voice echoed throughout the house.

Disappointed, Lucian let her skirt fall and leaned back on his feet, his lips at a full pout.

Serina tousled his hair, and whispered, "Big baby."

"We'll be right there, Duncan." Lucian hollered. "Serina is just packing a few things in case she wants to stay on a few days."

Serina threw Lucian a look of total surprise. He returned it with one solid smile and asked, "What? Can I help you get anything?"

"Go lock up the back of the house for me? Although it's overkill since the front's wide open. I'll be down shortly with a few things."

Thirty minutes, umpteen nails and a sore thumb later—Duncan's, when Lucian hit the wrong nail with the hammer—they headed out, Serina's front door fixed.

****

Crabapple trees dripping with fragrant delicate pink flowers stood beside monstrous maple trees and smaller Japanese dwarf maples acting as sentinels along the road to the manor. A white picket fence hid behind overgrown rose bushes, their thorns a deterrent to any sane person. Wildflowers scattered themselves into the mix. Serina couldn't figure out if the landscape fell into the category of gardener's delight, or absolute nightmare, depending on how much work was needed. And who cared for it. Serina wondered if Lucian had an ulterior motive for asking her along.

Nearing the end of the driveway, Serina realized this house was the same one she admired last night. Surrounded by tulips, a stone path wound its way from the water's edge to the back veranda. Lilac bushes created a giant tapestry of both beauty and fragrance. Sticking her head outside the carriage, she inhaled the light scent. About to say, "Umm," she instead swallowed a bug. After gagging and choking on the vile insect, she hollered to Lucian, "You could have told me, you know—about the house."

Witnessing the ordeal as Lucian leaned over the side of the carriage, he tapped his finger to his teeth, laughing. "You have something stuck."

"You're not funny."

"He thinks he is and that's all that matters," Raven added.

In front of the manor, Serina sat speechless at what most likely would be her new home. She adored the thatched roof, the way it hung over ivory stucco walls, plopped on top of the house like dollops of cream on custard. The leaded glass windows scaled the walls from the floor to the ceiling. The thick glass, double door entrance had fleur-de-lis designs forged throughout. Looking through the doors, Serina felt as if she were looking in a carnival mirror; the glass distorted her, made her even smaller and wider. She turned away, repulsed. That was the last image she needed to see. However, Serina discovered the inside of the home was more beautiful than she could have imagined. Thick Persian rugs lay in front of a settee and chairs in the main parlor. She was relieved not to find any animal heads hanging off walls. Trophies, she despised them. It seemed a criminal end to a beautiful life. The main entryway's walls reminded her of a museum. Not a naked spot on the wall to be found. Paintings of Lucian's heritage adorned the walls as reminders of those past and present. A portrait of their parents, Lucian, Raven and another young man identical to Lucian hung above the alcove of the upper hallway.

"Lucian, is the boy in the pictures your cousin André? He really could be your twin. You three could pass as triplets." Serina admired the painting. Someone else as gorgeous as Lucian. Her eyebrow lifted once again in a non-prim, non-proper fashion.

Lucian added, "Yes, that's André. It is astonishing how we look so alike, but look at our mothers. Our mothers were also twins, although not identical, but they resembled each other closely."

Serina cast a glance 'round looking for someone equally as beautiful as his mother. She noticed a waif of a woman wearing a tiara with a thin moustache and light beard appearing quite miserable beside his mother.

Serina pointed to the painting. "Her?" He nodded. "You're right. They aren't identical, but Lucian, I don't want to be the one that breaks it to you, toots, but you and your cousin are identical. You're twins, trust me. Someone's snookered the two of you."

Lucian gave Serina a serious look only for a moment and with a slight annoyance said, "We're not twins, Serina. We'd have known. Why would—ah, never mind." Serina's words struck a raw nerve. The idea that André was his twin and raised as if he wasn't, well Lucian found it ludicrous.

"Ladies, I'll take your bags up to your rooms while you look about. Make yourselves at home. 'Tis now yours."

Serina gave Molly and Raven a quick glance that held more questions than answers looking at the portrait of Lucian and André.

"They're twins, Molly, which actually makes them triplets," Serina whispered to her.

Molly nodded. "Indeed they are, Doctor."

Raven too, oddly brushed off the comments and continued her tour with her new friends. When they reached the front library, Raven noticed a man on a horse riding up the pathway.

"Who could he be?" Raven asked with her nose pressed to the window. "He's rather handsome. Would you look at those curls?" Her breath fogged the glass. As she wiped it away, the glass made a squeaky noise.

Serina joined her at the window. "He's the cook from the restaurant last night. Your brother offered him a job as your personal chef."

"Really?" Raven mumbled, never taking her eyes from the man as she spoke, lost in thought.

"Something was said about none of us being able to cook. I guess the man decided to see if the offer still stood."

"I'm an absolute disaster in the kitchen. Did you hear of the fire at Oxford a few years back?" Raven raised her hand. "Guilty. Lets go see what he can cook. I'm famished. Come to think of it, I never received me mint cakes last night." Raven tapped Serina's nose in passing. "I'll bet you're not hungry!"

Serina gave her a sheepish grin. "Sorry," she said, but she didn't mean it. The dessert was decadent. Serina turned and followed to finish her tour.

From the looks of things, the kitchen was next. Things around this manor seemed to be cooking up faster than she could've imagined.

Chapter Seven

After careful consideration, Serina sent a letter of resignation to the hospital, telling them she had to live her life, not lose a little piece of herself each day to the dead. She took over the gardens around the manor, tending the weeds that threatened a coup. Some days she declared a stalemate as to who won the battle, her or the meddlesome plant-life. Her arms were torn open from thorns and welts covered her from bugs who seemed to find her a tasty treat. Lucian never veered far away from her, because apparently he too found her his tasty treat. She swatted either at him or the bugs trying to get her work accomplished.

****

The day before the wedding, Serina found Lucian in their bedroom looking over the lake, deep in thought.

"Lucian, I need to go to town today. Molly, Raven and I have all but finished my gown, but I need a few little things from home. Would you come with us? She slid her hands over his back and down to his buttocks. "I adore the feel of this." Serina pinched him.

Lucian closed the distance between them and kissed her nose lightly. "I adore the feel of this inside you." He bumped his growing fondness into her.

Outside their door, Raven raised her voice so they'd hear her. "Sorry to interrupt, you two. Duncan's ready. Luce, you up for the ride? Molly's going to bring her kitties back here to stay. Payton said we've three hours till supper. He's prepared something special for us tonight. Unfortunately, I'm not at liberty to discuss what it is."

Lucian opened the door. "As long as you didn't have a hand in its preparation I don't care what it is." Lucian ruffled her hair as he walked past her.

Raven conceded, "That was uncalled for Luce...but true."

"I'm going to stay here and dream of your speedy return, ladies, one of you in particular."

Raven teased, "You must stop dreaming over me, Luce. Your bride will grow jealous and find out how deranged you really are." Seeing his large hand coming at her again, Raven twisted and sidestepped Lucian's attempt to swat her.

Lucian glanced at Serina and blew her a kiss. "I've got some work to do around the place before the ceremony." He closed the distance and drew Serina against him, trailing little kisses around her neck. "You and I have unfinished business in here this night, my love. Be safe."

"I will. And this business between us," she said a hair away from his lips, "will never be finished." Serina pulled away from his attempt to kiss her. She turned and headed out the door, with a little wiggle in her step.

Lucian called after her, "Serina, why do you even need a dress? You'll just be begging me to rip the cumbersome thing off you. I say we do the whole Garden of Eden scenario. Everyone naked."

Serina stopped dead in her tracks and turned to him, her face a cross between shock and repulsion. She reclaimed the distance between them. "Lucian, think about that for one minute. Do you really want to see Father Butler naked?"

Lucian closed his eyes and shook his head no.

"Or better yet, your sister?"

Once more, his facial expression changed as he toyed with Serina, a mischievous smirk plastered on his lips.

"Lucian St. James! Ewh!" Serina punched his stomach. "You just want to show off your crown jewels and hope no one's dowry comes close to matching yours." She grabbed his chin and tugged it down to gaze into boiling-blue eyes. "I wouldn't mind seeing if 'tis true what they say about identical cousins." Serina's smile reeked of roguery.

"Right then. The dress it is, but I—"

"I know, m'lord, 'tis good to want." Serina stood on her tiptoes and kissed his nose. She spun and walked away.

"You're walking out? Just like that? That's wrong. You're really leaving? Serina?" Lucian waited, his mouth wide open, his hand over his heart, watching her disappear down the hallway. He started to laugh, but stopped. When she didn't turn around he yelled, "You owe me. I'll have you over my lap tonight."

She had no intentions of turning back. Over his lap sounded devilishly good.

****

After leaving All Hallows Church, the carriage rolled to a stop in front of her home, or what was left of it. Someone demolished her house. The front door lay on her lawn with all of her belongings strewn about, picked over by scavengers. Every window shattered. Her player piano sat in a heap, waiting for a spark to end its misery. All her family photos had been reduced to broken memories. Serina gingerly stepped over the broken glass from the picture frames. The photographs of two of her beloved children from the orphanage, Avery and Sydney, were shredded. Anger replaced fear, leaving her as broken as her belongings. She held up the remains of a once ornate perfume bottle, and threw it across the room in heated rage.

Upstairs, she lifted a garment from the rubble.

Threads from a skirt disintegrated, and fell to the floor. Her jewelry—gone, the box empty. Her grandmother's cameo, her only memento of her—now as absent as her grandmother. She picked up one of her favorite winter boots, now without a heel and open toed.

"Bastards!" She dropped it into a waste can. Her books—fragments of some author's blood, sweat and tears reduced to meaningless dribble. That's when the tears started. She could deal with almost anything being destroyed, but not her books or her flowers. *Lucian, if you can hear me, someone's flipped me home upside down.*

Raven stuck her head in the bedroom. "Serina?" Her voice held caution. "What can I do?"

"Stay out of me way for a bit." With sure-footed steps and anger controlling her, she traipsed down the stairs and through the kitchen, headed toward her garden, petrified to see any damage to her beloved roses.

Her roses were the only things untouched. "Molly," Serina screamed to her, "go check on your home. Check on your kitties."

"She's there, Serina. She left a minute ago." Raven walked to her with her arms wide open. "Come here, Sis."

Serina glanced at Raven through blurry eyes and flung herself into the woman's welcome embrace. Raven tightened her grip and hugged her close.

"Is this how you live every day of your life? Fearful that someone wants you dead? That everything you've built your life around could be ruined in an instant for no apparent reason? My God, Raven!" Serina backed away and began to pace, talk and gesticulate. "I had a quiet life before this. No one knew me or suspected anything. I was invisible. Safe! I hadn't used my powers for years. I hadn't needed to or even wanted to. Everything I touched when I was younger just ended up being an experiment gone awry. I gave up on many things for safety reasons. Mine!" She plopped on the ground amidst the debris that had once been her home through a watershed of tears.

Raven sat next to her and started playing with Serina's hair, twisting it into a braid and talking, in an effort to release her own nervous energy.

"Serina, you don't give yourself enough credit. Lucian and I wouldn't be here right now if it weren't for you. You can't live your life invisible or trapped in that morgue. What you've been given is a true miracle. Can you honestly tell me you were happy before you met Lucian? Trust me, I know what you're feeling. You feel you've been violated and you have, but when I tell you there are much worse evils out in the world to deal with, you must believe me. You still have your health, the love of my brother and myself, Molly, and Duncan. We will watch over you. We are your family now. The house, your clothing 'tis the least of your worries. 'Tis naught but material things, all can be replaced, but my brother cannot replace you. I know you read my mind and know what happened to me a few years ago. I lost so much with that incident. But I had my brother, André, and Duncan. And now, with you in our lives, I have hope again. I feel the love he shares with you and for the first time, I actually want to try to have a relationship with a man. Please don't give up on him or us." Raven took Serina's hand and gave a gentle squeeze. "We need to go see if Molly's all right. Do you want to walk with me or stay and have another cry?" Raven made her best pouty face trying to get Serina to attempt a smile, and it almost worked.

Serina thought Raven was just the most beautiful woman she'd ever encountered. "Raven, before you go and I start crying again, you need to know something that is rather important to your future. It slipped my mind until just a moment ago. The night in the carriage..." Serina scooted closer to Raven and gingerly placed her hands on Raven's stomach. Serina found her mouth bone-dry and yet mist leaked from her pores. How that worked she'd never know. She knew Raven would want a child, but would this come as a complete shock? Most likely. "After I gave you a blood transfusion, I fixed your womb. The doctor that performed your surgery after your attack saved your life, but left you unable to give life back. I reversed that. You should be able to have children when you're ready."

The words filtered in, in slow motion one at a time. *You-can-have-children!* Raven didn't know whether to laugh or cry, whether to believe Serina or not. For four years she'd lived with the knowledge that she would never have her own family, and now this woman was telling her she could hope again after so many years of grieving. Raven toppled Serina and rolled her onto the ground hugging and kissing her, hysterical.

Lucian approached them, and watched his two women rolling around in the grass covered in rose petals.

"What the hell did I miss?"

No response came.

"Uhm..." Lucian cleared his throat. "*HELLOOO!*" Lucian raised his voice a bit more with still no answer. "It's a bloody good thing I'm not a bad guy." That got the two of them to look up.

"Lucian, I'm going to be a mother." Raven jumped up and hugged him.

"What? Who's the father? Ray, when? How? No, don't answer that last one. Is it Payton? I'll kill him with his own set of carving knives! What's the little bastard been cooking up?" He had more questions than he could spit out of his mouth. This was the last thing he expected to hear. First he gets an urgent message from his beloved bride-to-be, then he finds them in hysterics laughing and crying over ruins and then Ray blurts out she's to be a mother. Lucian dropped to the ground next to Serina, holding his head in his hands.

"Lucian, I didn't mean this instant, you imbecile, I meant in the future. Serina fixed me. How? I don't know. I just know I'm the happiest woman alive." Raven bent over and kissed Serina on the cheek again. "I'm going to check on Molly and Duncan. Take care of her, brother."

"Please explain what's taken place here today." Lucian looked at Serina, his face filled with questions.

"You and I are getting married in the morning. I went and saw Father Butler, and he'll be there with bells on. Someone kindly gave me a housewarming present, although I must say it's not my cup of tea." She held up a shattered teacup by the handle showing him. Without thinking, she tossed the broken china against the back of her home and watched it disappear. Serina bent over and kissed Lucian. Just his presence made her feel safe once more. "How did you get here so soon?"

"You called, I came. Some things I can do with the speed of lightning," he said as he ran his fingers tenderly down her arm. "Other things, my wild rose, I take meticulous time and accuracy in doing, ensuring complete and utter satisfaction." He displayed a toothy grin then kissed his way down her arm to her hand. "What really happened, m'lady? Are you well?"

"I am as long as I've you by my side. I will, however, need some new clothes unless you really want me naked all the time. Lucian, take me home, now."

Lucian stood and extended his hand. Once up,

he embraced her with all his strength, afraid to let go. "I'm so sorry about your home. I'm sorry I didn't come with you. We'll get the place redone. New furniture, whatever you need or want."

"I need only you."

He kissed the top of her head and then grabbed her hand and began walking to Molly's. Trying to lighten her mood he added, "Oh, about being naked..."

Lucian never got to finish his sentence. She elbowed his side and kept walking as if he said nothing. He, on the other hand, doubled over, the wind knocked out of him. "Ouch!"

****

Serina finally got what she'd asked for only a month or so late...the trip to the constable. There, they spent quality time trying to convince everyone listening that they were not runaways from the insane asylum. Serina resented the constable's snide, cavalier attitude. She witnessed Lucian's temper for the first time, actually using his stature within the royals to get the lazy man off his wide derriere and do what he was paid to do, investigate and find the villains behind the break-in. Lucian could be intimidating if he wanted to. She found that watching him in control made him even more desirable. When they returned home, she intended to show him just how desirable.

Chapter Eight

Back at the manor Serina, Raven and Molly went to work finishing Serina's wedding dress. As Duncan worked in the garden setting up a few tables and chairs, Molly watched him with reverence through the window. Her mind was as far away from dressmaking, as from the moon itself. "Raven? You've known Duncan forever right, dear?"

"Yes, why?" Raven asked with a wink to Serina.

"Do you think enough time has passed for him to begin to heal? I don't mean to say that he wouldn't still hurt over his loss, but do you think he could move on?" Molly found Duncan exceptionally handsome. She had a hard time getting past his eyes due to their distinct difference. He owned one beautiful brown eye that she was sure he'd stolen from some poor deer and his other eye was the shade of jade. Then there was his hair; long, lustrous brown curls that he always pulled back. Molly was jealous of his silky strands, never having fancied her own color. Hers was too red, too thick and too much the color of tomato sauce. She'd always wanted brown hair just like his. Well now she may just get it, just not in the manner she wanted, but she wasn't complaining.

"Molly, I believe he has already taken that first step. Can't you feel it or see the man has feelings for you?" Raven crossed the room stepping over Serina, the dress, and thousands of tiny pins just waiting to sink into someone's feet. Raven despised sewing so this matchmaking effort came as a welcome distraction. "The way he watches you when he thinks you're not looking? It was his idea to move you and your kitties here so you could be closer to him. Yes, Molly, I believe Duncan is moving on in his life and with you. I won't kid you, he was devastated when he lost Jane and the baby. We all were. But maybe time does heal all wounds with some help, and some very special people you meet along the way." Raven looked directly at Serina when she said that. She walked over to her and gave her a giant hug.

"Don't you dare make me cry again." But the tears flowed, regardless.

"There will be no tears, Sister. Only the finest champagne and whatever our handsome chef whips up. Speaking of the little devil, is anyone else famished? How close are we to finishing your gown?" Raven asked.

"We?" Molly asked wide-eyed. "Serina just needs to try it on and make sure it's perfect. Why don't you head to the kitchen, you know, just oversee the chef's progress, so to speak."

Raven dashed out the door without so much as a word or a glance back.

"Just don't touch anything," Molly called after her.

"Everyone's a blimey court jester 'round here," Raven yelled back.

****

Payton arranged for dinner in his favorite room within the manor, the atrium. The odd-shaped room held five walls. A black granite fireplace, tall enough to walk into occupied the only solid wall. A mirror etched with tiny flowers, matched the brass embossed ceiling tile. The remaining walls held French doors that led out to the veranda overlooking the lake. The room's showpiece was a glistening chandelier of fine leaded crystal. Payton had been told the light dated back to 1815 when Napoleon fled

France and sought refuge on one of England's islands. Napoleon had brought it as a gift of thanks for the shelter.

Candles and sconces scattered across the room, brought the walls to life as the shadows of the approaching night danced across them. Payton arranged a large vase of white lilies and bluebells to grace the oval mahogany table.

Six place settings awaited their dinner guests. As each person entered the room, Payton filled a glass with bubbling spirits and escorted them to their seat. When everyone had been seated, one empty place remained.

"We're missing one seat, Payton. You are most welcome and expected to join us this evening." Lucian said as he grabbed the bottle from Payton. He filled Payton a glass.

Appalled, Payton grabbed at the bottle and tugged it away from Lucian. "The last seat, my Lord, is for your cousin. Word came earlier he would arrive by dusk. I thank you for the invitation, but who would serve you if I join you? 'Tis most inappropriate."

Lucian looked at Raven. "I don't know, I think we're all pretty capable of getting our own plates, right? You need to know, I've never been comfortable having others doing things for me that I'm more than capable of doing myself. I just can't cook. And it's only right you share this meal you've prepared for us, with us. And if you're to be part of our family then you'll dine with us. Fair enough?" Lucian snatched the bottle back with a smirk.

"Yes, Sir. And thank you." Payton held up his glass to Lucian and Serina and toasted them. "There is nothing more noble than two people willing to give their lives to one another, to share their home to delight their family and friends and confound their enemies. Remember, if you put your marital problems on the back burner, they surely will boil over."

"Thank you, Payton." Lucian shook his head with a grin before he asked, "Does it always come back to food with you?"

"That it does, Sir. If I could quote a person I admire? 'A man's gotta eat and then there's dessert!'" Payton glanced at Raven and gave her a quick wink.

Serina leaned into Lucian and whispered, "His hearing is exceptional. We weren't even in his kitchen the evening you said that to me."

"Payton, one last thing—stop calling me Sir."

"Yes, Sir, I mean Lord St. James."

Lucian shrugged his shoulders. "Baby steps."

The rest of the night went smoothly. The six of them devoured fish and chips, fried to a golden perfection. It wasn't what Payton had planned by any means to serve, but then he hadn't planned on Raven sabotaging his beef Wellington either. He had asked her to watch the stove for just one minute, while he ran to get burgundy for his sauce. When he returned flames engulfed his entrée giving the term "blackened" an entirely new meaning.

No one said anything to Raven about dinner. For once, everyone behaved...well almost everyone.

Duncan remarked, "Raven, just because it's called beef Wellington doesn't mean it has to be well done, overly done, burnt-to-a crisp-done, Beauty."

"Oh, Duncan?" Raven smirked before she flung a chip at him. The fried potato smacked his cheek.

Duncan filled his fork with mushy peas, took aim and launched them back at her. Covered in malt vinegar, potato remnants and green vegetables both excused themselves to go change their clothes. Upon returning, the two still snickered like children, provoking each other all over again.

Serina looked around the room at her new

family and noticed one chair still vacant. "What do you think happened to your identical cousin, Lucian?" she asked straight-faced.

Lucian purposely ignored her. He was not going to justify that comment or acknowledge her crazy claim. *Identical cousin! The woman's insane.* "If he's anything like me, he probably hit one of the pubs on the way over. Paris is quite a journey in short notice."

"Luce, how long has it been since we've seen André?" Raven asked. "I probably won't even recognize him."

Everyone except Raven burst into laughter with that comment, seeing their last dinner guest slip into the room where Raven could not. While she stood with her back to the door, trying to figure out what she'd said that seemed so funny, a pair of arms wrapped around her waist and hoisted her off her feet. She sent a shrill scream into the air.

"Raven, it's been way too long since I've heard your beautiful voice or your silly comments, or seen the sincerity and innocence your eyes behold. Four years is much too long." André turned Raven in his arms.

Another scream filled the room, only this time it wasn't a shriek of horror, but one of joy. Raven threw her arms around André and hugged him as if her life depended on it.

"Oh my sweet, André. I've missed you. Bloody 'ell, you're the spitting image of me Lucian." Raven cocked her head to one side, studying both men for a moment and then continued, "Although I suppose I just forgot that one little fact. How are you? You're still beautiful." Raven glued her lips to his cheek.

Lucian and Duncan approached. Serina stared at the man in total disbelief noting the undeniable resemblance between the two men. They were more than just cousins. Serina knew something was amiss. Her nose twitched sensing something vaguely familiar. Black magic's fumes scented the air. Hopefully not her mother's because it had her mother's stench all over it. Her stomach knotted.

"Lucian, you're looking dashing as ever and rather fit." André held out his hand. "Does the beautiful woman at the other end of the table have anything to do with this?"

Serina's face warmed. Quickly she fanned herself with her napkin.

Lucian pulled the man to him in a warm embrace, with Raven sandwiched between them. "André, this is Serina. And you too, cousin, look quite fit and debonair."

"Are you two done patting yourselves on the back about your looks? My God, it's bad enough with just Lucian here but now with the two of you!" Duncan threw his arm around the man and hugged him. "How's our ponies?"

"Good to see you, Duncan. You are truly the one person I missed. You always seem to keep me in line, and as of late, my line's been a bit crooked. The little fillies are fine and gaining strength and speed. Next year Saratoga shall be exciting." André hugged Duncan all the while still holding Raven, and Lucian. "Serina, I would offer my hand to you, but then I would drop our little beauty on her *arse* if I did so, not that she probably doesn't deserve it occasionally."

"That was uncalled for, André. Now put me down—gently." Raven ran her hands through André's hair, studying him. She turned a cheek taking in Lucian, like she'd never really seen the two of them before today. "It really is uncanny," Raven mused. Without a care, she dragged André first to Payton. "Ands, meet our new chef, Payton."

"Pleasure, Payton. Hope this crew doesn't scare you off."

Raven added, "Nothing is scarier than his ex-boss. Luce stole him from our aunt's club house. He's an excellent cook."

"When Ray doesn't get involved," Molly snuck in.

"The feisty redhead is Molly. Duncan's lady." Raven blew Molly a kiss.

André waved a quick hello while he was being dragged toward Serina. Raven grabbed Serina's hand and placed it in André's. "Ands, meet my new sister. She is a doctor and a chemist. She also sells a smashing perfume called, Eden's Black Rose." Raven turned, walked back to Lucian and hugged an arm around his waist.

"A chemist, hey? I know the scent well. Very alluring." André looked back and saw Lucian and Duncan wryly eyeing him. With a shy wink he asked, "What?" He knew both men wondered why he would know of a woman's perfume. "I love women and they love perfume. 'Tis as easy as one plus one." André held two fingers to Lucian and in a low voice said, "The answer's two, Luce," then bared all his teeth at the other man playfully.

Raven blurted out, "This is perfect."

André gently kissed Serina's hand and then let it go. "I should have come sooner, but so much has happened, Lucian. We need to talk after you and your bride return from your honeymoon. Where are you planning on taking this fair maiden?"

André never took his eyes from Serina as he spoke to Lucian, which made Serina uncomfortable, sensual and mystified at the same time. A wanton goddess. That, she decided might be a bit over-the-top but still, her lips curled into an unstoppable smile. It was one thing to have the most beautiful male on the planet wedding her in the morning, but then to see an identical replica standing in front of her, with his black eyes scorching her soul and pouring heat over her body like wax from a melted candle was an entirely different story. Again, she realized her thinking might be a bit exaggerated, but she smiled regardless. The idea of two of them moistened her drawers. *You need to forget that line of thinking, Serina, or you'll be divorced before you're married. Two men at once would most certainly be the sin of the century.*

Lucian asked, "What is the grin for, m'lady? I certainly hope you're not thinking what I think you are."

Serina watched Lucian as he stood across the room rubbing his fingers over his chin, wearing a grin as evil as she felt at that moment. *He knows, dammit!* His twinkling eyes held her secret. Instantly, her bottom lip became a target for her top teeth to gnaw.

Lucian shook his head, amused.

Overwhelmed with the wedding, the new family, and the new identical twin/cousin, and her home's recent destruction, Serina stood and excused herself. "André, 'tis a pleasure to meet you. Raven, sweet dreams. Molly and Duncan, thank you for everything and Payton, sorry I'm bailing on you and not helping clean up. Lucian, would you escort me to my room?"

Once alone in her bedroom with him she said. "I am so sorry.... I don't know what came over me."

Lucian nudged Serina against the wall, dragged her hands up over her head and held her there as he kissed her fast and hard with such force she'd have sworn he passed right through her. The kiss stole her breath.

"Remember whose lips just tasted you, just loved you. Never say you're sorry to me. André and I are actually used to the exact thoughts you just had. You'd be amazed how many women want a set of twins at the same time. Me more than him, of course."

Serina rolled her eyes.

"Ah—but then we are not twins."

"Oh, about that, Lucian! I don't know what to think just yet but I'd bet my powers you two are twins. I don't know how or why but I've never seen cousins resemble each other like identical twins before. Of course, anything is possible. Vampires prove that. Will you tuck me in? I really am tired and want to look like a blushing bride for you tomorrow." Serina slipped out of Lucian's hold and patted the bed. "Come sit by me."

"Keep having thoughts like the ones you just had about André and I and you'll be blushing again."

"Lucian..." She tried to sound appalled, but it was a wasted attempt.

"I couldn't resist that, m'lady." Once tucked in, Lucian sat on the edge of her bed and brushed her hair. After he braided it, he gave a little tug of her tail to land her in his lap looking up at him. "I would love nothing more than to make love to you now, but for this night only I'll be the gentleman and wait. Serina, I will call for you in the morning." He bent down to kiss her goodnight and Serina snaked her arms around him and pulled him down to her.

"Kiss me once more, Lucian. Lay with me 'til I drift off and dream of you, or your twin/cousin, whatever he is."

"Serina!" Lucian slapped her bottom.

"I owed you that one. Not to worry, my love, it is you and only you I shall spend my dreams with. Until the sunrise, m'lord."

****

Each with a glass of brandy in hand, Lucian found Duncan and André in the atrium catching up on old times. He listened with reverence about their escapades in Paris the previous year and how they ended up buying the thoroughbreds. Lucian basked in their laughter. Up until then, he hadn't realized how much he actually missed André. They'd grown together as brothers, learning to ride, hunt, use a bow, and fence. Both were excellent marksmen; neither man better than the other, yet they professed to best the other at every opportunity. Lucian claimed it healthy competition.

"André, tell me of your life these past years. Have you met a woman who can put up with you yet?"

Lucian sat and flung his feet over the arm of the chair. His long, lanky legs hit André's chair. He tapped his foot purposely, nudging André's arm.

André growled, "My, what big feet you have." He laughed when Lucian looked curiously between André's feet and then back at his own.

"That's not all that's big," Lucian jested.

"Other than your sense of self," Duncan tossed in.

"Lucian, you probably wouldn't believe me if I told you, but I've been slaying vampires now for the past few years. It seems someone out there wants me either dead, or undead. I'm not sure which yet, and hope not to find out."

Lucian sat up, processing the information while he rubbed the stubble on his jaw. "Try me. Raven and I were attacked this past month and all but killed. Serina saved us. She's a doctor. Did I mention that to you before?" Lucian beamed with schoolboy pride.

"Oh, Lucian, how she has you strung like a puppet." André turned his attention to Duncan. "Is he always this bad?"

"More so, usually. I never thought I'd see it with mine eyes, but the boy's beyond words."

"What can I say?" Lucian shrugged his shoulders.

André tapped his fingers on the table

repetitively. "Maybe together we could find out who is behind these attempts on our lives. We will finish this conversation when you and Serina return from your honeymoon. You never answered me before. Where will you go?"

"Virginia Falls in Surrey. The falls are beautiful this time of year, and there are some hot springs too. Remember the cabin?"

André laughed. "Remember stealing your parent's clothes from the rocks by the springs?"

"Do I? I couldn't sit straight for a week when father caught us. Mother laughed ridiculously, but he was upset. He screamed, 'A woman's pride is worth your heart.' Funny, I finally understand that now. Will you be staying long with us?"

"If you'll have me—"

Lucian cut André off, "Of course. We want you back home with us. We should never have been separated. I never understood mother's decision, but I'm grateful you've returned. And you never answered me. Is there no woman yet?"

"Too many to choose from." André went quiet deciding on whether or not to tell his tale of woe. With both Lucian and Duncan bent over in their seats awaiting an answer, André opened up. "Four years back there was a woman, an insanely, bold blond." André visibly blushed thinking of her.

Duncan smirked. "Oh, I've seen that look before."

Lucian cut in, "Yes, old man, on you at dinner tonight, beside Molly."

"I noticed it too, Luce." André raised a brow to Duncan and continued, "My lady disappeared right from under me. I searched for an endless year. A detective I'd hired gave clues to her whereabouts with none ever panning out. Lousy detective if you ask me. Went by the name of Holmes. Sherlock, I believe."

Duncan burst out laughing. "Ands, he's fictional. 'Tis no wonder you never found your lassie."

"I just wanted to see if you were paying attention. I met her at a train station in a tiny hamlet after Raven's attack. Had a torrid affair with the woman and left my heart in her hands. I told her I'd return in a fortnight, but when I did she disappeared. I received one letter from her a few months later asking me to join her in Paris. I was there, in her empty hotel. However, I did encounter an over abundance of vampires waiting for me on every corner. I've lost count of how many kills I've made, but I've become rather proficient with my new career...Fell head-over-heels in love with her. And four years later nothing has changed. If I saw her tonight, I'd ask her to marry me." And if she was already married? She wouldn't be. He knew it deep in his heart that she felt the same way he did. André rolled his eyes towards Lucian, a smirk covering his face. "Laugh and we'll duel here and now, I swear." André turned to Duncan. "So—old man, see you've gone and found yourself a pretty lady as well. Saw you at dinner holding hands with her under the table."

Duncan studied the two men in an entirely new light, as if he'd never really seen them before today even though he'd spent his entire life with them.

"My, my Ands, you don't miss a thing. Then, you never did. Molly is Serina's neighbor." Duncan continued to eye the men oddly. First one then the next and blurted out, "Holy God, you two are identical. I never noticed it as much when you were growing up, you know with awkward growth spurts, weight gain—Lucian, and pimples—André, and the dreadful haircuts Raven gave each of you, but it is undeniable now." Duncan grabbed one hand of each of the men and flipped their hands over, palms up.

Lucian accused, "You're hanging around my

fiancé too much, old man."

Duncan ignored him. "Did you know Scotland Yard is working on a new way of detecting crimes and *who-done-its*, so to speak? They say each of us has our set of fingerprints, unlike anyone else's. There's this detective, Sherlock..."

André socked him in the arm. Duncan ignored the shooting pain riveting up his arm and continued, "Doctor Henry Faulds. He states you can grease up your fingers and put them on a glass and you can see your fingers printed on the glass. He said identical twins are extremely similar, so close that you can barely tell them apart. You two up for a test?" Duncan wanted to know if his feelings were right. This was just too much of a coincidence for them not to be twins. But that left many unanswered questions. Duncan thought for a brief moment that Pandora's Box had been delivered to him. "No, we won't do this now." He let go of the two men's hands.

Both men sat with the same puzzled look.

Lucian, fighting a smirk asked, "I don't mean to be rude, but how do you know these things, Duncan?"

"Lucian, when you look at me, all you are able to see is beauty and brawn and rightfully so." Duncan doubled over and laughed hysterically at his own joke. He spit out, "Young man, there happens to be a very intelligent brain that goes with this *oh-so-manly* body." Duncan took a deep breath, puffed out his chest while stiffening his arms to show off his finely whittled muscles.

After the laughter died down, André added, "I'm glad one of us thinks so." Then he gave Duncan a mischievous smile that Duncan had seen plastered on Lucian's face a million times before.

Lucian and André turned their attention to their hands, and then each other, both making "humph" sounds.

"How do we do it?" they asked in unison.

"Each of you slip your finger into a bit of lard then hold a glass. That's how they described it at the Yard. One of the constables said it's truly amazing."

"Duncan, you amaze me." Lucian's tone serious.

"Oh, like that's so hard to do," Duncan rebutted.

André grabbed Lucian's shoulder laughing, as tears welled behind his eyes. "Oh, I miss you. Good one, old man."

"You two are more like peas in pod." After Lucian ran and got the butter, he and André stuck their fingers in it and then pressed their fingers onto a glass. Duncan pulled out a magnifying glass and they each stared in silence. There was no telling the prints apart. The men had no knowledge of this training, but the evidence before them was undeniable. Silence consumed the room.

Raven walked in carting a champagne glass half-full, glassy-eyed and smiling. "What's up, me boys?" Raven threw her slender frame on top of Lucian, squashing him flat into the chair cushion. "What is it that has you all looking like you've seen a ghost? You've not, have you? Vampires, ghosts, werewolves, what's next? Fairies?" Raven pushed herself off Lucian.

No one answered.

"Someone had best spill the beans. Come on then, out with it." She bent over and pressed her nose up to Lucian's looking him directly in the eyes, spilling some of her champagne on him.

"Oops! Luce, tell me what's going on."

Lucian closed his eyes.

She proceeded to Duncan. He shook his head no. Last, but not least, she went to André who never lifted his gaze from his fingers or the glass.

"Have I lost me charm?" Raven positioned herself next to Duncan watching them closely, the way a cat does a mouse just before it pounces. Each looked guilty, Raven was positive of that, but what?

André looked to Lucian. "You want to tell her or shall I?"

Lucian pointed to André.

"Ray, did you ever just once think I could have been your brother? Really? Did it ever occur to you that Luce's and my resemblance wasn't just a coincidence? Did you ever think in the grand scheme of life that the three of us had totally been snookered—lied to our entire lives?" André was very close to losing his edge. His sight became blurred, and he stood in haste, shrugging his shoulders as if he could dismiss the overbearing pain and humiliation so easily. He took long, heavy strides to the windows that overlooked the lake and he watched as the moonlight danced alone off the waves effectively shielding his pain.

Antsy, Raven waited for someone to make some sort of sense, because André certainly didn't. She tapped her fingers out of annoyance on the back of the chair and watched Lucian cross the room to André, place his arm around the other man, and share the window with him.

"Oh, blimey already. Would one of you talk?" Raven shot across the room, nudging her way in between the two men and looked from one to the other. "What did I miss? Please tell me. I feel like a small girl all over again asking you two to give me the time of day."

Lucian whispered to André, "She's your sister." Then patted his back.

André produced a smile, real and sincere as he glanced over to Lucian. "God help us."

"How much brandy did you three get into?" Raven asked, annoyance heavy in her tone.

Duncan started talking again and what he said would leave all of them with more questions than answers since the only people capable of answering them were long gone from this world. "When you three were born, I was ten. I honestly don't remember Chyna being pregnant, André. Chyna was always the tiniest, frail creature. Lorelei was enormous, even in her early stages of pregnancy, unnaturally so. She'd been restricted to bed rest for the last four months of her pregnancy. I remember because I was the one who had done all the running for her. One day Mum, Chyna and Lorelei took off for a fortnight then came home with all of you, all three of you. Oh, and some midwife. The midwife came 'round religiously. Every month she would pop in and give everyone in the home medicinal potions and herbs, claiming it kept everyone's health up. It did help, because not a one of us ever had any illness. Chyna always had you, André, in her care. I guess I always suspected something deep down, but never thought too much about it. I just figured you were her baby because what woman in her right mind would give a baby away? I don't know why I thought of it now. It must be seeing the two of you together again. When Chyna turned up missing, Lorelei...she went berserk. She didn't let any of you out of her sight for months. The three of you actually slept in her chambers. Your mum figured she and your father were next on the list and damn if she wasn't right. Just like that. Life gone in the blink of an eye. Maybe that's why she separated all of you. Maybe she thought you all had a better chance at living apart from each other. I know separating you all took a terrible toll. I even felt it. I felt sick for you André." Duncan shrugged his shoulders. He went on to explain the fingerprint theory to Raven.

After absorbing Duncan's explanation and another glass of champagne, Raven cried, "I don't understand. I feel so cheated." Raven looked to Lucian out of habit. She looked at him for everything in her life and didn't realize how much she actually depended on him until that second. "André, I'm so sorry you've been alone for so long." Raven placed both her hands on his face and held him steady, gazing into his deep blue almost black eyes. She kissed him chastely on the lips and then hugged him with as much force as she could muster.

"You're going to love me to death, little beauty," André whispered, as he returned her hug.

Lucian and Duncan joined in, all of them crying like a bunch of drunken fools.

After a moment of awkwardness, realizing how they appeared, Lucian backed out of the group and with a giant grin and reddened eyes said, "This is the best night of my life. I'm going to bed now before anything happens to change it. See you all bright and early for my wedding."

He heard Duncan snickering as he left, saying, "Hopefully, tomorrow night will top this one."

Chapter Nine

When the front door opened and closed, André stuck his head over the upper balcony and watched a man, he assumed to be Father Butler, his white chasuble and bible in hand being a dead giveaway, examine all the pictures in the main entry. He yelled down, "Good morning, Sir."

Father Butler looked up. "Lucian! So good to see you, son. Are you all prepared for today? Do you and I need to have *the chat*?" Father Butler asked, sincere.

André choked back laughter as he hurried down the stairs to greet the man. "Father, I'm sorry, Lucian is still upstairs. And not that you heard it from me, I believe you're a day late on the chat, Sir." André extended his hand to the priest. "André St. James at your service."

"Lucian never told me he had a twin brother."

"No one bothered to tell us either, Sir." Father Butler gave him a quizzical glance. "'Tis a long story, Father. When we've more time I'll explain it to you. May I escort you to the gardens? Would you enjoy a glass of champagne? Molly, Duncan, and Payton are all ready out there waiting for our bride and groom."

"Where's my girl?" Father asked wearing a smile fit for the bride's father.

"Hopefully up. I've not seen her yet."

"I'll wait here for her. Thank you. And I'll have that champagne." The twinkle in his eyes shone bright.

****

Serina wasn't sure how she ended up here...in

this enchanting home with a man that she had fallen head over heels in love with in a matter of weeks. Oh, but she did love him. He gave her a feeling of warmth and security she'd never known. And when he kissed her...

Deciding she had to make this a reality, she picked up her pace and stopped her daydreaming. Padding over to the dresser, she noticed a small, white silk package with a note beside it.

August 30, 1896
M'lady, Serina Spencer,
This morning you will fulfill my destiny. You are my treasure, which I will protect, love and cherish with my heart, my soul and my life. You are my very heart's desire. My eternal love is forever yours. You are my Garden of Eden, Serina.
Lucian

Within the box, lay a strand of pearls with a trillion shaped solitaire that hung from the center of a gold slide. Serina stared in awe at the necklace and smiled. She set the necklace aside, got cleaned up and started doing her hair which was never an easy task. The length alone became a battle as she pulled it up into a Grecian style twist with long loose tendrils falling down and framing her face and longer curls sweeping down her back. Make-up came next. No easy task again, especially when she rarely wore it and had no idea how not to end up resembling the circus clowns or worse, the corner tart. Her mother taught her what to wear and made her memorize each compartment of her compact so she would know where to apply what. When she finished, she glanced into her looking glass and prayed.

The dress was the last thing to do battle with,

and there was, indeed, a battle. Raven and Molly insisted that the gown be just a bit on the snug side, to hold a few things in place. There would be no repeat of Lucian and hers first meeting with the robe. After some very intense minutes of wiggling, stuffing and cursing, Serina triumphed and managed to get into the dress and still be able to take a deep breath without losing any buttons.

The champagne satin, two-piece dress had been in Serina's family from the sixteenth century. The princess-cut undercoat gave her the appearance of being slightly taller. She loved that. The back of the gown had ruffled layers that cascaded the way a soft waterfall would flow behind her. The sheer lace overcoat fastened in the front with one pearl button and it lay just off the shoulders. Marching back and forth in front of her mirror, and doing an occasional spin to see the gown's swirling movements, Serina admired her reflection, then glanced at the wall clock, which ticked towards her future.

****

"Knock, knock, Luce. Can I come in?"

"When did you start asking, Ray?"

"I'm practicing so I don't waltz in on you or Serina. I've witnessed enough of you two, and I'd rather save my eyesight. Going blind by your own overactive sex life is one thing—losing your sight because of someone else's, well 'tis wrong."

Lucian opened the door to see his sister standing on the other side looking more beautiful than he ever remembered. "What may I do for you, my little beauty?"

With a quick kiss on his cheek, she began fixing his buttons on his cuffs, then she moved on to perfect the knot on his tie. "Today's only the most important day of your life. Are you nervous?" she asked as she plopped down atop his feather bed and sank a good six inches into the mattress.

"Not when you put it like that! Ray, what do I do about André now that we almost know for sure he's our brother? I asked Duncan to stand up for me. Now I feel obligated to have André. Help?" Lucian sat down on the bed next to Raven holding his face in his hands.

"You have a very nice option, dear brother...ask Duncan if he wouldn't mind sharing you. I'm sure that with everything that happened last night he would completely understand."

Lucian wrapped his arms around his sister and held her for a few minutes without either of them saying anything, or needing to. "I'll ask Duncan. Ray, you know just because I'm getting married it doesn't mean..."

Raven tapped her fingers to her brother's mouth.

"Shush, my favorite imbecile. We really need to get you downstairs. There is this woman waiting for you, and I fear if you don't light a fire under your arse, she'll marry the wrong man. Your twin, my twin, our twin, what the hell do we call him?" She pushed at him to get up.

Lucian got up off the bed and held his hand out to her. "Shall we?"

"Thought you'd never ask. I love you, Luce."

"You better!" Lucian answered following on her high heels.

"Imbecile."

****

In the garden, Lucian approached Duncan. Before he could get a word in edgewise, Duncan jumped in. "Luce, we need to talk. Can I ask you something most personal?" Duncan tossed his arm around Lucian and walked him to the water's edge so they could have some privacy. "How would you feel about two best men? It wouldn't be right to leave André out. Luce, you've been like my little brother since the day you were born, and I'm honored to stand up for you, but André really is your brother."

"Old man, your generous offer leaves me speechless."

"I'll believe that when I see it."

Lucian laughed hard. "I'm the fortunate one to have you by my side today and in my life." Lucian embraced him as if he never wanted to let go of the man. "I should go speak with my twin. Oh, that's going to take some getting used to. See you at the podium in a few moments?"

"Luce, if you say anything to make me cry, so help me God."

"Duncan, you're the best. I mean that." Lucian swatted his friend's back as he walked away.

Duncan turned away wiping his eyes.

****

Concealed by thick pricker-bushes, Olivia Spencer dabbed at the bloody tears that stained her cheeks with her black hankie as she watched her daughter's wedding get underway. How could her daughter do this to her? Not invite her own mother to her wedding? She'd bloody well waited twenty-one years for this day! She'd almost gotten over the fact that Serina threatened to call the Sorcerer's Squad on her. She knew Serina would never really do it, not to her—her own mother. Olivia worked up a mist as she swatted at bugs, trying to get a glimpse of the man that had stolen her daughter's heart. "Blimey, if this doesn't warm me cockles, nothing will!" Olivia blinked and rubbed her eyes. On the opposite side of the lake stood two identical men, both who looked hauntingly familiar. Then Olivia remembered them.

Royals! Holy shite!

Thinking back she remembered their aunt had been a wretched creature, full of guile. *Oh, what is her name? She's named after a flippin' tea cup or a plate—got it, Chyna! I should have smashed her to smithereens. Wench never paid me for my potions.* "My dear daughter, you need to learn if you're to make accusations you need to follow through with them. Life is full of consequences and this is a hard one you'll learn." Requital time approached as Olivia weaved her hands in the air, and directed a curse that would put a halt to the royal bloodline for some time to come. Serina would learn one way or another to respect her mother and the royals would soon find out money couldn't buy everything. Still perturbed, Olivia closed her eyes and fashioned a dress worthy of a royal wedding. With a snap of her fingers, she glanced down at the luxurious gown and its accessories.

"Damn, I'm good." Olivia evanesced.

****

"Serina," Father Butler yelled at the top of his lungs, "move your dainty arse, little girl, if you'll still be wanting to wed the poor, wilting man outside. 'Tis rather warm out." The pounding of the knocker called Father Butler towards the door.

"Father, who's here?" Serina peeked over the banister.

Father grabbed the handle and pulled the heavy glass door inward. Squinting away the sun's rays he focused on a woman dressed in a black satin gown, a black veiled hat that could have used trestles for support. It was that bold. A frilly, black lace parasol twirled above her. At first he thought the glass distorted the woman's figure, then upon taking a closer look, he realized it was not the case.

"Oh dear Lord! Livvy?"

"Thomas, you know the lord has naught to do with the likes of me."

Father Butler gripped the knob tighter.

"Are you going to just stand there or allow me in, Thomas?" She prodded him with her parasol.

"Mum?" Serina's throat tightened around the

very word. Her eloquent descent down the stairs took a nasty turn. Before Serina blinked, she was moving faster than a snowball on a mountain barreling down the slopes going head over heels.

With the flick of her wrist, Olivia plucked Serina from mid-air before she splattered upon the bottom step.

"Such a graceful entrance, Serina. Did I or did I not try to send you to charm school?"

Disoriented and disheveled, Serina wobbled to the hallway mirror, one shoe on, one shoe lost. "You look as if you're dressed for a funeral, Mother. Did someone die?" *Or am I about to?* Serina didn't give her a second glance. With no time to waste, she redid her hair, straightened her gown, and climbed half way back up the steps after her shoe. "I feel like bloody Cinderella. Don't you dare turn me into pumpkin."

"Weddings—funerals, they'll both be the death of you at some point. Oh, you're welcome, Serina, for saving you."

"I wouldn't have fallen if you hadn't shown up. What do you want?"

"What every mother wants, to walk her daughter down the isle and meet the new in-laws of course."

"I'll be taking that trip down the isle with Serina, Livvy."

"How utterly inappropriate, Thomas." The woman stomped her umbrella on the floor, hitting Father Butler's toes on the last blast.

Father Butler cast a scornful shot her way.

"Oops!" Olivia gave Father Butler a side-glance, pulled her shoulders back, and said, "Let's get this fiasco over with."

"To argue would only hasten the inevitable. 'Tis either her way or no way. Right Mum?" Serina looked at Father Butler with a grim face. "Shall we?"

Serina held her hands to Father Butler and her mother. "This day started out so nicely."

"I'll not ruin your wedding, Serina. I'm just curious."

"Curiosity killed the cat, Mum. How many lives have you got left?"

"Enough!"

Lucian, André, and Duncan stood at the podium, waiting...

Within moments, Lucian caught sight of Father Butler as he escorted his blushing bride...And some strange woman dressed like the Grim Reaper's mistress, down the garden path.

Serina gave Lucian an ill-fated grin.

Serina?

Don't ask, Lucian. Pretend you don't see her.

Hard not to. Serina?

My mother.

Splendid, I'd love to meet her.

You say that now. Serina rolled her eyes and trudged forward trying not to allow her mother to mar her day. She set her sights straight ahead and focused on Lucian. He was the only person here who mattered.

I did not think it possible for you to look any more stunning, beautiful, radiant, gorgeous...

Flattery, my love, will definitely get you everywhere this night. Sorry I'm running a tad late. You see—I had a minor spill when Mummy popped in. Thank you for the note and necklace this morning. I can't wait for this to be over so you and I can, well, you know.

I do...Wait, that part comes in a few minutes. I know exactly how you feel, trust me.

Serina could feel the color rising to her cheeks, and she didn't want that to happen. She already had enough make-up on to paint her portrait. And that wasn't the only place the heat pooled. The whole idea of not wearing any drawers to surprise her new husband may not have been in her best interest when she realized how very moist she'd become. Suddenly she didn't think she could hold out until after the ceremony.

Serina leaned over and whispered into Father's ear, "Father, could we pick up the pace a bit?"

"My dear child, did I not teach you patience is a virtue?"

"Did you?" She laughed heartily. "I'll work on the patience part; you work on your speed. Do we have an accord?" Serina gave Father a little tug.

Father giggled as he quickened his step. "Come on Livvy, lose the hat and lighten your load."

"Thomas!" Olivia gasped as Serina jerked her forward to keep up with them.

Serina laughed. "I can't believe the way you speak to my mother and get away with it."

"Dear child, your mother has been my dearest friend since childhood. Right, Livvy?"

Olivia peeked out from under her veil, her emerald eyes glistening. "The fool's demented. He's been around too many spirits, and I'm not referring to the holy ones." She dropped her shield.

A few feet from the podium, Father Butler stopped. He whispered to Serina, 'I just want you to know how proud this old man is of you. You've truly been a great joy in my life, the best part of my life."

"That goes both ways, Father.'

Olivia elbowed Serina.

"What?" Serina asked agitated.

"Don't you have anything you'd like to say to me?"

Serina lifted both brows to the woman. "If I've nothing good to say..."

Olivia huffed, blowing the black netting on her hat out.

With a shrug of his shoulders, Father Butler

nudged Serina toward her new life. "How's that, little girl."

Serina grabbed the portly man and kissed him leaving a set of peach lips upon his cheek.

"I do believe, my dear, I'm the one who is supposed to kiss the bride." And he did along with a hug that stole her breath. Then Serina turned to her husband-to-be.

"Lucian, this is my mother. Mother, Lucian. We'll do all the formalities after the ceremony, all right?"

Lucian greeted her with a warm smile. "Pleasure to meet you."

"You say that now," Olivia retorted. She nodded, and Serina ducked avoiding the ridiculous obstacle atop her mother's head.

"Your daughter has your sense of humor. Would you remove your veil so we might meet eye to eye?" Lucian asked politely.

"My lord, 'tis vanity that shields me this day. Seeing my only child wed has taken its toll on me. Another time, perhaps." Olivia realized if they recognized her there would hell to pay, and she did promise no trouble today. Olivia leaned close to Lucian's ear and whispered, "Break her heart once, and it shall be yours I replace it with."

Caught off guard by the woman's bold remark, Lucian took a step back. "'Tis a great thing you are here with us today, Olivia. We both have Serina's best wishes in our hearts."

Serina looked at Lucian curiously.

Not now, my lovely bride.

Father Butler cleared his throat and placed Serina's smaller hand into Lucian's, their fingers entwined and the ceremony took place.

Just before Lucian placed Serina's wedding band on her finger, he asked her to read the inscription inside the ring.

Serina held the tiny gold band in front of her and read, "Eden 1896."

Lucian laid a gentle kiss upon her hand and placed the ring on her finger. "This is inscribed because since I've met you, I feel as if I'm in the most mystical garden on earth."

Not a dry eye in the bunch could be found.

When it came time to kiss the bride, Lucian was all lips, literally. He arched Serina backwards and dipped her low to the ground. He whispered, "I love you, Serina St. James," just before he claimed possession of her soul and her heart.

Lucian's kiss left Serina lying in his arms wanting him to finish what he started right there, crowd or no crowd, mother or no mother blocking out every ray of sunshine with her bonnet.

"You and I have unfinished business, my dear husband. I love the sound of that."

How long can you wait, m'lady? Can we at least share some champagne with our family or would you prefer I escort you out of here like a caveman, saying nothing? Shall I throw you over my shoulder and drag you off? Your choice. Lucian held a hungry grin for his new bride.

Oooh...definitely like a caveman!

"Champagne sounds divine, Lucian." Serina bent her head back and waited for him to close the distance again.

He accommodated her in one long, hard-pressed tonsil-tickling kiss.

"All right you two, I can see my timing on the chat came a day late," Father Butler interrupted. "Let us toast to your new lives together." Everyone held up champagne glasses as Father blessed their marriage. "Lucian and Serina may the wind always be at your back, the heavens at your gate, love in your heart, and more children at your feet than you can remember their names. Cheers."

Olivia patted her chest and cleared her throat.

Bags packed and ready to get her honeymoon underway, Serina scurried to Father Butler, with a grin that Father recognized as trouble —for him.

"You, dear old man, lost a bet we made. Remember betting me I'd never find meself a man in this century? I even had four years to spare. All my gardening tools are in the greenhouse. I know you know how to weed even if you've never done it, you've seen me do it a thousand times. Watch out for the thorns and bees. Love you."

"Serina Spencer!"

"'Tis St. James now," Serina corrected.

"You honestly expect me to keep your roses alive?"

Teasing him she said, "You'd better. I've got a few spells up my sleeve me mum taught me."

"Blackmail, child? I never thought I'd see the day." Father swatted Serina's bum. "Go now to your husband, my girl. Enjoy your new life." Father grabbed Serina and hugged her once more. "I love you."

"Love you more." Serina's fingers lingered on his chubby cheeks before she left.

Lucian watched Duncan and Molly dance, holding each other closely. Lucian would treasure that sight forever.

Now he had to see his sister as happy. He watched her with Payton, laughing, cuddling with him. He felt good about that one giant step.

He kept wondering, what would have happened if he and Raven had never been attacked? He would never have met Serina. In a strange way, Lucian was thankful for that fateful night.

He sought out Serina's mother to get better acquainted, but the woman and her hat had vanished.

He glanced around for André and found him

with Father Butler.

Lucian waltzed across the veranda, grabbed his new bride, tossed her over his shoulder, and headed for the train station.

Chapter Ten

The carriage ride to the station allowed no time for even the quickest little tryst...but then there was the ride to Virginia Falls. Between the Pullman Limited Express train, which began its routes in 1883, and horseback up the mountain they'd make time. Lucian made certain their private car came with a butler, bath and bed. He asked the room be filled with fresh flowers, champagne, chocolates and berries, and luxurious sapphire-colored silk sheets with white rose petals scattered across them to welcome his new bride.

Entering their car, Serina pointed to a gift that lay in the center of the bed. "Lucian, really you shouldn't have." Regardless, she wasted no time picking the gift up and rattling it. "This is the most stunning closet-sized room I've ever stepped foot in. Did I ever mention I am claustrophobic?" She wasn't kidding. Her heart kicked up a notch. Even though the tiny boxcar had all the amenities of home, it was crammed into a eight by eight foot room. The bed, the loo, the shower and a table with two chairs filled every square inch. She looked up at her husband with eyes wide. "The rose petals remind me of home, flowers all over the bleeding place. The strawberries are nice, but I have afflictions to them. I'll turn into one giant hive if I eat them. The silky sheets look dangerous. Slippery when wet comes to mind. Guess I'll have to hold on tight to you." She shifted her brows in her non-prim non-proper motion.

Not quite the reaction he was hoping for. She sounded skeptical. He wanted her bubbling over with joy so he could do the same. He had his work cut out. "Go on, undo this one." He tapped on the gift.

She pulled out a sheer, black lace negligee that looked very close to the one she had on the first night they had met. Her green eyes smoldered when she turned to him. Just as he'd hoped. Maybe this would take her mind off her worries. She could place all her energies to use in other areas...Him.

She bit her bottom lip as she squeezed around the chairs to the edge of the bed. She sat down and held her hands out to him.

"Would you undress me, m'lord, if it's not too much trouble? I'm feeling rather overdressed for the occasion at hand. This little lace coat is beautiful. I can't wait to put it on."

"I told you you'd want out of that cumbersome dress." Lucian's husky voice offered a warm entanglement of their bodies with passion steaming the windows of the car. He stood Serina with her back to him and began to undo what seemed like an infinite number of buttons. "Did I mention to you today that you are the most beautiful goddess on the planet?"

"I'm easy. Keep 'em coming. One more won't hurt." Serina laughed.

He edged her gown from her shoulders, but stopped the dress from falling just short of her breasts. All in due time! Her eyes held fire and brimstone when he faced her. That glance caused his gut to tighten and his loins to feel more like watermelons tucked in his trousers. "I'm enchanted by the fact you are indeed my wife, my lover, and my heart." He let the dress slip down over her breasts.

Every nerve in her body reacted to his touch, his scent, his caress. Her breasts became firm, her nipples hard peaks with each breath that passed over her.

He captured her at her waist, and when his lips met her skin a flame scorched its way to the juncture between her thighs.

That fast. Foreplay? Yes, it was indeed torturously fun, but she was already there. He began at her wrists, moving lazy little kisses upward. Anxious, she drew Lucian's lips to her chest and looked down to him, pleading without words.

He shook his head no. She grunted.

Lucian wanted to take his time with her. He kissed his way over her shoulder and worked his way to her neck. Once he found that spot she seemed to adore, he nipped hard. More sounds slipped from his new bride as she dug her fingers into his hair and crushed him to her.

"Lucian..."

"Not tonight, Lady St. James. I will not give you what you want until I am more than certain you cannot take one second more. You told me I could have my way with you, so I am holding you to your word." As he kissed between her breasts, he slid his tongue over her beaded nipples, Serina's knees began to shake.

"You're taunting me."

"Indeed I am, m'lady. I've only just begun." Tiny tremors rocked his body from anticipation alone. What she experienced, so did he. Lucian tightened his hold.

"I'm already nearing the end, Lucian, and you still haven't gotten me out of this cocoon. This is not fair." Serina's voice came out low, a complete seductress at work. She began to try to wiggle her way free when Lucian shackled her hands behind her.

"Soon enough, my love. What did Father say about patience being a virtue?"

"That in all likelihood it would be the death of me since I have none! Do you want me to die, here?

Now?"

"Oh, my little drama queen." Lucian never missed a beat. He took her breast to his mouth and puckered his lips around her nipple. He nibbled, sucked, and as she put it, taunted the ripened bud then he sat back and admired his handiwork. Two perky mountains of creamy flesh awaited his next move. He lowered her dress.

"Lucian, I can't stand any more."

"Yes, you can."

"No, I mean I can't stand, my legs are threatening to give way."

"I did not realize I married such a whiner." Lucian blew her a kiss. As the dress slipped from her hips Serina's own little surprise was revealed. Not a stitch of clothing to be found under the dress. His eyes couldn't have shown more delight. "Tell me you've not been like this all day?"

She grinned. "I worried slightly when you went in search of me garter, that you'd find me surprise a bit early."

"Damn shame I didn't." With his hands on her hips, he drew her to him then nudged her thighs apart and let her straddle one of his legs. He slid her hips back and forth across his thigh, rubbing softly over that one spot that could satisfy her and drive him insane. The movement wasn't enough. He wanted his shaft trapped between her delicate folds of warm skin and having her ride him as she was now.

"How close are you, my luv?"

The velvet-trousered leg that caressed her mons was pleasurable, but not enough. She wanted it all. She swallowed a scream. Every cell within her overheated little body was on the verge of madness. Serina groped at Lucian's loins until she found the buttons on his pants, then ripped them from him. As the material fell away, Lucian's bulge pressed hard into the air.

Oh it's like a jack in the box. Pop goes the penis! Lucian read her mind. *Oh, you are a rare gem.*

"Care to buffer any rough edges you might find with your tool, Mr. Gemologist?" Serina slid her hands down and stroked his engorged shaft. From the corner of her eye, she watched Lucian quiet. Seemed he enjoyed the way she dominated him. She shoved him onto his back.

His eyes closed and his hands clasped behind his head, he said, "Do what you must!"

Serina bent and kissed him long and slow while she climbed atop him. She slid his solid muscle between her legs, rubbed his head between the folds of her skin to tease them both. Already slick from his earlier ministrations, Serina's impatience won out. Her husband gasped along with her when she shoved him inside her. She didn't move for a minute, afraid to. Her pleasure-pain receptors were busy trying to figure out which way the scales would tip. Right now, she was leaning towards this was not the smartest move she'd made to date. Father Butler's little "patience is a virtue" proclamation just came back to bite her where the sun didn't shine.

"You all right?" she asked. "Did I break anything?"

Lucian didn't say a word. He just gritted his teeth and growled.

Serina started again with a slight shift sideways and then worked her way into a easy rhythm of rocking back and forth before she went full speed ahead, riding him hard and fast. Every time she ground down on him, Lucian stilled her hip's momentum and eased his way out, all but making her scream. She wasn't certain who'd go insane first...him or her if she kept this up. She wanted these sensations to never end, and at the exact same time, she wanted to reach that peak and have the grand finale. Maybe it was just the position, but he filled her in ways she never knew possible. Overwhelmed, Serina started to cry.

"M'lady, I didn't hurt you did I?" Lucian pushed off the mattress and sat up taking Serina with him. He held her so she wouldn't topple backwards.

She wrapped her legs around his waist, securing her body to him. Crying or not, nothing would stop this climax. She had priorities.

The change in position finally tickled that one spot deep within her and ripped the orgasm from her with Lucian's release immediately following. She held on to him as her body erupted into a giant frenzy of pulsing waves and contractions taking them both a ride for their lives.

Spiraling out of control, Lucian rolled Serina over onto her back, never losing his position within her. He brought her arms up over her head and held them in place.

"I do believe I've got you right where I want you, my little bride."

"Actually, dear husband, 'tis I who has you right where I've wanted you all day. Took you long enough to get here." Serina tried to reach up to kiss Lucian, but he kept her pinned and moved his head back out of reach. He smiled showing her that perfect grin of pure white teeth that seemed to say he could eat her alive, and she'd willingly allow it.

"Not so fast, little one. I wasn't finished with you when you assaulted me. Might I add, that was a nice touch?"

"Thank you. I rather liked that position too."

"I noticed." Lucian moved his hips back and forth, in and out of Serina, all over again, surprising both of them.

"Where did that come from? Are you never sated? Not that I'm whining mind you." Serina wrinkled her nose at him.

Lucian bent his head and kissed her little nose softly. His thrusts, however, were the exact opposite, hard, primal. He shoved his hands under her bottom and pulled her derriere up to him. Every time he penetrated her the sounds of flesh slapping together echoed in their compartment.

Caught by surprise, Serina raked her fingernails into his back, his bottom, his arms leaving thin trails of blood behind; she needed an anchor. She heard herself crying his name over and over, but couldn't stop. She gave in and simply closed her eyes. "The conductor of the train is going to find us in this exact position when we arrive at Virginia Falls. Lucian, I hope our butler isn't a prude because I think we're stuck in this position, although I happen to fancy it."

"The train hasn't even left the station yet. You're in for one hell of a ride, little bride. People are still boarding." Lucian pressed his lips to her neck and kissed her again.

"You couldn't possibly be ready again," she asked. "Could you?"

"How badly do you want to find out?"

Lucian gave her a slight push with his hips. He wasn't fooling.

"How? How is it possible? Don't you need a recovery time of some sort?"

"Apparently not yet. You ready or do you need a breather?" Lucian pumped his unfaltering erection into his wife, inch by tantalizing inch and watched her face fill with astonishment. He bent forward and kissed her until he couldn't feel his own lips any longer. When Serina's petite body shook a third time under his weight, Lucian finally collapsed on top of her.

"I think that one did it, luv. Are you all right?"

Serina grabbed a handful of his hair and tugged, trying to lift his head. "We're stuck."

He nuzzled his nose into the crook of her neck

and closed his eyes, making no attempt to move.

With the train conductor's call of, "All aboard," the train started a slow roll out of the station toward their destination. Lucian smirked, thinking, yes, she was in for one hell of a ride.

****

Jasper Black put all his effort into climbing the stairs to board the train. Not being a morning person, and completely out of his element, he petered out. And the midday sun sure as hell didn't help. In fact, he felt an obscene sunburn penetrate what was left of the three layers of his skin. If the sun didn't do him in the heat would, especially sporting a long black coat and top hat just to keep the blasted rays off. It may have been overkill, but he thought he looked quite dashing. He and his assistant sat in coach waiting for their opportunity to meet face to face with Lord St. James. Their business was with him only. His new bride was merely a small potato about to get mashed. Although, he recognized the need to use extreme caution with her having dealt with her mother in the past.

He watched with disdain as passengers boarded. Some would look directly at him, and just as quickly cast their gaze elsewhere. He was used to it. All seats close to him remained vacant, which was fine by him. Gave him extra leg room.

Jasper's assistant, Jonah, was handsome in a rugged way, and Jasper loathed the man for that very reason. Jonah's long brown hair hung low, just short of his hips. He always kept it tied back with a strap of leather. Reminded Jasper of a horse's ass. Beneath Jonah's coat hid a fine, muscled body, the exact opposite of his.

Jonah spoke to people on the train; he enjoyed their conversations. He sat opposite the man he despised, yet could not physically leave, bound to his companion for better or worse. Worse being his choice. Every time he'd tried to break their connection the other man had brutally retaliated against him, leaving him for dead on more than one occasion. In the back of his mind, all he wanted was to get through this trip in one piece, without any threat to his life. Too bad, he couldn't say the same for Lord St. James.

Chapter Eleven

Lucian handed Serina the reins. "The only way up the mountain is by horseback. Giddy-up!" Lucian interlaced his fingers and said, "Place your foot in my hand, and I'll help you up."

Serina rolled her eyes. "I can't."

"You've ne'er ridden before?"

"No, but I can't regardless. Pretty certain I've already gone bare-back with a stallion." Serina inclined her head towards her groin. No matter how sweet the endings, when Lucian and she finished their marathon lovemaking, between her thighs needed some time out. What in Goddess' name would a horse do to her? The honeymoon was finished, caput, over before it began.

"Side-saddle, luv. You'll be fine." Her skeptical look said otherwise.

Making their way up the overgrown trail, Serina followed Lucian's horse careful to stay away from the edges. Jagged cliffs dropped abruptly to a shallow brook filled with unfriendly rocks. A spare horse tagged behind carrying their supplies for the next ten days. Serina marveled at the surroundings. She'd never set foot out of her city. The forest was alive with lush foliage and small animals hopping from one rock or bush to another. She saw her first doe and fawn and giggled like a small child. "Lucian? Can I try something with you?"

Lucian turned back and pulled up on the reins of his horse.

"Anything, anything at all!" His tone dripped of a steamy seduction.

"One track mind you've got. Can I merge my mind with you and attempt to see the colors surrounding me?" Serina watched Lucian's eyebrows shoot up.

"Will it work?"

Serina shrugged her shoulders. "I haven't got a clue. Never tried it before."

After a moment of silent meditation, Serina locked into Lucian's eyesight and almost fell from her horse when a kaleidoscope of colors exploded in a mad rush around her. Lucian jumped from his horse and caught her before she tumbled off.

She covered her mouth trying to hold back a joyful scream. No use. "Oh mother of God," she shouted. "Life is beautiful! Lord in heaven, you are beautiful." Serina remained wide-eyed for the next hour as Lucian taught her all the different colors for everything they encountered: trees, wildflowers, birds, rocks, moss, shrubs, bugs, the horses——everything—her clothing! She couldn't absorb the information fast enough.

An hour later, Serina no longer focused on the beauty that surrounded her, but rather the nagging soreness where direct contact with the saddle lay. And keeping her mind merged with Lucian she found depleted her energy.

"Lucian, I need to walk for a while. Between you and this horse, I'm rather worn out. Thank you for the opportunity to see through your eyes."

"What's mine is yours, Serina. Use me anytime."

Serina read between the lines with his last statement, knowing full-well innuendos were laced throughout. She slid from the horse, reins in hand and started tugging at the large animal behind her. "Please come," she begged. She'd have had better luck if she talked to a brick wall. This animal was stubborn.

Lucian slid off his animal. After coaxing the

animals to a nearby tree and tying the horses up, he pulled her into his arms. "Would you like me to kiss you better, m'lady?"

"Your kisses, m'lord, are what started this trouble. "

Lucian gave Serina his best sad face.

"Don't even think about giving me those radiant blue eyes of yours—that is what you called them, right? And trying to look all innocent. You know I can't resist. Aye, Lucian!" Serina screamed and laughed when he picked her up and tossed her over his shoulder.

"I called them brilliant."

Carrying her up the mountain path, he slid his hand under her skirt, and massaged her bottom and with a gentleness he hadn't shown since they boarded the train he stroked and stimulated her private lips until her soreness was replaced by an insatiable need.

Two could play that game. She slid her hand down his trousers and pinched his bum. He roared with laughter, but that never stopped him from caressing her as they trudged their way to the base of the falls.

"You'll wake the bears with that laugh of yours. Set me down foolish man. This is the most bizarre position you've had me in yet, Lucian. I must say, you make a walk in the park an altogether new experience. Maybe the cavemen really knew what they were doing."

Lucian removed his hand from under Serina's skirt and brought her around to his chest. Sitting down on a low boulder, he sat her on his lap and gazed into her eyes. A tender kiss, he placed upon her lips. "Lay back and let Dr. St. James take care of you."

Serina's jaw dropped. "What—your title of Lord isn't enough, so now you pinch mine?"

"I pinched something else as well." He found Serina's neck and ran his tongue along it. "I've always wanted to play doctor. I have a special serum I can inject into you to make you feel like you're atop of the world."

"I can only imagine." He isn't playing fair, she thought. "Can we please rest for now?"

Lucian stood and set Serina on her feet. He pointed to a soft grassy patch a few feet from the edge of the cliff. "Come and lie down." Lucian walked to his horse, pulled a blanket from his pack, and spread it on the ground.

Sprawled out on her back, Serina merged her sight with Lucian's again and looked up to the waterfall; its beauty left her in awe. Tiers of rocks blanketed in green moss gave the precipice of the falls a warm, earthy appearance. Vines both brown and green, some with tiny, white flowers hung suspended over the ledge. Leaves that swooped and fell from the light blue sky, landed in the water and were swept away to a mystical place, just as Serina was.

Lucian closed his eyes and listened to the falls, Serina tangled within his arms. The power and endless rush of the water as it plummeted to the ground gave a flagrant display of force. He found the roar of the falls luring him into a sleepy state.

Serina started to stir, but Lucian tightened his hold on her, not ready to relinquish her. *Just a while longer, luv. Let the horses rest and me.* Lucian curled up around Serina and inhaled her scent. The fragrance of black roses filled his soul. "I love you, my wild rose. I will love you with my dying breath."

Serina turned, and looked at Lucian, her expression most befuddled. "Lucian, that may have been nice in your mind, but once out in the open, it came out cryptic. With my dying breath?" She shoved at his chest.

"My apologies. I meant I'd love you till the day I died."

"Cryptic again. Let's change the subject." Serina slowly undid her husband's trousers.

"I think a change of subject is doable. Let me help you with that, dear." Lucian winked.

The wolf watched as the horses threw their heads into the wind, and their nostrils flared in search of a scent.

His.

Well concealed in the thick brush, he bided his time as dusk encroached. Watching the two lovers awoke a distant pang of emotion that pierced his empty heart better than a dull arrow.

Annoyed for a few reasons, he couldn't fathom why watching them would bring back an emotion he snuffed out long ago. How long had he been the beast that killed for no other reason than to feel the raw surge of power, caught between a man and wolf? When did he turn into the ruthless murderer that had taken his life in the same manner? Was he so far gone that he no longer knew himself? And more important, did he want the answers?

The answer to that he knew—no he didn't want to know. Ignorance is bliss on the rarest of occasions and this was one of them. He certainly didn't need Sigmund Freud sitting across a cold room staring him down for answers into his personal psyche of hell.

He knew of Lucian, although never formally introduced. They attended the same university, but traveled in different circles. He often thought of the twins as recluses, together always, letting only a few people into the trust of their lives, and he now understood why.

He watched Lucian and his new bride making love. It wasn't just sex, but truly, they loved one another. He knew he violated their privacy, but still...watching them excited him, sickened him, and confused the dickens out of him. This was a job, pure and simple, wasn't it? Would he be here now if he were not called upon by the pestiferous rogue he traveled with?

No. He knew he would never kill these people of his own hand if he were of free will, but free will hadn't been an option for five long years.

Do not deny me this fun tonight, Jonah. Someone's going to bloody well die tonight. Your sister and brother would love to meet me, would they not?

Jasper's laugh cut to his very core better than a guillotine splitting him wide open could have.

Lucian and Serina stirred. The sky's faint hues of orange and red faded through the treetops as the sun set. From the corner of Jonah's eye, Jasper materialized from a thin mist back to his hideous form. It startled the wolf setting off a chain reaction of events that time could not turn back.

Unable to break free and spooked, the horses kicked up their back legs in self-defense. Hearing the commotion, Serina jumped to her feet and doubled over. A noxious gas plugged her nose better than clay could have.

With smell being the strongest human sense and links to memories, Serina recognized the repulsive odor from the first night she'd met Lucian and Raven.

The vampire was back.

With a scan of her surroundings, she saw nothing except a thick fog coming toward her. It made absolutely no sense until she looked through the fog and stared into the most virulent eyes she'd ever encountered. Flames darted out at her from its pupils. She ducked to avoid their contact. Behind her a small bush burst into flames. Her old ticker picked up its pace.

Lucian grabbed Serina hard, and threw her between himself and the horses. *Get on the horse and ride. Do not look back.* Lucian looked into Serina's eyes and with that one look, an eternity of unspoken words, unrealized dreams, love, life and hope passed between them.

He untied the horses' reins. *I found love with you once, my wild rose. What is between us is never finished. Go now to our family and see them safe. My promise to you, Serina, I will come back to you.*

Lucian, that promise is not one for you to make. Only God can.

'Tis not my time, m'lady. We still have our destiny to fulfill—together. Death cannot separate us, Serina—only time and circumstance. Dying now makes no sense.

Nothing makes any sense, Lucian. Life...death.

No, Serina, you and I, we make sense together. Forever. I will accept no less.

Lucian slapped the horse and screamed, "Be gone." His only thought was to see Serina to safety. Her life was all that mattered to him. He could do no more than try and save her from the same twisted fate he faced. He had to, because to live knowing he'd failed her would be a fate far worse than death.

"Lucian you'll get nothing more." Jasper remarked, after reading Lucian's mind.

****

Crouched against the ground, the wolf crawled out from the brush. Yellowish saliva gooey and hanging off his lips like a rabid animal. He erected his awkward shaped body directly in front of Serina's horse, causing the horse to rise up onto his rear legs again. Serina tightened her grip on the reins, her fists white. She clamped her thighs to the horse's large trunk praying not to fall and opened her mouth to scream, but the sound she made could only be compared to a death rattle, the last noise someone makes before their soul leaves their body. Right here and now, she wasn't sure her soul didn't flee. If it was smart, it did.

The horse clipped the wolf's head and knocked him off balance. The beast's retaliation came fast. He sprang at the animal using powerful muscle-clad hind legs and ripped directly into the mare's chest with his teeth. When he finished a large hole lay where the animal's heart once beat.

Stunned by the fatal blow, the horse stumbled head first to the ground, and catapulted Serina into a boulder, head first.

Serina now saw two wolves, both with malice in their yellow eyes. She saw the colors without Lucian's help. She shook her head to clear her vision, only to have pain radiate to every distal nerve in her body. Her only thought, save Lucian. If he died—well he just wasn't going to. Life without her husband was not an option. Before she could formulate a plan, the wolf pinned her wrists and rubbed his large, wet muzzle over her face. He sniffed at her the way a dog does hot on a trail of a bitch, and left behind a sticky trail of snot. His jaundiced eyes never blinked. Neither did she. Growling, he displayed numerous teeth, stained red from the dead horse. Spittle dripped into Serina's eyes, and burned as if it were acid.

Lucian. She cried over and over. Serina couldn't see him but she could hear the struggle between him and the vampire as tree limbs snapped, cries of pain echoed out and the vamp's cackle trumpeted. *Lucian, please hear me. What do we do to save ourselves?*

Lucian had no answer. He didn't understand why this was happening to him, or how to get away from the situation. A skilled fencer, he'd never been equaled with a gun nor bow. His marksmanship held him high honors. Unfortunately, he had neither a gun nor sword nor bow on him. His horse, for all the good it did, stood heavily armed and unattainable on the opposite side of the path.

The vampire's blaring gaze followed Lucian's every step. Blisters formed on his person, as if he had been struck with a hot poker repeatedly.

"What is it that you want from me? If it is just me you're after then let the woman go unharmed," Lucian pleaded.

"Do you not mean your wife?"

Lucian stared in disbelief at the physical condition of this vampire. That it could speak, think, and live boggled his chaotic mind. Lucian fully understood the phrase, "a walking nightmare," now. With every breath it took, grayish skin sloughed off like the worst case of dandruff he'd ever seen.

Having a slight tickle and feeling something warm and wet dripping from his head, Lucian touched his finger to his ear. Blood. If that wasn't enough, Lucian watched horrified as the vampire licked his thin, pale, blue lips.

Oh shite!

With each step closer the ghoul took, Lucian stepped back.

"I see you saved the last dance for me. Thoughtful, but I do not care to dance with you, Lucian. That was your wife's job at one time, not that she's much of one."

Lucian avoided eye contact. If the tales were true, he certainly didn't want to get snared in its web. He focused on its mouth, which he found no easier to look at. Jasper's grin displayed an excess of twisted, decayed fangs that left Lucian wondering how many people before him had met this very fate. His heart rate increased tenfold and the vamp dropped his gaze to Lucian's chest and laughed.

His mouth now bone dry, he was barely able to ask, "How is it you know my name? Or anything about my wife?" If the vampire wanted money, he could pay him one hundred times the bounty offered.

"I do not know you, Lucian, but the man that bid me to do his dirty work knows you well. When I last saw him, he was dying to meet you—" He paused to pick at a rough growth on his cheek. "—and you too shall have the same fate." The vampire brought his finger into his view, inspected the chunk of dried up flesh and then popped it into his mouth.

Lucian's stomach churned.

Jasper leaned against a tree, both legs stretched in front of him and crossed at the ankles. "Lucian, I will tell you my plans for this night go far beyond just you. How you and the little enchantress want to set up housekeeping after tonight is naught to concern me, but you will be needing new accommodations if you make yet another miraculous comeback. And one more thing, I must say you look bloody well from the events of the past. How is that you fared so well, after I did such a divine job ripping your throat out?"

"You?" Lucian asked astonished.

The vampire saluted him with two fingers.

"I am a fast healer. You're a lousy vampire. Your choice. Why did you do this to us? And who is this man dying to meet me?" Lucian asked, as he searched for Serina, trying not to back himself into a corner between the boulders or fall off the cliff by the waterfall's edge.

She'd been on the ground not a minute ago and had simply vanished. Terror was about to bury him alive with no hope of breaking open ground. He needed to get her the hell away from here.

Serina, where are you? Please answer me.
Lucian?
Has he hurt you?
No. The wolf has me pinned behind a boulder off to your right. Lucian he could have ripped me to

shreds a hundred times over, yet he just keeps looking into my eyes. Do you still have the cross Father gave you? If you do, aim for his blackened heart. I have mine on me, but it does no good where werewolves are concerned unless I can get him to swallow it. I don't suppose we have any silver bullets or wooden stakes in our picnic basket? Serina actually tried to joke in the midst of the wolf looming over her even with their lives in mortal danger.

Whatever that stuff is Raven made in the basket could possibly kill him. Lucian too needed humor regardless of the circumstances. It proved futile.

Conflicted, Jonah could not decide what exactly he wanted to do with Serina. The wolf wanted blood, pure and simple. He wanted to rip her apart limb by limb, prance off with one of her legs, and gnaw on it all night. He watched the blood trickle down her neck from her head wound and he smacked his lips together a few times. Inhaling, he scented her fear but it didn't stop him. Her blood awakened a visceral hunger. The wolf wanted her heart, not to love, but to devour. Such a tasty, chewy treat.

The man trapped beneath all the fur wanted her too. Carnal pleasures were forthright in his mind, because beneath him lay a ravishing beauty. He wanted to taste her sex and watch her writhe beneath him as he licked every inch of her delicious body with his long tongue, between her breasts, between her thighs and take her body again and again. He wanted to sink himself deep within her and watch her green eyes glaze over from the ecstasy. He wanted her locked away from everyone. He wanted her to fill his empty soul.

He could have both.

Reading his mind, Serina couldn't decide which fate would be worse. Being ripped apart and eaten alive or being raped at his every whim, with no way out. Although, if she were made to choose, the ripped apart really held no appealing qualities. She had to try something and fast.

"You'll die from a broken heart before you have any part of me," she screamed. Serina exerted as much pressure as she could muster and blasted it towards the wolf's heart, in an attempt to shatter it. She imagined her nails digging into his aorta, gouging large holes in the intima, in hopes of a swift closure to this hideous abomination to life.

His eyes grew wide with disbelief, or something Serina couldn't understand. Pain? The wolf faltered and within that second, she used the opportunity and brought her knee up into his groin. The wolf toppled backwards, whimpering. Serina scrambled to her feet and fled.

"Lucian?" Serina screamed in a blind run, ending up directly in between the vampire and her husband. Both of them reached for her at the same time making her the prize in a tug of war.

Just bloody dandy. I'm going to be ripped in half regardless. "Let go of me," she screamed at Jasper. "Dear God, you're hideous." She kicked at his loins repeatedly, but he didn't flinch.

Jasper circled his free finger in Lucian's direction and levitated him while maintaining his grasp on Serina. He blew a hard rancid breath and watched Lucian careen through the air and impact a tree, the bark splintering under pressure.

With the flick of his wrist, Jasper tossed Serina on her bottom. He watched her crawl to her soon-to-be-extinct husband, cradle his head in her hands, and then do what he hadn't done in centuries—pray. "I'm about done playing this game you two. I've had my fun. Now kiss your husband good-bye and let me get the hell out of these woods." Jasper took a step back, then swatted in front of his face at a swarm of angry insects. "Is it just me the bloody flies want?" he screamed. He evanesced from tree to tree trying to escape them, ending up beside Serina again, the pesky nuisances close behind.

Serina covered Lucian protectively and didn't budge. She sent her powers into her husband to heal his head with no one the wiser. The bleeding stopped, but he didn't regain consciousness.

"Do you have a name?" Serina asked as she wiped away a stray tear. She stood, wearily, holding her arms crossed over her chest, no longer afraid but angrier than the insects were.

"You are too stubborn for your own health, Ducky, just like your Mum. I shall indulge you this one last time. Jasper Black. You've met my companion, Jonah. Why would you care?"

Serina felt ill as she took in the rotted piece of flesh before her. He even had the audacity to mimic her stance. "Didn't I autopsy you once already? For the love of God, how are you still on this earth? 'Tis neither here nor there. I've two reasons you fetid bastard. My first, if I live to see tomorrow, I'll know who to come looking for. My second, if I don't then I'll know who to spend an eternity haunting and make your bleak existence on this earth a hell beyond that which you already believe it to be. And stop calling me Ducky." Serina bent to Lucian again. She held his face tenderly in her hands and kissed him.

"Lucian, you need to help me," she whispered. His glassy eyes stared straight ahead. Once again, Serina let her spirit move throughout his body before Jasper grew weary. So focused on Lucian, she never saw the wolf come up behind her.

"What did you do to my wolf, Ducky? He's walking with a distinct limp." Jasper looked between Serina and Jonah and let out a loud blood-curdling snarl. He was on the wolf without warning and bit him. Jonah gripped Jasper's hair, and almost scalped him to get out of his clutches, but the vamp clamped down harder. When finished, Jasper shoved Jonah to the ground and accused, "You are weak, my friend. A puny woman did this to you? Maybe I should spare her life and end your useless one."

Jonah stood and stumbled from blood loss. He pressed his hand over his ravaged neck.

Serina shouted, "I'm not bloody puny." *Who the hell does he think he is?*

Jonah struggled to breathe. "She is not" pant, "human, Jasper. I think" pant, "witch. She tried—to kill me." He doubled over.

With a pound of sarcasm, Jasper responded, "Really? A witch?" He glanced to Serina and Lucian. "Jonah, what rock have you sought shelter beneath all these years? Her mother is only the most powerful seductress in this hemisphere, if not the entire world. Of course she's a bloody sorceress."

And here I thought my secret was safe. Ha!

Out of her element, she needed help.

Raven, I have no idea if you can feel me. I only pray you do. Please watch out for yourself and André in the days ahead. Lucian and I have encountered a vampire, Jasper Black. He travels with a werewolf, Jonah. Watch for them. Their sole intent is death. I fear the worst for your brother and myself. I'm so sorry I failed you. Know that your brother is valiant, and holds a love for you with no boundaries.

Careful not to be seen, Serina reached into her blouse for her cross while the wolf and vampire hashed out their differences. She stood and took a step toward the vampire. As she closed in on him, the cross took on its own identity, shining so brightly it looked like the North Star on a clear night.

Jasper wailed like a baby when he caught sight of the religious symbol. He plowed into her faster than he had attacked the wolf.

Serina went down. She held the cross for dear life in front of her even as he bashed her a second time with the back of his hand. The blow wrenched her head to the side with a loud snap.

I'm going to feel that later. I hope!

"Ouch! You scoundrel. Beating up women make you feel like a man? Because you sure as hell don't look like one." With a quick jab, she landed her cross on his ankle. A loud sizzling sound just happened to coincide with the lovely scent of burnt flesh. "God wanted to give you a reminder who the real boss is."

He grabbed her shirt, lifted her and sent her directly into the arms of the wolf.

"Ducky, that was not nice. You don't play fair. I have been more of a gentleman than you deserve. That time has ended." He strutted to Lucian, who still lay unconscious, and hoisted him to his chest. Jasper held Lucian at an odd angle, which caused his head to fall backwards exposing his neck. Jasper licked his thin lips. "Breakfast the royals would die for."

Lucian lay like a broken rag-doll in the arms of the beast. That's when the full-blown panic hit her harder than Jasper had. In that one second, she watched helpless, as this monster destroyed her beloved husband.

Serina kicked, screamed, punched at anything, dug her nails into the wolf's arms, and tried to bite any part of him in which she could to make contact. She had to get away from the wolf and get to Lucian.

"Lucian wake up. Wake up," Serina screamed to him over and over, leaving her throat raw. Her desperation turned to tears. Her heart thudded so loud even the wolf looked at her chest. She watched mortified as the vampire's leather-like tongue tasted Lucian, his vacant eyes laughing her.

"Why?" She was barely able to whisper.

Jasper paused. "Why does anyone do anything, Ducky? Power and money, and that whole do unto others as they do unto you line. I had neither money nor power when I lived. People would just as soon spit on me and walk over me rather than to see if they could offer assistance or a kind word. Neither ever came. I've been walking this God-forsaken land since the birth of Henry the VIII. I was the hooded bloke on the chopping block that whacked off Anne Boleyn's incestuous noggin, and Catherine Howard's as well. Although, I never fancied her as much. People avoided me altogether as if I were something contagious..."

"You are the black plague," she blurted.

Just never know when to shut up do you, Serina?

"You are beyond the realm of medical science. What could you possibly gain from killing us?"

"I want England, Ducky."

"But you're dead."

"Define dead. Am I not up and walking about?"

"All right, I'll cave on that point but, well, there's really no nice way to say this, you look dead, like shite really." Would nothing stop her mouth? she wondered. "I can see blooming grey matter between your sparse hairs."

"Ducky, technically I was dead three days. You want dead? Look at your lover. He's dead. I'll have his heart before I leave this time."

"You pompous corpse. Over my dead body." Serina spat on him.

Jasper licked her saliva from his cheek. "Ducky, that's already been arranged. I think I'll miss you. You're a spry one."

"When I'm done with you Jasper, you'll wish you never met me."

"Did your mother teach you naught? Your spells do not work upon the undead. I am invincible. Sticks and stones won't break my bones and your word shan't ever hurt me."

In a bitter tone, Serina turned her head and asked the wolf, "Why would you do to us that which was done to you? Was your life not taken in such vile circumstance?"

"My life is none of your damn business." Jonah knotted his fist in her hair and twisted her head back in Jasper's direction. He crooked her arm back behind her so she couldn't struggle without injuring herself and then he mirrored Jasper, licking her neck in slow strokes up to her cheek.

Serina's rage boiled. Despite the pain from her hair being ripped out, she turned and chomped down hard, severing his tongue. She spat the still-twitching chunk of meat onto the ground. The wolf attempted to scream, but it came out jumbled. And honestly? She didn't care what he had to say.

Jonah cranked her neck back to face Jasper.

Serina watched horrified, as Jasper's jaw stretched open like a boa constrictor's so wide. Was he going to devour him whole? In a panicked state, Serina screamed, "Take this rotted creature without a soul, and place him heartless in a six-foot hole. Remove his head. Render the bastard dead, dead, dead."

"I'm all ready dead, Ducky, but 'twas a valiant attempt." A second later his teeth disappeared. Lucian never knew what bit him.

Serina felt Lucian's heart skipping beats, missing many altogether. Her heart followed the same path. Serina corralled her energy and pictured a bullet piercing Jasper's heart. In front of Jasper and Lucian an explosion detonated, never reaching the vampire.

Jasper paused, looked up and smiled. "Good try, Ducky. Invincible!" He wasted no time ripping two new holes in Lucian's throat.

Again, she allowed her spirit to join Lucian. In him, she tried fiercely to keep his blood circulating by softly pumping his heart. The exact opposite of what she'd done to the wolf. She knew as long as

Lucian had a pulse, he had a prayer. Serina had one last hope. Maybe the Gods, all of them from every religion and cult, would hear her pleas and help her.

"Papa Legba, great Lord, please open the gate so that I may speak with Baron Samedi, Lord of death. Hear me. Help me. God, you out there? Anubis? Atum? Isis? Ra? Some assistance, please? Do not allow Lucian St. James passage through to you. His destiny has yet to be fulfilled. He sits now at the crossroads. Return him to me." Serina turned her focus back to her husband and through waves of tears she decreed, "You will not die, Lucian. Do you understand me? Lucian, you are my life, as I am yours. I am your lifeline. You are mine, Lucian. Mine. Hold onto me, to us. Lucian, whatever you do, do not follow the light. No bright lights, m'lord! Follow my voice, my heart, our love. I'm so sorry I can't stop him from doing this to you. Please don't leave me..."

From within Lucian's body, Serina witnessed his heart quiver then stop. That's when the burning, crushing pain consumed her. She couldn't breathe, could barely form a coherent thought. She numbly asked the wolf, "Please just allow me to touch him. I have to touch him." Oddly, Jonah obliged and set her down.

Jasper cast an estranged eye at Serina and his wolf lending his allegiance elsewhere. He swung his free hand through the air and began to orchestrate an unforeseen peril.

Before Serina could say anything exceptionally unladylike, charcoal-colored vines with glistening thorns pushed their way through the earth. Each gnarly root wrapped around and pierced Jonah's feet into the ground.

Hearing a high-pitched clicking noise coming from behind her, Serina whipped her head around and saw blood-red beetles the size of mice with fangs and needle-sharp pinchers headed for her. They reminded her of ladybugs with lobster claws, two of her favorite things she'd never ever look at the same way again. "What in the name of God are those?"

Jonah answered, his voice quickened. "Just what they appear to be—blood beetles. They'll skin the flesh from a carcass in no time. Get up here."

Serina found herself back in Jonah's arms after he yanked her from the ground. Jonah held her easily in one arm, while he swatted the insects with his free arm, crushing some with his bare hand.

In a low voice Jonah said, "We have to get away from this," he yanked the vine-like garrote from his foot and calculated each step, trying his best to avoid the beetles and vines. One of the barbed roots filleted a large area of his flesh down to the bone.

Jasper erected himself. "Do not take that siren, Jonah; I want the witch's essence." He tossed Lucian to the ground as a child bored of his toy does, and stepped towards Jonah and Serina.

"It'll be a cold day in hell before you sink your rotted fangs into me, you giant louse," Serina screamed.

"As you wish, Ducky," Jasper retorted. Again he waved his hand to the heavens and commanded the sky. "You're going to be sorry you didn't wear your coat and galoshes, Ducky." With a quick snap of his fingers and a rolling wave, Jasper pointed to the heavens.

As ice-cold winds surrounded her, Serina buried her face in Jonah's furry chest. Blizzard-like conditions turned the mountainside a blinding white within minutes.

Then a loud rumbling shook the earth as ice bolts penetrated the hard ground.

The wolf tried to dodge the daggers, but it was of no use, Jasper's expertise triumphed and the icy spears impaled him.

Although he bled profusely, Serina wasn't too much worried for him after seeing how quickly he healed.

His tongue had already regenerated.

Her husband on the other hand...

Chapter Twelve

Blanketed in a snowy grave, ice chips clung to Lucian's eyelids and lashes, and his perfect pouty lips turned a non-kissable shade of ebony.

Serina wanted to die with him. She had no idea what real pain felt like until she saw the man she'd given her heart, her soul, and her dreams to, dead. She couldn't breathe, and she didn't care if ever she did again. She looked to the wolf and with quivering lips begged, "Kill me, Jonah. Please?"

"I can not, Serina. I shall attempt to protect you from Jasper, but he has proven his strength and powers. He may just keep you around to see if you'd be of any use to him. I know for a fact he does not care for women, so it would not be sex he craves. I wanted that," Jonah admitted. "There are givers in a relationship and there are receivers. Jasper likes being on the receiving end, if you understand me."

Could this conversation honestly be any more bizarre? Serina's new outlook on reality took an unbelievable twist. In the arms of a half man/half wolf, and having a conversation with him about the sexual preferences of a vampire no less, made her wonder if straight jackets came in her size.

What's left of my life has become stranger than fiction.

At least all the remaining beetles lay frozen under the snow for the time being.

I found the silver lining. Too bad I can't decipher the bloody color once again. She laughed hysterically knowing shock would be a blissful welcome.

"How sweet, Jonah, you protecting our little

Ducky. How quickly you forget she just tried to knock out your manhood, bite off your tongue and—oh, try to rip out your heart. There must be something sweet running in her veins. Bring her to me, Jonah. Now!"

Jonah closed the distance carrying Serina to him, apologizing with a pathetic excuse with each step.

Futilely, she kicked, screamed and bit her way through the wolf's fur, spitting out chunks of it, getting some strands still stuck between her teeth. Anything...She could handle anything, but that vile, noxious creature touching her. She fought twice as hard when Jasper had her arm behind her back, and pinned her face-first up against a tree.

"Jasper, may my blood solidify in your veins, and leave behind permanent stains. I'll see you disintegrate into a pile of ash, to be disposed of with the trash. May holy water boil away your rotted skin, ridding us of your evil sins. I can only pray someone takes you apart limb by limb."

"Oh, like I've never heard that before! That's a thought out anathema, Serina. Pity it shan't work. You're persistent if nothing else." Jasper knocked Serina's head with one powerful blow into the solid bark and then ravaged her neck. Blood splattered and covered both men when he tore open her jugular vein.

Trapped, just as her husband had been only moments ago, Serina felt as if she'd ingested Laudanum. Nothing seemed real. Hallucinogenic thoughts and feelings flooded her as the vampire fed, sickening emotions she couldn't understand and sure as hell didn't want.

Serina knew the tales, read the books about a vampire's bite being so erotic that people would do anything for the next encounter, becoming a wanton creature of habit, even from the most heinous beings. And now, trapped firmly in his grasp she understood. The damned tales held truths. Her slovenly body deceived her—rejoiced as he drained her life. Confusion and guilt ripped a larger hole in her heart.

She wanted him to continue, and on the flipside of the coin, she wanted to rip out his blackened clump of flesh he had the nerve to call a heart. If this wasn't the epitome of a love-hate relationship! She tried to scream his name belligerently, "Jas-per..." Instead, languorous little syllables slipped softly from her lips. She cried out the last bits and pieces of her withered soul.

Serina fought the orgasmic convulsions, except struggling intensified them. The hot, wet sensation between her thighs clawed its way up to gnash at her nipples. She vomited.

The wolf coughed and distracted Jasper. When the vamp looked at him, he asked, "Good to the last drop?"

Jasper rolled his eyes towards the wolf, and as fear rapidly replaced arrogance, he dropped Serina on top of her husband's lifeless shell.

Not quite himself, Jasper cried, "What has she done to me, Jonah? Incantations don't work on the dead." Jasper looked up to see the wolf looking like the picture of health, and knew he'd made a fatal error. "How?" he screamed, as smoke flowed from his mouth. "Witch!"

Jonah noticed where Serina's blood sprayed Jasper, more holes bore through his carcass. Jonah just needed a clean set of clothes. "How did that saying go? 'Sticks and stones can break my bones, but words can never hurt me.'" Jonah laughed and clapped his paw-like hands together as flames exploded from Jasper's nose, ears, and mouth. "It wasn't her words, Jasper. It was her blood. Serina, you've turned him into a fire-breathing dragon. Jolly good show. Unless, of course, he doesn't disintegrate."

Serina teetered between lunacy and lucidity. Coming in and out of her dark shadows she witnessed Jasper bend over, holding his stomach and groaning as he smoldered. She prayed the images were true as the overbearing weight of her eyelids stifled her view.

With his clothes melted to him, Jasper rolled around in the snow, and left once pure, white, sparkling flakes, charred, and unsightly. He grabbed handfuls of the frozen crystals and stuffed them into his mouth, only to have the smoke effuse thicker. He coughed and choked up actual lumps of coal. Gingerly, he picked one up, looked at it, and took flight, headed toward the falls. Behind him, a dark polluted trail spoiled the skyline.

Jonah watched the vampire turn mid-air and plunge headfirst into the water. Bubbles of steaming vapor erupted, and boiled the vamp's skin. He covered his ears from Jasper's heinous bellows as they echoed into the night.

"Holy mother of God, all her wishes are taking place," Jonah noted.

At the water's edge, Jasper yelled, "I am going to kill the witch, you, and then your family." Defiant, he glared at the wolf, before he shifted into the form of a black raven and took to the sky. Circling the area once, Jasper plummeted towards Jonah, turned and disappeared.

Jonah headed toward Serina. The snow crunched under foot with each step he took. He bent over and brushed the remaining flakes from her face. Moving slowly down her body he removed the snow from her chest and allowed himself the stolen luxury to feel the fullness of her bosom, and the firmness of her nipples under her shirt. Ashamed, he stopped, picked her up and walked away, leaving

Lucian alone, to rot. He couldn't help what happened to him. But he could do something about Serina. Just what, remained to be seen.

****

A feeling deep within Serina tugged her from a dark wasteland. Drained didn't touch the way she felt. All she wanted to do was close her eyes and dream of Lucian, yet something dragged her back from the black abandonment where she hid. Her eyes fluttered a few times before she was able to focus on her surroundings. Back in the arms of the wolf she felt safe, until she realized he carried her away from Lucian.

"Put me down. You cannot take me away from my husband. We cannot leave him here like this, please," Serina whispered. She didn't have much strength left, and she wasn't about to waste it screaming. "Please, please do this for me. He deserves so much more than this."

"Your husband is dead, Serina. He has neither a pulse nor blood to bind him to this earth."

She cried, "He has me." Then grief got the best of her, and her world darkened.

Jonah covered much of the mountain's rugged terrain easily as if he were out for his evening constitutional. He found them shelter inside a cave. He knew he had a few days of safety until Jasper would come looking for them and he would come. Of that, there was no doubt. Jasper stole Serina's blood, which almost killed him, and the bloodsucker would want revenge. Jonah also knew the blood-bond between Jasper, Serina and him made them an easier target than pickpockets working the London Tower on the tourists.

Unconscious for hours, he didn't know if Serina would wake up wanting blood in the same manner as a vampire, or if she would be an indentured servant as he was. With no medical background

Jonah had no idea how to replace blood loss, but his only option was to give her his blood and with that came the question of how to and how much to give? He gave up thinking about what-ifs, and pulled a pocketknife from his satchel. With one quick flick of his knife, he sliced his wrist open, pressed it to Serina's mouth, and watched as his blood flowed from his wound and ran down the front of her neck, and saturated her shirt. The what-ifs he wondered about were about to come back and bite him in the arse, because seeing all the blood on her tickled his senses, and subsequently enticed his own hungers and desires with a murderous intensity. He fought the urges even as his fur stiffened and stood on end. Other areas of his anatomy became aroused as well. He looked down at his tattered trousers, and saw a giant bulge protrude that threatened to shred the last threads that held his pants together. To say the least, he couldn't think, his heads hurt so, both. The one on top his shoulders felt as if he had a vice grip around him, squeezing the daylights from him. The one beneath the trousers wanted a vice grip on him squeezing him...period.

His good intentions backfired when Serina's soft lips lapped at the fluid. Her mouth covered his skin like a warm blanket with each sweep of the tongue. Oh, what he wouldn't give to have her mouth elsewhere on his body, sucking on him as she was now.

Getting a little tipsy, Jonah stepped back, his arm very much caught between her teeth like a bear in a trap.

Exquisite!

He hadn't suffered pain like this in years. Just how far gone was he to enjoy this torture. He knew he always enjoyed sex rough, but even this pushed the envelope. This snapped him out of his ethical dilemma, whether to let her finish her snack before he had his—her, or wait like a gentleman. After prying his wrist from her mouth, it resembled a dog's chew toy, a mangled mess of torn flesh and bone. For once he was grateful of the powers that came with being a werewolf. He stood and watched his arm rejuvenate itself before his eyes.

Chapter Thirteen

Mid-afternoon, Raven coaxed André out for a ride to enjoy the crisp September air, the sunny skies and his company. She couldn't have been more content. She had her two brothers, a new family of friends living with her, and life was splendid until she heard Serina's exigent pleas for help in her head. Raven's world turned hazy without clouds.

"Ands," she panted, "listen!"

"Listen to what, little one?"

"My head, you dim-wit limey. Listen to what's in my head. Serina and Lucian are in trouble." Chills engulfed her, as if she'd fallen within the thrall of a seizure.

The exact moment Lucian's heart stopped, solemn agony swept through her soul faster than a tsunami devouring the earth and with deadlier intent. This couldn't be happening, not to Lucian. She would die without him, without her best friend, or confidant, or the world's worst joker. There would no longer be a reason to laugh...or live.

Without time to think, André jumped from the stallion and caught Raven to his chest. Touching her intensified the visions she witnessed as he merged his mind with hers. Overcome with images of death, he cursed his psychic abilities.

Concern for Raven's wellbeing weighed heavy upon him. He feared he could lose her as well due to the deep bond she and Lucian held. After a slight struggle with Raven's dead-weight, André placed her over the horse then mounted himself. Shifting her into his arms, he headed home, praying they'd make it because he wasn't feeling so great either.

By the time they reached the stables, André was slumped over the horse with Raven crushed beneath him. "Duncan, help," André barely whispered. He held his head up long enough to give Duncan a shortened version of all that had happened and then he collapsed to the ground, dragging Raven atop him.

Duncan got them into Payton's room and sent Payton to retrieve the doctor and Father Butler. Not thirty minutes passed, Payton returned with Father Butler and Dr. Jones, both wind-blown, and disheveled. The doctor gathered what materials he needed for blood transfusions in swift fashion. Oddly, he told Duncan, "They both show all the signs of blood loss and shock. Both are pale and unconscious, yet there is nothing to substantiate these findings, no visible trauma." Dr. Jones touched Raven's chest with his stethoscope and listened. "Their respirations are irregular and shallow, yet their hearts race like the devil chases them," he said wearily. "Father, I do not understand the ways of God. I can only see the science behind this mystery. And my hypothesis makes me no sense." The doctor shrugged his stocky shoulders.

"This is in no way the work of God, Doctor Jones. The evil is so thick it chokes the very life from them." Father never looked up at him. He focused solely on Raven and André trying to save them. Because to save them meant he'd save his Serina. Nothing or no one else on this earth mattered more.

André fought his way back from an unfathomable abyss and latched onto Raven. He held her close uncaring that anyone saw him weep. The lines of blood that ran into his arm, he tore away. A splattered trail of crimson drops stained Payton's crisp white linens.

André only just found out he had a family and

now, that part of him stolen. Gone, his identical brother. This creature that threatened his sister's life had to be destroyed. He had to find Serina too, for Lucian.

André whispered to his sister, deep in her mind, *My little beauty, you must wake up. Do not let this monster take you from me. I could not bear to lose you as well. I know I'm not Lucian but I love you Ray. Please...stay for me.* After laying a gentle kiss upon her lips, he rolled over to face his friends. "I know where Lucian lies, and I know where Serina is. I need help."

Numb to his very core, Duncan held Raven's hand. "What do you need from us, André?" He wiped at the steady stream of his tears, never looking away from Raven. Duncan never thought he would have to live through something so traumatic again. First his wife and child, now Lucian and possibly Raven.

Not Lucian, not his best mate, his confidant, his little brother. They grew up together, taught each other about life, and laughed often for endless hours. He loved Lucian and the mere thought of him no longer showing his smiling face, with his ridiculous jokes and sense of humor to brighten everyone's day, his day—crushed him.

Raven. My God, what would Duncan do with out her? Her smile warmed him on the coldest of days. Her gentle nature, the way she cared for everyone so meticulously. Her natural disasters in the kitchen, even with the best of intentions...Duncan smiled at that thought for a second then the tears carried it away. His family lay dying in front of him, and he was unable to protect them. Tremors slowly crept from Duncan's shoulders to his hands, and he started to shake.

Dr. Jones instructed, "Take slow deep breaths, and focus on anything other than Raven."

With a methodical twist of his head, Duncan

gave the man a vexatious glare.

Even Molly scrunched her face with the doctors words. She took Duncan's hand. "You're not alone. You've got all of us here. And you've got me." She gave his hand a strong squeeze.

Duncan glanced at Molly, and wrapped his arm around her waist. He pulled her as close to him as he could get and attempted a grin that said he appreciated her, but his lips remained paralyzed, much like his heart.

André knelt before Duncan. "Old man, we need to find Serina. She is in grave danger and any time we waste is precious. Somehow, she is connected to Raven, and in order to save Ray we need to save them both. We can do no less for Lucian or for Serina. Payton is preparing the horses as we speak. Please, dear friend, help me save our sister and sister-in-law. We will bring Lucian home to us."

Too little too late, André realized he probably shouldn't have mentioned bringing Lucian home, because Duncan growled and pushed himself off the chair abruptly. With one swipe of his arm, everything on Payton's dresser (books, glasses, and a cologne bottle) smashed to the floor. He stormed from the room, never looking back. André was left on his knees beside an empty chair.

Wearily André stood and strode to the door. He turned to Father Butler. "Please take the women to the church and keep them under your protection. Do not allow them to leave and allow no one inside your parish you do not know."

Father Butler handed him a cross and a bottle of blessed water and wished him, "God speed, son. Bring my girl home to me."

****

André, Duncan, and Payton rode in silence, never breaking their stride. Through his and Raven's link, André reached the area where the ambush took place but after that it became sketchy trying to find Serina since she'd passed out after contacting Raven. André stood on the very ground where Lucian lay covered with snow, but the snow had disappeared, as had Lucian.

With nightfall closing in, Payton reached into his satchel. "Who's hungry? I'm going to start cooking up my specialty for camping. Any takers?"

"What is it?" Duncan gave him a wistful smile. "I am famished."

"Smoked pork and beans with garlic. I brought a lot of garlic...You know, just in case." Payton shrugged his shoulders. "It is true about garlic and vampires, isn't it? Well if not we'll eat well and scare the creatures with our breath alone."

André answered, "I believe the garlic may actually help our breath at this point, not hurt it. And yes, Payton, garlic doesn't make them jovial over-grown mosquitoes. Their sense of smell is more than that of a bloodhound, and garlic mimics acid. A lot like humans and onions. We turn into blubbering idiots when we cut them up, except we don't shrivel up and die."

"Speak for yourself, Ands. I've turned out to be a blubbering idiot without the need for the offensive little veggie. Cry, cry, cry..." Duncan's laugh had an intoxicating quality to it and André drank it in.

Too close for comfort, the cries of animals cut through the stillness of the night, settling in uninvited.

Payton wiped the sweat from his brow. "What's that?" he asked as he scooted closer to André. Payton didn't budge when the taller man threw his arm around his shoulder.

"That, little friend, are some animals mating, some in anguish, and some screaming for their lives. Feel better?"

"Up 'til you said that last part."

****

Curled in a fetal position and desperate to stay warm in a damp, musty cave, Serina knew the signs of hypothermia, and she had them all. She may not have been able to feel her fingers, but she knew they hadn't fallen off. Shackled with one short chain binding her arms to her legs, she was stuck in one position and continued to poke herself in the eye as she shook. Her hair reminded her of a mop left outside in the cold—stiff and stringy. Body fluids stained her clothes, leaving her wet and foul. She recognized the scent all too well from working in the morgue, but this time it was her own scent she had the displeasure of inhaling, not some poor dead bugger. Although, soon she'd be the poor dead bugger if things didn't turn around and give her the happily ever after so many of her favorite books always did. No, this certainly wasn't the fairy tale ending she'd envisioned, but it did fit *Grimm's Fairy Tales* version.

Beyond hungry, the growl of her stomach should have warded off anything that dared come near her. Never-the-less, her company for the most part had been some creepy-crawly things she tried to ignore yet she failed miserably because the insects took chunks out of her and scurried off content, their bellies full. "You're welcome!" she admonished.

The damned wolf left her for dead in a *tiny-closed-in-no-god-damned-windows-no-god-damned-furnishings*, three-by-five-rock abode with a mud floor. The ceiling, if that's what it was seemed to breathe. The rocks shifted in unison. She'd found out the hard way it was bats when they dropped into the air and filled the enclosure with the deafening sound of wings flapping and screeches.

The werewolf slept curled around her the first night in the cave, kept her warm, even though she detested the physical contact. Then, the bastard bound her so she couldn't free herself from another animal that might wander into the cave seeking shelter or food.

When Serina touched Raven's mind, the overpowering loss her sister-in-law experienced with Lucian's death stymied her. As if her own agony wasn't bad enough, now she had Raven's suffering compounded. *Misery loves company, Serina!*

Through their mind merge, Serina found out André, Duncan, and Payton searched for her. So it was a good thing she didn't gnaw off any body parts yet to free herself. A fleeting idea she'd toyed with if no help came.

Chapter Fourteen

At the sound of twigs snapping, Serina jerked her head towards the cave's entrance. Pain radiated the length of her neck and spine with the slightest of movements. Her pulse pounded in her throat. She pictured an animal slinking into her forced shelter, hungry. She rolled her eyes. Petrified, her current condition left her helpless for whatever or whomever crawled through that hole. Even though her night vision had become exceptional in the past few days, she closed her eyes.

"Serina..."

She felt the pressure of brake pads clamp down on her throat. Hope flew out the cave door quicker than the bats. Mister werewolf returned, not her rescue squad. He came back for her, but with what intent? Sex? Food? An all out smorgasbord? Reluctant, she peeked. There stood a man she did not recognize, all for his piercing yellow eyes. They oddly cut through the darkness. She reeled in the fact she could see colors. Lucian had left behind a piece of himself.

The man knelt over her, and fumbled as he pulled a key from his trousers pocket.

"Jonah?"

"Yes, Serina. I look a tad bit different now. Although my eyes are peculiar at all times, they do lose the feral appearance when the moon is no longer full. And lucky for you, I am no longer having thoughts of you as my main course. I'm sorry I left you, but I needed to regained control of my head. How are you?"

"You even have to ask?" she responded with a fair amount of rancor. "I see the prodigal child has returned. Why are you here? What do you possibly see happening between us? No, wait—don't answer that. Will you return me to my family?"

"Serina, the only reason I didn't eat you, was because I found you very sensual and I wanted to take advantage of you. That saved your life."

"Honesty, how damned quaint," she chided with indignance. "So what's changed, Jonah, other than my current state of personal hygiene? The wolf liked the blood and guts smattered on me, whereas the man finds it distasteful?" Serina couldn't help the bitter edge that slid into her voice. It felt good to be angry and lash out at someone.

"I have no idea what you did to me. You invaded my soul, I think. Not that there's much left to it. Yes, I'll return you to your family. I looked for Lucian. It is as if he never set foot on the mountain. I'm sorry."

Those words ignited a raging storm. The vampire was dead, all over again.

"I need to know how you did the things you did to Jasper? I've wanted that bastard out of my life five minutes after I met him. Are you really a witch?"

The shackles from her ankles and wrists thudded to the ground even as the key twisted in the lock. Serina lifted her arms into view and noticed deep purple imprints embedded into her flesh. Open lacerations covered her flesh, some weeping purulent, green pus.

Once free, she was both perplexed and perturbed. "What do you think?" Her claustrophobia getting the best of her, she asked, "Nice dwelling you've got here, but can you get me out of this dungeon? I can't straighten my legs. Damn you! As far as Jasper is concerned, I simply wished those things on him. I had no idea I could actually make it happen. Temper tantrums seem to spark my creativity, so you'd be best watching your furry little tail doesn't go up in flames because I won't extinguish it."

"You don't have to remind me. I witnessed your wrath firsthand." Jonah tried to lift Serina into his arms but she cried out in pain.

"I'm so sorry I did this to you, but it was for your own interest. Will you turn me over to the Yard?"

"Aye, but you did it just the same, didn't you?" Serina looked long and hard at Jonah. She filtered through his mind and found her captor sincerely regretted the past days events. Now what to do? The man seemed easy enough to control, but the wolf? She feared that if the same scenario were to repeat itself, things might go worse. Then she wondered, what could be worse than watching a vampire drain your husband's life on your honeymoon? Not one damn thing.

"I know for a fact that the Yard will skin you and stuff you. Maybe my entering your body tampered with Jasper's stranglehold over you. I'm not ready to condemn a man so easily that saved my life, even if it wasn't the most orthodox way. Carrying me off and locking me in a cave without food or water won you no favors whatsoever. Right now, you're like two different people. If I'd just met you on the street I'd never have said, 'He's a murdering sod, watch out for him.' I'd have foolishly introduced you to my sister-in-law. Your life must be beyond reproach. A living hell."

"And then some," he added.

Outside and free, Serina glanced up. The sky supported a barren canopy of dull, non-twinkling gaseous bubbles. She went back in thought to the first night she spent with Lucian by the lake. Her heart yearned to relive that night and the beauty it held. Nothing could ever recapture the special moments and memories she shared with Lucian.

"Can you set me down on the ground? I've a monster of a Charlie horse in my back and legs." Jonah set her down on her side and gently kneaded her muscles, trying to ease the kinks. Serina felt the warmth of his hands and she had to admit to herself if no one else, it felt good, as much as she detested the idea of him touching her.

"Serina, I'm going to lift your skirt up to your thighs so I can get to the muscles. I promise I'll behave."

"Peek—and I'll burn out your eyes. Just do what you must so I can walk out of here on my own accord. How did you end up a werewolf?"

Jonah's grip tightened, and she tensed.

He stopped his ministrations. "Have I hurt you? My apologies."

"No Jonah, 'tis not you. I just—there's never been another man touch me." Serina choked on anger. Once again, the tears assaulted her. Where did they keep coming from? Was there no end to the flogging of tiny beads of water?

"Do you want me to continue?" he asked with sincerity. When she made no protests, he did. He liked the feeling of her skin against his. She was cool to touch still but slowly warming up... to him. He studied the woman lying beneath his hands, and he liked what he saw. Her hips were slim, her legs muscular, and her breasts—they just didn't seem to go with the rest of her body. They belonged on top of a woman with ten babes suckling at them. He liked them though. "Do you really want to know about my life?"

"Yes. I want to know, but only if it causes you pain. Whoops! I mean no pain."

"Be at least honest with yourself, Serina. You meant pain, and I don't blame you one bit. Five years ago, my wife and I were out celebrating. She had just told me we were with child. We lived in the Brahmall area and had gone for an early evening constitutional by the water's edge at the park. We laughed and joked about what kind of parents we would be, and how we would have the most intelligent child on the planet, and of course the most beautiful. We watched the swans floating across the lake as if magically propelled through the still water, grace and elegance surrounding them." Jonah raked his hand through his long dark curls, as his other hand meticulously continued at the knots of Serina's legs. "Then the swans became spooked, their squawks high pitched, fearful."

"Just as the horses did," Serina whispered.

Jonah's grip tightened to the point of cutting her circulation off.

"You don't have to tell me anymore, Jonah. You don't need to relive what happened again. I can feel your pain, especially in my legs." She had meant it as a means to ease his burden.

Jonah never acknowledged her concern. "We watched the swans swim further out. Not a cloud in the sky, nor a ripple in the water. No sign of a storm. Only the beauty of the sun setting. The shades of orange painted across the sky matched Jezzie's silken tresses. To this day, I still cannot look at a setting sun. My heart sighs."

Serina found herself in wonderment of this man living two separate lives, obviously educated and once deeply in love with a woman, now torn between two separate worlds. One, the human nature in him, to be a loving caring man as he seemed now, then, during the cycles of the moon or under a vampire's compulsions, a wild dangerous beast fighting for supremacy.

Serina lay on her belly both dazzled and dazed by his words, and his life. Groaning, she shifted her body a bit to ease a root pressing into her ribs.

Jonah moved to her feet, warming them between his hands. He carefully squeezed each toe, to press the blood to color the tips once again instead of the bloodless-white color they'd become.

"We never saw the wolf. It came with such force and speed, a blur really. Within a split second, my life as I knew it ended. My Jezzie lay dead before me. Her throat torn out, her life and my child's ripped away from both of us." Jonah wiped a stray tear from his cheek. "It's been five years since I shed these. I shut all the people in my life out for fear of hurting them. I've a younger sister and brother to keep safe. I'd die a thousand deaths before ever hurting them or having Jasper find them. All three of us are one year apart in age. My grandparents raised us after our mother mysteriously passed away. Never knew our fathers."

"Fathers?" Serina turned her head to watch Jonah.

"Me mum, she held the same gifts you, Serina, but she was never comfortable in own skin, which affected her relations with men. She never committed to a relationship. Hard to love someone when you have no clue who you are."

"Does your sister have her powers?"

Jonah lied and shook his head no. "Don't believe so." He wasn't about to cast his little sister to the wolves, so to speak. Her secret was safe with him.

"So you haven't seen your brother or sister in five years? Do they know you're alive?"

Again, Jonah shook his head no and continued. "A constable happened by and heard my pleas for help, and he became entwined in the struggle. He took me to the hospital, and the staff put me back together better than Humpty Dumpty. On the next full moon history rewrote my life."

You've read Humpty Dumpty?" Serina's eyebrows shot up.

"Hasn't everyone?"

"No, not everyone." Serina groaned. She'd planned to read that fairy tale to Lucian. She'd packed the little book in her bags. Frustration mounted in her gut. She wanted to scream, but she was both physically and emotionally withered. "I'm sorry for your loss, Jonah." She truly meant it. She knew exactly what it was like to have her heart, life, and dreams ripped away for some fathomless reason.

"You have some rather strong powers yourself," he said as he poked his finger into her side a few times. "They may save you again, or in the end, be the very death of you if the wrong people learn of you. Now that Jasper has fled to London there will be talk. More of the undead or the Sorcerers Squad might knock you up. You'll need to keep your eyes open at all times and your senses finely tuned. You have two more problems you may not have thought about yet..."

Serina cut him off, "Trust me, Jonah, being locked away in that dark, damp, bloody bug-infested cave I had plenty of time to drive myself insane with different scenarios. First and foremost is Lucian. What happens if he comes back as one of the undead? A vampire himself? Honestly, I don't know. I told him I would follow him anywhere our lives led us and I meant it, but this line of thinking is too bizarre. But trust me, I would welcome him with open arms." She swatted at a few tears. "My second problem being that blood sucking creature Jasper may now have compulsion over me. Right?"

"Indeed."

"Well..." Serina thought about it second. She tried pulling her hair up twirling it into a bun so it would be off her body, but her hair could have been used as mortar. Her once silky strands were caked with mud, and only God knew what else and no longer flexible. "Ugh! I'll bet Blythe wouldn't like my hair down today!"

"Who?"

"A friend." Miffed, she gave up. "I almost took that fetid-breathed bastard out. I'm rather confident I can inflict some form of necrosis into him."

Once more, the effects of the cold damp ground chilled her. She shifted, and that left Jonah's hand precariously close to her bottom. She didn't notice.

He most certainly did.

Working on her thighs, he moved slowly upward, enjoying the view of her ass. Soft yet firm. Something he could sink his teeth into. His heart picked up its pace.

He skimmed his hand across the swell of flesh, purposely. He hadn't touched another woman in years. Hell, he hadn't touched another human, except with ill intent. She felt warm and alive. She brought back emotions buried deep within him that he had made a solemn oath he would never again allow to surface, hope and lust. Love was nowhere near the equation nor would it ever factor in again.

That slight touch sent raking claws down Serina's spine. Confusion and guilt weaved a web around her. Was her captor now trying on a new hat? To be her lover?

"Touch me like that again and I'll have your fingers dismembered at each joint. You have no right to..."

"I'm sorry." Jonah offered flatly.

So consumed by grief, she never heard the rush of leaves or branch's rustling as André, Duncan and Payton snuck up on them.

****

Time hung in the balances. André eyed the stranger with fevered caution. The hairs on his neck stood straight up. Bells and whistles blew in his head. There was more to this gent than met the eye. Serina resembled a forgotten doll in the bottom of the toy chest as she lay in the dirt. Had the man hurt her?

About to ask Serina if she needed help, André gave pause when he saw a look of sheer horror consume her. She stared at him wide-eyed, and he watched the color drain from her face. On hands and knees, she attempted to crawl away but she kept falling face first into the dirt and leaves. He realized his appearance spooked her, but there wasn't much he could about that. He was who he was, Lucian's identical twin.

Serina rolled her eyes up and locked them on André, opened her mouth, and roared indiscernible words as if she'd never get another chance to speak. Absolutely nothing she said made sense.

Behind him, crackles grew steadily louder, then his nose twitched, scenting smoke. Apprehensive, André turned around. Fire spread from one tree to the next, with one thunderous clap after the other as the lush evergreens burned faster than a wick on stick of dynamite. "This isn't good."

Serina screamed louder, pointing at André in an accusatory fashion.

"And that definitely isn't good." Being a rather quick study, André put some distance between her, seeing her hands tightly fisted, her nails sinking into her palms, drawing blood. "Serina, I know this is a shock seeing me standing here. Please listen when I tell you we need to get you back to the safety of your home with your family, our family. Serina?"

Serina twisted away from her brother-in-law and hugged her knees to her chest, then began to rock and sob. "I have no home, André." She kept her face concealed. "My husband is dead. I can't look at you every day of my life and see him. I'll go insane. I believe I've already begun the process." She tried again to look at him, but she saw only Lucian's silvery blue eyes looking back at her. Flashbacks pummeled her broken heart with memories of the two of them laughing, holding each other, Lucian kissing her...She blinked and saw André standing there looking helplessly alive.

Duncan stepped forward and bent to her. When he placed his hand on her arm, she froze. She slowly faced him, and he gasped.

"Those are the eyes that attacked Lucian, Raven and myself the first night we met you, Doc." Duncan had a sinking feeling he just got a glimpse into the porthole of Hell.

Serina hissed, "It would be in your best interest, Duncan, if you backed away from me. I seem to be having issues with my powers, and I'd never want to hurt you."

Duncan swallowed hard. "Doc," he attempted an ill-fated grin, "no hissing. Really, it doesn't become you. I know you would never hurt me, but you seem to be doing a great job at digging up your own body. Please, allow me to help you." Duncan gently pried each fingernail out of her skin. He ripped a hankie from his pocket, tore it in half and wrapped her bloodied hands.

Serina threw her arms around Duncan, and buried her face in his shoulder. He hoisted her from the ground and began a retreat without a look back.

"Who, Sir, might you be?" André asked the stranger.

Jonah eyed the man discerningly. He knew only that Lucian had a twin sister, and this man was a healthier spitting image than the man he'd just left for dead.

"Jonah. And you, Sir?"

Eyebrows pinched, André took in the stranger. The stranger's height didn't match André, but his build certainly did. André kept his stance ready for an attack should one ensue. He whispered the man's name, Jonah! 'Twas the name Raven whispered just before she collapsed. He reached for his gun.

Serina stiffened, which caused Duncan to pause his steps. She didn't know whether to say naught and keep him safe, and save her own men from a fate worse than death, because she knew without a doubt things would turn ugly fast if they threatened Jonah.

"André, this man found me chained up here in the woods. He helped me. The werewolf and the vampire left me here to die." There, she attempted to kid herself, it wasn't a complete lie. *The werewolf did leave me, but the man came back.*

Serina tried very hard to censor her thoughts so Raven wouldn't pick up on that last remark, and get back to André with the truth.

"Oh, Serina!" André mumbled. "Do not forget I know my sister's thoughts." He squared his shoulders.

Serina tilted her head to face Duncan. She gave a silent plea not to start another war. Even with Jonah no longer in wolf form, he wielded inhuman abilities.

"I'm sorry, Serina." Duncan answered. "The man cannot live. He's taken my best friend, not to mention your husband from you and yet you seek to protect him. Why?" Duncan turned to face his adversary and his companions. He set Serina down on the flat surface of a boulder near by.

Serina caught Duncan's wrist. "Duncan, listen, he had no choice. The vampire owns his mind. He is the werewolf, but he is also a man, just like you. He said he would return me to our family."

"And you believed him? Do not place us in the same category with that scoundrel. I do not howl at the moon nor do I hunt humans," Duncan lashed out, his tone harsh. "Why would you shelter him?" Duncan got in Serina's face, his forehead pressed to hers. He held her chin in his hand, gently caressing her cheeks, while anger flared through his body.

"I don't want anyone else hurt, Duncan. I can't take another death." Serina wrapped her arms around Duncan's neck, and looked deeply into his soul trying to convince him to stay silent. "Please? Do this for me and if not for me, for our family."

"For our family, you say?" His voice shot up in octaves. "And what if the vampire is using him as a puppet? What if he comes into our home some night and destroys one or all of us? I must take this risk...him, from our family, Serina. You must see that." Abruptly Duncan pulled away from Serina and headed for the men.

Chapter Fifteen

With sure and steady steps Duncan moved towards Jonah and pulled a gun from his boot top. With the barrel of the gun pointed between Jonah's eyes, Duncan accused, "You are the wolf, are you not?" Duncan spat on the ground. "Serina for some reason fears for his life, and ours as well, but he must die."

At that exact moment two things happened. In a blinding blur, Jonah turned and grabbed Payton by the throat. He threatened, "His last breath is here and now if anyone moves towards me. Test my will, if you dare," as rocks, higher on the mountain loosened and tumbled to the ground.

Serina pointed to Jonah, then André to warn them of the debris headed straight at them but before she had a chance to utter a word, sparks discharged from the tips of her fingers, like bullets from a gun. Energy bolts of red and blue in color soared past them. The aftermath left her fingernails charred and bloody. One boulder she hit disintegrated. Buckshot-like pebbles sprayed in every direction.

Duncan lost his grip on the gun and the weapon landed conveniently beside Jonah's feet. Other than dodging rocks, no one moved.

Jonah shot Serina a wide-eyed look. "For the love of God, Serina, put your hands in your pockets and think happy thoughts." Jonah turned to face Duncan and with sarcasm-coated words asked, "Did no one ever teach you playing with guns can be deadly?" He kicked the gun farther from Duncan still holding Payton as if he had a garrote around his neck. "Do not do this. Your mate will die. He means naught to me." Jonah pressed his talon just above Payton's heart.

Payton gave no struggle, but got a better grip on his silver pocket/paring knife he'd tucked up his sleeve, Jonah none the wiser.

The earth shifted underfoot and sent everyone sideways. In one swoop Jonah's nails shredded Payton's shirt and chest open. Payton plunged the silver blade into Jonah's abdomen, in self-defense. Jonah scrambled to a boulder, fighting to stand, until his knees buckled, and he slid down to the ground panting.

Payton attempted to hold pressure over his chest, but it was useless. Blood seeped through his clothing and from between his fingers.

André and Duncan placed themselves between Jonah and Serina.

"All of you stop now. Sit!" Serina screamed. André and Duncan ended up on the ground whether they intended to or not. "This is exactly why, Duncan, I asked you for your silence. Look what has taken place. You'll all end up dead if you keep this up. We need to get away from this place now. It is no longer safe. André, pick up Payton and get him away from here. Duncan help Jonah," Serina ordered.

"No." Duncan defied her. "I will never help this man. Serina what the hell is wrong with you?"

Through gritted teeth, Jonah answered, "The first is easy. The vampire wills her to do so even as she is unaware of his presence within her mind. Trust me, he is there."

Serina burst into a mixture of tears and laughter talking to herself, "Is this how I sounded the first night I met Lucian? Trust me vampires are real?"

A few glances were exchanged between the men.

Jonah continued, "Secondly, Serina is pure of heart and incapable of killing another." Jonah looked into Serina's eyes and finished speaking directly to her, "It is not within you. That is why I still stand, Serina. When you tried days past to crush my heart, you felt my life slipping, and you withdrew yourself. I felt it." Jonah closed his eyes, and toppled over sideways next to Duncan. Blood stained the corners of his lips and appeared like lipstick smeared from a lover's kiss.

Duncan scooted farther away from him. "You should have finished what you began, Serina. Your better judgment has failed you, and now we will all pay for it. Let us get Payton to a safe haven and then you can heal him." If looks could actually kill, Jonah may not have been the only one Duncan wanted gone from this earth as he glared at Serina.

Serina had never seen nor heard Duncan act in such a hostile manner. She always found his nature soft, gentle. This new side to the man she didn't particularly care for one iota. Who did he think he was ordering her around? Even with that thought eating at her, she knew she could do no other than help the men. "Get the men further down the mountain, and I will help them, but hurry. Duncan, what happened to you?" Serina had to know where the aggression came from.

Was the woman daft? Exasperated, Duncan held his hands palm up. "You, Serina. You're the problem. I thought your love for Lucian would never fade away, and now you treat the very man that helped kill your husband with tender care. 'Tis bloody revolting. Lucian's probably rolling in his grave right now." Duncan stood up and stomped the grounds to Payton. Gently, he picked up the smaller man, and hurried away.

Back on his feet, Jonah clung to anything in his path to help steady his gait. He trailed yards behind

Duncan and Payton. Already, his wounds had begun to heal. The silver blade did some damage and would leave a nasty scar, but it wasn't a mortal wound, and he had longevity rooting for him whether he wanted it or not.

Up to his eyeballs in uncharted water, André saw Duncan's point so very clearly. He wanted to leave Serina on the mountain, but then he heard Jonah explain she could be under the vampire's compulsion. All right, that only compounded the problem at hand but as he looked over his little fireball of a sister-in-law an irresolvable conflict mounted. Out of honor for his brother, he would bring Serina home, but in doing so, he also brought home the possibilities of more trouble. What if Serina turned on one of them? What if more werewolves and vampires ended up dropping in for tea or something with a bit more sustenance? More meat, less potatoes? What if?

"Serina? Can you walk?" he asked, his voice on the tremulous side as he skirted around the situation. His fingers were crossed praying she could. He already had a blazing inferno glowing around him. He didn't want to set off another storm, unless maybe the forecast said showers. A small curve of his lips crept in. "Can you do a rain dance and extinguish these flames before we all burn to a crisp?"

"I can't dance. Period!" Serina focused on the ground as she tried to stand. Not used to being on her feet, her thighs burned and shook and she landed flat out on her bum. Curse words chomped at the bit for release. In a heated tone she stated, "André, I can't walk. And I 've no clue how I started the fires. I thought I might spontaneously combust when I saw you, not Lucian. I've never experienced such rage. I'm so sorry." Massaging her temples, she hoped to alleviate the constant berating of Jasper's cackles as they bounced off the grey matter in her head. "The vampire made it snow on the mountain a few days ago. I could try," she said even though she held little hope.

Behind closed eyes, she imagined a blinding downpour of large droplets of rain to extinguish the fire...not a bloody drop of water. "Come on already, rain." Concentrating so hard, she turned three shades of red.

"Serina, it's not working. You're just sitting there and..." André turned away from Serina.

"And what, André? Just say it."

"You're very red. You look like you're having a bowel movement." André had the audacity to snicker under his breath.

She found no humor.

"He must have had a magic wand or something, Serina."

"Magic wands aren't real!" she chided.

"Are you sure?"

She slapped her hand to her chest, asking, "Who's the witch here? Just shut up before I turn you into a ugly, drowned rat."

And then a light rain trickled from the heavens into the trees and the grounds. "Oh my God, André! This is unbelievable. How did I do that?"

André lifted his hands to catch the falling drops. "I believe you threatened my life." He grinned. "Come on." He leaned over and lifted her into his arms. "Serina, please forgive me because I know I'm about to offend you, but—you look pitiful and you smell like shite."

Serina bowed her head in shame. "My apologies, my Lord."

"My name is André, Serina. Never address me as My Lord again. I am not your master. I believe no man shall ever be."

After a few minutes in her brother-in-law's

arms, Serina stirred. Uncomfortable and wanting to break the awkward silence between them, she had no idea what to say. Her breath caught in her throat. If she didn't look into his eyes she would never know it wasn't Lucian, well except André held her as far away as possible where Lucian would have had her crushed to him with his luscious lips glued to her somewhere. André didn't return her gaze. He just trudged along the trail stoic, with his stiff upper pouty lip.

That damned lip. She wanted to bite it from his face.

Serina wiggled a bit more, still trying to elicit a response, a word, a glance, a grunt…anything to show the man had a pulse. His inattentiveness irked her. Serina shuddered as a sick visceral sensation clamped down on her. And then, just as quickly, it passed.

Let's play a little, Ducky. Entertain me, why don't you, with your new friend. And look at this— he's the same make and model as the last one we just offed. Cheaper by the dozen, hey?

Deciding another tactic might benefit her, she placed her head on his shoulder and buried her face in the crook of his neck. She inhaled him without censor needing him to smell like Lucian. He didn't, and he certainly didn't react like her husband. André physically turned to stone. Ah! A response after all. Fear. She smiled, but it wasn't one André would appreciate.

A dark fever crept through André. Right now, he wanted to toss her on her luscious little bottom and be rid of her, but he had to be honest with at least himself, sick as it was, a quick thrill shot down his spine.

Eyes locked shut, he counted to ten, hoping whatever she had up her tattered, little sleeves would end. When he first laid eyes on Serina desire filled his lonely heart, the complete contrast to the here and now. The first vision of her, wearing her emerald dress, her bosom pressing through the satin, ummm! He had wondered how it would feel to have his face buried between her creamy mounds of flesh suffocating him, what her nipples would feel like ripening inside his mouth and here and now, he still had the same perverse thoughts. Oh, he was going to suffocate all right. Lucian would gladly snuff out his last breath.

Confusion wove a stealthy trap around him. Serina tightened the ropes. Did he free himself immediately or fall prey to this enchantress's lure?

"Serina...I don't think that you should be doing this," he whispered, nervous. His hair stood on end, and that wasn't the only thing stiffening up on him. His trousers felt uncomfortable, snug. He repositioned her a few times and tried to hold her even farther away from him, knowing full well he wouldn't walk right for a month of Sundays.

"Then do not think, my Lord." Serina/Jasper understood all too well after they shared his thoughts. She stretched her arms over her head, and hooked him.

Serina licked the saltiness of his coarse stubble away and pursed her lips as if she'd sucked on a lemon. His heart thumped so hard she heard it through his chest. She threw her head back to see the look on his face. She liked what she saw. André turned a ghostly white.

Think, André. She is your brother's wife, first and foremost. He would never breach that confidence between them, even with Lucian gone. Never!

But, then again, when cleaned up, she is ravishing. But still, there it was again, like a fly he just couldn't swat away...his brother's wife—his dead brother's wife, he tossed into the pot to make himself feel lousier. And still, here she hung in his arms with her soft lips sucking on him, her breasts cozying up to him.

Serina moved again, and wrapped her legs around his waist, anchoring them together. Her laugh, a purely sensual melody, tore through him like a tornado. André found his hands massaging her bottom gently. He didn't remember moving them there. Skillfully, she teased her womanhood over him, just enough to arouse the dead. *What is Serina doing? Why now? Why her? Why me? Why?* He threw his head back and choked back a scream.

Gazing into her black obsidian eyes, his soul slinked away, one bit at a time. Guilt clobbered him again, as would Lucian if he were to witness this twisted entanglement of bodies as this possessed woman rode him. André tried to drop her, but her strength waxed as his waned.

Kiss him, Ducky. Taste his lips, take his essence from him; make him want me—I meant you of course.

She rubbed her most intimate parts over him with vigorous enthusiasm, trying to scratch that annoying little itch between her thighs. She closed the distance and covered André's mouth chastely. There was nothing other than the cold, foreign, firmness of his lips. He didn't return her favors. She pushed at his mouth with her tongue and forced entrance. Sensing something irrevocably wrong, Serina hesitated. "André get off me," she bit out, her voice sounded estranged to her and just as detached as her heart.

Frustrated, André laughed, though it was not a jovial burble, but the exact opposite, hard, distant and cold. "If only I could." Certain beyond a reasonable doubt he wouldn't have answers that would exonerate his behavior if anyone were to witness this, André tried again to peel her from him, with what was left of his strength. He pulled, pushed, twisted her and yet there she was—slinking her hips in a circular motion over something that was mere seconds away from making a mess of his trousers. She physically bested him. André dropped to his knees taking Serina down on her back.

"Oh! This is an exquisite position," Serina purred in a voice that sounded nothing like her, but much more raspy, masculine. She yanked his hips down to her and ground her pelvis without mercy into his erection. "Come for me, Lucian, crash into me. Take me here, now, like this. I need you, I love you...Lucian..." Serina yelled in anguish, "Please don't leave me." Tears rolled from behind her closed eyes.

André found his will and strength quicker than lightning striking. "Serina, I am not my brother. You're acting like two totally different women right now."

"You think? Help me, André!" Serina cried. "Drop me."

In her next breath of air, her voice dropped to a baritone. "You want to be Lucian. Kiss me, André," she growled and yanked him to her mouth, jammed her tongue deep into his mouth and came close to eating him alive. He fought for freedom.

She cursed, "Coward!"

A split second later, Serina ran her fingers through his jet-black curls and yanked him away from her. "Kiss me again, André, and I'll bite off your tongue. Ask Jonah. I got his."

This insanity had to stop.

"I love your pouty lips, Lucian."

Oh Christ, not again. His heart pounded its way past ribs and sinew looking for a way out. However, lower body parts also sought release. André peeked down at his erection. He thought about whacking it off himself.

With a machete.

Serina/Jasper read André's mind and offered, "Let me do that," as she reached between his legs.

"Oh, in the name of the Queen, Serina, stop!" He ripped her hand from his pants and then remembered something. He dug in his pocket and yanked out a small bottle. He brought it to his lips, bit down on the cork stopper and opened the bottle. He wasted no time dowsing Serina with the blessed water.

Raven screamed in her head, *Serina, André, stop what you're doing now.*

Serina, listen to me. André is not Lucian. Stop your assault. The vampire is playing you both. Listen with your heart, Serina. I would not lie to you.

Jesus, André, get off her!

André fell backwards onto his ass and took in a huge gulp of air when she released him. He touched his lip and his finger came away covered in blood. She bit him.

Confused, Serina shot her brother-in-law an unfavorable glare. "Ouch, André, what just happened? I don't remember anything at all. My head feels like a punching bag. That may not be the only part of my anatomy that is bruised, besides my ego?" Serina looked down at the position of her body...lying beside André with her skirt wrapped around her hips. A warm rush of color raced up her neck to her face. "What did we do?" She yanked her skirt back down to her ankles. "Did we? Lie to me if you must!"

"No." André felt like an awful cad. He had almost taken her, but he ignored the signs. *Take me Lucian...I love your pouty lips...*

André whacked the side of his head repeatedly with his palm. "How could I be so callous? Serina, the vampire that killed Lucian and attacked you—" André ran his fingers gently over the deep, purple holes in her neck. "—has one hell of a stranglehold over you. None of us are immune. Most assured we would have had sex just now if Raven had not gotten into our heads, and Father hadn't given me the holy water. Forgive me?"

Serina grabbed his face. "André, do not place blame on yourself. You and I both are strong-willed. We have loving people who surround us yet Jasper has found entrance to our bodies, not our hearts. We need to find a way to combat him. He cannot destroy what we have left."

Determination to bring Jasper to an abrupt end took precedence on Serina's do it tomorrow list. He'd met his match, and she was the spark waiting to incinerate him. She needed to protect Raven and André at all costs. Now Serina understood why she lived.

Jasper. It was all about Jasper now.

"You look so much like him, André. It hurts so. That is why I went a bit ballistic on the top of the mountain…"

"A bit, Serina?" André interrupted. "Look behind you. The trees exploded behind us. The earth shook."

Serina shrugged her shoulders and kept talking. "I thought about you…I didn't think I could ever look at you again, and not have my heart fragment into a million pieces."

"It works both ways, Serina. I look at you and will always wish to see my brother at your side."

"Payton!" Serina gasped. "Jonah ripped him open. Do you know what that means?" Serina gave it her all, attempting to get to her feet, yet she stumbled the second she stood.

André caught her and balanced her. "André, he'll turn into a werewolf. Is there anything we can do to prevent it? Can you get me to him?"

André pulled Serina up into his arms and headed down the mountain. "His fate will be determined in a few weeks. Serina, you don't mind if

I drop you in the creek when we catch up to everyone do you?"

"That bad?"

André nodded. "Worse. Tell me about Jonah. Why did you want to protect him from us?"

"I knew if confronted a fight would ensue. He told me about his past, and I suppose I have sympathy for him. He lost his wife the same way I lost Lucian." Serina clammed up and buried her face into his shirt. For a brief moment, Serina could speak of Lucian and not turn into a babbling idiot. That time had apparently ended.

André pulled her closer to him and held her as they continued down the mountain. "I see Duncan, they're just past the turn."

Payton fought to remain conscious. Duncan cautiously looked at Serina, then to André. "Serina, please help Payton. I know what you did for our Lucian and Ray. Can you help him?"

Serina set her hands on Payton's shoulders and explained her intentions so she wouldn't give him the fright of his life. "I'm going to enter your body now. It may feel awkward at first, but it shouldn't cause discomfort. Don't panic." Serina kissed his forehead. "And Payton? You've got us, always, no matter what."

"Thank you," came through chattering teeth.

Serina shed her earthly body and became pure kinetic energy. Focused on the damage done to the interior of his chest wall, he'd been most fortunate Jonah had missed his lungs. He did however make quite a mess of his abdomen and sliced into his liver. Meticulous at her work, she mended all torn parts with great certainty that Payton would live to see the next full moon. After that, it was out of her hands. When she finished, she passed out, with not a word.

Duncan caught her and held her, uncertain

what to do with her or what to feel for her, but he held her all the same and didn't let go. He ran his hand over her face tenderly. "Someone needs to get her water and food. She's completely depleted of energy." And without missing a beat he added, "This is indeed my fault, André. Payton would never have gone through this if I'd listened to her. I was so certain we'd lost her along with Lucian that my temper took over my better judgment. I am so sorry, Payton. Please forgive me. If I could trade places with you, I would do so in a heartbeat."

"Careful what ya wish for, Duncan. Next month Payton might be needing some company when he's out roaming the woods," Jonah muttered.

"Well then, he should be thankful he's got you to show him the ropes, hey?" Duncan harshly added, "He was a good man until you did this to him."

Jonah pugnaciously replied, "Payton still is a good man, Duncan. Just different now. He's still a man, with a heart and a conscience." Saying that, he hoped it would sink into Duncan that, he too, owned a heart and a conscience, although he wasn't sure why he cared an iota what any of them thought of him.

André looked around their makeshift camp, and seeing no food or water, said, "Hold the fort, Duncan. I'll be back. You two, kiss and make up before I get back."

"You first, Ands," Duncan shouted.

"Not on your life."

Chapter Sixteen

He placed a ladle of water to her lips, but Serina didn't stir. He looked at her lying in Duncan's arms and asked, "Can I take her?"

Duncan looked up through tired, smoke-filled eyes, and reluctantly handed her over. "André, did you change your clothing?"

He gave Duncan's question some serious thought. "I don't recall." He then did the one thing he'd wanted to do since he'd found her. He waded her into the water. Slowly the cooler fluids rose to her neck and rushed over her tiny body. He ran his hands across her skin where all the debris of the past days stuck to her fragile bones. Cradling her head in one hand he washed her hair, knowing soaps would still be needed, but he had to start somewhere. His touch was gentle, intimate. She felt wonderful in his arms. He closed his eyes holding the tears hostage. No tears today. Feeling her heart beating through her shirt, allowed him a moment's respite, even if only temporarily. He prayed she'd open those emerald eyes for him soon. He needed to see that sparkle she held for him alone. Would the gleam still be there? Or had he already been replaced?

And just like that Serina opened her eyes. She all but jumped from the water onto his shoulders laughing.

"What is with the St. James men and water? I hate water. Get me out of here." She laughed heartily, showing off a beautiful grin and soft lips that he had to have.

"Not that fast, little luv. You need a good rinsing off, and then we'll see what we can dig you up to dress your little body in. Usually you're a beautiful woman, except at this very moment." Pulling her off his shoulders and back into his arms, he said one last thing to her as they both went under the water, "Hold your breath."

"Wha—?"

Under the water, Serina clamped her eyes shut. Being scared of the water as it was, she didn't need to see any fish or sea serpents swimming by her with large fangs directed at her body.

As he crushed her tightly against him, a stinging sensation in her chest perplexed her, and just as quickly, the pain was replaced with an undeniable need. She shook, saturated with pleasure. Her lower muscles gave off little tremors, creating waves in a still lake, releasing all the horrid memories of the past days.

She had no idea of how or why this orgasm came about, but she welcomed it. Even knowing she desperately needed oxygen she let him hold her under the water. That too heightened her orgasm. She wanted to get to the top of the water and gulp in as much air as she could force her lungs to take, but at the same time, she couldn't release her body from the intensity feeding her. She never opened her eyes; she didn't want to wake up and have her dream be that, a really wet dream. Right here, like this, she decided she had a newfound appreciation for water.

Serina came up and sought to see the glimmer in his eyes, remembering the intense beauty they held and how she felt when she gazed into them. She rubbed water from her eyes trying to focus, as she clung to him in a death grip.

His words, just before he dragged her under...he'd said the exact same thing to her the night they'd spent at the lake. Coincidence? She thought not, but she had to ask. "Lucian?"

Damn the moon for disappearing and stealing all the light. It had to be him. She knew at that exact second, she didn't want to live without him. She tried to kiss him but he pulled away from her.

"Sorry, luv." He carried Serina back to the edge of the water, set her down and left, never speaking another word or glancing back.

"Sorry luv," Serina mimicked as she sat on the muddy shore and picked up every last stone in her reach and flung each one harder than the last into the lake. "How could I have been so delusional?" She'd have bet her life Lucian returned. Now this orgasm left the bitter taste of guilt. Getting up, Serina wobbled sideways and stumbled over a few rocks making her back to Duncan. She plopped down next to him with a thud, and soggy butt. Gathering the ends of her dress, she wrung the water out. Duncan looked at her from the corner of his eye as the excess drops rolled to his feet. His nose twitched.

"Feel any better? I must say you smell much better."

"One out of two isn't bad." She turned to Payton. "How are you doing?"

"I'm no longer resembling a stuck pig, nor am I chasing me tail so I suppose I'm just ducky too."

Serina snapped, "Don't ever say that word again."

"What word," Payton asked. He glanced at Duncan and mouthed, "What did I say?" Duncan shrugged his shoulders.

"The one that rhymes with lucky and quacks." Watching Payton mumble through the alphabet until he reached that word, Serina couldn't help but laugh.

André returned with cans of beans, fresh raspberries he'd picked and canteens filled with water. "Anyone hungry?" Glancing at Serina he eyed her from head to toe. "Serina, you're soaked. What, did you fall in the water? We'll have to get you some dry clothing."

The air stilled. Not a one of them budged. Serina looked from Duncan, whose mouth hung open, to Payton, who held his chest, to Jonah who turned a pasty white and rested her eyes on André. Her hands went to her mouth as if trying to contain the scream that would come out regardless. "Lucian," she squealed. He'd made it back to her. She didn't care how he got there, only that he had.

Duncan bounced to his feet and searched in and around their campsite. "Serina? Am I crazy? Please tell me I'm not clinging to a dream. Please tell me we both saw him."

"Would one of you please tell me what in hell I just missed?" André faced Serina, then twisted his body around to follow Duncan zigzagging between trees and brush. "Hello! What happened?" André dropped the food in haste and held his arms wide open with a questionable look on his face.

Wearing a grin from ear to ear, Duncan answered, "Lucian. We think."

"You've all gone insane. I leave for one second, maybe two and you're all seeing ghosts." Regardless of his words, André wasted no time to join Duncan. "Serina, tell me what went on," André yelled from the top of a boulder trying to get a clearer view of the area.

"I stayed put. I passed out after healing Payton."

"I was there for that part," André answered.

"I passed her to you, I thought," Duncan piped in.

"Wasn't privy to that part," André added.

Serina wondered aloud, "Then where did he go? Why would he leave me?"

With restless passion, André headed for the woods once more and scoured the mountainside for his brother.

André finally settled by the fire beside Serina, drained. He glanced around. Each of his family were spread around the fire at various angles trying to get close enough to stay warm through the night, but far enough from the flames not to end up singed come morning. He lay on his side next to Serina, his one arm bent under his head, focused on the flames and things that one could not see or feel except him.

He'd come very close to having sex with Serina. That would haunt him all the days of his life. He'd lost faith. The vampire got to him, which had never happened. That too bothered him, because his will was unbendable. "This vampire must be ancient." André said it more to himself.

Jonah offered, "Jasper? He's crafty, but he's a peon. His strength is gained through another vamp. This other demon lives without consequence. He is immoral and his appetites go far beyond blood lust. Been told he's cannibalistic by nature."

"Lovely. How is it you know so much of him, yet you have no name to stake him with?" André chuckled. "What a great metaphor."

"I have only heard mention of him by way of others less fortunate. Forgive me, I meant no harm."

"You've already caused enough of that now!" Duncan, obviously still awake and still very angry piped in. "Why is it you lie here with us?"

"I stay for Serina, to see that she makes it home safely. If Jasper returns, you'll need help."

"She doesn't need you. We do not need or want you here, Jonah. You will leave us in the morning." Duncan's voice reached new octaves surprising even him.

"Ease up, old man. Serina says the man means us no harm and I believe her. I think it's in our best interest to keep him close at hand or under foot, whichever way you choose to look at it, but this way we can monitor him as well. I think it makes more sense to keep your friends close and your enemies closer."

"Means us no harm, does he? Ask Payton that why don't you."

"Duncan—please, let it rest for tonight. Payton's alive. We found Serina, and Lucian's somewhere—or so you keep saying. Tomorrow, if Jonah barks or snips at you, you can neuter him with Payton's silver knife." André winked at Duncan then gave a slow lazy stretch of his arms over his head with a loud sigh. "Who's got first watch? We've still three hours before sunrise."

"I'll watch for awhile," Payton offered. "I can't sleep just yet any way. My stomach is rumbling so loud it's keeping even me awake."

Huddled close to the fire, Serina basked in the warmth, as it soothed her tired bones. Even sleeping on the ground didn't bother her tonight. The flame's reds, blues and oranges sparks dazzled the night. Serina laid back and listened to the crackles and pops of the logs burning. The crisp, woodsy aroma should have relaxed her but she couldn't let her guard down. Lucian was out there somewhere alone. She hadn't dreamed him up. She knew when he could, he would return for her. He'd promised her that. He'd told her death would not separate them. Even though he made his way back, Serina had questions. What happened to him? Where did he go? Was he actually dead? She shook her head a steadfast no. Everything her sciences taught her said this was implausible. But medical science had some catching up to do with real life, it seemed. Look at her—she was a walking anomaly of life. Ah, but she was still alive. Well, now, didn't Jasper pose an unsettling point. He was technically alive, although for how long once she was through with him remained to be seen, but he was on her side of the ley lines causing all sorts of havoc. And now, her dear husband followed in the heathen's footsteps. Ugh!

She wanted to dance and sing to the world that the love of her life lived, but she smartly knew her limits... Singing and definitely dancing was not her forte. When a sharp stab in her chest demanded her attention, she crossed her arms over her breasts and that one tiny movement sucked her last molecule of oxygen she had stashed in her away. A tingling, tickling sensation wound around her nipple and dove down past her abdomen and stopped right between her thighs. She touched her breast again and the same thing happened. It was where she'd felt the undeniable pleasure radiate through her body when she went under the water. She looked around the camp to see if anyone watched her. André lay beside her snoring. Duncan's eyelids fluttered in deep sleep. Jonah slept with knees pulled tightly to his chest, his arms welded around them and his head at a crooked angle to the rest of his body's alignment. Serina snickered. He was going to have one hell of a stiff neck come sunrise. No sign of Payton, but she assumed he was out picking berries or bugs to eat.

Serina pulled open the large shirt Duncan gave her, and she gasped when she found two tiny holes in the center of her breast. She immediately placed her hand over her flesh, unsure what she felt other than a deep curiosity. She pulled the edges of her shirt closed hearing Payton's whistling.

When Payton returned he stood over Jonah and stared at the man that possibly infected him with the lycan virus. Serina channeled him as he watched Jonah for signs of anything different, finding none, all for Jonah's yellow eyes. Those eyes stood out like a dinosaur on an ant farm.

A handsome, striking dinosaur, her thought, not Payton's.

She pulled away from him and observed him like any other person without the ability to read his thoughts. He lay down and curled up next to the fire then closed his eyes lightly just for a minute, to relieve the tension. One minute turned into two and then four and then he lost count. So did Serina.

Concealed by the darkness just beyond the campsite, he watched them sleep. A grin slowly worked its way to his face when his eyes lit upon Serina. He moved closer and added more wood to the fire to keep them warm and to keep animals away.

André.

He stifled the desire to throttle him. André lay protectively next to Serina, circling her with his body, yet not touching her. Close, but not too close. After the entanglement between them today on the mountain, they'd have to be watched. Can't have your brother sleeping with your wife. Doesn't make for pleasantries, period.

Witnessing them together earlier stopped his heart, for a second time. He'd never lived through anything so painful. Jasper's bite didn't hold a candle to watching his beloved bride come close to getting full carnal knowledge of his twin. Even knowing Jasper caused this didn't lessen his anguish. Hearing Serina calling André by his name, eased his burden some, but none-the-less, it left a bitter taste upon his lips. He couldn't intervene, couldn't stop the struggles between Serina and André because his needs overrode his emotions. He needed blood and seeing his brother's hands on Serina's ass made him want to rip out his twin's throat and drain his last drop from him. And dear God, how close he actually came to doing it! He left to regain what precious little control he owned. He would not turn into the monster that did this to him.

Jonah.

He cast an unappreciated glance towards the

werewolf. He still couldn't get over the word belonged in his vocabulary along with vampires and witches. Curled up in a ball, knees to chest, and no headrest Jonah's neck looked broken. Maybe Duncan snuck in and got him after all. He waited for the rise and fall of Jonah's chest. He knew Duncan would never kill him, but he could hate him to death, for all the good it would do. He wasn't at all sure what to do with Jonah. The werewolf didn't stand a chance against the vampire's enthrallment. He held remorse for the man/wolf. Lucian read Serina's mind and heard of his life's tragedies. Jonah seemed stuck in a cyclic intrinsic volatile atmosphere. Oddly, he categorized himself in the same sphere. They'd become two peas in a pod, like it or not. As far as Jonah's welfare went, he would make no decisions in haste. With time now on his side, he would wait and see how Jonah played his hand. Even though Jonah did nothing to stop Jasper from killing him, the man helped Serina and that alone won his respect.

Duncan.

He eyed his best mate, his body guarded, rigid, his breathing rough and ragged. He appeared completely uncomfortable, as if plagued by nightmares. "What to do with you, my old man?" he wondered aloud. "I need you to know things will work themselves out." He wanted to wake Duncan and hug the man, but he resisted. He had other needs that required his full attention. The little woman lying in front of him being his first concern.

Serina.

She resembled a living angel asleep with a trace of a devilish grin on her lips. *Be still my beating heart. The course of love never does run smoothly.*

After sitting by the fire for an hour, he carefully sauntered to her side. Nothing stirred under foot. He placed his hand over her hands. Her warmth reached up to touch him.

She wrapped her fingers around his, held him close. Serina never woke, unaware her dream stood before her. He bent to her and inhaled her scent, held it deep in his lungs until they burned for release. Her body shivered beneath his touch as he skimmed over her cures. With his lips on her neck, he waited to feel her pulse ebbing. He found it and reeled back, almost landing in the fire. It was too dangerous next to her. She was warm and alive.

He wasn't sure what the hell he was.

Her pulse lured him to her. She was the siren, he the enthralled vampire too new at this to understand a damned thing. This undeniable urge to take her regardless of consequence pummeled his will to a mere thread. He'd bitten her once already. He told himself he'd done it out of necessity to try and protect her from Jasper. Was he kidding himself? In all likelihood yes, but he had to get control of her before he lost her to that hideous beast. What would happen if he bit her again? His incisors lengthened.

Only one way to find out!

Lucian hung his head in shame. He lacked the strength to walk away even as his body screamed for sustenance, for his wife. He couldn't move, he felt caged, with nowhere to run. Then she stirred. She rolled over, her eyes blanketed by thick dark lashes, and her lips curled, into a smile he would treasure for an eternity. Her beauty melted his being, and brought him back to life.

Serina stretched her arms out over her head slowly, not really trying to catch anyone. She wrapped her arms around his neck and reeled him in.

Her fingers gently twirled through his silken tendrils. She took a deep breath and recognized his scent—so sweet, so damned close her heart flip-flopped.

Serina pulled his face next to hers and brushed her lips against his cheek. He felt so real she didn't want to wake up. She didn't want to lose the closeness she now had with him. She would not live through the loss again. "Take what you need from me, Lucian. My life is yours, my love is yours, my heart is yours. Always, I am yours," she whispered lost in her dream. "I love you."

"I love you too, m'lady." Salt-laden tears spilled and wet his lips. He tried wiping them away before they reached her, but a few slid onto her cheek. With a gentle caress, he brushed them away. As he bent forward to kiss the corner of her mouth, she turned into him, her warm lips touching his. His body shuddered, his heart slammed in his chest, and his penis turned to solid rock. *Thank god it still works!* Yes, it was on his top-five worry list. The remaining four seemed moot at this point. As he met her lips she opened her mouth, her tongue teased.

Eyes open, Serina smiled as if she'd never seen anything more beautiful or precious in her life. She hadn't. "You kept your promise to me. Or I must be a pretty good witch to have dreamt you up and made you real. You're definitely better than Pinocchio."

"Harder too!"

She couldn't help but giggle. His sense of humor was still intact. "If you are just a figment of my imagination and I've gone totally bonkers, please don't tell me just yet, let me finish my dream and kiss you one more time, fair enough?"

"Fair enough, m'lady," he whispered as he swept her off the ground and crushed her against him. "Oh, m'lady, your scent—I—" He walked them away from the fire, away from everyone. "I need things tonight, Serina, that you do not understand, and I am only just learning. You know how you have issues with patience? Well, so do I, and I am not faring well." Lucian found a pine tree with a plump cushion of pine needles and dropped them onto it.

Serina leaned back in his arms and kissed his bottom lip, his face, his eyelids, his chin, and back to his mouth. "Oh, how I love your lips." Deciding she wasted precious moments with words she went back to kissing him...touching him. Seeing wasn't always believing. She needed concrete proof he was beside her. "Lucian please tell me this is real, you are real. I cannot lose you again."

As her finger tips brushed over his lips, he took her hand, slid each finger past his lips and kissed them.

"Lucian, did you wake me up to talk, or to kiss me, or to bite me, or all of the above?"

He laughed, a low sensual tone that wrapped her in ecstasy and pressed every button on her female form.

"I'm real. And yes I plan on kissing you, talking to you and," he hesitated, "we have things to discuss."

"I've got so many questions for you. Are you all right?"

"Let's say yes for now." Lucian turned Serina around in his lap. "Wrap your legs around my waist."

More than willing to accommodate the new position, she did a little happy lap dance for him, and ground her pelvis shamelessly into him. Lucian, in return, showed her just how happy he was to have her there. His erection grew with as much if not more need than his new dents.

"Hold that thought, luv." Serina got to her knees, straddled him and got directly in his face. "Did you die? Did you see the proverbial white light at the end of the tunnel? Did you hear me? Is it true what they say about hearing being your last sense to go? Did you meet God? What's she like?" Serina held no judgments only a need to sate her inquisitive mind. If Lucian actually died and came back a vampire, she'd find a way around it, no ifs, ands or buts about it.

"You know deep in your heart the answer. It's so bloody strange. I can't put my thumb on it, but something is different. As for the white light, yes I did see a light at the end of a long garden passageway, but as I went toward it, I heard you and then saw you lying on the ground above me praying that I stay with you, and then suddenly, luv, an invisible wall halted my passage. I had to turn back to you. I had no choice. I wanted none. Serina, listen to this…when I hit the transparent wall my mother stood on the other side looking as beautiful as she did the last time I saw her. She smiled and told me to return to you and my family. God, she is beautiful. I wish Ray could see her."

Serina reached up to Lucian and wiped a few tears from his cheeks. "Do you have any idea how much of a miracle you were given?" Serina sat there for a moment letting that sink in. If people knew their loved ones waited for them to cross over it would make death so much more peaceful and beautiful. Well, as long as you liked those you were about to run into. Otherwise, that could be hell. Hump! Serina thought, two sides to a coin.

"Do you have any idea how much of a miracle you are to me?" Serina kissed him softly and as she did the hardened, jagged, pain that tortured her the past days dissipated.

Lucian nuzzled her head with his chin. "I think you've got the miracle part backwards, my wild rose. You're mine. I don't feel evil, although I know I'm going out of my mind with the desire to taste your blood again. How ludicrous is that?"

"Take what you need, Lucian." Serina meant it. She focused on his lips, and kissed him hard, almost to the point of bruising her own. As she thrust her tongue into his mouth, she caught the edge of something very sharp, causing two things to happen at once. She tried to pull away to assess the damage to her sore tongue, and he latched onto her even tighter.

After a brief duel, Lucian relinquished his grip. She started to laugh.

"That hurt. You could have warned me about those things."

"You should see the inside of my mouth. I look like a drunken, blind dentist had his way with me." Lucian stuck his tongue out at her. Sliced up and raw he was. "We both have some adjustments to make. I'm petrified of attempting to kiss you in any of your favorite other areas. You'll end up looking like a leaky hosepipe."

Serina muttered, "There must be a way around this." Because she'd grown quite accustomed to his lips everywhere on her body.

"Serina, I have to leave you again..."

"No! Absolutely not! You can't leave me again, Lucian. I'm not that strong. I don't ever want you away from me, ever again. Follow me anywhere, even into the loo if you must." Serina would have crawled inside him if physically possible just then. She sat down again and tightened her legs around his waist knowing she couldn't keep up the pressure without becoming a human pretzel.

"God, woman, I love you. I thought I'd never see or feel you again." Lucian kissed the corner of her mouth. "I cannot live without these lips either, luv. " He kissed the tip of her nose. "But I have things to do to protect you that require I go and get a few things under control first." He continued to kiss her before she had the chance to argue with him. He should have known better.

Serina squashed his lips together. "Lucian please...you and I, we're a team. Together we are unstop—"

He wiggled from her trap and eased his tongue into her mouth. Then he pulled away from her. "Don't get too close to the teeth just yet," he warned, "I know vamps have fangs, but, Serina, these come and go. I thought they were supposed to be a permanent thing, not that I'm an expert on vamp dentistry, but it's different. They seem to lengthen when I get aroused or hungry and then recede afterward. And there's something else, little luv. This is the big one…"

"You're already big, Lucian, and apparently aroused." Serina winked. She had her husband back and wasn't about to lose him ever again. She swiveled in his lap, and pressed her private lips against his growing fondness. Definitely enjoyed the little ripples of pleasure that found their way between her thighs.

"Hold that thought." He grinned, with a flash of fang just a bit lengthier than before.

"My, what big teeth you have!" She slid her hand down the front of his trousers and grasped onto the solid length of him. His body shuddered when she gripped and squeezed his hot shaft. His breaths came hard and fast and his head dropped back spilling black silken curls into disarray behind him. In that moment, the man looked wild and untamable. Serina never remembered him looking more desirable. Even the new teeth and the knowledge of what passion they possessed drove her to the edge of her precipice.

"Please—" Lucian gasped between clenched teeth. "—don't." He took possession of her hand, hoping to stop her before this finished all too fast. So very close to release, urgency and pleasure battled his body. A thrill coiled through him from his groin to his stomach. His last plea fell on deaf ears. "Serina, st—"

Serina finished his thought for him, "Stop? Never, m'lord." His hand with hers, she made swift strokes over the length of his penis. His beautiful silvery-blue eyes glazed over.

He fastened his mouth over hers, and whispered, "I love you, m'lady," through his kiss.

"I love you too, m'lord." Curious, she pulled back and peeked into his mouth, and sure enough the incisors had lengthened. "Wow! That's bloody amazing. What other tricks do you have stashed away?" Serina raised her brow to him. She felt like a small child watching a magician pulling a rabbit from his hat.

Lucian snapped his jaw shut with a loud chomp and sent her backwards with a gasp.

"You're an idiot!" Serina shoved at his chest.

"I'm not sure if I've any other tricks. There isn't a book out on the best ways to nurture and coddle vamps yet. How did you like being in the water?" He couldn't help but grin. He knew fully well she liked the water. He kissed the side of her neck gently and her breath stilled. Uncertain whether it was from fear or anticipation he pulled away.

Never fear, Lucian. I know you would never harm me.

Serina nuzzled into the crook of his neck, and settled her head on his shoulder. With the intent of luring him back, she tossed her hair over her shoulder out of the way, giving him a glance at her neckline.

"My skillful, little seductress." He hugged her to him and felt her warmth, her strength, and her love for him regardless of the uncertain future they now faced.

"You had something else to tell me before I so rudely distracted you." Purposely she swirled her tongue over his neck, working back up to his lower lip. Covering his lips with hers, she felt him smiling as she continued to seduce him, and oh, how it was working.

"If we want to finish this we'll be needing a tad bit more privacy, m'lady. Do you think you can do this quietly?"

She shook her no while whispering, "Yes." Hearing leaves and twigs cracking, both Serina and Lucian looked up.

"Oh my God, Lucian!" André pounced atop his brother crushing Serina beneath them both. "Duncan's really not batty. You're here, you're alive." He caught his breath and quickly asked, "You are alive, aren't you?"

"Not for long with you smothering me."

"Please, forgive me." André stood and offered his hand to Lucian. "Serina? Oh, lord. I didn't realize you were under the rubble. Oh, I'll turn whilst you redress."

"Obviously." Her cheeks burned a deep shade of red. Serina stood, straightened her clothes and brushed off the dirt and pine needles that clung to her. Giving herself a quick glance over, she cringed seeing her blouse (Duncan's actually) unbuttoned. *Nimble fingers, m'lord. I never even saw you undo them.*

Vampire! Lucian shifted his brows up and down.

André grabbed Lucian's forearms and hung on. "Luce, what happened? Tell me everything. Have you killed anyone yet?"

"That's random." Lucian had to laugh, because if he didn't there would be an endless stream of tears from the frustration beleaguering him. "No one's dead—yet." *Your future is very much up in the air, though.* "I'll tell you everything, I promise, but let me have some time with my bride. Wake no one. It shall be my surprise." Lucian embraced André and with him that close all Lucian wanted was his blood. He shook off the first instinct to clamp down hard and fill himself on his warm, wife-stealing brother. When his second wave of need bashed him, he bit his lip and pushed André from him. "Go, Ands. We'll talk soon."

Serina paused when she realized something, something that seemed most urgent to her but evaded Lucian. "M'lord?" Serina stood with her head cocked almost in the same fashion Jonah had slept in, her hand on her hip. "That one thing...that one big thing you started to mention a while ago."

Lucian winked at her. "You just took care of that."

Serina walked over to her husband and looked into his serene, mesmerizing eyes and forgot what she'd started to say. Trapped. The man had trapped her mind.

Lucian pulled her close to him. "Don't do that, m'lady. Don't look me in the eye like that unless you want me to take over what's in your head. I can do it. I've spent the last few days practicing on animals. Watch yourself around other vamps as well. They can take your thoughts and twist them to their advantages."

Serina shook her head to clear it. "That enlightening vampire book you spoke of? Shouldn't it say somewhere that you're not, how shall I say this?" Serina yelled the rest loudly, so even people on the next mountain may have heard her. "—supposed to be able to walk about in the sun? Do I need to point out the obvious that 'tis daylight? That you're up and basking in the sun and not broiling in it?" Annoyed, she brushed her hair from her face. "And I'm not under any spell you think you may be able to weave over me, you *eejit*."

She indignantly stomped away from him, swaying her hips just a little more than usual. How dare he think her lesser than him and unable to handle herself around a vampire. He hadn't been around when she sent old Jasper off all hot and bothered. Serina amused herself with that thought, and suddenly stopped walking. Two things occurred to her, neither of which made her insides all warm and fuzzy. Lucian was able to hold her mind, even briefly, but he did it. She wasn't about to tell him that one little fact.

You just did, m'lady. If you're going to censor your thoughts from me, you'll need practice. Along with my funny fangs and the ability to walk in the daylight, I've acquired a few more things, you'll find most interesting, but I'll save those for later. And when did you start speaking broken Scottish calling me an idiot? Now, weren't you in the middle of storming off back to the campsite?

Serina felt him laughing, not a taunting laugh that made her blood boil, but one that melted her heart. When she realized she wasn't ready to face André yet, or any others he may have over-shared her indignant position with, she daintily plopped her bottom down in the middle of both places, between Lucian and the rest of the men. She wasn't sure which fate was worse, being caught indisposed, or facing Lucian with his new lease on life. She didn't have to choose.

Lucian sauntered to her graceful and silent as a great cat, strong, sinewy, and sleek; one she wanted to pet. God, she thought, he's so beautiful. That one little thought made her smile.

Thank you. Your big kitty has some catnip you can play with later if you wish. Lucian wrinkled his nose at her and held his hands out to help her. "You aren't really upset at me are you, m'lady, for charming you just now?" Lucian bent and kissed her cheek. "I don't ever want you angry with me."

"Lucian, you charmed me the second I saw you in the carriage covered in blood and guts. I thought I lost you. You were gone. You died on me, you bastard! I saw your heart stop. I tried with everything I owned to keep you alive and yet you left me. I've never felt anything so profound or devastating." Serina buried her face into his chest, not wanting him to see the fear in her eyes, or the tears but her body's tremble betrayed her. The events of the past days finally caught up to her, and she couldn't look back, her past was forever changed. Looking forward, hers—their future, teetered on shaky grounds. If he disappeared or died again, she die without him.

You won't, m'lady.

Lucian strengthened his grip around her while she cried like he'd never seen her do before. His heart ached for the trauma she'd witnessed. God help him, he'd give her the world if it was possible, but the tears had to dry up.

I'm sorry. I've been a soggy mess since this happened.

He slid his thumbs along her cheeks and wiped away the little beads of water. When that didn't seem like enough, he covered her mouth with his. He whispered to her mind, I love you, over and over until the tremors stopped. Lucian sat on the ground and pulled Serina into his lap and rocked her as if she were a child after a nightmare in an effort to console her. "You need to get some rest, m'lady. You are withered."

Serina started a protest of sorts, but stopped. She hadn't really slept in days, and her mind and body felt like that frozen custard she'd left forgotten in her icebox. "Lucian, I'm sorry."

"Do not apologize, Serina."

"I am petrified."

"Jasper made a claim on you, and until he is truly dead, he'll have a part of your mind to control and play games with. Games you don't want to play, nor have any chance at winning."

"Together, Lucian, we can get rid of him. All of us together. André, Duncan, you and I, we can do it." Serina knew it would be easier to wrangle an alligator out of his shoes than getting Lucian to give an inch, but conceding wasn't her nature.

"M'lady, Duncan could not kill an ant. It is truth. He has the tenderest heart of us all."

"You haven't seen him the past days, Lucian. He's become rather hostile, mostly toward Jonah and me."

"And why is that?" Lucian knew the answer, but wanted to hear her version.

"Because I protected Jonah even after he tried to kill us on the mountain."

"And why would you seek protection for this man after this act of violence against us?" Lucian dangled the bait and she ran with it: hook, line and sinker.

"Because he was under the compulsion of Jasper. He would not have tried to kill you otherwise. I know he wouldn't have."

"So, this evil vampire, unlike the beautiful vampire that holds you safely in his lap..."

"*Eejit!*" Serina sniffled and shoved at his chest of steel. "Stop reading all my thoughts. Let me have a few secrets."

"Anyway, this evil vampire, as I was saying before I was assaulted for a second time—" he tugged her hair lightly, "—has the ability to capture minds, even those of a werewolf. He must be rather powerful and dangerous. I would think it would be in our best interest if you would let me take care of Jasper. And yes, before you run your little luscious lips at me, I will consider asking André to help. But you are not included, Serina. I will not place you in harm's way."

"I already am, Lucian. Look at my neck." Serina stopped talking mid motion, and placed her hand gingerly over the marks Jasper gnawed into her. "Lucian, when Jasper bit me..." Serina lowered her head, ashamed to tell Lucian what Jasper's bite did to her, but she had to tell him the truth. There would be no lies between them. She knew lies in a marriage were as evil as the vampire himself. And then came André! That conversation, she decided, would come at a later date. She needed time to think. Jasper was the ground-breaker. André would be the dirt atop her casket once she told Lucian.

"I am most aware of what that bastard did to you. Serina, listen to me—you are not what that creature made you feel. Without our love, he had nothing to work with. That is why he must be stopped. There will be no third party in our bed, unless we invite them."

Serina snapped her head up at Lucian. "Who—what?"

"That piqued your interest!"

"I'm willing to try anything with you once." Serina mustered up a smile for him. "How did you know what he did to me?"

"You've already accused me of sneaking into your mind just now, need I say more?"

Serina sighed, and nodded her head no. "Lucian, what do we do about Jonah? Do we trust him? Do we bring him home with us? We'll end up looking like a band of merry misfits. One witch, one—possibly two werewolves, a sun-worshiping vampire, and three scruffy mortals. It's the stuff Geoffrey Chaucer would have killed to write about." Serina sent her hands back into her hair making it even more of a tangled nest.

Lucian grabbed her hand and steadied her as only he knew how. He brought her hand up to his lips and kissed each knuckle gently. As he slid his tongue over each scrape, the saliva acted as a soothing agent, healing her.

Dazzled, Serina watched him. How did he learn these things so fast? Did all vampires have the ability to heal, besides the viler one, to destroy? A little flustered, she tried to shake her hand free, but somebody had them in his mouth sucking on them. "Lucian, stop."

"What?" he sheepishly asked, one finger still between his lips.

She gave him a slight shrug of shoulders and tried again to yank her hand free. "Jonah, what to do with him?"

"I was enjoying that."

"Yes, well so was I, but I cannot concentrate when your lips are on me."

"We'll bring him home with us. It'll give Duncan something to do while André and I are gone. And as long as he doesn't turn rabid, it'll give you and Raven some extra security at home."

"He'll drive Duncan mad. 'Tis cruelty. How can you be so forgiving of Jonah?"

"Because I also read his mind. He's an absolute mess. He needs us more than we need him. Being around you, Raven and Payton may help him. Also, if Payton does turn in three weeks? Never mind, I can't think that far ahead. Serina, we won't have all the answers this day, but for now rest."

"Will you be there when I wake?" She cuddled in closer.

"You've my word." Lucian kissed Serina one more time before she relaxed enough to close her eyes. With Serina tucked in his arms, he relaxed as well.

For now, she was safe.

Chapter Seventeen

With leaps and bounds, Payton approached Lucian throwing caution to the wind. Duncan kept his distance.

"So much for my surprise, Ands." Lucian feigned disappointment.

Palms to the sky, André asked, "Have you ever known me to keep a secret?"

Payton scratched at his whiskers. "I'm not certain whether you're a ghost or a true miracle."

"That makes two of us, Payton. Glad to see you're well."

"As well as can be." Payton shrugged his shoulders. "Do you want blood or tea or me?"

Lucian almost fell over with laughter. "I'll have your blood later," he answered. "I asked Raven the exact same thing after she was attacked." He noticed Duncan standoffish and quiet. In a calm tone, Lucian told him, "Duncan, I'm fine. I have not turned into what you witnessed that evening in the carriage. I've got some ambiguous issues that I need to address, but you and I are fine. My solemn word, I won't hurt anyone."

Duncan placed his hand on top of Lucian's then choked out, "Bloody right!" He managed to flash him a brilliant smile, but it faded fast when he realized what he'd said. "I'm sorry. I didn't mean to bring up that word. Luce, are you truly one of them?"

"Duncan, like I said, I've got a few things to resolve." He smiled for everyone showing off his new set of choppers.

Duncan stepped back and turned fast. He

suggested, "Let's get out of these woods for now, and we'll talk once we arrive home."

****

"André reserved two coaches for the ride home. Lucian and Serina have a private coach and the rest of us get to squeeze into the other one. Should be most pleasant," Duncan grumbled. He gave Jonah a venomous glare. "I don't understand why he's coming with us. I just don't understand why we would invite the devil's advocate into our home."

"Play nice, boys," Lucian shouted over his shoulder as he carried Serina over the threshold to their cabin. Lucian regretted leaving them with the issues they had concerning Jonah, but he was quickly persuaded to let them figure out how to deal with each other when he felt his wife's lips attached to his neck.

Lucian tossed Serina onto the tiny mattress and watched her bounce. He plunked down beside her, and that sent her body back into the air from his weight landing on the bed. Once settled his mood changed to somber. "Serina, do we start over? I'm so worried what our future holds. What happens if this is permanent? Or what happens if I drop dead tonight? Or if I go ballistic and kill all of you from bloodlust or something." He stared into her eyes in hopes she'd have all his answers.

"Not start over, m'lord." Serina stroked his curls from his face, tucking them behind his ear. "Just pick up where we left off before our lives were so rudely interrupted." Serina placed Lucian's hand against her heart. "If this situation is permanent then we have time on our side to figure out how to live with it. And I'd worry more about me going ballistic and killing people. You missed my little temper tantrums between Jasper and Jonah, and then again when I saw André." As Serina spoke, the color literally drained from his face. "You look wearied. What can I do for you?" In a seductive manner, Serina undid the buttons on her new sweater, edging it open to expose the part her breast where he'd left his mark. She gave him her sultriest smile. "Anything at all?" She brushed her fingers across her bosom drawing his attention to her soft curves.

"Wicked little witch!" Unable to resist, he bent over, and kissed her breast over the exact site he'd bitten previously. Quick little flicks of his tongue brought hot, wanton sensations traipsing through her body. "I can't do this to you again so soon, Serina. I just bit you last night. I know I need more, but I won't endanger you. There's no way of telling what the outcome will be if I take your blood. You may end up tied to me for centuries."

Serina lifted her ring finger into view. "Marriage ring any bells, luv? Lucian, I gave you more the night you were attacked, along with Raven, and I fared well."

"Yes, Doctor, I do remember. You passed out in my lap that night and threw up all over me the next morning. Quite the first impression."

Serina wrinkled her nose at that. "It was sort of like a dog marking her territory."

"Serina, can you see me going about town biting poor, innocent, unsuspecting people, or better yet, asking them if they wouldn't mind donating for a worthy cause, with me standing there looking like some deject that escaped Charitable Guy's Asylum? What am I going to do? I'm not vampire material. I don't even make your cross flare. I can see it now, I'll be the last vampire picked for all the blood games, not scary enough, not mean enough, not dead enough, too much bronzed to perfection skin tone."

"Vampire vanity has arrived."

Lucian buried his face in Serina's chest and lay motionless while he listened to the ebb and flow of her pulse. This was pushing the envelope. "The thought of tasting anyone's blood other than yours revolts me. I feel like a giant mosquito." He was serious, but he was laughing.

"Lucian, what am I going to do with you?" Serina kissed the top of his head, and then worked her way down his face to his eyelids, then the tip of his nose. "You know André and Raven would give you whatever you want or need without asking. So would Duncan. You've got four willing donors at your beck and call. We can all take turns and then there will be no endangering any of us. Now, do as I say and bite me you big bug before I swat you away." Serina kissed him. "I don't want to sound desperate, but what you made me feel last night overwhelmed me. I'm more than willing to be your sole donor. You said you'd never make me ask." She pulled his head up and looked him straight in his lost eyes, then kissed him as gently as she could, knowing he treaded thin ice. He was not a vicious killer and even turning into a vampire wouldn't change that. "I believe you hold the key to our future. To bite...or not to bite...that is the question." Serina slid the rest of the shirt off her shoulders, leaving herself bare for her husband to admire, to fondle, to tease and have his way with, if only...

Lucian leaned back, a small curve perched on the corner of his lips. Seemed the flirting worked. The teeth lengthened and without further ado, he dipped his head back to her invitation. His fangs disappeared deep beneath her flesh.

Intense pleasure pervaded her. Warm tremors tickled her insides educing urgent demands from her body, lower, right between the thighs. She lay beside Lucian joined, the connection and bond between them growing stronger with every drop of her blood he took. She closed her eyes in the midst of pure ecstasy and one hell of an orgasm, as he ravaged her.

"Ugh! More, Lucian. Whew! Take your trousers—"

Lucian jammed his fingers into her mouth in hopes this would keep her voice busy, but it was not meant to be.

"Ooh! Sweet!" she hollered. Her nails dug deep in his arms, holding him for her anchor. "I wish I could suck on you this way."

So did he!

On the verge of abandonment, he voraciously drank Serina's life essence. He hung onto her body as her excitement mounted again and her eyes rolled back into her head. The only thing that snapped him back to reality was the loud pounding on their cabin wall from their boys next door.

"Lucian, Serina, knock it off. These walls are paper thin!" André yelled, choking with laughter. "Luce, you've a queue waiting for their turn after you're finished with Serina, although none of us can hit the high pitch she just did, well maybe Duncan can."

Duncan slugged André.

"Ouch, old man! You hit like a girl."

Duncan slugged him a second time. André laughed harder. "A little girl."

Lucian lifted his chin and kissed her breast where he'd bitten her to stop the bleeding. He was totally in awe of his newfound powers and that he was able to coagulate the blood flow. "Aren't I just a little walking science project? Wonder if 'tis vampire powers or because I now carry my wife's blood? Hum!" Only the faintest purple trace remained. Aloud he exclaimed, "I like the private tattoo I've marked you with, wife."

A few crackling noises were followed by his fangs retracting. That one sound he could do without as it reverberated inside his head. It reminded him of a tooth extraction. "Serina? You're awfully quiet. Are you all right?" Lucian cradled her head in his arm, and with the back of his fingers stroked her cheeks.

"Oh indeed, m'lord." Serina's words slurred as if she had a mouth of marbles. "Could you make love to me, Lucian."

"No, not now!" That came from someone in the cabin next to them.

Lucian laughed, both from embarrassment and frustration. Serina never noticed and kept talking.

"This feeling within me is overwhelming. I'm not sure what you just did to me, but whew, don't stop!" She tried to raise her hand and run her fingers through her hair, but her fingers got tangled in her mane. "I seem to be stuck." She giggled as Lucian set her free.

"Little one, this one time I can't. I love you, but I'm not up for the occasion..."

"Awe, too bad," came from someone who Lucian would have bet the farm was Duncan.

Lucian laughed even more knowing his entire life was being monitored. He played it just a bit, and raised his voice. "Let me rephrase that, Serina, I am definitely up for the occasion." More grumbling seeped through the walls from the boys next door. In a serious tone, he lowered his voice. "My control is in serious jeopardy now. I could hurt you. And then there is the issue of all the extra ears." Lucian inclined his head toward the wall behind him. "In a few days we'll do this again when we can have some privacy, but for now let me just hold you until you fall asleep. Drink some water. I was a tad bit greedy, and you'll most likely feel it when you try to walk. My apologies."

Languorous, Serina reached up and kissed Lucian, and with a gentle whisper in his ear, told him, "I'm holding you to your word." It took more effort than she had realized and her head thumped backward into Lucian's waiting arms.

Lucian shook her once. "Little one, wake up. Come on. Please don't tell me I hurt you." Fear spiked when she didn't stir. "Oh Christ, Serina— wake up!" He shook her again, tapped her cheeks, shook her once more and then panicked as he tried to figure out a way to get her to come around. He silently prayed he hadn't done to her, what Jasper did to him—bleed him to death. His mind went back in time to a book he'd read when he was but a child, *La Belle au Bois Dormant* (Sleeping Beauty), by Charles Perrault.

Kiss her Lucian, a small voice screamed. "It can't possibly be that simple," he whispered. "Can it?" *Kiss her and save her.* And so he did because he didn't have any other tricks up his sleeve. When her lips met his in a passion-filled, hungry kiss, he burst into tears. He proclaimed, "I must really be Prince Charming." He watched Serina eye him oddly, and he laughed more. "I am going to go get some food and more water for you. Do not attempt to leave the cabin, fair enough?"

"Fair enough. Lucian, I can't even lift my head. What just happened?"

"You passed out on me again. I won't be long." About to walk out the sensation of being smothered in maggots squirmed up his spine. Someone had to have boarded the train with them at the last stop, and that new someone was not so friendly, nor alive. *André how is everyone?*

Payton and Duncan finally fell asleep after you two quieted down. André snickered. *Jonah has the appearance of a caged rat. He's a barrel of laughs. Why?*

Have you spoken with him? Has he said anything?

He started getting restless when you and your

wife...

I get the point. Do you think a walk would do him some good? Would you sit with Serina while we go?

What's going on, Luce?

I think something's on the train with us. Maybe Jonah feels it too.

****

"Jonah?" André nudged him with his elbow.

Jonah jumped as if he'd had a bucket of ice dumped down his back.

"Sorry," André added.

"What?" Jonah faced André.

"Lucian wants you to take a walk with him. You up for it? Stretch your legs a bit?"

Jonah gave him his full attention. With his hands on his knees, he bent forward and asked, "Why? Is he going to throw me off the train?" Jonah actually tried to smile, but his face twitched instead. "André, I know you've no reason to trust me, or believe me, but you must listen to me now. Something dead just boarded this train. I can feel it all over me, like bugs crawling all over my body with little pinchers digging into me. Trust me, I know the feeling." The attacks of the beetles on the mountain were going to stay with Jonah for a long while to come.

"Thank you for painting such a clear, unforgettable picture, really." Andre rubbed his legs and arms.

"It's not Jasper. I'd feel it if it were, and so would Serina and your brother, but it is dead, and it travels with a sentinel."

André's interest piqued. "How do you know this?"

"Animals can sense things humans can't. With the mix of both bloods, I don't miss much. André move, I'm not feeling so well." Jonah doubled over.

Upon entering the cabin, Lucian gave a wink to André when he saw Duncan sprawled across Payton crushing him into the window. Lucian commented, "There is a sight for sore eyes. Can Payton breathe?" Concern crept in when he noticed Jonah. "What's going on?"

Jonah answered, "I'm good. Just a stomach grumble. Lucian, we've got company on the train, but I guess you already know. Am I right?"

Lucian nodded. "Yes. Do you want to walk with me?"

"Let's go." On his feet, his stomach cramped like a woman's in full-blown labor, and he bolted through the door. After a few tumultuous heaves, a soured puddle of vomit covered the floor and stunk up the hall. "Sorry." Jonah apologized as he stepped over the mess and continued on his way.

André stepped over the puddle and said, "Mind the muck. I'll go keep your wife out of trouble, Luce, but hurry back. She's more than a handful."

Lucian immediately thought, you would know, but said naught, piercing his tongue with his newfangled incisors. Now was not the time to bring up such matters. Then Lucian wondered, would there ever be a right time to bring up his brother almost getting full carnal knowledge of his wife, enthralled or not!

Lucian and Jonah swayed with the train's jerky movements down the aisle in single file. The setting sun cast dusky shadows on people. Some of the passengers slept, while others chatted quietly between themselves. A few children sprinted up and down the aisles without care that they might disturb someone else. Oblivious to the children's antics, their parents were probably happy to be rid of them for a short respite. Lucian briefly thought about showing the little wildebeests his not-so-funny fangs and watch them run screaming back to their seats, but then decided it was best to behave. Sometimes he found being an adult absolutely no fun.

Outside the baggage car Jonah whispered, "It is in here, Lucian. Do you see anyone you recognize or looks abnormal, anxious, or panting like a dog in the dead of summer?"

"You sure you're not describing me?" Lucian flashed Jonah a quick smile. That's how Lucian dealt with stress, humor first, and then if that didn't work, then he'd get serious, or as serious as he could muster.

No deranged, psychotic serial killer jumped up to greet them or chuck them from the train. A few women actually flirted as they passed by, finding them remarkably attractive. Lucian enjoyed his new ability to read everyone's mind. Before the attack, he was limited to his siblings and Serina's mind. Now the world was his playground. So far, other than the *whole-have-to-have-blood-or-die-diet*, Lucian found his new lease on life interesting.

Getting the uncomfortable feeling of eyes burning a hole in him, Lucian's gaze was drawn to a man sitting next to the window in the last row of seats, watching him and Jonah with a menaced glare. The man was huge—Sumo wrestler huge.

"I think we're at the wrong end of the train for food and beverages," Jonah said with a slight tilt to his head in the direction of the man at the window.

"It appears so. Want some air? I believe the caboose is through that last door."

Once inside the pitch-black car, Lucian bumped into Jonah then grabbed the door and held it to allow light to filter in. At a first glance the room looked like one giant booby-trap. Open boxes overflowed with baubles and beads. Trinkets of every size, shape and color threatened to spill out. Rolled carpets leaned against the walls at impossible angles. One wrong touch and they'd tumble like giant dominos. Suitcases were stacked uneven one atop another against the walls and there even sat a crate carrying two pigs, which began squealing when they realized they had company. Then, Lucian saw their treasure, tucked neatly into the corner, a black tin casket, with more suitcases strewn across it and a two seated tandem bike, both wheels flat, parked up against the side. Lucian's heart picked up its pace.

"What if it's just really a dead person, Jonah?" Lucian couldn't peel his eyes off the casket. "Damn, I don't want to sleep in one of them. Do you have your silver cross on?"

Jonah threw Lucian an unhealthy glare. "I don't do silver anymore, Lucian. Remember, the whole werewolf-silver scenario? How 'bout you? You got your cross on? Oh, I'm sorry, you can't wear a cross anymore, can you?" Jonah actually laughed at his snide remark. Then, remorse settled in. *What the hell is wrong with me? The man has taken me in, given me shelter and food even after all the events of the mountain.* Against all odds, Lucian showed he was a true gentleman, and Jonah was being a giant ass.

Lucian pulled his cross out from under his shirt and gave Jonah an empty smile.

"That's impossible, Lucian. How?" No vampire he'd ever met had ever been able to wear a cross.

"Sorry, Jonah, you've had a few more years of practice at this way of life. Should we open the casket, or one of us stay here and keep an eye on it tonight?"

Jonah's voice came out thick with sarcasm then. "And do I get to guess who's going to babysit the box? I'm not back here for the night, Lucian. Send me some relief in an hour or so. I'm not the big bad wolf you all think."

With that and remembering the tragic events on

the mountain before he passed on, Lucian's blood boiled. "I beg to differ. I know you saved Serina from Jasper and for that I'm grateful. I understand Jasper had you by the cockles, but you dealt with him in the first place. Correct me if I'm wrong, you made a deal with the devil, and now your payments are due." Lucian's temper continued to escalate. He backed Jonah into the suitcases. "And one more thing, wolf, as long as I'm breathing, stay the hell away from my wife. Don't you ever think of taking advantage of her, ever again! Touch her and I'll rip your throat out. It'll make what Jasper did to me look like he was toothless." Lucian waited for some reaction or response, but none came. "I'll send Duncan back in an hour to relieve you." Lucian squared his shoulders, turned and left. He didn't know he could harbor such contempt or empathy for the man at the same time, but he knew he was right concerning his wife. Jonah would die a thousand deaths by his hands if he touched Serina.

When Lucian reached the boys' car, he woke Duncan and Payton and asked them to join him with Serina. Both Payton and Duncan exchanged a tired, aggravated glance.

****

With only the sound of his heart slamming into his ribs to keep him company and darkness breathing down his neck, Jonah hugged his knees to his chest. If he'd shifted, he was certain his tail would be tucked between his legs from fear. What had happened between Lucian and him? For a fleeting moment he thought they'd all end up friends. *You're a nutter, Jonah.* Everything Lucian said held truth and the truth hurt. So lost in his thoughts, he didn't see the casket start to open with skeletal-like bony fingers prying their way out from under the lid.

****

"Duncan, will you go back and relieve Jonah? He's in the very last car. We're keeping an eye on a box."

Duncan shifted a brow towards Lucian. "What kind of box, Luce? A small box?" Duncan spread his hands out about six inches apart. "Or a big box?" Again, Duncan spread his arms out a tad wider, apprehension covering his face. "What's in the box, Luce? Or don't I want to know?"

"Don't ask questions you really don't want the answers to." Lucian never broke a smile.

"All right, I'm asking, against my better judgment. What do you believe is in the box? Should I be worried?"

"Yes, old man. There is a casket on the train accompanied by some man that is very big, ridiculously big." Lucian spread his arms out very wide and attempted to smile. "He's in the second to last car, and I believe he is a sentinel. The casket is in the last car." Lucian paced the tiny room talking to everyone and no one in particular, explaining what he and Jonah saw. Attempting to sit down he found no empty seat, so he grabbed Serina, swung her in the air and pulled her onto his lap. He wrapped his arms around her waist, and held her against him. With his face buried in the crook of her neck he whispered, "You feeling better, my wild rose?"

Serina gave him an affirmative nod.

Duncan commented, "You didn't call us over to watch you two, did you?"

Lucian ignored him and purposely continued to kiss Serina.

Don't start something with me you can't finish now, dear husband.

What's between us, m'lady, will never be finished. Lucian closed his eyes just for a second, his head resting on Serina's. She was his anchor. She was the one and only reason his heart beat. She gave them a second chance at love and a life together, and he was never going to let her down again. Peeking around his wife, he suggested, "Ands, maybe you could go with Duncan. Check on Jonah. We don't need him growing fur on us now."

"And we don't need you looking like a saber tooth tiger either, Luce." André slapped his brother's arm trying to lighten his mood.

Lucian snapped his teeth at him. "You want to feel what my wife felt? I'd be more than happy to rip a—never mind."

"Some other night, Luce, when I'm totally pissed and have given up on all women, then, you tall, dark, drink of a man, maybe I'll let you sink your tiny, little, teeth into me." André laughed so hard he fell off the seat. "Come on Duncan, help me up and let's go check on your new best friend."

Duncan walked out alone.

Chapter Eighteen

"Do you see Jonah?" André asked feeling his way around in the dark.

"No time for puzzles, boys," Jonah whispered. He may as well have been invisible because neither man could see him even though he could see them perfectly. "We're not alone, and we've trouble."

André spun to find where the voice originated from, and he slammed into Duncan.

"Jonah, where are you? Who's here with us? Do either of you have a match?" Duncan asked.

"No! Don't light it." Desperation filled Jonah's voice. "I don't want it to touch me again."

"Again?" André reached blindly and gripped an arm, hoping it was Jonah's. "Jonah, what happened?"

"It brushed up against me, and I felt a thousand snakes biting me. Then it hissed, just as a snake would, only meaner, I'm sure of it."

"Oh, Christ, no more nasty things," André muttered.

She watched them fumble, trip over bags and each other, a malicious curl to her lips. Her indefectible night vision kept her alive; it was where she lived. She sat perched on top of her polished black box waiting for the precise moment to strike. After a few awkward minutes and her inability to control her impulsiveness she spoke.

"Hello, André. 'Tis been years since I've heard your angelic voice. I thought I might go mad from missing you, but what fate we have, you and I, to end up here together again on this train."

André could not breathe. Funny thing, he never really thought too much about air until there was none. Now, he missed it—miserably. He was certain fingers choked the very life from him, even though no one touched him. He was positive his chest had just been ripped open and his heart torn out—still beating. This was the part of the stories he despised as a small child, where the monster came to get him, and twenty-four years later, that damned beast still plagued him.

The voice could not be the person he knew it belonged to. She'd been long gone from this world. His mouth went bone dry. A week prior...hearing her voice, he would have welcomed her with open arms. Things had changed! After the past week's unveilings he wanted the woman as far away from him as possible and yet now here she was, somewhere in the room with him, speaking to him as if it was yesterday.

Duncan corralled André and Jonah and backtracked to the car door. About one foot away from freedom, the door opened in and a very large male shoved through the opening, hogging any trace of light that may have filtered in from his presence alone.

"Good evening, my Princess. I see we have company. Splendid."

André mouthed, "Princess," to a blackened room.

The large man's delicate voice sang like a soprano's, soft, feminine. The body was anything but. He resembled a bull, castrated, and full of ire. With a light clap of his hands, he smiled, displaying an empty toothless grin.

"I don't know about you," Jonah yelled, "but we need to get out of here. She's got fangs, this one. Big healthy ones. And he's flippin' toothless."

"Silence, little mutt. André, how is it you travel with this sorry excuse of a werewolf, and Duncan?

Let me guess, son, where there's Duncan, his little lamb Lucian's sure to follow. Didn't we slaughter him? Am I right?"

"Who are you, lady?" Jonah snapped. "Let me try again boys, we need to get out of here, now!"

"André, why is it you do not speak to me, my love? Has it been so long that you've lost your manners? Introduce me to your mangy little pet. I might be wanting one of my own some day. I'd like very much to teach him a new trick or two—roll over...play dead." Chyna St. James hissed through her teeth looking directly at Jonah. "I can smell your fear, mutt."

Jonah countered, "Trust me lady, I smell like bloomin' roses compared to you."

"He's not a mutt, Mother. Or at least that's who I thought you were." André added, "Jonah, meet my mother, or my Aunt Chyna or whatever the hell you are or were." He turned in Duncan's direction, his facial expression plagued with that *oh-my-God-what-the-hell-just-happened-and-how-do-we-remedy-it* look. "Duncan, I'm positive you need no introductions." André tried to place where the voices came from, while waves of bile sloshed around inside his stomach making his disposition all the more miserable.

Luce, help! Chyna is on the train and not quite dead, but dead all the same, if you understand me. Sadly, you two seem to have some common ground now.

I'm on my way. André, are you all right? Where is everyone?

Define all right.

Things were not well in the rear of the train.

Lucian looked at Serina and that look said more than words ever could have. "Stay put. I will be back. Let no one through that door other than those who boarded the train with us. Understood? Get your crosses out. I love you." Lucian bent down and kissed her hard then went out the door in a blur.

Reading Lucian's mind as well as Jonah's, Serina explained to Payton what had happened.

"Have a look-see at this, Serina." Payton pulled his and André's packs from the overhead compartment and displayed a small arsenal, silver knives, a gun loaded with silver bullets, a gun that launched wooden stakes, a hammer, a crossbow and garlic. Lots of garlic.

Serina hugged him. "Where were you on my honeymoon? Where did the crossbow come from, Payton?"

"Don't look at me, Serina. I'm just the cook, remember? I brought my knives and garlic. Figured if we never got us a vamp, we'd at least eat. Garlic goes with anything."

Payton's amber eyes lit up his face and lightened Serina's mood.

"André brought the crossbow. Said he's used it on many occasions. My personal favorite is the gun that shoots stakes. It's like a spear gun for whales, except much smaller." Payton scratched his head. "What happens next?"

"You ever make bat stew?" Serina raised her brows to him.

****

"Who is the oaf you travel with?" André asked.

"You need to show some respect to your mummy, André," Chyna chided. She waved her arms in circles and levitated off the floor, floating over André, hoping to show off her talents, but when she realized her efforts were wasted in the dark she laughed.

An ungodly shriek echoed in the compact room. André and Duncan covered their ears. Jonah howled himself hoarse.

"Do I need to show you that I command respect

now?"

"You're not my mother and respect is earned. And when did you start using your title, princess? Little late for formalities isn't it? Why did you lie to us all these years? What did you possibly have to gain?"

"You, son."

"Stop calling me your son," André pounded his fist into the wall.

"Your mother was weak. You were special to me. I could not have children and when your Mum sired three, things worked swimmingly to my vantage. Our dear Queen ran about telling everyone I used a potion, of all things, to get what was rightfully mine. She sounded truly insane. She did however, tell your mum she could have me head if she'd liked, but your mum was such a soft-heart, she neither believed her sister or wanted me dead. Pity the feeling wasn't mutual."

André listened to the woman who raised him, whom he once loved as a mother and understood that he had to come to terms his entire life had been based on a lie and that this frail creature was well past her due date and rotted.

"Mo—Chyna, you just admitted to killing Lorelei and Christian. How could you?" André felt Duncan throw his arm around his shoulder for support. Or at least, he really hoped it was Duncan's.

"No, I did not. Did I?" Her sentinel shook his head no.

"Chyna, where have you been all these years?" His attempt to come off chipper sounded lame, and Duncan cursed under his breath. Chyna was the one and only St. James' family member he didn't fancy before she disappeared. Nothing had changed over the years as far as he was concerned. "Would someone please light a lantern? 'Tis been far too long since we've seen you." Tongue in cheek took on a new meaning for him as he tried very hard not to insult or upset the delusional vamp who still believed she could sit upon the throne one day.

"You were too young to remember what happened the last day I was with you, but since you're here, I'll tell. Lorelei and I had a nasty parting of the ways. She informed me she was going to have the Queen lock me up for—" Chyna paused and picked at the dead skin from her chafed lips.

As easily as snapping her fingers together, she lit the lantern and then everyone became visible, like it or not. She laughed at their shocked faces. "I believe she used the phrase, 'Until hell freezes over.' I remember being in the Queen's garden and receiving an offer from a very radiant, young woman telling me she could make all my dreams come true. All she wanted in return was one kiss. Sounded fair. Pity she didn't bother telling me it would be the kiss of death."

"Her name," André demanded.

Chyna smirked. "Her surname came from some sort of cow. And as my recollection tells me, she looked like one too."

Duncan and André exchanged a knowing glance.

"Contessa?" André said under his breath. "How?"

Duncan shrugged his shoulders.

"Anyway, your dear mother won that battle, but I won the war. How do I look, André?" She stood directly in front of him and gave a quick spin around.

Holding up the wall with nowhere else to turn, Duncan answered for his mate.

"Better than he does at the moment. This may be the one and only time I say this but Contessa has you beat." Duncan noted André had gone whiter than a sheet of virgin paper.

Duncan studied the one woman whose havoc

seemed to follow her better than a shadow. Chyna's glazed-over and emotionless eyes resembled those of a fish packed in ice at the market. Her orange-crepe cloak with its high collar, once her favorite, was now filthy and tattered. No amount of lye could bring it back. The pristine white gown she wore to her sister's coronation now held stains of red and brown—from what, Duncan didn't want to venture a guess.

But, the icing on the cake was the diamond and ruby tiara that topped her head. The prongs poked into her scalp to steady it. She'd worn it many times dancing around the manor, not a care in the world. Now, patchy wiry strands of dull brown and grey hair poked through the crown like antennas on a bug. Duncan rubbed his eyes. What he thought he saw and what he actually saw had to be two different things. It just had to. Open sores spread across bald patches, maggots and larvae residing within. Duncan spun fast and vomited on the strange man's feet. He offered no apology after wiping his mouth on the man's sleeve.

"Someone please turn the lantern off," Jonah moaned as he turned away from everyone holding his stomach. He too heaved into the contents of one of the open boxes filled with trinkets.

"Some lucky bloke is going to get more than they bargained for once home," André added.

Duncan grinned at the odd man about ready to come after him. "So tell us, Chyna, who is your sentinel or should I say companion…"

André cut Duncan off, "I liked oaf better."

Duncan wanted to hug André for attempting to make him laugh.

"Boys meet Phillip, my companion. Phillip has been neutered by me," she announced. Her smile reeked of pride for a job well done. "I'm rather proficient at the surgery and require all my men nipped and tucked."

André shot a glance to Duncan who in turn looked at Jonah and just as fast offered, "Him. Castrate him if you must." A low steady growl at his back, Duncan was happy he'd hit a nerve. The werewolf he could do without.

"Phillip is indispensable to me, so I suggest you not try anything stupid. Duncan, darling, didn't anyone ever tell you it's not polite to stare? Especially at those superior to you? You never were too bright." Chyna turned her full attention to the man and walked within inches of him. "Or do you think you're stronger willed than I? Care for a challenge?"

Duncan stepped forward.

André grabbed his arm. "Old man, don't prove her right!" Knowing or at the very least hoping she wouldn't harm him, André sought Chyna's attention. "Chyna, please—" André found if he concentrated on just his breathing he could speak and think clearly. He was able to do two things at once. Joy all but bubbled from him. "It's just such a shock seeing you after all these years. You can't imagine what I thought thinking my mother dead and then being raised by my aunt, who was indeed my real mother and now seeing you again—it's such a shock." Albeit a repulsive one.

"Yes, my love. I do know how you feel. I'm sorry Mummy scared you."

Chyna's voice made André want to vomit.

Jonah did just that for him.

"I would never hurt you, André."

Seeing her arm coming straight at him, André sidestepped her attempt at contact.

"Naughty boy." Chyna made some little tsk, tsk noises, as she waved her index finger back and forth in his face. Her hand moved so fast no one saw her grab him. Chyna wrangled him into a choke-hold and held him at an angle that left his neck unprotected. He fought, but even with her demure stature, she wielded inhuman strength. "I think I'm in need of some new company in my travels, Phillip. I'll be keeping my son with me."

Ridicule coated Duncan's tongue. "What was that saying Lorelei used on you? When hell freezes over. I believe that was it."

Duncan grabbed for André just as the train screeched and lurched forward and then jerked backwards. Everything in the car went airborne, people, boxes, baggage, the pigs, tiny vomit-covered trinkets, all spilling over and everyone landing into a big displaced pile.

Lucian blasted through the door, his grip tight on the handle so he didn't end up in the mix. He reached out, grabbed Duncan's arm and yanked him backwards.

Jonah tripped over the loose beads and went into a nose-dive. Lucian crouched and latched onto the back of his shirt and pulled him to his feet.

Phillip fell on André, who had Chyna flattened beneath him. An avalanche of suitcases dropped atop the three of them and broke open.

Endless squealing alerted everyone that the pigs weren't thrilled with their topsy-turvy environment either.

"Phillip, make some bacon for yourself and put an end to their misery and ours," Chyna screamed, her timbre no better than the swine. "And both of you get the hell off me."

Lucian waved his hand at the hulky man and sent him sailing. Phillip somersaulted across the rubble and landed flat on his back. When his forward momentum came to an end, Phillip resembled a turtle stuck on his shell, arms and legs kicking in the air.

"Hello, Auntie. You've looked better. Time has

taken its toll." Lucian simpered, finding he had new hidden strengths he might just have to thank Jasper for.

"Lucian? Damn!" A faint voice came from under a pile of rubble. "Get off me, baby." Chyna shoved at André. Impetuousness getting the better of her, she unleashed her powers and flipped André on Phillip's head. "Can't say it's good to see you either, Lucian," Chyna countered. "What exactly have you been up to, nephew?" She sat up and straightened the eyesore of a cape. "Help me, Phillip. My God, man, show respect. Some day I'll be Queen."

"You, Queen? Have you lost what feeble mind you had? I don't see a vampire ruling England anytime too soon."

Chyna remarked, "Well then, that makes two of us, hey?"

Oh how he loathed the woman for stealing his brother, and ruining their childhood.

Outside the door, chaos claimed the isle of the train. People lay piled atop other passengers they'd never met. There wasn't a child awake that wasn't making full use of his or her vocal cords, crying. Lucian closed the door. "It sounds like Hell's Bells out there, Auntie. They ring for you."

"You've yet to experience the underbelly of the world, Lucian, but soon."

"If creatures such as yourself crawl out from the bowels of such a place, I'll pass."

Chyna ignored Lucian. "I hear you had the pleasure of meeting an associate of mine these past weeks. How is old Jasper? Isn't he just the stuff nightmares are made of? How you sleeping these nights, Luce? Got your own little black box tucked away 'round here somewhere, do you?" Chyna snickered, her arms crossed under what little there be of breasts.

"You are more the stuff nightmares are made

of." Lucian laughed at the very sight of her, thinking she looked like a child riddled with leprosy, digits missing, emaciated to the bone.

Serina, I know I told you to stay put, but now I'm rethinking we need you and Payton and André's bag pronto.

We are on our way. It may take a few minutes. The train conductor's thoroughly upset with whoever pulled the emergency stop cord. You wouldn't have had a hand in that now would you?

Little one, no time to talk. Got a psychotic vamp, a hyperventilating werewolf, a Sumo wrestler and two other men who can't seem to stop digging their hole deeper for themselves.

Are you the psychotic vamp? Serina sent Lucian an image of himself looking quite disheveled running around chasing after her snapping his teeth.

She laughed hysterically until Payton jabbed her side. "Payton, I'm not crazy, I swear. I was just talking to Lucian and..."

"Serina, you're not helping your cause. He's not here and not too many people know you guys can communicate from a distance." Payton gave her a shove toward the other end of the train. "Put one foot in front of the other, Doc."

Lucian replied to Serina, laughing too. *Only where you're concerned. Could you please get down this train aisle as fast as you got down the aisle to marry me?*

Did you say Sumo wrestler?

If you ever show up, I'll give you a formal introduction.

"Auntie, so nice of you to be concerned over my welfare. I sleep just fine in a bed and today I went for a nice hike with family and friends. I'm not the rabid chiropteran you are. Yes, I did meet Jasper. Seems he flew off in a puff of smoke."

"How is that, Lucian?" Chyna snapped. "I don't

believe you. Jasper would not lie. It would cost him dearly."

The tremor in Chyna's voice was music to Lucian's ears. Her face however...He gawked, couldn't tear his gaze away as she pulled an eyelid up with her fingers and pushed and shoved the loose skin harshly into the bony socket, like one does with the last pair of socks they can't quite stuff into the drawer to get it shut. With her occupied, Lucian whispered to Duncan, "Get Jonah, I think you two might want to get out of here while the getting's good. Serina and Payton are on their way."

"I'm not leaving you, Luce. There'll be no further mishaps or disappearances from any of us. All for one, and one for all and all that. Except him." Duncan shot an angry glance towards Jonah. "He can rot here."

"Oh, Duncan. Back up then." Lucian sighed. Testing his new powers he waved his right hand at his aunt in a counterclockwise motion hoping to send her rolling over, but what he got was Phillip rolling over again.

André snapped his head at Lucian with a grin that stretched ear to ear, and quickly got to his feet. *Do that again, only with her.* André inclined his chin towards Chyna.

That's who I was trying for. My aim is off. Both men smirked.

"It's all fun and games until someone gets hurt, boys." At the far end of the car, Chyna began to straighten out her hair, but a clump fell to the floor. She glanced down and dismissed the fallen locks just as quickly as it fell. All of the men in the car with the exception of Phillip turned their heads in repulsion.

Once again, Jonah vomited.

"Jonah? What's going on with you? You're not faring too well here tonight. Is your stomach usually this upset?" André asked. If Jonah continued to retch his insides out, André had an uneasy feeling it could start a chain reaction. His stomach wasn't made of cast iron either.

His head between his legs, Jonah answered, "André, I'm a werewolf. I have eaten live animals in the past, without so much as batting an eye. This is new and most unappreciated. I've been poisoned."

"So it's not Chyna that's bothering you? Oddly, that makes me feel better."

"You two all right back there?" Focused on his aunt, Lucian heard mumbling and didn't need the distraction.

"Jonah's just baptizing everything within his proximity," André answered.

Duncan added his two pence, "Good. Let the miserable turncoat rupture."

Lucian turned and stared at Duncan with disbelief. Serina hadn't exaggerated when she'd said Duncan didn't like Jonah. Lucian moved Jonah and André behind him, and edged them slowly to the door.

From the corner of her eye Chyna glanced at the men and believing they posed no threat, she spun around to face the rear of the car. She weaved her hands at the back wall in a zigzag pattern and as she did flames burst out along the wall. A huge chunk of the wall simply fell away onto the tracks below. She spun back around to see the faces of her guests. Lucian and Duncan gaped at the hole. Jonah and André stood behind the two men peering out over their shoulders.

"Can you do that?" Duncan asked Lucian.

Brows pinched and pouty lips pursed, Lucian answered, "Of course—not!"

"That was nothing, boys. Watch this," Chyna went to wink, but the skin she'd previously jammed into place stuck. Upset, she pointed to Duncan and

Jonah, and levitated both men. With the roll of her finger, she flipped them upside down and careened them into the carpets. The men just missed the hole in the wall.

As Duncan sat up, his left arm crumbled beneath him. It took all of two seconds for shock to set in. He methodically poked at the protruding bones. A small steady giggle leaked from his lips as a warm fluid dripped down his arm and painted the floor red.

An ostrich-sized egg hatched from the front of Jonah's skull. Concussion, Lucian thought. The vomiting would definitely continue.

Any chance you'll be joining us tonight, Miss Serina? My dear Aunt just injured Duncan and Jonah. Duncan's pretty bad. Jonah's napping against his better judgment.

Lucian wasted no more time and moved forward to Duncan to stop the bleeding and wrap his arm, but Chyna was one-step ahead of him.

Lucian bounced off a solid invisible barrier. He pounded his fists in the air hitting something solid, but nothing happened. "This can't possibly be good," he exclaimed.

Serina, how would you get rid of an invisible barrier?

I'd simply picture a door dead center in it and walk through. Payton and I are going to be a bit. I'm sorry. The train conductor and his cronies confiscated our crossbow. We are in the process of negotiations for its swift return. Hold the fort, luv.
Serina showed Lucian what she meant about breaking the barrier, and then she was gone.

"I'm sorry, André, that you had to witness that. But your brother needs to learn a few things around here, like who's actually in charge. And that would indeed be me, your princess, soon-to-be-Queen." Chyna snorted and with a quick snap of each hand tossed her hair behind her back.

Half-paying attention to his aunt, Lucian silently concentrated on Serina's suggestion. Briefly, he closed his eyes and envisioned a giant door to get through to Duncan and Jonah.

With a sharp inhalation, he focused and held his breath. Through pursed lips, Lucian blew hard and directed the force toward the invisible barrier. As the energy intensified a glossy bubble-like barricade burnt bright red as it mixed with oxygen. Lucian blazed a trail as if a charge of gunpowder had been lit, in the outline of a door. He stood there in awe of his work. *Jesus, Serina, this is amazing.*

I knew you could do it. We are going to have some fun if we get out of here alive.

Serina. The true optimist—once more.

I mean when—when we get out of here.

Feeling the train start forward again, Chyna widened her stance for balance and glanced out at the tracks below. A gentle breeze made its way inside the cabin.

Lucian approached his imaginary door and walked through to Duncan.

Lucian, the train conductor gave us back our bow. I had to persuade him it was in his best interest. Don't worry, I played fair. One car to go. See you in a minute.

You said that hours ago.

Payton reached for the door to the car, his palms a sweaty mess. His hand slipped off the handle at his first attempt to open the door. Serina quickly shackled his wrist holding him still.

"Payton, let me just get a feel for the room before we go blasting in there on basically a hope and prayer."

Lucian, we are outside the door. What is happening in there and what do you need?

A miracle.

I'm more like a great magician, not God, luv.

Let him decide that. Come on in and join the party.

A party? I love parties, Lucian. I'm not dressed for such an occasion.

M'lady, unless you're wearing the suit God gave you, you're not dressed correctly period.

Lucian gave Serina a mental picture of what lay on the opposite side of the door to prepare her for what they were walking into.

"Tea party behind door number one, Payton. Get the crossbow out and point it at the first ugly thing you see. Shoot anything with skin hanging off, falling off, sloughing off, not attached, or really huge. You get the picture right?"

"I was just stalling to see how many different synonyms you'd come up with before you shut up." Payton twisted the handle.

Lucian bent to Duncan and placed his fingers over the other man's lips, mouthing the word, "Shush," to him. Grabbing a piece of clothing from someone's suitcase, he wrapped Duncan's arm. Then he reached gently and tapped Jonah on the shoulder.

With a grimace, Jonah opened one eye and checked out at his surroundings, not certain he really wanted to know where he was. He caught sight of Duncan sitting next to him, propped up against the wall, panting like a dog, covered in blood, sweat and tears, his arm in a tourniquet saturated red.

The sight of the other man both frightened and excited him. The fresh scent of blood almost always awakened Jonah's beast. That's all he needed. Time to get the hell away from Duncan. Just as Jonah tried to crawl away, the cavalry arrived.

Chapter Nineteen

The squeak from the door's hinge grabbed Chyna's attention. The over-zealous vamp wrenched her head a full one hundred-eighty degrees around without so much as moving her feet an inch in any direction. Bones cracked and the unnatural sounds filled the car. Chyna stood there with her mouth hung open, her four carried fangs visible. "Lucian you were able to breach the confines I'd set. How?" she asked curious.

Too amazed at what she'd just done to her body, Lucian couldn't answer her. That she turned her head behind her was an implausible anomaly. That she stood in her current constitution bewildered the dickens out of him.

Duncan managed to whispered, "What Lucian did is nothing compared to what you just did. Trust me."

Lucian elbowed him.

"What? Luce, give it up. She one-upped you this time," he spit out.

Chyna gave a small curtsy to Duncan and then sent her sights on Serina and Payton.

Chyna's black eyes were a complete contrast to Payton's new stark-white color when he realized he was the new object of her affections.

Chyna held her finger to the small, blond chef. "Hold that thought, boy. You and I shall sink our teeth into something juicy in just a bit...That would be me doing the sinking and you being the juice." She turned and lunged at Lucian while ordering Phillip, "Get up off your corpulent back you oversized eunuch and help me."

Phillip rolled his eyes, and made no move to jump up and kiss her royal tush.

Lucian sidestepped to Duncan's left allowing Chyna the opportunity to slam head first into the same wall she had shown Duncan and Jonah.

"Turn around is fair play." Lucian laughed until he saw the malice in her black eyes.

Chyna let loose an ungodly cry as she ordered her sentinel to his feet. With no tolerance left for her bodyguard, she held her arms in front of her, and jerked them into the air. Phillip was ripped from the floor much like a marionette being tugged upward and suspended.

"You malicious bitch," Phillip swore, "I've given you my life and you treat me like a puppet."

"Seems the toothless one has a bit of a bite after all." Lucian studied Chyna's movements and what happened when she did. Like some old biddy with swollen ankles, he retained everything.

Just as Phillip's feet hit the floor, the train jolted unexpectedly forward and Phillip took a hard dive, taking André down with him, again.

Crushed beneath four hundred pounds or better, André could barely breathe, certain he'd received a few broken ribs in the fall because pain radiated through his chest. Panic hastened his ability to breathe more so. André did the only thing he could think of at that point and that was scream for help. The lips moved but no sound came forth.

Ands, relax. Inhale slowly. You're easier to read than Braille. Lucian knew André inside out. He had always been just short of fanatical when it came to his cleanliness. Despite everything going wrong, Lucian smiled. It really sunk in that he had a brother and that he was going to watch over him and enjoy him for a long time to come, of course, that was after he kicked the living daylights out of him for touching his wife. First things first! Then he'd enjoy him.

Serina watched with admiration the way Lucian handled his situation. So much on his plate and yet he remained true to himself and a gentleman. She noticed him smiling at his brother and before she knew it...*I love your lips. You are so handsome.* The thought came uncensored. No one needed distractions just yet, but maybe later.

I'm grateful you love my lips. Later, I plan to show you just how well they love you.

André rolled his eyes. Being able to read his brother's thoughts placed him oddly in the middle of what should have been a private moment between husband and wife.

Would you two save it for later? Can you not see me down here dying? André tried a smile but his chest really hurt.

Serina sent her powers to André and scanned his chest. Since she had no blood bond with André, she relayed her thoughts to Lucian.

Lucian, tell André, his ribs are cracked, but his lungs and heart are safe for now, as long as no further damage is done.

'Tis been nice knowing you, Ands. Serina asks if you have any last wishes?

"What?" Both André and Serina asked at the same time.

Lucian laughed. "You'll live to see another day, as long as we get off this train."

Serina turned her attentions to Phillip's wide girth. She needed a way around it, him, to free André. She dug through the larger man's mind in search of his fears. The strongest fear he held was Chyna touching him. Serina could fully sympathize. He loathed Chyna. He hated what she'd done to him, to his life, to his manhood, or lack thereof. He despised being tied to her for an eternal hell.

And who wouldn't, she thought. His second fear was of drowning. The big man would sink, not swim. Again she could sympathize. She couldn't swim either. He'd never been taught to swim, and he thought no one would willingly go in to the water and try to save him, knowing it'd be the last thing they ever did. Not much useful information thus far. Serina gave up because someone that big probably wasn't scared of too much.

What would scare her into running for her life? Easy, bees, spiders or...snakes. With a subtle mind prod, Serina implanted the notion in Phillip's head.

The yellow and black snake slinked across the floor, with red slanted eyes focused on one man. Its forked tongue stabbed into the air searching. The second Phillip realized he had unwanted company in his pants, he pushed off of André, and jumped up shaking his leg, groaning, "Ooh-ah—what in bleeding 'ell?" To no avail, he ran his hands up and down his leg searching for the serpent, desperate to have it gone.

Beads of sweat trailed across his forehead, matted down his thin grey hair, and soaked through his shirt as the cool scales of the reptile slithered towards his groin. "No!" he cried, "help me." The pants dropped to the floor, and Phillip began to flog at what was left of his genitals. The knobby, scarred protrusion bled out and he wailed like an insane man.

Not a one of them lifted a finger.

Once free, André rolled to his side and sucked in his first real breath. It was then that Serina wished the snake gone. Only the after-effects lingered.

Chyna's ireful eye tracked Serina. She snapped her bony fingers and pointed.

After being thrown up against the door, Serina now understood André's take on breathing. She ducked and covered her head when Payton's body headed straight for her.

Payton unraveled himself and then helped Serina up. He blurted out, "Should we take this as a sign and get the hell out of here?"

So intrigued by the events unfolding, she would not have left the car even if the Sorcerer's Squad arrived with an embossed invitation just for her. She felt right at home.

It was then that an epiphany slammed her upside the head. Serina now knew without a doubt why God had bestowed her with the gifts she held, the powers to heal with her mind, not medicines, to see without sight, to hear through the silence, and to feel without her hands, but with her soul. He silently asked for her help.

Bigger question she'd work on later—did she really have to go through all this rigmarole to figure that out?

Watching her sentinel display inept puerility, Chyna cringed. *Giant ass, enough is enough! Why did I tie that wooly mammoth to me and for eternity no less?* A mistake she would have to live with for the rest of her nights. Chyna thrust her arms above her head and reached for the sky. She floated to the ceiling and lay across it, as if she were lying on the floor, but above everyone.

Payton's eyes went wide. He reached for Serina. "Oh bloody 'ell, Doc! Would ya have a look-see at that?"

Chyna's clothing hung as a curtain from her body, giving all on the floor an up close and personal view of what she wore under the dress.

Nothing. And there in lay the problem.

Every one of them looked. Every one of them blinked and rubbed their eyes trying to either focus or forget.

Lucian stared perversely. Taking in the dark secrets of what lay hidden under her filthy dress, revulsion quickly replaced guilt. The images his brain sent him made no sense. Women weren't supposed to look like that. Serina sure as hell didn't.

Lucian. Stop being a deviant.

"Serina, no! Look. She's not normal. I mean really—not normal. It's as if there are two people under that dress she wears. A man and woman. She's got a bloody penis. Oh, thank God mine doesn't look like that!"

Payton and André both said, "Amen to that," at the same time.

Jonah's curiosity got the best of him. He cranked his head upward and felt his jaw drop. This time Jonah didn't vomit. He rolled over and laughed until he cried.

"How?" Lucian's voice carried across the car to his wife.

"Hermaphrodite," Serina answered matter-of-factly.

"A what?"

"She/he is a cross between a man and woman. Some people are born with both sex organs. Probably explains why she had no children."

"Probably?" Lucian gasped.

"You simpletons forget I can hear you? I'm not dead yet."

"I beg to differ," Lucian added.

Chyna's mouth twitched before she answered. "Your wife is correct. That is why I had only André. My poor husband got more than my dowry paid for," Chyna explained. "Poor, poor Jonathan. I wished I'd had a photograph of his face the first and only time he saw me birthday suit."

Her indifference astounded Lucian. It was as if she were detached from her body. Her ambiguousness was the work of a true charlatan, of that he had no doubt.

Serina stop talking to me out loud. No man in

his right mind would touch her yet she married my uncle.

And then your uncle died shortly after the marriage, didn't he?

The marriage was prearranged. Jesus, Serina, maybe his death was too.

Would it surprise you after everything she's done, killing her own husband?

No. Personally, I'd want to be dead too if I had to go home to that nightly.

No worries, luv. I've nothing hiding under my skirt like that. I'm going to cross to you and Duncan.

Her attention on Phillip, Serina slipped past Chyna undetected.

"Hello, lover." Lucian grinned as she closed the distance. "The plan is, you fix Duncan, and I'll fix the broken, battered fixture on the ceiling. Fair enough?"

"Fair enough." Serina ran her fingers across Lucian's jaw in passing. That little caress sent shivers down them both.

Payton remained close to the door. The phrase "scared stiff" painted a poignant picture. He gripped his silver knife as if it were gold, even while his knuckles burned white from tension. He knew he could not hold out much longer without releasing the knife but without it he might as well had been stripped naked, so the burning continued. And the monster cramp that accompanied it helped hold the knife securely in place. In Payton's other hand he held the cross bow tilted toward the ceiling and the creature. This, he had no knowledge of or how to shoot it. If they got off the train alive——

Serina read his mind and interrupted, "When we get off, Payton."

"You're not funny in the least, Doc." Payton discreetly tipped the bow in her direction. "I'm taking lessons when we return."

As he looked up to the woman he had once loved, once called his mother, André mourned her loss. She was no longer his mother, but a lying, conniving she-he vampire. He thought her dead for so many years and looking up at her now, he wished she truly were. Someone had to put her out of her misery.

André attempted to reach Payton, but the man was too busy trying to blend in with the wall. Groping blindly around the floor, he latched onto a shillelagh stick that poked out of the one of the boxes. André tapped the stick on Payton's toes. No response. Those amber eyes were thoroughly transfixed on the vampire watching them. André tapped the shillelagh stick again, harder this time. Payton jumped.

The look André received for making Chyna aware Payton was still in the car and once more a viable target wasn't the friendliest face he'd seen today, but then glancing between his aunt and her oaf, it wasn't that bad. Payton tilted the bow to him, in a menacing manner.

"What?" Payton mouthed to the man wielding the little magical weapon.

"Crossbow." André pointed. "Give me it, don't shoot me. I've a perfect shot at her from this position." André slowly reached out, and grabbed it from Payton.

Movement caught her eye, and Chyna spun around faster than a lightning bolt could ignite the sky. Mid spin another chunk of her scalp, flesh entwined with hairs, flew off her head and landed atop of Jonah's face.

Very carefully, with two outstretched fingers, Jonah grabbed the toupee from hell and flung it back in her general vicinity. Chyna looked at the knotted strands and then back to Jonah, smiled at him as she picked it up and tacked the chunk under the prongs of her tiara. "Ta," she said. The next blink of an eye she screamed, "Phillip, get Lucian. I want him gone from my life once and for all. Now!"

Lucian swung his head around to see where Phillip was, only to find him moving toward him with a gummy grin. Speaking before thinking, he lashed out, "*Hellooo!* Ever hear of dentures? Dr. Fonzi didn't make porcelain teeth for his own good. Toothless ogres are about scary as toothless vampires."

Phillip stopped and blankly stared at Lucian with his head cocked to the side. "Well then," Phillip added, "Let's see what we can do to remedy the situation."

Phillip opened his mouth wide and to Lucian's horror spiked grey teeth popped through his gums at different angles.

"Best be careful what ya wish for, Lord St. James." Phillip finished with his all too feminine tone.

Serina knew from the events unfolding her time with Duncan would be precious little. After cauterizing his arteries and veins, to stop further blood loss, Serina inspected the broken bones. They appeared jagged and would require much more effort and time than what she now had. Bones, she knew from past experiences, were hard, tricky immobile objects, with tendons, ligaments and muscles attached that required two sets of hands to reset them correctly. She could start the repairs to save Duncan's arm but if it weren't set soon, he'd have permanent damage and that was the good news. If it wasn't set in the next few days he wouldn't have to worry about it at all. It'd be on the chopping block.

After securing that Duncan would not bleed to death, she glanced at him. His eyes were both bizarre and beautiful, she didn't know which eye to focus on when she spoke to him.

He shyly winked. "I see you finally noticed me

eyes."

"Hard not to, Duncan. They're exceptionally beautiful and very rare. It's called heterochromia, if you wanted to know. Anyone else in the family have them?"

"Me grandmother and a cousin. I've never met me cousin, only heard of him. Lives in Brahmall with me Grandma. I feel better. I know me arm is still needing work to be done on it, but the pain is diminished," Duncan whispered. "Thank you."

About to interrupt their conversation, Jonah held his tongue and looked at Serina in a whole new light. His comments could come later.

Serina planted a quick kiss on Duncan's cheek and abruptly backed away from him. A familiar, tainted feeling rolled over her and made her stomach knot.

Duncan's mouth dropped. Serina's green eyes were fading to black pools of hatred. "What is it, Doc?"

"I've company boys, most unwanted. I've got an ugly little incubus attempting a visit. What better timing?" she bit out heavy with sarcasm. Then she began to laugh to the point of hysterics.

Hello, Ducky. Playing without me? Awh, I feel so shunned. Jasper's voice inside her head was about as pleasant as being autopsied when you're still quite alive.

"Lucian, help me," Serina begged.

Lucian turned from Phillip and glanced into two black, empty eyes that didn't belong on his beauty. Her teeth chattered as if she were freezing to death. Serina extend her hands to him, pleading for rescue.

Before he could catch her, Serina spiraled face first into the floor, and began to pound her head against the floor's wooden planks. As she lifted her face her nose oozed blood, and shards of broken glass and splinters projected from her eyebrows and cheeks. Her lips were swollen and purple.

Lucian crossed the distance in the blink of an eye, and grabbed her. The assault had to end.

Duncan lent his one good arm to cradle her face from the floor each time she thrust her head down. His arm wouldn't be the only thing she fixed...if she came out of this. His good hand was no longer good.

Serina didn't want Jasper anywhere near her especially in her head. Her only idea was to knock herself out. The last time he got in her head she almost had sex with her brother-in-law. Goddess only knew what could happen this time—so many men in the room and one vulgar vamp. She wasn't about to find out. At least Phillip wasn't a viable candidate! Her optimism hit a plateau.

Chyna watched Serina knock herself senseless and more than amused, she was outright jovial. Chyna undulated her head a second time a quick one-eighty degrees. Finished, she placed her hands on each side of her head and with a slow methodical twist, tried to wrench it back into place, pushing up on one side, tapping down on the other side, tilting it forward just a bit, rocking her skull back and forth until it was level, and she had a straight view. When she could see straight she adjusted her tiara, making sure it was perfect, believing appearances were of the utmost importance.

Mesmerized, Lucian couldn't tear his gaze away. This creature was not for the faint of heart.

Lucian!
Oops.
Do something!
M'lady, how can I aid you? Just as Lucian tried to reach her, Jasper locked down her mind tighter than a bank vault.

"She's busy now, Lucian."

Lucian heard the voice. Everyone heard the voice.

Hearing it, André visibly paled. "Not again," he mumbled.

For the time being, Serina was the center of attention. Even Chyna's interest piqued. "Jasper?"

It, the raspy male voice, sputtered from Serina's lips as if she were trying to spit him out. "You look ravishing, Princess. Lovely to see you."

"Yes, it is, isn't it?" Chyna wrinkled her nose towards Serina. "I thought you weren't fond of being inside women, Jasper?" Chyna snickered alone.

"You are my one exception, my lady."

"Enough!" Lucian yelled. His fangs exploded inside his mouth, and sliced the insides of his cheeks. He spat a large chunk of blood onto Chyna and then watched with disgust as she sucked it from her gown. The overwhelming urge to protect Serina from Jasper was foremost in his thoughts, but how with that bastard in her body?

"Phillip, get Lucian you moron. How many times do I have to tell you?" Chyna roared.

Phillip did a slow calculated turn of his head toward the ceiling. "What would you have me do, my princess?" Chyna pointed towards Serina. Phillip followed her finger.

Serina grunted with each move. Her eyelids now swollen, she struggled to see. Spanning the breadth of the room, and ready to report her findings to Jasper, her gaze fixed on the large blur she claimed as her husband.

"Oh, no!" It was all Lucian said.

Serina cocked her head to one side and lifting her hand to him, she shooed him off. Hurled him sideways into Chyna's casket is what she did.

"You're getting better at making me fly, luv, and look at that, no rhyming this time." Lucian shook off the pain and stood.

In her own voice, Serina screamed, "Lucian, get away from me. He wants you dead."

"So do I, dammit," Chyna yelled. "Phillip, need I repeat myself? Get Lucian or you will pay dearly for your insubordination with me in these matters."

"I have paid dearly. Repeatedly, Princess." Phillip grabbed André and placed him in a strangle hold. Breathing hot and heavy into his ear just for the hell of it, he laughed when André's body shuddered the way a dog does coming in from the rain. "Just give me a reason, lad. The quicker you are all disposed of, the quicker I can get the 'ell out of here."

André dropped the cross bow.

Payton grabbed the weapon and took aim toward the two men. He swallowed a good chunk of fear and shouted, "Hey, Princess, call off the mastodon or I shoot."

"Just shoot the damned thing, Payton," André yelled back. "Don't announce your intent. What happened to the element of surprise?"

Payton shrugged his shoulders. Having never shot a bow before Payton was confident he could indeed hit something as large as the one standing before him holding his friend prisoner. There was of course a slight concern for the welfare of André if he missed.

Looking down the long end of a silver-tipped arrow, André's eyes grew wide. He wasted no time trying get out of the line of fire. He twisted and turned in Phillip's clutch to no avail. The solid oaf had him pinned.

Chyna wailed, "I said Lucian not André you impotent fool."

That high-pitched screech startled Payton, his finger twitched and the silver tipped arrow carved a path through André's shoulder.

Lucian stepped toward André until he saw Payton reloading.

"Payton, no!" Lucian stated in a calm tone. Sure

as hell didn't want to startle the man again.

For Payton, time stood still. He looked upon his wounded friend remorse-filled for what he'd just done to him, but he was now past the point of no return. He had to see this through. "Forgive me, André. Possibly want to back up, Lucian." Payton swung the bow at the vampire hugging the ceiling.

"Try it, little man, and it'll be the last thing you ever do," Phillip mused.

Phillip tightened his grip on André, careful not to catch the edge of the arrow jutting out from his shoulder. Nor did he allow André movement to inspect the wound. He reached around the front of the spear and flicked the end of the arrow back and forth causing a shearing of more flesh. André never made a sound.

Not enjoying the display in the least, somewhere deep in her depraved mind, Chyna still loved André and seeing him in pain triggered some lost emotion to protect him.

"Phillip—hurt my child, and I'll make what's left of your sex life total misery."

"It already is," he squealed. "You've personally seen to that. I believe this is retribution, Princess!"

Payton pointed the bow directly at Chyna's chest. "This nonsense can not continue, you broken tea cup. Your hold over this family ends today." In a flash, he swung the bow around and fired it toward Phillip.

Lucian sprung through the air and slammed into Serina hurling the two of them onto the floor in front of Duncan and Jonah, just in case Payton's aim had not improved.

Shock covered Phillip's face when he realized he was the hit. He dropped André.

Chyna laughed, pointing to the arrow piercing Phillip.

Ducky, this car is too crowded. Let's get a few

people out of here, shall we?

"Lucian, get off me." Serina spat at him. "He's got me. Get away from me." She struggled to free herself, except her demure frame didn't stand a chance against her husband's six-foot-four blanket of muscle.

Lucian pinned her to the floor, stretched her arms high over her head, leaving her to resemble a sacrificed goddess. His goddess and he'd be damned if anyone took her from him. Her small rib cage, her firm, full breasts waited for him like the gold ring on the merry-go-round to reach for, to covet. Oh how he wanted her, even here in the midst of all this chaos. Having no formal training on demons or exorcisms, he did the only thing he knew how. He bent to her mouth and fastened his lips over hers, taking command of her mind, her heart, and her soul as he whispered, over and over in her head, You are my love and my life. Don't leave me. Come back to me.

Unable to withstand the overwhelming emotional bonds between husband and wife, Jasper cowered in retreat. He thought he was hot and bothered when he'd first encountered Serina's wrath on the mountain. It was nothing compared to the two of them joining forces. For the first time in his lonely existence, he had a bittersweet taste on his lips, death.

Chapter Twenty

Olivia followed the trails of thick, black smoke back to the mausoleum in the oldest graveyard in White Chapel. Stupid ignoramus of a vampire might as well have left an ad in the Daily Tribune with a map to his little slice of Hell. The ground's dewy cover would soon be burned off after the sun rose. Olivia bit her nails as she waited. Just a few more minutes and on old Jasper would be getting a little more rest than he planned. Clutching her satchel, Olivia pried open the heavy wooden door and placed a large brick in front to keep it open to allow the twilight in. The stagnant, musky air turned her stomach and made her eyes water. She fumbled her way to the large mahogany casket and placed her equipment beside her feet. Reaching inside another bag, she retrieved a jar of concentrated garlic juice mixed with blessed water and a blunt wooden stake. Olivia wanted Jasper to feel the full weight of her wrath. She took a deep breath knowing once the casket opened the fumes that poured out would be no match to her surroundings. She tapped on the box. "Knock, knock!"

With a slight delay and grumbling coming from under the lid, Jasper's fingers edged their way out.

Jasper peeked out seeing a petite woman with auburn curls spilling down her back. "Olivia Spencer, the pleasure's all mine."

"You say that now."

Jasper laughed.

"It weren't meant in jest." Olivia reached into her pocket.

Jasper went to move his hands in self-defense, but Olivia doused him with the juice. Between his screaming and sizzling Olivia went on a little rant of her own.

"I hear you met my daughter, you demoralized piece of rubbish."

Frantic, Jasper wiped the liquid from his face and neck as he bellowed out threat after threat promising retribution. "You bitch..."

"Shut up, peon." Olivia plunged the stake into and through Jasper's chest, paralyzing him as he attempted to sit up. The last thing she needed to do was chop off his noggin. But that fate would be too swift, too merciful, and Olivia wasn't in a forgiving mood today. No, Olivia decided to make him suffer.

"Jasper, you messed with the wrong witch."

"I thought Serina called the Squad on you. I thought you..."

Olivia twisted the stake, and ground it farther into him. "Tip number one, save the thinking for someone who actually has a brain. Have you ever heard blood is thicker than water? She's my child. I'll do what I see fit for her and no one else. She almost got you. She may be more like her old mum than she realizes. See you in Hell, Jasper."

"You can't leave me like this, I'll die."

"You're already dead, remember?" Olivia reached into a second bag and gingerly pulled out a black rose, its thorns numerous and sharp. "I do believe the prickers on the flower have yours beat." She tucked it down the front of his trousers, slammed the lid shut, picked up her belongings and sealed the crypt. Closing her eyes she whispered, "'Tis the least I can do for you, little girl. I do love you. It's all about consequences." She evanesced with the blowing winds.

****

Lucian broke away from Serina and watched the

earthly green of her eyes replace the bottomless black pits of Jasper's. Duncan's tap to Lucian's back alerted them to turn toward Chyna, finally coming down from her high perch.

With casual ease, Chyna fluffed her orange cape into the air and pussyfooted on over to Phillip. Her grin held malignant intent. She flicked the end of the spear that had already collapsed one of Phillip's lungs back and forth and watched Phillip twist and turn in agony as he tried to escape her taunts. "You've been most disingenuous to me today, Phillip. Maybe this shall help ease my saddened state from the harsh things you've accused me of. Then again, maybe not!"

He backpedaled. She followed. He took another step back. She another forward. Backed against the wall, he'd run out of options.

She'd simply run out of patience. Chyna viciously tugged to bring the arrow out through the same hole it entered.

Phillip's effeminate cries bounced off the interior of the walls. The fool bit his bottom lip until it bled to replace one pain with another.

Chyna crooked her head sideways, and watched with deep enthusiasm as the ruby-red fluid flowed down his chin and dripped onto his shirt. She anticipated each drop, her head bobbing with each droplet that splattered and soaked in to his clothing. The blood distracted her with a deadly enthusiasm.

Without time to blink, her nostrils flared and her fangs filled her mouth. Flesh tore open around her lips as she stretched her jaw to accommodate Phillip's tree trunk of a neck.

Before Phillip had time to react, she was on him, her stained, yellowed posts embedded and sucking him dry.

Fully aware if Chyna drained her body guard, he could come back with an even meaner disposition in life, Payton lunged forward, his silver blade extended. He plunged it deeply through Chyna's left back, aiming for her heart. Through a bone-chilling cry, Chyna released Phillip and turned on Payton, her face a collage of mangled nightmares. Her attempts to get the knife from her back proved futile. Her arms were too short, the blade embedded just out reach, like that annoying little itch dead center in the back that's never quite attainable. Her piteous wails clashed mercilessly with Phillip's.

Looking at the arrow projecting from his shoulder, André quietly stated, "Stick to the knives, Payton. Those, you know how to handle."

Payton gave him half a smirk.

When Phillip staggered toward Chyna, Lucian thrust a force field around his aunt. He watched Phillip pound the wall until his fists came away raw. Phillip picked up the arrow and tried to jab a hole in the barrier. After a display worthy of a warrior's last stand, he dropped to his knees and sobbed.

The aversion playing out between the odd couple was more than Serina could take. She headed to Phillip, uncertain what she would do when she reached him, but something had to stop the grown man from crying inconsolably. Evil or not, the man mourned the loss of someone, even if he loathed her. Even if it made no sense. She knew many times the heart spoke love, the mind of hate and that people were driven insane by both. Here and now, she witnessed it first hand.

"Serina, no. Stop!" Lucian chased her across the car.

Phillip turned and wrapped his bloodied hands around her. He jerked her body from the floor and proceeded toward the hole in the train.

Lucian blocked Phillip before he knew what hit him. With one hand around Phillip's neck, Lucian squeezed the two sides together until they met in the middle unyielding to him.

Phillip took one last shot at Lucian, with a knee to the groin, refusing defeat.

Lucian never flinched. He just wanted Phillip dead.

Duncan attempted to free Serina one-handed, and Jonah added his two pence and managed to vomit on Phillip's feet. For the briefest flash, Duncan found his smile and directed it towards Jonah.

Lack of oxygen or not, Phillip's grip on Serina was solid.

"Release my wife," Lucian screamed inches from his face.

"Over my dead body," the die-hard ogre choked.

"That's a given," Duncan hollered. Then he noticed the shillelagh stick. Duncan grabbed it and swung the wand hard across the back of Phillip's Achilles heel. "Make him kneel and squeal. Seal his fate, turn him in to fish bait." More pitiful wailing followed. Duncan knew the words were rolling off his lips, but he wasn't in control of them. He glanced at Serina, her lips moving in a fevered state. He looked directly at her and said, "I will not ask how you managed that. Ever!"

André added his two pence, "You told me there was no such thing as magic wands, Serina."

Busy trying to save herself, she didn't respond.

With the train back to full speed, the rocking and swaying motion gave Lucian and Phillip a test of balance. Lucian had André for an anchor. Phillip had Serina and only one leg, thanks to Duncan's precision placed blow with the shillelagh which severed Phillip's tendons. Outside the train, the ground gave way to a large expansion bridge that spanned a dark murky river about fifty feet above the river. Winds whipped into the car from outside as a storm shifted in. Dangling and stuck, Serina took a moment to look around and regretted it.

Peering out of the hole, she saw the swift moving current of the river below. That's when she screamed, "Lucian...I don't do water. Get the oaf off me. I'm not going in that muck. Now, m'lord!"

Swearing non-stop, with an arrow stuck through his shoulder, André had a painful reminder that he would have to teach Payton how to shoot a crossbow.

André reached for the crossbow, but caught sight of Chyna. He watched her trapped inside her glass prison that his brother some how concocted. She pleaded with him, her words landing on deaf ears, as he took aim with the bow and aimed the weapon on Phillip. His aunt's face turned to stone as the arrow pierced Phillip's back, a direct hit on his heart. André never lost sight of her dead black eyes as he delivered a fatal blow.

The arrow forged through the front of Phillip's chest. Between Lucian's chokehold and the arrow bulging from his heart, his number was up.

Lucian glanced down to the proximity of the tip of the arrow...A few more inches and André would have skewered two for the price of one. Lucian bent his head around Phillip and asked, "Explain this."

André returned the look with a mocking, "What? I missed you. It's more than Payton can say."

Wilting fast, Phillip dropped Serina. With the knowledge he was indeed dying, Phillip decided he wasn't going down alone. He bent over and grabbed Duncan's long brown hair in one fist and Jonah's dark brown curly hair in his other and leapt through the hole in the train dragging both men kicking and screaming over the side with him.

"Duncan! Jonah!" Lucian, André, Payton and Serina all screamed in unison, as they rushed to the opening.

Leaning dangerously outside of the train, and grabbing at air to attempt to bring the men back to her, Serina lost her balance and almost fell a second time.

Lucian yanked her back in, and wrapped her in the safety of his arms. Serina fought him, yelling, "Help Duncan and Jonah." They looked out, seeing nothing but a fast flowing river beneath them.

With less than a split second to think of something Lucian surged forth every ounce of energy he owned in attempts to slow their descent, which almost dragged them from the train and hastened Duncan and Jonah's fall. Backfired! Yes, there seemed to be a learning curve to his newfound power.

He created a reverse vacuum sucking out anything that wasn't nailed down. All the suitcases, boxes filled with trinkets were lost to the river below. The carpets proved there was no magic in them as they tumbled through the air to a watery grave.

Payton clung to Lucian and Serina for dear life while André held the back of his pants to keep him from falling as well. The area where the arrow pierced him oozed the more André struggled to save his family.

Lucian changed his train of thought immediately to envision a leaf sifting down to the water and floating safely to the shore.

Serina read Lucian's thoughts and added her own, sending a blistering heat to Phillip's hands. He relinquished the death-grip on Duncan and Jonah. They watched as the men crawled from the river. Phillip never resurfaced.

Lucian shook Serina. "Never scare me as you have just done, ever again. My heart is too fragile where your wellbeing and life are concerned. I would not choose to live without you. I would have no choice but to join you somewhere in the heavens, because I will not live with out you, Serina." Lucian secured his grip on her.

Her temper one degree hotter she yelled, "We have to stop the train, Lucian. We have to go get Duncan and Jonah. And you bugger—don't you dare reprimand me. Lucian, you almost tossed us off the train as well!" Serina pointed her finger at him. Her favorite emotion had resurfaced, panic. How could they have lost Duncan and Jonah? She was so upset there was no thinking straight. She headed out the door of the car but stopped in her tracks and looked at Chyna. Really studied her. Lucian threw his arm around Serina and André and Payton joined her.

Trapped inside an invisible prism, Chyna resembled a wild, exotic animal. She pounded on the barriers until blood covered her knuckles. Then she stopped, sniffed her hands and licked them clean.

"Someone should put her out of her misery." Didn't matter who said it, because they all thought it.

"You'll see the sunrise alone, Chyna." Serina said before she turned to leave.

Lucian grabbed Serina's wrist. "We will not stop the train again. Duncan and Jonah will be fine as long as they don't kill each other. The poor people aboard this train have already endured much too much from this trip. I can only imagine the looks we will encounter when we exit this car." Lucian looked at André and Payton, and started to laugh because at this point, if he didn't laugh he was going to cry.

Serina turned to face the others. "André, let's get the arrow out. Sit." Serina squeezed Lucian's hand. "I need you to remove the arrow, and I'll go inside and make certain the lung is fine."

Concern etched into every line of his face. Never mind having an arrow ripped out from his body—going in was bad enough—but André wondered more what it would feel like having another person inside him. Crowded came to mind, especially after witnessing Serina with Jasper. The whole body/mind snatching escapade left a bitter taste in his mouth.

Serina placed her hands on his shoulders. André mirrored her actions bracing himself for whatever happened.

"Ready?" Serina asked

With a solid, "Just do it," André closed his eyes and waited.

Serina told him, "Count to ten—"

Lucian butted in. "He can't count that high."

"Imbecile," André muttered. "Why do you want me to count?"

"The element of surprise."

"One…"

Lucian snapped the arrow at the tip and pulled the arrow out backward with such speed André didn't realize the arrow was out.

"Jeepers, Luce, I never felt a—how'd you—"

"Vampire!" Lucian's impish grin took up his face. Then witnessing the way André looked at his wife, all misty-eyed, with a sappy infatuation, alarms began to chime. Lucian dragged her back to him.

"What is it, m'lord?" Serina asked.

Lucian's cheeks flushed. "I am ashamed to admit I am jealous. I am sorry."

Serina looked directly into his beautiful silvery eyes. "Never apologize to me, Lucian, for wanting me close to you. I want and need the same things. I'm not going anywhere, husband." Serina tugged Lucian down to her height, and gently kissed him, not caring there were still others in the room with them.

Chyna watched them carry on as if she didn't exist and from the looks of things she only had a short hour to go before she didn't. Sunrise was well on its way and thanks to Chyna herself, the sun would shine directly through the hole she'd knocked in the train car's wall. Frustrated, she tapped her twisted nail on the wall of her prison. She hated it when things backfired.

Serina pondered aloud, "Poetic justice is about to be served. Sun's almost up. Let us leave her to her fate."

Lucian headed for the door.

"Should we leave Chyna alone? What if something goes awry?" André asked. "Don't take this wrong, Luce, but you're a fledgling at the whole vamp business. It takes most of them a few hundred years to perfect some of their techniques, not a few days. The reverse vacuum being case in point, not that I'm bringing it up, mind you."

"We've only got two stops left on this holiday from hell. As long as I'm breathing, she's not going anywhere. And I'm finished making objects float, Ands, so if you end up in water I hope you can swim." Lucian flashed a smile towards his brother. "Once we get Serina safely back to Raven and Molly, we can get fresh horses and retrieve our two boys. Hey, did any of you notice the resemblance between Duncan and Jonah? It doesn't jump right out at you, but there are similarities between them that are rather obvious."

"What? Similarities like identical cousins? You'd definitely be the first to take note of that," Serina teased, then paid for it when Lucian gently paddled her behind. She just laughed and nudged her body closer to his.

"Luce, you know you're right. Aren't they 'bout the same age too?" André asked.

Chyna stood up, shook out her orange cloak with the large silver knife still wedged in her back. She moved onto her tiara and yanked it from her scalp, huffed on the dull gems and spit-shined them clean. When finished, she pushed the ends of the comb back into her scalp as one would a thumbtack into a wall. She didn't even flinch as the prongs penetrated her flesh. She turned to them, both hands pressed on the see-through enclosure and pleaded for André to rescue her. Chyna did not want to die like this. Hell, she didn't want to die period. But then she still believed she would be Queen some day soon.

Lucian tried to ignore her. "No. They're eight years apart. Jonah graduated two years before Ray and I did."

"I must go. I've seen more boogey-man, hocus-pocus than my brain can register, and I'm hungry. I'm going to the food car to make breakfast for whoever is left aboard." Payton walked out.

Lucian leaned against the makeshift prison, his legs crossed at his ankles. He tapped back at Chyna. "Auntie, I believe farewells are in order. 'Tis that beautiful dawning when the sun kisses the night adieu. You however, shan't be kissing anyone anymore and especially not Phillip. What an odd couple you made! André, I would think it best if you went with Payton and take my wife with you. Oh, before I forget, although I seriously doubt I'll forget it any time to soon, please keep your nob in your trousers and try to keep your hands off my wife's ass!"

André and Serina froze.

With a slow turn and a guilt-ridden expression, André started to explain, "Lucian—I'm—"

Serina cut him off. "Not here. Not now." She pushed him out the cabin door toward Payton.

André opened his mouth to say something, closed it and turned back around. He shoved his way back into the cabin to face his brother. "Lucian, forgive Serina. She had nothing to do with what went on between us. Believe me when I tell you that the vampire had complete control of her. Her heart remained true to you. I have no excuse. I will leave the manor when we return if that is what you wish. I am no gentleman. If you knew, why wait until now to say something? Why didn't you attempt to intervene on the mountain?"

"You don't understand!" Lucian yelled his fists knotted tight to his side. "André, do you have any idea what it was like finding my wife in your arms and on my honeymoon no less? I wasn't even cold and yet you wasted no time making a claim on my wife." Lucian spun away from the two of them. "What you did was worse than what Jasper did to me. At least I saw him coming. Betrayed by my own brother." Before anyone had a second to react, Lucian turned on André and pinned him to the door, his fist blowing past André's face and punching a hole in the wall next to his head. He spit in his face, "I wanted you dead on that mountain that's why I never interfered, because I wasn't the only one. Jasper was in my head egging me on. You and I will talk much about this, André, but you will remain with us. Get out now!" Lucian dropped him to the floor and dismissed him. The scars carved into his soul would be there for some time to come.

"André, I need to speak with Lucian." Serina showed André out of the car a second time, then she turned toward her husband. How did she tell her husband she'd almost had sex with her brother-in-law due to some vampire's morose sense of humor, not out of lust. She loved Lucian with all her heart. His brother was just that, his brother. "Lucian—" Serina still couldn't look him in his eyes, and she loved his eyes. She felt unworthy of his love. Of his trust. Tears welled up behind her closed eyes.

"M'lady, look at me. Please?" Lucian tickled her under her chin.

Serina's bottom lip quivered, and she knew she was out of her element. She'd hurt Lucian, and she'd never intended to.

"Serina," he whispered, "I love you. Please, my wild rose, look at me. I know you did none of that with André from desire." He trailed kisses down her cheeks, chasing each teardrop with his lips. "I love you."

He said it again. Maybe he really did mean it. Serina opened both eyes, her bottom lip still making her teeth chatter.

Lucian placed both hands on her cheeks to steady her jaw and then he did the only thing he knew how to do to stop the rattles. He flashed his fangs at her as he shifted his brows mischievously.

Serina unclenched her fists and hugged his waist. She pulled him to her, and kissed him while, trying to avoid the incisors that had sprouted in the past moments.

"Lucian—ah—"

Lucian put his fingers back over her mouth stilling her. "Please forgive me, Serina. André and I shall speak of this later."

"You're just like Raven you know," she said. "Such compassion. If I never had that one random thought of André and you together nothing ever would have happened. And you try to ease my burden when 'tis I who should ease yours."

"I appreciate your honesty." He deliberately kissed her neck, thinking it was a safer area.

Not quite.

Serina looked up to Lucian with that one look he knew so well, that look in her eyes that begged him to take her.

"Do it."

"What about," Lucian nodded towards Chyna, "you know who?"

"Do it now."

All right then. He wasted no time and did as he was asked. Passion, relief, power and trust flooded his injured soul. He felt what he was doing to her as she merged her mind with his. Her orgasm came fast and hard and left her breathless in his arms. Just once, he wanted her to bite him like this, instead of someone trying to rip out his throat, so he could experience the sensation first hand, although he thought this was pretty darn good.

He drank carefully, only taking a little from her then closed the wounds in her neck.

"Thank you. You've no idea how I fancy what you do to me."

"Anytime."

He faced Chyna when he noticed the sun inside the cabin.

Chyna watched horrified, as her shelter slowly evaporated into the light. Backed up as far as she could go, her screams fell silent.

Lucian and Serina watched. Chyna tried to hover off the floor, as the morning sunbeams inched closer and closer to her, resembling the incoming tides of the ocean eating up the sand as it washed ashore.

Chapter Twenty-One

Serina had that nasty knot in her stomach again. A knot of guilt...the knot that would not allow Chyna to die this way, at the hand of her husband and she. For as much as she wanted Chyna a pile of ash, and she did, she knew this would not be the day. It was a horrible way to die. To slow and too smelly. People burning up—charred flesh...Ewh! It hit a little too close to home. Serina scrunched her nose at the very thought.

"Lucian—" Serina looked at Chyna. "We can't do this. There must be an alternative."

Chyna stopped her whining and stared at Serina as she hung in the far corner of her prison, her orange cloak pulled around her as a shield.

"I agree, luv. I will allow her access to her casket. Once in, we will bind her with chains and crosses and deliver her to the queen. Let her sister determine her fate. I'm so grateful you spoke up, Serina. I really wasn't up for the show either."

"You'd best expand her barriers before our good intentions go up in smoke, so to speak. She's beginning to singe, Lucian. Hurry up." Serina half screamed and half laughed.

Lucian closed his eyes as his fingers weaved through the air in methodical pattern. When he finished the two of them watched Chyna dart across the car to the safety of her bleak confines, the knife still protruding from her back. She thumped her back into the base of casket a few times until the blade pushed through to the other side of her chest. The hole in her chest healed as if it were a mere scratch.

After securing her coffin, Serina and Lucian headed out after André and Payton.

****

Once they gathered their belongings, Lucian stopped and sent a telegram to his aunt, the Queen, that read:

Dear Auntie Mattie,

Soon you will be receiving a large black box, a casket actually. To open it at night would be a fate far worse than opening Pandora's box. 'Tis your last sister. We traveled with her for a night that was unforgettable and unrewarding by most standards. She does not travel lightly. Please, do not unlock the wholly evil that lay locked within this box, unless 'tis high noon. Keep her guarded at all times. It has been many years, give our cousins Deidre, Devona and Deba our best.

Lucian

Serina wasn't happy with the way Lucian closed his note, thinking it sounded so informal and distant. She asked, "Why not sign it, With love, Lucian?"

"I have no love for the woman. Nor she me."

"How about, sincerely?"

"There is nothing sincere about her. Or my feelings for her."

"Best wishes, then?"

"Serina, the only wish I have for the woman is that it was she on the mountain with Jasper."

Serina's last attempt made Lucian smile. "Have a nice day," but still he signed only his name.

****

The sight of the small church stole Serina's breath. It was her home away from home for so many years, her refuge. It hit her then; she missed Father Butler more than her own mother. He always held a smile for her. And his hugs, they held a warmth that saturated her soul. Serina hopped out of the carriage and ran up the five steps to the church. She burst through the heavy wooden doors, acting like a child running home and happy to be there.

"Father Butler?" Serina's voice echoed across the vacant room. "Lucian, maybe he's at the rectory. It's out the back door, come on." Serina grabbed Lucian's hand, and dragged him through the church. "See, m'lord, you're not evil, not at all. The roof's not come crashing down around us." She winked and tugged a little harder on him.

Lucian tagged along, happy to be on the backside of his wife so he could enjoy the view.

"We're in church you evil scoundrel. I got that thought." She wiggled her backside quickly in a teasing manner.

"You just told me I wasn't evil." Lucian pinched her bottom.

"Lucian St. James, I'm appalled at your behavior." She spun to him, a grin growing. "But I like it."

"Me? Who just taunted me with that little dance?" He raised an eyebrow and quickly drew her to him for a small kiss.

Licking her lips she asked, "What if Father Butler saw you do that?"

"I'd say he's a very lucky man to have such a beautiful wife."

Serina's heart skipped a beat. She knew that voice. Serina snapped her head around so fast her hair swished Lucian across the face.

"Father." Serina dropped Lucian's hand and backtracked across the church. She threw her arms around the portly little man, with huge blue eyes and squeezed him.

"Good graces, Serina, what's gotten into you child? Not that this old man doesn't love the affections!" Father Butler held onto her for dear life, hoping to ease her fears and his as well. Seeing her battered and bruised body he wanted to cry. "Serina, now don't go setting a little bon-fire off when I say this, but you seem a tad bit insecure. Come on, show me my green eyes." Father tilted her chin up to him and kissed the tip of her nose.

"Father, 'tis been the longest days of our lives, and I do suppose I'm just tickled to be home again with my husband." Serina reached for Lucian as she talked with Father and they made their way to the garden.

Father Butler turned to Lucian. "You look well son, but I understand you'd nearly lost your life this week. Please tell me what happened. Raven told us bits and pieces, but then she was no longer able to communicate with you or Serina. She, we thought we'd lost you all. André too when we hadn't heard from him."

"If you've a few minutes first, Sir, I really need to see my little beauty. I can't imagine the hell she must have been put through these past days, or she put you through as well. Then you and I shall have *the chat*." Lucian's grin widened. "Not quite the one you were thinking of, but…" Lucian's voice trailed off.

Father blushed and made the sign of a cross saying, "This one's for you son. If I had a sixpence every time I said that around Serina I'd be richer than your aunt."

Serina nudged Lucian in the ribs as he spoke with Father.

"Boo!" Raven threw her arms around her brother's neck and hung on for the ride of her life when he picked her up and swung her around in circles. "I knew you'd come back to me," Raven said dizzy, her eyes filled with tears. "Put me down, you imbecile." Raven clung to Serina for balance and said, "I knew you'd take care of him, Serrie. Do you like that nickname? Serrie, you've a colored eye. What happened to you? You've even cut up your face. Do you hurt?" Raven ran tender fingers over Serina's cheeks as she inspected the damage.

Lucian threw his hands in the air. "What about me? I'm the one dying."

"Imbecile. You look healthier than before you were married. And, Lucian St. James you're never dying on me."

So it seems, he thought.

Raven turned back to Serina. "You never answered me about your name."

"I've never had a nickname before, other than the ones your brother calls me. I like it. As for my face, the train made a few unscheduled stops. The old mug will heal." For now, Serina knew she could live with her avoidance of Raven's questions until Lucian and André were ready to tell her all that happened. Serina hugged her husband, silently thanking each and every deity, she was able to do just that.

Enjoying being the topic of conversation between his two favorite women once more, Lucian decided it was true what he'd heard about vampires being vanity stricken. At the moment, he found no fault with it.

Raven put her worries behind her for the time being and flashed her brother her best smile.

Serina looked around and asked, "Where is Molly?"

"Over at the orphanage helping out with the younger children. It's where we've been since you two disappeared on us. I think it was Father Butler's way of getting two grown cry babies out of his hair. Serrie, do you want to come to the orphanage and meet the children? They're amazing. I'd no idea how many poor children and babies had no homes.

Lucian, we need to make this home a better environment for them. What good is our money if we can't help people?"

"Actually Raven," Father Butler added, "Serina has been coming here to our home for many years now. So many indeed I've lost count."

"I was around four. I taught some of the children how to read and do mathematics and garden when I got older."

"You were younger than that, Serina," Father added. "I'd been bringing you here since the day you were born. I actually delivered you. Did you know that? Right up there on my alter."

"I believe I've heard it once before." Serina pat his shoulder gently. He told the story of her birth with pride every chance he got.

"Yes, Raven, the children are amazing. They are all so different and all carry strengths and weaknesses in different ways. A complete mishmash of personalities live here. Some of the children are drowning for attention; others cower at the slightest touch. Every one of them different. Have you met Avery and Sydney yet? They are comical and so beautiful. I hope that when someone adopts them, they find a home together, because to separate them would be tragic. They remind me of you two. Avery is an overbearing older brother who wants his sister to do as she is told without question, and Sydney knows she's holding Avery wrapped securely around her finger. "

"I am not overbearing, am I Ray?"

"Not in the least bit, my handsome knight." Raven turned away from Lucian and winked at Serina. "Come on. Let's go see Molly. Where are Ands, Duncan and Payton?" Raven grabbed both Serina and Lucian's hands and tugged.

"They had to drop off a package to the castle."

Raven gave her brother a look that held a giant

question mark. "The castle, as in our aunt's humble abode?"

"It's a long story, Ray, and I'm only explaining it once." Lucian sighed. "I'm waiting for André and Payton, then we'll talk."

"But you didn't say Duncan. Where is he?" Raven's voice changed dramatically to that of a whisper.

"He's alive, Raven." *Shite! Why did I phrase it like that?* "We just need to go pick him up at another train station. He jumped ship so to speak on us. He departed two stops short of our station. That's all."

"Yeah, but your tone Luce, you didn't say he was well."

Damn, when did Raven get so intuitive? "Let me rephrase myself. Duncan is well and we will be picking him up at the next train stop."

"Why didn't he just get back on the train when he'd realized he got off at the wrong stop? Out with it, Luce. What are you hiding?" Raven stood on tiptoes and looked him squarely into his eyes.

"Ah, bloody hell. Forgive me, Father." Lucian gave Father Butler a quick bow from the hip. "Can you please wait until Payton and André return? They'll be along shortly. Please, Ray?" Lucian attempted to smooth the worry lines away from her face. "I promise the last time we saw Duncan and Jonah they were fine, a little soggy, but fine." Lucian wondered why women were so difficult?

"Jonah? Jonah is with Duncan? Isn't he the werewolf from the mountain? What in bloody blazes is going on?" Raven's voice filled the church each time she said Jonah's name. Grabbing her brother's shirt collar, she dragged him back to her eye level. "Out with it. Now."

The moment Molly walked in with André and Payton, Raven ran to André.

"André, you'll tell me what's going on here, won't

you? Lucian is evading me, and rudely I might add." She hugged André, and flashed Lucian a snippy grin, her nose in the air.

"Hello, little one. I see absence makes the heart grow fonder," André teased with a hint of sarcasm. He planted kiss on the top of her head.

"Luce, the package has been delivered, and is safely tucked away." André peered over the top of Raven's head to his brother. *You haven't told her yet?*

"Raven and I were just about to have a conversation of our trip to the mountain and our ride home."

"Where's Duncan?" Molly asked.

Raven pointed her index finger at Lucian. "I asked the same thing, Molly." She gave Lucian one more look that he recognized as trouble for him.

Lucian scratched at his beard. "Father, have you a place we can all sit and talk privately?"

"Follow me. What is said within these walls, stays within these walls. House rules. It's been this way for centuries." Father Butler led them all to his favorite room within the church, a glass atrium which overlooked his garden off the back of the church. A play-yard surrounded by a small moat filled with lush white sand had a little drawbridge to get to the miniature castle.

Father Butler excused himself for a few minutes and returned with a tray full of fruit, cheese, bread and wine.

As the food and wine disappeared, Lucian told every detail of his greatest tale to date. Silence hung in the balances.

Raven moved in very close to Lucian, her gaze locked on his. She'd heard so many stories about vampires and now twice one had bitten him as well. And here he sat, her beloved brother, telling her that he was a mutated version of one.

"Open up." It was an order. No please or would

you, just "open up." Raven moved her fingers to Lucian's mouth ready to pry open his lips if need be.

Lucian found the situation absurd and started laughing. He'd never seen her as resolute in a decision for many years. It made him proud she was gaining her self-confidence back, but she could've chosen someone else to pick on for starters. But then he knew she would start out on him as a testing ground. A trust existed between them that held no boundaries.

Raven peeked and saw only his pearly-white teeth. No fangs, no bewitching her with his silvery blue eyes, just Lucian, her beloved imbecile.

With her English accent in high gear, Raven spouted, "Ah bloody 'ell, Lucian St. James. You're pulling me leg. I'm findin' ya not the least bit funny. You've no fangs. You're no blood sucker and 'tis broad daylight you daft sod. If you'll be tryin' to pass as one of those vile creatures then ya best be tellin' such tales at night, with the moon full and your furry little friend that I've yet to meet—ah excuse me—pump full of silver." Raven swiftly turned her full attention to her sister-in-law. "Serrie, please tell me he's full of shite."

Serina's lips thinned as she glanced to Lucian.

Lucian finished his tale of woe explaining that Payton had been seriously wounded and would most likely turn in three weeks to a werewolf.

Raven switched gears. She studied Payton. A werewolf? She jumped from her seat by Lucian and slumped beside her personal chef on a big plump, cushy daybed. With a hand atop each of his shoulders she shoved him on his back so he had to look up to her. Without thinking of consequences, she hiked up her black silk skirt to give her legs room and straddled Payton. It started off as a joke, but once she sat across him, she found her feelings a little more intense than she expected.

Then she felt his feelings becoming more intense, right where she'd plopped her dainty little self upon him, he began to sprout a new limb and without the need of moonlight. She wiggled slightly, trying to adjust to him, not to cause any more arousal, but it backfired. He was solidly pressing into her most feminine parts which left her both mortified and aroused. If she jumped off him, well...her brothers and Father would know something was up and once off him, they'd see exactly what it was. So she stayed put and tortured both Payton and herself in a fun yet strangely aggravating sense.

Payton blushed. "I'm so sorry," he mouthed to her, "but you really caught me off me guard. You, on top of me was the last thing I expected and the first thing I dreamt of." Payton enjoyed the attention, even with an audience of their closest family and friends, all on the edges of their seats leaning forward, watching intently. And they were.

Raven's long jet-black tresses created the perfect backdrop for her gorgeous blue eyes. It brought out the stark vivid sapphire hue. He could easily lose himself in the depth of their beauty nightly. Her lips silently beseeched him to reach up and close the distance between them. He'd wished they were alone when he did this, but the way he saw things, it was now or never. Raven showed concern for him. Maybe, just maybe it meant she had feelings for him. He was certain she knew he had feelings for her by now.

Looking into her eyes with a smile that he couldn't control, he brought his finger between them motioning for her to come closer.

She did. No questions asked.

He ran his fingers through her hair with his one hand and when she didn't flinch or try to pull away from him, he brought his other hand up to her face, and caressed her cheeks. "Raven, no matter what happens to me in three weeks, I'll be fine. You'll just have to learn how to cook one night out of the month. That's probably the scariest part of this deal."

Raven punched him in the stomach. Payton found his laughter made his own worries less intense. Now he had to find a way to do the same for Raven, once he got back his wind.

"It's not funny, Payton. None of it. You, Lucian and Ands don't seem much worried. I suppose I'll have to be the one who worries for all of you." Her tears fell from nowhere.

Payton reached up and brushed each and every tear from her face. Conjuring up all his nerve, he brought his body up to meet her and kissed her gently.

Raven froze, her body more rigid than the protrusion between her thighs she sat perched on. She stared straight ahead, focused on nothing. She didn't kiss him back, but she didn't pull away from him either.

Raven didn't know what to expect, but this wasn't it, especially in front of her brothers, not to mention a priest. She knew God would strike her down—any second now. Waiting with her lips still glued to his, she actually looked up to the ceiling and around the room.

Reluctantly, Payton broke away from her. "Raven, look at me, not the ceiling." He whispered, "I will never hurt you. Your family knows this or they never would have allowed me to touch you, let alone live under your roof with you." He bent his head back to hers to kiss her once more but stopped just short of her mouth. In a low voice he asked, "Kiss me back this time, so I won't look like a complete fool, but only if you want to."

Raven let out a nervous little giggle and smiled

as she closed the distance between them. She knew Payton would never hurt her, and she trusted him. For the first time in many years, Raven trusted another man.

She enjoyed Payton's lips. He was soft, sweet, tantalizing, and made her want more, even if she wasn't ready for the next step. Their kiss had no tongues—not this time, not her first time. She was content with the fact she'd let him kiss her. Maybe, in time they could experiment, slowly, and see what came of it.

Father Butler stood and excused himself, making excuses that the garden needed weeding.

Oh! Like he does the weeding. Serina bit her cheeks. Father patted her head in passing, laughing.

"You need not say what you're thinking, child. It is written as plain as day all over your precious face." His hearty belly laugh echoed in the hallway.

Molly stood up, fanned her cheeks and excused herself, mumbling something about dirty nappies.

In complete disbelief, André and Lucian went back and forth between looking at each other with the exact same stunned mask and staring at their sister, her lips melded with Payton's.

Serina grabbed both brother's hands, and dragged them from the room. "You two act as if you've never witnessed a kiss before."

Raven never noticed she and Payton were alone. Oblivious to everything except Payton's gentleness and his lips on hers and his hips pressing gently into her sensitive spots, she opened her eyes to find him smiling. "What?" she shyly asked. "Did I do that right?"

Before Xavier attacked her, she had wanted the first man, the only man in her life to be just that, her first and only man. She wanted to save herself for her marriage. Could Payton be the one? She wasn't sure, but now she was willing to experiment.

She knew Lucian was absolutely positive about Serina. He never second-guessed anything in his life, ever. Raven, however, second-guessed what day of the week it was. Xavier made her doubt almost everything in her life.

"You are beautiful, Raven. You have the kiss of an angel. Although maybe I feel that because we are in a church, but I do believe it is of your doings."

"You Sir, have the grin of the devil plastered about your face. Maybe we should leave here and make our way home, before the roof comes down upon us. No, wait. Am I right in assuming you won't let us go home until Duncan and your attacker, Jonah, are back? When is everyone leaving to go find Duncan and the other one?"

Raven didn't like the other man they were about to bring home with them. He'd hurt Payton, he'd kidnapped Serina, left her alone and chained in a cave, and God help him if he so chose to, he'd had a hand in her brother's death/rebirth. And for that alone, she knew she'd never forgive the man.

"They're leaving very soon. But it's just André and Lucian going to find them. You've got me to watch over you. Doesn't that leave a warm, fuzzy feeling all over you?"

"Yes and at the same time, no. This feeling you describe scares the daylights out of me, Payton. What happens if you really turn into a warm, fuzzy, snarling thing? I really can't cook." Teasingly, she smiled at him. "I won't lie to you. We need to do baby steps. I hope you're a patient man. But just so you are aware of what just took place—"

"Raven, I will never force you to do anything you're not comfortable doing. Ever. I want you to trust me and until you do, we will have fun finding out ways to get around it."

"Nicely put. And then you as our bodyguard, I don't know about that either. André showed me the hole in his chest." She poked her finger into Payton's chest right where the arrow pierced André. "I thank God we've got Serina. We've definitely kept her busy since the day we met her."

Shooting an eyebrow up a few times and flashing a smile, he eased her fears. "Your brother says he will teach me how to shoot a crossbow when he returns. I did hit one of the targets I sought you know," he added, trying to reclaim his confidence in his own abilities more so than trying to reassure Raven he wasn't a blundering idiot on the loose with weapons he'd no knowledge of, other than a set of carving knives.

"Payton, what happens if in three weeks…?"

Payton leaned into her and whispered in her ear, "Do not spend the next three weeks worrying over something that neither of us can control. You'll make your self sick for no reason. Worrying is like paying for something you've not yet purchased, and I sense you spend your money wisely."

Raven threaded her fingers with Payton's and tugged at him. "Garden, come on. Let's go get Duncan. I want my family home again under one roof."

****

Serina took the opportunity to spend some quality time with her husband before he left her. In the playground, Lucian sat curled on a swing, his knees crushed into his chest. The swing scraped the ground from both his weight and height each time he passed the starting point.

Serina took one look at him and laughed heartily. "The swing is built for people the size of fairies in mind, not giants."

"Give us a shove, luv," he said with a straight face.

Valiant in her attempts, she stood behind him, trying to push him, her feet buried in the sand.

"Higher, m'lady," he teased. "I want to experience the wind in my hair."

She yanked him backwards through the chains to the ground and jumped atop of him.

"Or not. I like your idea better." Lucian ran his hands up her thighs.

Perched on his stomach, she smiled. "We made it home, luv. Together. I didn't think we would, but someone was listening to me on that mountain after all."

"Serina, I failed you up there. I should have been able to kill that monster."

Quickly, Serina grabbed his cheeks and held his face so he couldn't turn from her. "We had no idea what evil we were up against, Lucian. There's no way we could have been prepared for that. You have no reason to feel guilt. I think under the circumstances you and I did all right. You got a bit more than you bartered for, but we're together and that's all that matters." Serina bent over to kiss her husband.

With one swift roll, Serina was on her back looking up at him and the sky's radiant array of color behind him. This time he bent to her, and placed his lips ever-so-gently on her neck, the epicenter of her sensual awareness and watched a grin working its way onto her lips.

"A quickie here?" she asked eyes wide.

"Oh, how I love your scent woman. You mesmerize my soul, you make me whole and give me faith in myself." His lips covered hers with a warmth that would never cool. "No, m'lady, not here. We are open for many eyes to see. I will make endless love to you this evening and well into the morrow upon my return then you and I can begin our own family. I've heard it said, practice makes perfect. Now that I think about it, tonight sounds awfully far off. Would you care for a quickie before I ride off into the sunset?"

"I thought you'd never ask. Follow me. I've the perfect place. No one will find us. Or hear us." She winked.

Lucian stood, and pulled his wife up. As he brushed the sand from her dress he copped a lustful feel of her lush behind in the process.

"You're a cheeky bugger."

Walking back through the gardens, they smiled to everyone and continued straight past each and every person in their family.

"Hey you two, hold up. We should get going soon, Luce," André insisted as he stood ready to follow on his brother's heels. "A telegram arrived minutes past that Duncan and Jonah made it safely to a small village a few hours from here. Won't take long at all to grab them. We'll be home in time for dinner, Payton." André turned towards the blushing chef. "Unless, you've cooked up other plans for the evening."

"Dinner tonight, my Lord will be a feast, a celebration for our family." Payton lifted Raven's hand to his lips and kissed her, then excused himself.

Lucian yelled back, "Half past noon, Ands. We need to take care of one or two things first."

"Where are you going?"

Raven jabbed André in his ribs, giving him a look that he was indeed an imbecile, not Lucian this once. "Did you forget he's on his honeymoon?"

André blushed. "I did. My apologies," he yelled after them, but they were already out of sight.

****

"Where is it you're dragging me to?" Although it didn't matter. As long as he was with Serina, nothing else mattered.

"You'll see." Walking back through the church, Serina took Lucian through a back room. She opened a small door to an even smaller staircase. The opening barely allowed Lucian entrance. He squeezed his broad shoulders into the confines not much wider than a ladder grunting and groaning.

Climbing the stairs Lucian stopped a few steps down from his wife and shook his head.

"I see London. I see France. I see my wife's wearing nothing under that skirt at a glance." He slipped his hand up her thigh and pinched her bottom.

Serina stopped. Playing it up just a bit, she hiked her skirt well past her hips and finished her climb. The view left her husband doting over her little rump and her bigger sense of self.

"Oh you're a tease."

"Get up here, and we'll see what else I am." In the short amount of time it took Lucian to scale the remaining ten stairs, his little tease of a wife was stripped of every stitch of clothing she wore.

Ducking into the bell tower for lack of standing room, Lucian looked over the small space. A catwalk roughly three feet wide encompassed the bells. Splinters would be a worthy adversary, as the floorboards were made from rough unfinished pine.

"That was fast. What did you do? Wiggle your nose and wish yourself naked?"

"Lucian, if I could do that, you'd be in the same predicament. How long have we got till noon?"

"Why?" he asked both amused and aroused. With a quick glance at his timepiece, he answered, "Three minutes."

"Quick, lose your trousers and then put that finely chiseled tool of yours to work right here." Serina lay atop her clothing, pointing to a destination south of her belly button. She began to move her body in a suggestive manner, caressing her private lips as she waited, her impatience for some company testing her will.

Lucian was so taken at the images in front of him that he couldn't move. All blood flow on his body diverted south, and the levee was getting ready to break.

"Pushy, aren't we?"

"Time's a ticking away, toots. You know I have patience problems." She giggled. "Come on. I want us joined when the bells chime. It's been a fantasy I've had for years."

"Some say a person can go blind from too much sex. Not us. We'll end up deaf. But who am I to deny you ecstasy?"

She shook her curls out. "There's that vampire vanity I've heard tell of. Now...let's see if you're all talk or all action."

Lucian accommodated his wife's needs and fulfilled her fantasy, delivering a heated passion that rang louder than the bells.

On the twelfth chime and his twelfth pass through her thighs the deafening bells filled the air as Lucian's hips stilled, the vibration of both the bells and their lovemaking lingered sweetly between them.

"That, St. James was a record," Serina hollered.

Lucian yelled, too. "You said you wanted a quickie. Next time be careful for what you wish."

She looked appalled.

He looked amused.

Lucian nudged his lips to the small crook of her neck and kissed her lightly. Without warning, he sent his new shiny fangs into her neck, and drank her in.

Serina's orgasm started where Lucian's left off. She wiggled her hips and pressed into him, trying to get a response from him.

Slowly breaking away from her, he licked his lips behind closed eyes. "M'lady, I love you more than life itself, but the whole quickie thing, the bells, you with nothing on under that dress...well, let's just say I'm all chimed out. Are you upset?"

"No. It was fun. We can try it again tonight. When you return, we can fulfill one of your fantasies if you'd like."

"M'lady, you are my fantasy, my wildest dream, my life, my love and my reality. Sadly, speaking of reality..."

Lucian escorted his blushing bride back through the church and passed her hand to Father Butler. "Take care of our girl while I'm away, Father."

"I always have, Lucian. Go now and bring home your Duncan. We'll all be here when you return."

"What?" Lucian glanced to Serina seeing if she'd heard him.

Father repeated himself, watching both Lucian and Serina rub their ears and scratch their heads. "You two've been in the bell tower, haven't you? There isn't a sacred spot on this land you two haven't covered."

"What?" Serina asked.

Father Butler walked away making the sign of the cross over his chest.

With a cat-like crawl, Lucian snatched her body and whisked her to his.

"I love you, Serina St. James." A breath away from kissing her, he told her, "Remember what I said in another lifetime? Death cannot separate us. Only time and circumstance. And since I've already covered the death part, now it's just the time and circumstances." Lucian covered his wife's lips gently, loving every sensual cell of her that he came in contact with.

"Lucian, I—"

"I know, m'lady. Until tonight, my love." He set her down and walked out of the church with André by his side.

A word about the author...

Jaclyn Tracey's life began in merry old England on an American Air Force Base, giving her dual citizenship to both beautiful countries. Although she grew up as an only child, she is blessed with an amazing family she cherishes.

She grew up in Saratoga Springs, NY, where she met and married Steven, her best friend. They have been married twenty-four years. He is employed as an engineer, developing and manufacturing digital mammography detectors that are improving women's health care. They have two beautiful children, Caitlyn and Christopher, who are now in college. Caitlyn and her pitbulls, Damon and Dalton, live in Delaware and Christopher goes to college locally.

Jaclyn graduated from Ellis School of Nursing as a Registered Nurse. She works for Living Resources, a community of dedicated people caring for the mentally disabled. Her hobbies include hiking, skiing the bunny hill, four-wheeling in the winter with their jeep, traveling with her family and reading. Black-and-white photography was and still is one of her passions.

January 1, 2005, Jaclyn sat down and began writing *Eden's Black Rose*, after the Boston Red Socks won the World Series. She figured if they could win the series, she could write a book. She's grateful it didn't take 86 years to get published! (Thank you, dear editor, Callie Lynn Wolfe, and The Wild Rose Press!) Oh, and for the record, she's a loyal Yankees fan. Jaclyn belongs to a local chapter of the Romance Writers of America, the CR-RWA, and the RWA.

Thank you for purchasing
this Wild Rose Press publication.
For other wonderful stories of romance,
please visit our on-line bookstore at
www.thewildrosepress.com

For questions or more information,
contact us at
info@thewildrosepress.com

The Wild Rose Press
www.TheWildRosePress.com